Iris Murdoch was born in Dublin of Anglo-Irish parents. She attended Badminton School, Bristol, and read classics at Somerville College, Oxford. During the war she was an Assistant Principal at the Treasury, and then worked with UNRRA in Belgium and Austria.

She held a studentship in philosophy at Newnham College, Cambridge, for a year, then in 1948 returned to Oxford where she was for many years a Fellow and Tutor in philosophy at St Anne's College. In 1956 she married John Bayley, professor and critic in the field of literature.

For her highly acclaimed novel, *The Sea, The Sea*, Iris Murdoch won the Booker Prize in 1978.

Also by Iris Murdoch

Under the Net
The Sandcastle
The Bell
A Severed Head
An Unofficial Rose
The Unicorn
The Italian Girl
The Red and the Green
The Time of the Angels
The Nice and the Good
Bruno's Dream
A Fairly Honourable Defeat
An Accidental Man
The Black Prince
The Sacred and Profane Love Machine
A Word Child
Henry and Cato
The Sea, The Sea

Plays

A Severed Head (with J.B. Priestley)
The Three Arrows
The Servants and the Snow

Philosophy

Sartre, Romantic Rationalist
The Sovereignty of the Good

Iris Murdoch

The Flight from the Enchanter

**TRIAD
GRANADA**

Published by Triad/Granada in 1976
Reprinted 1979, 1981

ISBN 0 586 04429 9

Triad Paperbacks Ltd is an imprint of
Chatto, Bodley Head & Jonathan Cape Ltd and
Granada Publishing Ltd

First published in Great Britain by
Chatto & Windus Ltd 1956
Copyright © Iris Murdoch 1956

Set, printed and bound in Great Britain by
Cox & Wyman Ltd, Reading
Set in Intertype Lectura

To
Elias Canetti

ONE

It was about three o'clock on a Friday afternoon when Annette decided to leave school. An Italian lesson was in progress. In an affected high-pitched voice the Italian tutor was reading aloud from the twelfth canto of the *Inferno*. She had just reached the passage about the Minotaur. Annette disliked the *Inferno*. It seemed to her a cruel and unpleasant book. She particularly disliked the passage about the Minotaur. Why should the poor Minotaur be suffering in hell? It was not the Minotaur's fault that it had been born a monster. It was God's fault. The Minotaur bounded to and fro in pain and frustration, Dante was saying, like a bull that has received the death blow. *Partite, bestia!* said the mincing voice of the Italian tutor. She was an Englishwoman who had done a course on Italian civilization in Florence when she was young. Virgil was speaking contemptuously to the Minotaur. Annette decided to go. I am learning nothing here, she thought. From now on I shall educate myself. I shall enter the School of Life. She packed her books up neatly and rose. She crossed the room, bowing gravely to the Italian tutor, who had interrupted her reading and was looking at Annette with disapproval. Annette left the room, closing the door quietly behind her. When she found herself outside in the heavily carpeted corridor, she began to laugh. It was all so absurdly simple, she could not imagine why she had not thought of it long ago. She crossed the corridor with a skip and a jump, making a tasteful vase of flowers rock upon its pedestal, and went down the steps to the cloakroom three at a time.

The Ringenhall Ladies' College was an expensive finishing school in Kensington which taught to young women of the débutante class such arts as were considered necessary for the catching of a husband in one, or at the most two, seasons. The far-sighted mammas of the social group from which Ringenhall recruited its pupils were not by any means as rich as they used to be, and they wanted quick results. Ringenhall was geared to the production of those results with the stringency of a military operation. Annette had been a pupil at Ringenhall for about six months. Her father, who was a diplomat, wanted her to 'come out' in London, and had taken the view that a short period at an establishment of this kind would produce in his 'cosmopolitan ragamuffin', as he called Annette, sufficient of the surface of a young English lady for him to be able to pass her off as such during the social season which he felt to be a necessary part of her upbringing, if not exactly its crown. Andrew Cockeyne, who had not lived in England himself since he was twenty-three, and indeed thoroughly disliked the place, which he found, though he would not have admitted it, both tedious and oppressive, had nevertheless taken care to send his son to his own public school. Annette's education, which was less important, and in the course of which she had learnt four languages and little else, had been picked up *un peu partout*; but it was essential in her father's view that it should reach its climax in no other place than London. Annette's mother, who was Swiss, had spread out her hands and assented to this arrangement, and if she had felt any scepticism about it she had kept it to herself.

Annette was nearly nineteen. Concerning Ringenhall she herself had not experienced a single moment of doubt. She had loathed it from the very first day. For her fellow-pupils she felt a mixture of pity and contempt, and for her teachers, who were called 'tutors', contempt unmixed. For the headmistress, a Miss Walpole, she felt a pure and disinterested hatred. 'Disinterested', because Miss Walpole had never behaved unpleasantly to Annette or indeed paid any attention to her whatsoever. Annette had never hated anyone in this way before and took pride in the emotion, which she felt to be a sign of maturity. Against the Ringenhall curriculum she had fought with unremitting obstinacy, determined not to let a single one of the ideas which it purveyed find even a temporary lodgement in her mind. When it was possible, she read a book or wrote letters in class. When this was not possible, she pursued some lively daydream, or else fell into a self-induced coma of stupidity. To do this she would let her jaw fall open and concentrate her attention upon some object in the near vicinity until her eyes glazed and there was not a thought in her head. After some time, however, she discontinued this practice, not because the tutors began to think that she was not right in the head — this merely amused her — but because she discovered that she was able by this means to make herself fall asleep, and this frightened her very much indeed.

Annette put her coat on and was ready to go. But now when she reached the door that led into the street she paused suddenly. She turned round and looked along the corridor. Everything seemed the same; the expensive flora, the watery reproductions of famous paintings, the much admired curve of the white staircase. Annette stared at it all. It looked to her the same, and yet different. It was as if she had walked through the looking-glass. She realized that she was free. As Annette pondered, almost with awe, upon the ease with which she had done it, she felt that Ringenhall had taught her its most important lesson. She began to walk back, peering through doorways and touching objects with her fingers. She half expected to find new rooms hidden behind familiar doors. She wandered into the library.

She entered quietly and found that as usual the room was empty. She stood there in the silence until it began to look to her like a library in a sacked city. No one owned these books now. No one would come here again; only after a while the wall would crumble down and the rain would come blowing in. It occurred to Annette that she might as well take away one or two books as souvenirs. Volumes were not arranged in any particular order, nor were they stamped or catalogued. She examined several shelves. The books were chaotic, but in mint condition, since reading was not a popular activity at Ringenhall. At length she selected a leather-bound copy of the *Collected Poems* of Browning, and left the room with the book under her arm. She was by now feeling so happy that she would have shouted for joy if it had not been for the delicious spell which she felt herself to be under and which still enjoined silence. She looked about her complacently. Ringenhall was at her mercy.

There were two things which Annette had wanted very much to do ever since she had arrived. One of these was to carve her name on a wooden bust by Grinling Gibbons which stood in the common-room. There was something solemn and florid about this work which made Annette itch for a blade. The wood was soft and inviting. However, she rejected this idea, not because

7

the name of Grinling Gibbons carried, when it came to it, any magic for her but because she had mislaid her pocket-knife. The other thing which she had always wanted to do was to swing on the chandelier in the dining-room. She turned rapidly in the direction of that room and bounded in. Tables and chairs stood by, silent with disapproval. Annette looked up at the chandelier and her heart beat violently. The thing seemed enormously high up and far away. It hung from a stout chain; Annette had noticed this carefully when she had studied it in the past. She had also remarked a strong metal bar, right in the centre of it, on which she had always planned to put her hands. All about and above this bar were suspended tiny drops of crystal, each one glowing with a drop of pure light tinier still, as if a beautiful wave had been arrested in the act of breaking while the sun was shining upon it. Annette had felt sure that if she could swing upon the chandelier the music which was hidden in the crystals would break out into a great peal of bells. But now it seemed to be very hard to get at.

In her imagination Annette had always reached her objective by a flying leap from the High Table; but she could see now that this was not a very practical idea. Grimly she began to pull one of the tables into the centre of the room. On top of the table she placed one of the chairs. Then she began to climb up. By the time she was on the table she was already beginning to feel rather far away from the ground. Annette was afraid of heights. However, she mounted resolutely on to the chair. Here, by standing on tiptoe, she could get her hands over the metal bar. She paused breathlessly. Then with a quick movement she kicked the chair away and hung stiffly in mid-air. The chandelier felt firm, her grip was strong, there was no terrible rending sound as the chain parted company with the ceiling. After all, thought Annette, I don't weigh much.

She kept her feet neatly together and her toes pointed. Then with an oscillation from the hips she began to swing very gently to and fro. The chandelier began to ring, not with a deafening peal but with a very high and sweet tinkling sound; the sort of sound, after all, which you would expect a wave of the sea to make if it had been immobilized and turned into glass: a tiny internal rippling, a mixture of sound and light. Annette was completely enchanted by this noise and by the quiet rhythm of her own movements. She fell into a sort of trance, and as she swung dreamily to and fro she had a vision of remaining there for the rest of the afternoon until the boarders of Ringenhall, streaming in for their dinner, would make their way round on either side of her swinging feet and sit down, paying her no more attention than if she had been a piece of furniture.

At that moment the door opened and Miss Walpole came in. Annette, who was at the end of one of her swings, let go abruptly of the chandelier and, missing the table fell to the floor with a crash at Miss Walpole's feet. Miss Walpole looked down at her with a slight frown. This lady was never sure which she disliked most, adolescent girls or small children; the latter made more noise, it was true, but they were often in the long run easier to handle.

'Get up, Miss Cockeyne,' she said to Annette in her usual weary tone of voice. She always sighed when she spoke, as if wearied by her interlocutor; and as she never cared particularly about anything, so nothing much ever surprised her. This calm indifference had won her the reputation of being a good headmistress.

Annette got up, rubbing herself. It had been a painful fall. Then she turned and put the table straight, and picked up the chair, which was lying on its side. After that, she retrieved her coat and bag and the copy of Browning and faced Miss Walpole.

'What were you doing, Miss Cockeyne?' asked Miss Walpole, sighing.

'Swinging from the chandelier,' said Annette. She was not afraid of her headmistress, whose claims to moral or intellectual excellence she had seen through some time ago.

'Why?' asked Miss Walpole.

Annette had no ready answer to this, and thought she might as well skip a point or two in the conversation by saying immediately, 'I'm sorry.' Then she said, 'I've decided to leave Ringenhall.'

'May I again ask why?' asked Miss Walpole.

She was an extremely tall woman, which was also perhaps one of the secrets of her success, and although Annette, too, was tall, she had to throw her head back if she wanted to look into Miss Walpole's eyes. Annette took a step or two away and receded until the line which joined her eyes to Miss Walpole's

9

made a nearer approach to the horizontal. She wanted to look dignified. But as she moved away, Miss Walpole imperceptibly approached, gliding forward as if propelled from behind, so that Annette had once more to crane her neck.

'I have learnt all that I can here,' said Annette. 'From now on I shall educate myself. I shall go out into the School of Life.'

'As to your having learnt all that you can learn here,' said Miss Walpole, 'that is clearly untrue. Your style of entertaining is distinctly Continental, and as I had occasion to remark the other day, you still go upstairs on all fours like a dog.'

'I mean,' said Annette, 'that I've learnt all the things which I consider important.'

'What makes you imagine,' said Miss Walpole, 'that anything of *importance* can be taught in a school?' She sighed again. 'You realize, I suppose,' she went on, 'that your parents have paid in advance for tuition and meals up to the end of next term, and there can be no question of refunding that money?'

'It doesn't matter,' said Annette.

'You are fortunate to be able to say so,' said Miss Walpole. 'As for the institution which you call the School of Life, I doubt, if I may venture a personal opinion, whether you are yet qualified to benefit from its curriculum. What, by the way, is *that*?' She pointed to the Browning, which Annette was now slipping into her bag.

'That is a book which I wished to give to the library as a parting present,' said Annette. She handed it to Miss Walpole, who took it with suspicion.

'It is a handsome copy,' said Miss Walpole. 'We are grateful to you.'

'I should like a plate to be put in it,' said Annette, 'to say it is the gift of Annette Cockeyne. And now, good-bye, Miss Walpole.'

'Good-bye, Miss Cockeyne,' said Miss Walpole. 'Remember that the secret of all learning is patience and that curiosity is not the same thing as a thirst for knowledge. Also remember that I am always here.'

Annette, who had no intention of imprinting this disagreeable idea on her mind, said, 'Thank you,' and backed away rapidly towards the door. In a moment she was hurrying down the corridor and jumping into the street.

As soon as Annette found herself outside, she began to run. This was not because she wanted to get away from Ringenhall Ladies' College but because whenever she was feeling pleased and excited she would run: like Nike, she was normally to be seen in rapid motion, putting her foot to the ground in a swirl of drapery. Annette wore underneath her dress two or three coloured petticoats; so that as she ran, and as the April wind now did its best to sweep her from the ground, her long legs appeared in a kaleidoscope of whirling colours. Twice she dropped her books and had to go back for them. Three times she passed something which pleased her and had to run backwards until it was out of sight. Annette never minded turning round in the street and looking back. Her father had told her that this was childish and Miss Walpole told her that it was undignified. But her brother Nicholas, whom she admired more than anyone in the world, had said: 'People who never look round are always missing things.' There was nothing Annette and Nicholas feared so much as the possibility of missing something. Her father had laughed, and mentioned Orpheus and Lot's wife. 'I should have looked round if I'd been them,' said Annette. 'The most interesting things are always happening behind one.' 'The trouble with you,' her father had said, 'is that you want to be everywhere at once. One day you'll just explode into little pieces.'

It was beginning to rain. Annette shot round the corner from Queen's Gate at a considerable pace backwards, looking at a black man. Then she turned and pelted along Kensington High Street. She wanted to get home quickly and change and be ready to break the news to Rosa. 'I'm the boss now,' said Annette out loud as she ran past Barker's. Two ladies who were passing stared at her in amazement. Her eyes and her mouth were wide open and her petticoats were spinning like a Catherine-wheel. Trying to kick up her heels behind her like a horse, she nearly fell flat on her nose.

TWO

A door downstairs slammed violently. 'My sister is a brute!' said Hunter Keepe.

Calvin Blick was not interested in Hunter's sister, who was by then of a certain age. Besides, she was a plump woman; Calvin liked women, if at all, to be long-legged, pale, and slim, with very small feet. He had seated himself on the edge of Hunter's desk and was swinging his legs.

Hunter hated this familiarity. 'Need you sit on my desk?' he asked.

'There's nowhere else to sit,' said Calvin sulkily. This was true; there was no other chair in the room except the chair occupied by Hunter.

'There's the floor!' said Hunter.

This was true too. Calvin removed himself to the floor, where he reclined in the position of an Etruscan lying on his tomb. Calvin was a tall man, with pale eyes whose colour no one could ever remember.

'Need you lie down like that?' said Hunter. He found this posture equally irritating.

'Nothing pleases you, Mr Keepe,' said Calvin. 'Where am I to put myself?'

'You can sit there, with your back against the wall,' said Hunter.

Calvin put himself in the spot indicated by Hunter. 'This place is a pigsty,' he said. 'Look at the dust on my trousers already!'

'I can't afford a woman,' said Hunter, 'and Rosa won't clean up in here. Anyway, she's so busy at the factory now.'

'At the what?' said Calvin.

'At the factory,' said Hunter. 'Didn't you know? It all comes of being named after Rosa Luxemburg. She never had a chance.' He spoke with bitterness.

'Oh, I don't know,' said Calvin. 'What about me? I got on all right.'

12

'It's a rotten little factory anyway,' said Hunter. 'It makes sort of rollers and sprayers for painting with. It's not even exciting.'

'Well, it's useful,' said Calvin. 'We're all producers nowadays, as Saint-Simon says. But why does your sister do it?'

'She wants to be in touch with the People,' said Hunter gloomily, 'and to make her life colourless.'

'As for that,' said Calvin, 'most of us can manage it without taking so much trouble.' He wanted to bring the conversation back to the point from which Hunter had been leading it away. 'Tell me, do you edit the review from here?'

'Yes,' said Hunter. 'This is the office.'

'No wonder you've got a circulation of three.'

'We're doing all right.'

'You're nearly bankrupt,' said Calvin, 'and I just don't understand why you're turning down my proposal. You won't get an offer from anyone else for your dead-beat rag.'

Calvin was puzzled. Hunter had remained throughout the interview, not exactly adamant but apparently uninterested. He kept turning his head away like a sulky horse. The curious thing was that Blick was sure that his adversary was not a strong man. He had not expected this sort of resistance, and he was still at a loss to estimate its nature.

'I don't want to sell what you call my dead-beat rag to you or anyone else, so there,' said Hunter. He tossed back his rather long yellow hair.

Hunter was twenty-seven and was what some people would have called a 'pretty boy'. He had a very smooth face and a deprecating self-pitying smile. With his prettiness he had the untidy look not so much of an undergraduate as of a small boy. He took after his blond father, who had been a painter. Rosa took after her dark-haired mother, who had been a Fabian.

'It isn't even,' said Calvin, 'as if it *was* yours, the *Artemis*. Technically it belongs to your sister, doesn't it?'

'Oh, technically,' said Hunter, 'it belongs to a lot of old women who campaigned for Women's Rights back in nineteen ten. They were the original shareholders, and a lot of them are still around, tough as old boots. When our mother died, her shares came to Rosa. No man is allowed to hold shares in it, you know. That's in the constitution. But Rosa's only one shareholder among others.'

13

'So, strictly speaking,' said Calvin, 'it's the shareholders who should decide what happens to the review.'

'They don't matter,' said Hunter. 'They've forgotten about it long ago. The shares have been worthless for years. I call a shareholders' meeting at the prescribed intervals, and I bring a report and a financial statement, but no one turns up. The whole character of the *Artemis* has changed so completely in the last twenty years or so those battle-axes just wouldn't recognize it as the old suffragette paper. It's I who decide what happens now. I am the *Artemis*.'

'What about your sister?' asked Calvin.

'Rosa doesn't care a damn,' said Hunter rather bitterly.

'So far as the shareholders are concerned,' said Calvin, 'they'd probably be glad enough to be bought out. After all, they'd suddenly get some cash in return for those perfectly valueless shares.'

'Possibly,' said Hunter.

'So it's only you who's holding up the deal,' said Calvin; 'and what puzzles me is why? You don't even enjoy editing the thing. You don't make a penny out of it – and I can see from the appearance of this office that it's all a pain in the neck to you.'

'Don't talk about "the deal",' said Hunter. 'There's no deal. I'm not going to sell the *Artemis,* and that's that. Now be so good as to go away.'

Calvin rose and stared gloomily at Hunter. He had no intention of giving up, and he was certainly not ready to leave before he had thoroughly understood what was in Hunter's mind. He was prepared to stay there for the rest of the day if necessary. He started walking up and down the room, kicking aside the cardboard boxes, piles of newspaper and old numbers of the *Artemis* with which the floor was strewn.

'Don't do that,' said Hunter. 'You raise a dust.'

'Like to see a photograph of my mother?' asked Calvin. This was an old routine.

'I'm not interested,' said Hunter.

Calvin drew a sheaf of photographs out of his breast pocket. He showed Hunter the first one. It represented a well-proportioned girl dressed in a pair of black stockings and high-heeled shoes.

'Not bad,' said Hunter.

'And this is one of her after she dyed her hair,' said Calvin.

The next photograph showed a blonde climbing out of a bath.

'That's enough,' said Hunter. 'Where do you get those things, anyway?' Rumour said that Calvin Blick took all his photographs himself.

'Oh, just out of the family album,' said Calvin. He gathered the photos together like a pack of cards with a quick gesture of his pale, freckled hands. Calvin always wore several rings, not always the same ones. Hunter had noticed this and despised it. His own hands were dirty and his finger-nails cut roughly to a point. The two men looked with distaste at each other's hands.

'You understand,' said Calvin, 'that quite apart from any monies your sister might receive for her shares, you would be offered a certain sum, a sum in the fixing of which, I may say, we would be open to any reasonable proposal, as compensation for surrendering your editorial duties. Now, you're an educated man, Mr Keepe, you're not a socially unprotected man like me —'

'You're not socially unprotected now,' said Hunter spitefully. He was glad to find that he was able to put up this show of spirit. He concentrated his attention on Calvin's elastic-topped trousers, another item which he found thoroughly worthy of contempt. All the same, he had reason to fear the man, and he wished that he would go.

'I wonder if you realize that you are audibly grinding your teeth?' said Calvin. 'I knew a man who ground his teeth so hard for years and years that he ground them right down to the gum. It's a neurotic symptom, of course. Freud says somewhere —'

'Look here, Blick,' said Hunter, 'your boss already owns three newspapers and heaven knows how many periodicals and every kind of organized beastliness in print. What does he want the wretched *Artemis* for? Why can't he leave it alone?'

'He just wants it,' said Calvin. 'That's all. He just wants it.'

'Well, if he wants it, let him come and ask for it himself,' said Hunter, and his voice was trembling. 'Let him come in person to discuss it, and not send his servants.'

Calvin stared at him. 'Ah!' he said. 'Aha!' He had begun to understand.

At that moment the door of Hunter's office burst open and Annette entered like a small tornado. She seemed to fly in one bound from the door to perch on Hunter's desk, and her skirt

15

and petticoats fell in great multi-coloured folds all over his papers as she drew her feet up after her like someone taking refuge on a rock.

'Oh, Hunter,' cried Annette, 'do listen! I've left beastly Ringenhall!'

'Annette!' cried Hunter. 'How many times must I tell you not to enter this office without knocking? I'm in conference now, you must go away!'

Annette noticed Calvin, and fell off the desk. But it was too late. Calvin had jumped up and said, 'Don't go away yet, we haven't been introduced.' He was studying Annette with considerable interest.

Hunter looked furious. 'This is Annette Cockeyne,' he mumbled. 'Meet Calvin Blick.'

Annette bowed graciously to Calvin and held out her hand. His name meant nothing to her. She smiled her large joyful smile. Annette's teeth were set upon the arc of a circle so that as she smiled she revealed more and more and more small white teeth until the smile stretched right across her face. '*Enchantée*,' said Annette.

'Yes,' said Calvin. 'I thought I couldn't be mistaken. Your resemblance to your mother is very striking.'

'You know my mother?' said Annette. She was not surprised. Europe was full of men who knew her mother.

'I have had the honour of meeting her,' said Calvin. He was standing now with his heels smartly together, bending attentively towards Annette. The careless slouching appearance which he had had a moment ago was quite gone.

'Get out!' said Hunter.

'May I ask if your mother is in London?' asked Calvin, paying no attention to Hunter.

'No,' said Annette, 'she's still with Andrew in Turkey.' Annette had called her parents by their Christian names ever since she could remember.

'Are you staying long in London, Annette?' asked Calvin. 'May I call you Annette?'

'Blick, *will* you go away?' said Hunter.

'Don't be so horrid, Hunter,' said Annette. 'What's the matter with you? I'm fixed in London for this year. I've been at school here, you know. That is, till this afternoon.'

'Where do you live?' asked Calvin.

Hunter sat down at his desk and groaned softly as he began to pull the papers together into an aimless heap.

'Why, I live here,' said Annette, 'with Hunter and Rosa. Do you know Rosa too?'

'I have the honour,' said Calvin. He turned to Hunter. 'I see you've been keeping all sorts of things from me!' he said maliciously. He gave Annette a smile which lit up his colourless face with a sudden gaiety, revealing in it an unexpected amount of detail. 'Tell us about your school,' he said. 'What's this about having left?'

'Yes, it was wonderful,' said Annette. 'I just walked out!'

'Why did you do that?' asked Calvin. As he spoke, he was looking Annette up and down. He noted with approval her narrow long-legged build and the pallor of her face and the creamy smoothness of her bare legs. In Calvin's view a woman ought to be the same colour all over.

'I was learning nothing there,' said Annette. 'I have decided that from now on I shall educate myself. I shall go out into the School of Life.'

Calvin laughed. 'Well done!' he said. 'I trust that I may see you from time to time in the course of your studies!'

'You're to go now, Blick!' said Hunter, getting up.

'Do stop it, Hunter,' said Annette. 'Where's Rosa?'

'She's gone to see Dr. Saward,' said Hunter, 'and then on to the factory.'

'When will she be back?' asked Annette. 'I was wondering if I had time to go and see Nina.'

'She comes off early today,' said Hunter.

'Well, I'll go to Nina tomorrow morning,' said Annette. 'I do want to see Rosa as soon as she's back.'

'Is that Nina the dressmaker?' asked Calvin. His eyes were gleaming like a couple of sea-washed limpet shells.

'Yes,' said Annette. 'Do you — ?'

'Get out! Get out! Get out!' shouted Hunter. He began to toss the papers up in the air. A cloud of dust spread over the three of them. Annette began to sneeze.

'Get out!' Hunter cried again, and he started to push Calvin Blick towards the door. Calvin did not resist, but departed laughing, and could be heard laughing and sneezing all the way down the stairs.

Hunter came back. He looked at Annette with exasperation.

17

He was fond of her, but as he had said to Rosa when the latter had proposed that Annette should come to live with them he thought that she was likely to prove a trouble-maker; and, quite apart from his other worries, he had been far from pleased to hear her announcement about having left school. Now we're for it! thought Hunter. He looked upon the slim child with displeasure.

'You wait till Rosa hears about your trying to leave Ringenhall!' he said.

Annette turned a little pale. 'Rosa won't mind at all!' she said defiantly.

This was just what Hunter feared. He shrugged his shoulders. 'Now go,' he said. 'I'm busy.'

'What did that man mean about your having kept things from him?' asked Annette.

'I haven't the foggiest idea,' said Hunter. 'Just go away, will you? Go away!' And as the door closed behind her, Hunter said to himself again, Yes, Yes, now we're for it!

THREE

Peter Saward was sitting writing at a very large desk which was covered thickly all over with open books, photographs and printed sheets of hieroglyphic script. The surface of the desk was not visible. In places the books lay three or four deep. The floor was also littered with books. The room must have contained some three thousand volumes, of which at least a hundred were open, some lying horizontal, some at an angle of forty-five degrees, and others vertical, opened at a favourite illustration and perched on top of bookshelves or supported ingeniously by pieces of string. The shelves reached in most places to the ceiling. Any space which remained was covered with photographs of statues or reproductions of paintings pinned edge to edge.

The room was large, with wide casement windows which gave on to a dark green garden with tall walls and a single plane tree. Owing to the plane tree, the room was dark, and owing to the richly encrusted character of five of its surfaces, resembled an underground cavern. The ceiling alone had resisted Peter Saward, and his failure to cover it over with pictures and suspended objects was due solely to a lack of mechanical skill. Its pale surface, however, had in the course of the years developed first cracks and slight undulations, and later knobs, bulges and protuberances of all kinds, as if in irresistible sympathy with the walls and floor. Upon the mantelpiece, from which pieces of paper, pipes and boxes of matches fell intermittently, there stood an hour-glass which Peter Saward would thoughtfully reverse from time to time, and a photograph of Peter Saward's sister, who had died when she was nineteen. That was a long time ago. Over the mantelpiece hung a picture of Mommsen and beside the door a picture of Eduard Myer. On a table in the corner, in the middle of a pile of papers, sometimes visible and sometimes invisible, there was an anonymous-looking green plant, whose mysterious

19

vitality produced in this dark and dry interior a luxuriance of green leaves but no flowers.

It was early in the afternoon. Peter Saward usually divided his working day into four sections. In the morning he would remain quiet and receptive, almost in a dream, writing down ideas as they came to him. He would rise early and start work at once, postponing his breakfast until ten-thirty. What he wrote down during this time would be perhaps plans for future work, or intuitions about present problems, or else stranger things still, visions of the past, a knowledge which seemed to belong to the night, and a small portion of which could be caught each day before it fled away along the paths of sleep or became inextricably mingled with the phantoms of desire and anxiety. Peter Saward attached great importance to these intuitions; and at one time, before his doctor sternly forbade it, had extended this part of the working day into the night itself, taking a pad of paper to bed with him and continually writing upon it in the dark, as he woke intermittently in the night hours, and tossing the sheets on the floor, so that he would wake each morning surrounded by a sea of thoughts, many of which he would then have anxiously and often unsuccessfully to try to decipher. Since his illness, however, he had reluctantly abandoned this attempt to get twenty four hours' work out of each day. Yet he still made what he could of the night.

After ten-thirty, and during lunch, which he ate at his desk, and on till four he would work more systematically, writing perhaps a note or an article or some part of the longer work which had been in progress now for some ten years. In the evening he read sources, checked references, made notes, sifted and criticized his notebook of 'intuitions', and prepared material for the work of the following afternoon. After that would come the night again, which would be preceded by a period of contemplation, during which, in a kind of prayer, the problems were summoned up which were to be committed to the care of the darkness and put to the question during the hours of sleep. Normally every day would pass in this manner, varied only by occasional evening visits from friends. Peter Saward was a historian of the empires which rose and fell before Babylon.

Of late, however, Peter had become the victim, as he put it to himself, of an absurd obsession. The obsession was the deciphering of the Kastanic script, samples of which now littered his desk. Peter had used to hold the view that the deciphering of scripts was not a historian's job. He knew, from many distinguished examples, how easily such a thing can become a mania, and how the most sober and balanced of men, once this passion is upon them, can lose completely their sense of proportion and spend years in trying to establish a particular theory the evidence for which could be written upon a postcard. 'It's a mug's game,' he could hear his own voice saying out of the past, 'deciphering these ancient scripts. It isn't even as if historical knowledge could help you much. Very often it's better to forget what you know, or think you know, about who may or may not have written this language or what it's likely to mean, and treat the thing as a cipher or a problem in pure philology. Historical conjectures are so often wrong; and once you start to mislead yourself, you may work for years on the wrong track. Life's too short. It's not worth it.'

Yet now he had become mad himself in exactly this way. The Kastanic script had been known since the middle of the nineteenth century, when a number of tablets had been discovered in Syria; and in the years that followed, a small steady stream of tablets, monuments, seals, and dishes had turned up covered with similar characters, but so far the language had completely resisted all attempts at decipherment. Peter Saward had considered the problem of the script many years ago and had set it aside to lie among those many unsolved problems of ancient history which must simply wait upon the chance of further archaeological discoveries, in particular the discovery of a bilingual monument or tablet which, giving the same inscription in a known language and in the unknown script, would give a rational beginning to the task of decipherment. Without that, work on the script would be work completely in the dark, since it was still quite uncertain who had written this language, for what purposes, or even what type of language it was.

However, some eighteen months ago the Kastanic script had come once more to Peter Saward's attention because of two apparently unconnected things: one was the discovery of a large cache of tablets bearing the script on the site of an ancient city near the Bosphorus which was of particular interest to Peter; and the other was the appearance, again in Syria, of a number of tablets written in the cuneiform script, not in the

21

Babylonian language but in some unknown language. Immediately, for reasons which, he was well aware, hardly amounted yet to a historical argument, Peter Saward became convinced that the unknown cuneiform language and the language of the hieroglyphic script were one and the same. Further, the idea became lodged in him, and resisted all criticism, that the decipherment of the script, of which a very considerable number of items now existed, would bring him, and by the only available method, the solution of a number of problems which had troubled him for years. From that moment on he was lost.

Peter Saward knew very well that his intuitions about the script were exactly similar in type to those which he had, with pitying shakes of the head, observed to mislead and confound his fellow-historians in the past. And when he began himself to work seriously at the task he saw but too clearly how easy it was, in such a morass of imagination and conjecture, to attach oneself desperately to any idea which had even the faintest plausibility, to allow a conjecture, through mere familiarity and through the absence of rivals, to seem gradually more and more likely, and to become daily more in love with it because of the complete lack of even any rational starting-point to which one could return. Peter Saward was always fanatically systematic in his work. Although he knew how to invoke the darkness, he was rigorous in his criticism of his intuitions, and anything which could not fit into or modify the steady and continuous scheme of his work was ruthlessly discarded. In deciphering the script, however, the very problem was *how* to be systematic. The only thing that seemed clear about it was that it contained too many signs to be an alphabetic script. It might be a syllabic or an ideographic script, or a mixture of the two. It was not even clear whether the language in question was Indo-European or not. Anything was possible. Peter Saward proceeded at last by two methods: that of selecting names of gods and kings which might perhaps be mentioned in the inscriptions and trying, in some way or other, to identify some of the signs with these names, and that of studying the signs themselves, attempting to group and classify them and so establish in some way the structure of the language. He also hoped to get some clues, he hardly knew how, from a study of the cuneiform tablets. How happy he would have been if these procedures had yielded absolutely no results! Unfortunately although they yielded no results worth speaking of, they did seem to provide a number of hints or possibilities which always seemed to be worth following, without as yet leading to anything in the least conclusive. So, cursing himself, Peter Saward went on, until the task of decipherment encroached more and more upon his working day, and the mystery of his sleep was resolved into a dance of nightmare hieroglyphics.

Winter and summer a stove was burning in his room, stoked by Peter Saward's landlady, a Miss Glashan, who also brought him his meals and did the cleaning. In the course of time this lady had become expert in removing every speck of dust without disturbing the position of any object. She would dart about the room silently with the dexterity of a cat and the dirt would vanish as completely as if she had swallowed it. Miss Glashan never spoke, though she often smiled. She was in awe of Peter Saward, both because of those rather austere features of his character which inspired awe in most of the people who knew him and also for an extra reason of her own, because he was a sick man. Miss Glashan, who had never known a day's illness, regarded sick people with a mixture of reverence and horror which was identical with her attitude towards death. Peter Saward had an advanced but quiescent tuberculosis. As Miss Glashan told her friends with emotion, he had only one lung. His illness had been successfully arrested, but the doctors had sentenced him to a quiet life. Since then he had grown plump. Of the fine silhouette of his earlier youth there remained only the profile of his face. He had also, his friends noticed, grown strangely gay; and very often, when he had company, he would stretch out his long legs and throw back his big head and laugh till the house rocked, and Miss Glashan in the kitchen would say to her neighbours, 'Hear him laughing, the poor soul!' Peter Saward was forty-four years of age.

He was starting at the hieroglyphics; but it was now some time since they had become invisible. At last he thrust them aside. He was expecting Rosa. Peter could not endure the wasting of time. He would read a book while he ate his meals and even while he was shaving, with the result that he was usually as covered with scars as a Sicilian bandit. There were other special tasks which he saved up for times when he knew that he would be disturbed. While Miss Glashan was cleaning the room, he would work on his bibliography, sorting and indexing the innumerable scraps of paper on which he had written references to books and articles. But even this was too exacting for the times during which he was waiting for Rosa. After various experiments he had decided that the only thing he was fit for just then was cutting the pages of books. He deplored this irrational and continually renewed agitation, but was by now resigned to it. He stacked up the sheets of hieroglyphics, and reached out for the pile of volumes which he had been keeping ready for this moment. The soft hiss of the paper-knife made an accompaniment of his thoughts.

There was a knock at the door. Peter Saward lived on the ground floor, and as the front door of the house was always open, his visitors could come straight to his room. He dropped the knife and called out. But it was not Rosa.

The person who entered was a man called John Rainborough, an old friend of Peter Saward, but now a rare caller. Peter did his best to look pleased to see him, and succeeded. 'Come in, John,' he said. 'This is an unexpected treat. Sit down.'

'May I?' said Rainborough. 'I hope I'm not disturbing you. I just thought I'd drop in on the way back to the office.'

Rainborough held an important post in the Special European Labour Immigration Board, better known as SELIB, a body which had started life as a charitable organization supported mainly by American contributions and which now received a certain financial assistance from the British Government. He had the reputation of being a very clever man, though those who described him in this way would always add, 'Of course, he hasn't yet found his niche.'

Although Rainborough was younger than Saward by several years, he looked older. He had lost his hair almost to the crown of his head, which gave him the appearance of having an enormous forehead which was divided into two halves, a lower half covered with deep wrinkles and an upper half which was smooth and shining. He fidgeted continually and had restless brown eyes. He was embarrassed by his partial baldness and never ceased to envy Peter Saward, in whose great bush of brown hair, every time that he came to see him, he would look in vain for some traces of daylight. Saward was fond of him, although at that moment he wished him at the devil.

Rainborough sat down, screwing himself into the chair. 'How's the work?' he asked.

'At a standstill,' said Peter Saward.

'Oh, that language thing,' said Rainborough. 'Yes, I saw in *The Times* they'd found a bilingual.'

'It's not true,' said Saward. 'At least, it was only a seal with a single name on it, together with what may be, but probably isn't, one of my hieroglyphs.'

'I can't think why you bother,' said Rainborough.

Peter Saward shrugged his shoulders. 'A bilingual might turn up next week, or it might never turn up.' He suppressed the irritation he felt against Rainborough for expressing what he himself also felt, that he was wasting his time.

Rainborough was shifting in his seat and fiddling nervously with the edge of the chair. It was some time now since he had ceased to think of Peter Saward as a master from whom he might learn important truths, but he still bore him a slight grudge for having ever appeared, even momentarily, in that role. Rainborough respected and envied Saward's learning, which extended far beyond the bounds of the ancient world, and he disliked and was impressed by the simplicity of his life. He also and especially admired the way in which Saward was able to harness all the resources of his intellect to a single task. This was a thing which Rainborough had never been able to do; on the contrary, each project in which he interested himself would regularly turn out, after a while, to have 'nothing in it'. He gained, however a certain relief from reflecting on the peculiar pointlessness of the studies in which his friend specialized. Wherein, he asked himself, lay the interest or importance of the rise and fall of empires whose very existence rested upon a few unprepossessing stones and a disputed reference in the Book of Kings? Whole dynasties of princes with barbarous names and pantheons of gods dubiously identified with more respectable and better known deities, appeared to be supported only by the vigorous imagination of Peter Saward and his colleagues. And if Saward had in fact gone slowly mad and were inventing it all, Rainborough reflected, it would be years before anyone found out, even, he thought spitefully, his fellow-historians; and it wouldn't make any difference to anything.

Since Saward's illness, Rainborough had also been made uneasy by a change which he imagined to have taken place in his friend and which he found it difficult to diagnose. After he had been near to death he had become a jester. Rainborough had the impression that Saward had become deeply melancholy, and yet the only expression of this melancholy was a completely unforced cheerfulness. His personality had become in some profound way looser, less rigid; and yet the deep crack which Rainborough suspected had the strange effect of making Saward not weaker but more powerful. This change distressed Rainborough because in some sense it put the man even more beyond his reach than he had been before. He often wondered to himself, as he listened to Saward's frequent laughter, what it was that made him so conscious of the presence of something sad. It was only occasionally that Saward said something that revealed what Rainborough took, contrary to the evidence, to be the reality of the matter: as when he said once on a winter evening, 'When it is so cold I think often of those who sleep out of doors,' and it took Rainborough a moment to realize that he meant the dead.

'In fact, I'm making a little progress,' Peter Saward was saying. 'I'm almost sure now that certain signs represent grammatical suffixes — '

Rainborough, who had only made his inquiry out of politeness, hastened to interrupt him. 'Look, Peter,' he said, 'never mind that. I've got a piece of news for you. Mischa Fox is in England.'

'I know,' said Saward.

'You *know*?' said Rainborough, disappointed. 'How?'

'He called on me last week,' said Saward.

Rainborough looked annoyed. 'You're favoured!' he said. 'He hasn't condescended to call on *me*. I inferred that he was around when I saw that unspeakable man Calvin Blick in Oxford Street. I crossed the road to avoid him. Then I saw it in the *Evening News*. As you never read the papers, I thought you mightn't know.'

'Ah, well!' said Saward. His bush of brown hair had fallen over his eyes.

'It's all the more maddening,' said Rainborough, 'because I

have the reputation of being Mischa's friend, and the ten thousand people who want to see him will all start calling on me. I'm never so popular as when Mischa Fox is in England. Did he say anything about me?'

'No,' said Peter Saward.

Rainborough sat silent, frowning, his lower brow wrinkled up into a knot of lines. He would have said sincerely, and with a sort of pride, that Mischa Fox was one of his best friends; yet in his heart he now felt fear and almost hatred of the man. He never felt easy in his mind so long as Fox was in the country.

'I'm expecting Rosa,' said Peter Saward. 'You must stay and say hello to her.' He hoped that this indicated politely but clearly to Rainborough that he was not expected to stay longer than that.

'Rosa! Oh, good!' said Rainborough. A light gleamed in his eyes which was almost, but not quite, pleasure. Rainborough had known Rosa for more years than Saward had; and in the matter of Rosa he felt a certain resentment. Rainborough would have liked to play the role of being unhappily in love with Rosa, but it had been Saward who had set his heart upon her, meeting her after Rainborough had already known her for some time. Indeed, it was probably Saward's passion which had first revealed Rosa's charms to Rainborough. But it would have seemed to him absurd to love Rosa vainly, since his friend already did so.

Rainborough was not averse to being unhappily in love; indeed, an arrangement of this kind would have suited him very well. But he was reluctant to undertake the drudgery of an unrequited attachment if he was not also to have the satisfaction of being, in the eyes of the world and of the object of his love, a solitary figure. As a lonely and unfortunate admirer Rainborough could, he thought, have found in the tension of such a relationship a mode of being both apart from and together with the beloved: such a combination, in short, of security, yearning and rapture, as had now become his ideal conception of partnership with a woman. That Rosa could ever have returned his love did not enter his head, any more than it entered his head to imagine that she might ever return that of Peter Saward. It seemed to Rainborough now very unlikely that Rosa, who was a year older than himself, would ever get married. The beautiful possibilities of the situation had been spoilt by the unexpected and tireless way in which Saward had elected to love Rosa. Rainborough had no wish to be one of two people inspired by the same fruitless passion. In such a role he would have felt merely ridiculous. For such reasons he was not in love with Rosa. He had, all the same, a certain inclination for her. He admired what he took to be an ascetic trait in her character, and he liked her sulky pessimism, her sarcasm, even her rudeness, and her extremely long black hair.

'Has she seen him?' he asked Saward. 'Does she know he's in England?'

'I don't know,' said Saward. 'Rosa hasn't been here for ten days.'

'Did Fox mention *her*?' asked Rainborough.

'No.'

'Well, what the hell did you talk about? Never mind, don't tell me. I wonder ought we to mention to Rosa that Fox is here?'

'She'll certainly already know,' said Peter Saward.

'I don't see why she should,' said Rainborough. 'She might miss it in the papers, and, after all, the heavens don't turn red when Mischa Fox lands; comets don't burn in the sky, whatever some people may think.'

'She'll know,' said Saward, 'and it's better not to say anything.'

'Her kid brother never got over Rosa's turning Mischa down,' said Rainborough.

'Yes,' said Peter Saward. 'He was certainly fond of Mischa. Of course, Hunter was very young at the time.'

'The interesting question,' said Rainborough, studying his friend, 'is whether *Rosa* ever got over it.'

'Ah —' said Peter Saward. He had put the books aside, and was examining the paper-knife.

'It was a good thing she didn't marry him,' said Rainborough. 'He is a man capable of enormous cruelty.'

Peter Saward only replied by staring at the paper-knife and shaking his head slowly to and fro, and twisting his long legs into knots under the desk. 'How's the office, John?' he asked.

As Rainborough looked at him he felt a pang of pain and annoyance at his vulnerability. No man, he thought, had any right to be so vulnerable. He was letting the side down. All males have a right to a certain brutality, a certain insensibility.

28

Without this, Rainborough thought, we can be charged with anything. But Saward had foregone his right, perhaps never knew that he had it. Here was a personality without frontiers. Saward did not defend himself by placing others. He did not defend himself. It was, Rainborough thought, a scandal. He accepted the change of subject.

'The office,' he said, 'is appalling. The place is paralysed with boredom and inactivity. It isn't that there aren't plenty of things that need doing: half the staff needs to be sacked to start with. But it's partly that no one has enough real authority to do anything drastic, and partly that we're all so pleased at being in safe seats with large salaries that we daren't start rocking the boat for fear we fall out ourselves.'

'What are you waiting for?' asked Peter Saward.

Rainborough laughed nastily. 'I suppose,' he said, 'that I'm waiting until my own seat is made so impeccably safe that I can start making it hot for other people without needing to be afraid of the reprisals!'

'But you don't need the money, John,' said Peter Saward.

'I know,' said Rainborough. 'It isn't the money. It's just that one would have to be so bold and make oneself so unpleasant in order to get anything done. It's easier to sit still and hope for one's position to improve.'

'You hope to be Director when Sir Edward retires?'

'Yes,' said Rainborough shortly. He always found himself making damaging admissions to Peter Saward, and could not decide whether it was the manner of his friend's questions, or his own desire to strip himself before Saward, which brought this about.

Rosa came in. She knocked and entered in the same moment. Rainborough leapt up, took a step back, and stumbled over a pile of books. Rosa looked surprised to see him, and displeased. 'John,' she said, uttering the syllable in a colourless way which was neither an exclamation nor a greeting. It was as if she noticed his presence and murmured the word to herself. She paid no attention to Peter Saward, but sat down on a chair beside the door. Saward did not look at her, but bent his head lower over his desk.

'Don't mind me,' said Rosa. 'Go on talking.'

Rainborough sat down, kicking books away to right and left. 'Don't be absurd, Rosa!' he said. 'How can we ignore you?'

29

'I'm not asking you to ignore me,' said Rosa, 'but just to continue your conversation.' She turned her chair round so that she faced the bookshelves and began to examine the books. She selected a volume, and leaning a plump hand on the back of the chair, began to read. The two men looked at her back.

'What are you so cross about, Rosa?' asked Rainborough.

Rosa turned round far enough for him to see her profile. 'That man Calvin Blick is with Hunter,' she said.

Rainborough was very interested. 'Whatever did he want?' he asked.

'He wants to buy the *Artemis* for Mischa Fox.'

Rainborough exclaimed. 'How extraordinary! What is Fox plotting now?'

'Must he always be *plotting* something?' asked Rosa.

'Yes,' said Rainborough, 'I think so. Don't you think so?'

Rosa shrugged her shoulders. 'I don't like Calvin Blick,' she said, 'and poor Hunter is terrified of him.'

'Blick is the dark half of Mischa Fox's mind,' said Rainborough. 'He does the things which Mischa doesn't even think of. That's how Mischa can be so innocent.'

Rosa made a contemptuous gesture. Then she tossed the book she had been reading on to the ground.

'Pick it up,' said Peter Saward, 'and put it where you found it, or I won't know where it is.' Rosa replaced the book.

'But why in heaven's name should Mischa want to have the *Artemis*?' asked Rainborough. He was fascinated.

'Why indeed?' said Rosa. 'What is the *Artemis* good for?'

'I didn't mean that,' said Rainborough, 'as you well know. But why the *Artemis*?'

'The *Artemis* is a little independent thing,' said Rosa, 'it's very small, but it goes around on its own. There aren't many completely independent periodicals these days. Perhaps the sight of a little independent thing annoys Mischa. It's like the instinct to catch fish or butterflies. To feel the thing struggling in your grasp.' She stretched out her hand and closed her fingers slowly.

'Rosa,' said Peter Saward. He murmured her name like a magic charm to protect not himself but her.

'All the same it's odd,' said Rainborough. 'Hunter won't sell, of course.'

30

'I've no idea,' said Rosa, 'what Hunter will do. It's nothing to do with me.'

'Come, Rosa,' said Rainborough. 'You know Hunter will do whatever you say.'

'That's why I'm not going to say anything,' said Rosa.

'I only hope Hunter will be arrogant enough,' said Rainborough. 'It's not often anyone is in a position to be thoroughly disobliging to Calvin Blick. It's a chance not to be missed.'

'I don't see why Hunter shouldn't sell if he wants to!' said Rosa. Her hair hung in loops over her brow like a cloud of black thoughts and was wound upon her neck into a long heavy knot. She still sat turned sideways to the two men, looking at the bookshelves on the opposite wall. 'He's being offered a good price for the shares, and a compensation for the loss of a job he hates. I don't see why he should refuse just because some people think Calvin Blick ought to be taught a lesson!'

'Hunter should be too proud to sell!' said Rainborough.

'What do you mean, "too proud"?' asked Rosa. She was taut with irritation.

'Well,' said Rainborough, 'I mean – I should have thought you would have cared too much about the *Artemis*, Rosa, its traditions and so on.'

'It's clear you've never had to run a review,' said Rosa, 'or you wouldn't talk nonsense about "traditions". The *Artemis* is a wretched thing, it just manages to drag itself along from month to month. It's painful to watch. Perhaps it would be a good thing of Mischa Fox were to put it out of its misery. If he can turn it into a glossy magazine and make it pay, good luck to him.'

'You astonish me, Rosa,' said Rainborough. He was beginning to sound really angry. 'If I were you I'd rather kill the *Artemis* than let Mischa Fox have it. Whatever will the shareholders say?'

'They'll say what Hunter says,' said Rosa.

'If it's a matter of pumping some money in,' said Rainborough, 'I'm surprised you haven't approached the shareholders long ago with some sort of appeal. One or two of those old trouts are rolling in wealth. Camilla Wingfield, for instance. She's made of money. She could easily put *Artemis* in the clear. Have you never thought of that?'

'No,' said Rosa, 'I haven't. The old woman you mention is mad, incidentally.'

'She's not mad,' said Rainborough. 'I admit that she seems to be under the impression that she did in Mr Wingfield. But who are we to call her deluded? In any case, I think you ought to fight Mischa Fox.'

'For heaven's sake!' said Rosa. 'Under what banner?' She was rubbing her eyes and combing her hair with her fingers as if her thoughts were anywhere but with the present conversation. 'It's Hunter's business,' she said.

'Then why are you so upset about it?' asked Rainborough.

'I just feel ill from having had Calvin Blick in the house,' said Rosa. 'He is a horrible person.'

'I don't know —' said Peter Saward suddenly. 'He has a pleasant smile.'

'Peter, your good nature sometimes approaches imbecility,' said Rosa. 'Anyway, I don't want Blick to get wind of Annette.'

'Ah, Marcia Cockeyne's daughter,' said Rainborough.

'Yes,' said Rosa. 'Marcia wanted Annette kept out of Mischa's way. Mischa doesn't know the child's in England. And there's no reason why he should know, unless Blick smells her out.'

'I never met the legendary Marcia,' said Rainborough, 'but I remember meeting Annette when she was a child of fourteen, with that peculiar brother of hers. She was a striking kid. Her mother used to be a great friend of Mischa's. Have they quarrelled?'

'Of course not,' said Rosa. 'It's just that Marcia doesn't think Mischa would be the best chaperon for Annette in London.'

'I remember too,' said Rainborough, 'hearing someone speculating about whether Mischa wasn't really Annette's father. Do you believe that story?'

'I know it to be untrue,' said Rosa. 'Annette was about seven when her mother first met Mischa Fox.' She turned and looked at Rainborough, pushing her hair back out of her eyes. She was calm and grave now, the irritation was gone. 'Besides,' she said, 'Mischa would be too young.'

'Who knows?' said Rainborough. 'No one knows Mischa's age. One can hardly even make a guess. It's uncanny. He could be thirty, he could be fifty-five. Have you ever met anyone who knew? I'm sure even Calvin Blick doesn't know. No one knows his age. No one knows where he came from either. Where was he born? What blood is in his veins? No one knows. And if you try to imagine you are paralysed. It's like that thing with his eyes. You can't look into his eyes. You have to look *at* his eyes. Heaven knows what you'd see if you looked in.'

Rosa yawned ostentatiously. 'John, would you mind going?' she said. 'I want to talk to Peter.'

Rainborough got up. He still looked furious. 'You drive me mad, Rosa!' he said. He picked up his coat. 'I must get back to the office anyhow.'

'And I have to be at the factory at four,' said Rosa.

'Oh!' said Peter Saward. During the foregoing conversation he had sat contemplating Rosa's profile, and seemed not to be listening. 'So you're only giving me three-quarters of an hour!'

'That's right,' said Rosa, 'and Rainborough has already taken up twenty minutes of it.'

'All right, all right, I'm going!' said Rainborough. He moved to the door. Without looking up, Rosa held out her hand. He pressed it and then laughed. 'You drive me mad!' he repeated.

After the door closed, Rosa sat for some time still rubbing her eyes and rubbing her hand over her face. Peter Saward sat looking at the paper-knife. He heard her get up. Then she began to wander about the room. She always did this. It was a kind of dance. Peter Saward felt the whole room suddenly stiffen. The walls were full of consciousness and jerked themselves upright. The ceiling trembled. The space flung itself out like a fisherman's net and hung poised in an expanse of significant points. Still Rosa moved. She touched the green plant and drew her finger along the window pane. She stepped upon the books and breathed upon the pictures. It seemed to Peter Saward that she walked about in the air, and her shadow fell upon him from far above. He waited patiently. The circle grew smaller and smaller. At last he felt Rosa's fingers touch his hair. They touched it lightly at first, like birds not daring to land. Then they came back and plunged deeply in. Rosa drew her hands down the two sides of his face and lifted his head. She was standing above him. For the first time since her arrival they looked into each other's eyes. They looked gravely for several minutes, each scrutinizing the other, not with tenderness but with a puzzled curious intentness. 'Hmmm!' said

Rosa, and she threw away his head as if it had been a ball. Peter Saward caught her by the wrist as she was moving off.

Peter Saward was well aware that it is the illusion of the lover that love always consoles. Yet he could not help hoping that in some way his love was a benefit to Rosa. He had sometimes found, or imagined that he found, in her lately an increase of concern about him; but this might very well be a reverence for his illness and not a tenderness for himself. That ambiguity would go with him to the end of his life. It sometimes seemed to him that the continuity of his work in some way pleased her or healed some restlessness in her. When she expressed, as she constantly did, irritation with his obsession with the Kastanic script, he liked to flatter himself that this was the reflection of his own dissatisfaction, detected by the sensitive instrument of a true affinity; though at other times he was more inclined to believe that her annoyance with the hieroglyphs was simply annoyance with him and not an attachment to him that went deeper than consciousness.

He sighed and tried to look up at her, but Rosa moved behind him, and reaching over his shoulder pulled one of the hieroglyphic sheets into the centre of the desk. For a moment they both looked at it together.

'What does it say, Peter?' asked Rosa.

'I wish I knew,' said Peter Saward. 'Perhaps it's a great poem.'

Rosa always asked this question and Peter always gave the same answer, although in fact he did not think that it was perhaps a great poem.

'It's more likely to be someone's laundry list,' said Rosa.

'People don't carve their laundry lists on the backsides of stone lions twenty feet high,' said Peter Saward.

'Well, then, it's the dreary boasting of some king,' said Rosa — 'so many cities destroyed, so many men killed. I wish it were all over with! But maybe it'll all come to you in a flash.'

In such moments, with Rosa looking over his shoulder, Peter Saward did indeed feel that it might all come to him in a flash. But he shook his head. 'It's not like breaking a code, Rosa,' he said. 'Even if I got the elementary things right, I'd still have to build up the vocabulary bit by bit. Nothing can happen quickly. But I've told you this at least a hundred times.'

'Well, I can't listen,' said Rosa. 'I try to, but it bores me to death. Oh, I *hate* all this stuff, I hate it! Peter, why do I hate it so?'

Peter Saward wished that he knew. He sighed, and captured her hand again where it lay lightly on his shoulder. 'O Rosa —' he began.

'I see you've cut yourself shaving again,' said Rosa, who knew what was coming. 'Your face is covered with blood.' She could be very prompt in creating a distraction when Peter Saward wanted to say something serious.

'Rosa, I love you,' said Peter.

Rosa stroked his hair in a mechanical way with her free hand and said, 'I wish I had half a crown for every time you've said that.'

Peter, who was used to this, only replied, 'Stop hiding behind me. I want to look at you.'

Rosa ambled round his desk, picking her way between the books. 'I've got to go in five minutes,' she announced cheerfully.

'I wish you wouldn't come for these short times, Rosa!' said Peter Saward. 'You don't know how much your visits upset me. I lose hours of work. And then you're only here for a moment. And you leave me thoroughly distressed!'

Rosa turned on him at last the full power of her face, lit up suddenly with irony and delight. The love of Peter Saward was her only luxury. She never tired of forcing him to display it and lay it out for her like a rich cloth; but only when she had first protected herself by mockery and laughter.

'What!' she said, 'Isn't it worth it, to see me for half an hour? Think how much you can see of me in half an hour. I sneeze, I open and close my eyes, I stand up, I sit down, I walk, I talk! Even if you lost ten hours' work, wouldn't it be worth it for half an hour of me?'

'It would be worth it!' said Peter Saward. She gave him both her hands. Her smile came to him like a flame catching.

'Would it not be worth it for ten minutes?' asked Rosa. 'Think how much you could experience in ten minutes! Enough to think about for days!'

'It would be worth it for ten minutes, Rosa!' said Peter Saward.

'Wouldn't it be worth it for a second?' said Rosa. 'Suppose you were just to see me for an instant as a door was closing, just like a snapshot. Wouldn't that be well worth ten hours' work?' Her smile had dissolved into a look of delighted tenderness that pinned him down like an arrow.

'It would be worth ten hours' work, Rosa,' said Peter Saward; 'a hundred hours, a thousand hours!'

FOUR

Rosa ran down the road towards the factory. The big square building with its square windows grew larger and larger until it was looming over her. A tall chimney held a motionless trail of white smoke over three streets and the width of the Thames. Rosa's thoughts were moving as rapidly as her feet. At that moment everything in her life seemed to be a source of desperate anxiety. O God, as if it were not enough! she thought. Not only was there the problem of Hunter's future and the distressing decision about the *Artemis*. Her hair began to come down and she could hear the hairpins one after another pattering on to the pavement behind her. Not only were there the lies she had felt herself compelled to tell, by implication and omission, to Peter Saward. Not that in a way she minded lying to Peter Saward occasionally. He knew her so well that she assumed he always knew when she was lying and so that made it all right. She was late for the four-o'clock shift. Her life was in disorder. Her hair was in disorder. Would the handkerchief hold it? It would get caught in the machine. Caught in the machine. Not only was there the perpetual vague anxiety about Annette, who lived in her house as quietly as an unexploded charge of dynamite. Now there was Mischa Fox, whose rare presences in England never failed to disturb her even if, as usually happened, she did not meet him but was only distantly and indirectly aware of his coming. And there were the Lusiewicz brothers, which was the worst thing of all. They would be expecting her this evening, they would be waiting for her now. The last hairpin fell. As if it were not enough.

Rosa clocked in. Her hair was hanging down her back, still in a precarious knot. She supported it with one hand behind her and went to find her overall. Then she lifted her hair on to the top of her head and balanced it there like a bundle while she tied it securely about with a handkerchief. Then she ran into the workroom. The rhythmical din burst upon her as she opened the door. 'You're late, Miss Keepe,' murmured voices, which perhaps she imagined, amidst the machinery. She ran down an alleyway of contorted steel. The machines at the factory were in perpetual motion day and night. If the attendant of a particular machine was late the person on the shift before was supposed to stay on until he was relieved. So lateness was frowned upon not only by the management but by the workers. Rosa's breath came in gasps. The workroom was more than a hundred yards across, and her bench was on the far side. She ran upon a soft carpet of paper and steel shavings.

As she drew near her bench, she slowed down. Her predecessor had left, and her place had been taken temporarily by Jan Lusiewicz, who was tending the machine and looking out for Rosa at the same time. When he saw her coming, he waved to her not to hurry. His smile shone out like a neon sign. Rosa could see nothing else. She arrived panting.

'So. You hurry,' said Jan. 'Wait. Not yet. Sit.' He still usually spoke in monosyllables, except at peaceful moments when he had time to relax and think out sentences. Rosa could not hear his voice in the din, but somehow she knew what he said. Rosa seated herself at the bench and got her breath, and Jan continued to smile down at her while his left hand operated the machine.

'I'll take over now!' shouted Rosa. 'Thanks, Jan!'

'Don't say it!' shouted Jan.

'You mean, "don't mention it"!' shouted Rosa.

'What?'

Rosa shook her head violently. They were laughing into each other's faces. Jan still had his left hand on the lever; Rosa's hand covered his, and for a moment she felt the steel of the lever through his flesh. Then his hand had slipped away and he turned.

'What about it?' he called into her ear. 'Tonight, yes?'

Rosa nodded vigorously, and a sound rose up inside her head. She supposed it was 'yes'. Jan smiled and receded, waving, down the steel alley. Rosa glued herself to the machine, and the rhythm of it filled her body.

She called the machine 'Kitty' because it made a repetitive rhythmical noise which sounded to Rosa like *Kitty Kitty bang click Kitty Kitty bang click*. Kitty was rather tall and rose well above Rosa's head when she was sitting down – and as she sat, looking up through the steel body of the machine, Rosa would often try to find Kitty's face. But she could never decide what the face of Kitty was like. Sometimes she seemed to be all face, the big safety shields were her eyes and the shovelling back and forth of the tray was the insatiable movement of her jaw. At other times Rosa's attention fixed upon the motion of the steel arms above the tray, and the Kitty would seem like a contorted curling many-limbed creature with a tiny circular head, low down on the farther side, which spun madly round and round. At other times she looked different again. Only her voice never altered. When this became too monotonous, Rosa could produce a syncopated effect by introducing the suction device, which removed the steel filings a little off the beat; but she didn't like to do this too often, as it put a strain on the mechanism. An alternative way of distracting herself from Kitty's well-known diction was to try to listen instead to the din which the whole factory was making and try to understand its rhythm. But out of this deafening chaos of sounds Rosa was never able to draw any harmonious or repetitive pattern, although she felt sure that it was there, and that if only she could remember long enough and listen in the right way she would find out what it was. But it never emerged, and the only result of this entertainment was that she began to make mistakes with Kitty.

Today, however, Rosa had no ear for Kitty's music nor any yearning to catch Kitty's eye. She sat staring after Jan as she swayed slowly to and fro, hand in hand with the machine. Jan was as slim and as fresh and as gay as a silk handkerchief passed through a ring. His flesh was of an extraordinary whiteness and his eyes were of an unflecked blue, like the sky in summer or like a crystal-clear lagoon whose colour is built up from its depth, without content, planes or distances. His hair was a burnished brown, and as it swept on to his pallid neck it looked like a chestnut bursting from its white case.

He very closely resembled his elder brother Stefan, who also worked in the factory. The Lusiewicz brothers were engineers, and among those who had immigrated lately under the SELIB scheme and acquired their skills in England. Although it would have been difficult to mistake Jan for Stefan, who had very slightly more irregular features, the resemblance between the brothers was generally admitted to be uncanny – as if Stefan's face were a reflection of Jan's in water, just a little softer and hazier in line. The women who worked in the factory, who ran into hundreds, were divided into Janists and Stefanists, some exalting the neatly chiselled face of the younger, others praising the more rugged face of the older brother. But all were agreed that it was very hard indeed to say which of them was the more charming. They were both expert at their jobs and had soon graduated out of the enslaved group of machine-minders, to which Rosa still belonged, into the comparative freedom of the technical staff.

As Rosa watched Jan disappear round a corner fifty yards away down the workroom, she jumped violently to see his face materialize a few inches from her. It was Stefan.

'So. You come. Yes?' he said. 'It is for tonight, yes?'

Rosa nodded and again her tongue moved. Stefan's smile was like porcelain in the sun and his eyes caressed Rosa. He placed himself close up to Kitty so that the rhythmical return of the tray brought Rosa's bare arm into momentary contact with his. As the machine parted them again, Stefan faded away, his mouth opening in a laugh which fell inaudibly into the general noise.

'Oh, Kitty,' said Rosa. 'Kitty, Kitty!'

Kitty Kitty bang click, said Kitty, like a clever parrot repeating its own name.

The Lusiewicz brothers were Rosa's secret. She had discovered them when they first came into the factory about eighteen months ago, soon after their arrival in England, when they were a bewildered helpless pair of very young men. As no one else seemed to be interested in them at that time, Rosa had dutifully, almost sulkily, undertaken to be their protector. At that time they were dejected and colourless, like half-starved, half-drowned animals; and in a moment they had become completely dependent on her. They spoke practically no English and would sit together upon a bench, looking up at Rosa with their blue eyes full of confusion and sorrow. They would speak rapidly to each other in Polish. Then one of them, usually Stefan, would try to say something to Rosa in English. One mangled mispronounced word would come out, together with many gestures and an accompaniment in Polish from Jan. Rosa had never before seen a language appear so much like an instrument of torture.

40

She had protected them, guided them, given them money, and taught them English. During this period she saw them every day at the factory, gave them an English lesson almost every evening, and spent a large part of her week-ends in showing them London. They became her children and her secret. She had tried at first to make Hunter take an interest in them. Stefan was a bit younger than Hunter. But this was unsuccessful. For some reason Hunter had disliked them. Then after a while Rosa found herself becoming oddly secretive and possessive about the pair. She did not mention them again to those of her friends to whom she had described them in the early days. When people asked her, 'What happened to those two gloomy Poles you were looking after?' she would reply, 'Oh, they're all right, I think. They can manage for themselves now. I haven't seen them lately.' Even from Hunter she concealed the fact that she still saw the Lusiewicz brothers as often as ever.

The brothers had meanwhile been achieving a startling degree of success. They had both had some training in engineering before they arrived and they rapidly showed a remarkable aptitude with machines. They learnt to speak English with confidence and charm, though with a quaint and repetitive vocabulary and an ineradicable contempt for the definite article. Their appearance improved. Their hair, which had hung in muddy strands down on to their collars, began to arch up like a plant revived and gleam with brown fire: and the exceptional pallor of their skin now put the onlooker more in mind of Grecian marbles than of the symptoms of anaemia or undernourishment. Their blue eyes became filled with gaiety and ferocity and joy, and their mouths with laughter. At the factory, their beauty, their awkward English, which they soon learnt to make into an instrument of seduction, and their curious resemblance to each other soon commended them to the women, touched by an appearance of helplessness which was now comprehensible enough to be charming and by the mysteries of consanguinity. To the men, their mechanical skill and willingness to learn soon commended them just sufficiently to compensate for the irritations caused by their success with the women. They became popular.

Rosa watched this flowering with interest and pleasure at first, and later with sadness. There was no doubt that their arrival had transformed the factory for her. Rosa had been working in the factory for about two years. Before that she had been a journalist. Before that she had taught history in a girls' school. She disappointed her mother by failing to be a fanatical idealist, and she disappointed herself by failing to be a good teacher. In journalism she had succeeded a little beyond her expectations and even her wishes, but had never recovered from the gloom and cynicism with which she had entered the trade. She had come to the factory in a mood of self-conscious asceticism. Work had become for her something nauseating and contaminated, stained by surreptitious ambitions, frustrated wishes, and the competition and opinions of other people. She wanted now at last to make of it something simple, hygienic, stream-lined, unpretentious and dull. She had succeeded to the point of almost boring herself to death. Rosa did not imagine that the factory represented anything other than an interlude in her life; but then she had also ceased to imagine that her life would ever consist of anything but a series of interludes.

There had been a time when Rosa had been used to have one extraordinary thing happen to her after another. But since she had gone to the factory nothing had happened to her at all. It was as if whatever god she had invoked when she decided, in what her friends pointed out to be such a deplorably destructive and negative mood, upon this course of action had indeed taken her at her word. Her life became simple, with the simplicity hardly of beauty or goodness but of a monochromatic tedium. Where beauty and goodness were concerned, Rosa had of course had no particular expectations from her new life; she was far from sharing her late mother's urge to get in touch with the People. Deep in her heart, however, although she had not admitted it to anyone, she had hoped that she would get to know some of her workmates; she had even hoped that, somehow or other, she might be able to help them. But none of this had come about. She was on amiable terms with the men and women with whom she worked, but she remained at a distance from them, eccentric, solitary, only just failing to be an object of suspicion. At this Rosa had been not at all surprised and only a little disappointed. Life became impersonal and mechanical; and this even pleased her too, satisfying some deep and perhaps despairing desire for peace.

Rosa never wanted other human beings to come too near.

42

Her intimacy with the person closest to her, Hunter, inspired in her at times a certain horror. She was obscenely near to Hunter. For him she had no exterior. The shell of conventions and pretentions which enclose and define a person did not pass between Hunter and Rosa but encased the pair of them together. One's closeness to oneself, she thought, is made tolerable by the fact that one can alter oneself, the structure is alive. But for this other proximity there was no remedy; and this inspired in Rosa such a fear of any proximity as to console her for her increasing solitude. She would have welcomed the intangibility which was being forced upon her if it had not been that she was becoming thoroughly bored. So the time had passed and nothing had happened: nothing, that is, except the advent of the Lusiewicz brothers.

The brothers had treated Rosa at first with an inarticulate deference which resembled religious awe. They were like poor savages confronted with a beautiful white girl. For them she was from the start 'English Lady'; and they were very proud, as they told her later, that they had seen at once that she was 'Lady, not like those other ones, but lady.' She had had great difficulty in persuading them to call her by her Christian name. Their dependence upon her was complete and their respect for her abject. Rosa even became worried at the degree of her power over them. They asked her permission for the simplest things, they made no choice without her opinion, they were her slaves. Rosa feared this power, but she enjoyed it too. There were days when, contemplating the grace and vitality of her protégés, she felt as if she had received a pair of young leopards as a present. It was impossible not to adore them, it was impossible not to be pleased to own them.

The brothers lived in a cheap room in Pimlico. It was an L-shaped room, full of shabby furniture which had originally been stored there by a junk merchant who had died many years ago, and no one since then had felt inspired to clear the room. The brothers, in whom there was apparent, as soon as they had overcome their initial animal terror enough to display ordinary human characteristics, an exceptional degree of parsimony, were pleased with their junk-filled room, which they were able to rent for eight shillings a week, and whose bric-à-brac, once a senseless jumble, they soon set in order, giving to each decrepit object a proper use and significance.

The brothers had brought with them their very old and bed-ridden mother. This old lady they stowed in the recess of the L, where she lay upon a mattress on the floor. The brothers occupied another large mattress in the main part of the room. Social life normally took place upon the floor, since although there were a number of chairs, none of them was quite satisfactory for sitting on, and although there was a bed, even a large one, it consisted of the empty frame only. This large bed-frame was the central feature of the room. The iron side-pieces had long ago rusted into the head and foot boards, and it would now have been a work of considerable difficulty to take it apart. This, however, would not have deterred the brothers if they had not almost at once decided that the bed did very well as it was. Its presence was a joke of which they seemed never to get tired. As the centre part of the frame was entirely gone, it was necessary to step over the side pieces one after the other in order to cross the room. On the other hand, these iron bars were useful as seats, or for leaning against, or for hanging up washing – and so the bed was left intact. An unsavoury lavatory on the first landing provided water for the brothers and for all the other, extremely secretive inhabitants of the house.

It was not Rosa who had discovered this place. How the brothers had discovered it she never found out. They were proud of having found it and would only say again and again, 'We do it alone!' which in those days meant not with Rosa. The Pimlico room had given Rosa a shock when, in the early days of her acquaintance with the brothers, she had first come to visit it. The decrepitude of the objects, hardly one of which was unbroken, together with the spotless cleanliness imposed by the brothers, who had even managed to rid their room of the smell which pervaded the rest of the house, made it a strange scene. The clean-scrubbed colours and the air of neat deliberate management brought out with an odd emphasis the fact that nothing was quite the right shape.

Most of all, Rosa had not expected the old mother. The brothers had said nothing about her either to Rosa or to anyone else at the factory – and Rosa felt more inclined to attribute this omission to deliberate secrecy than to the lack in their vocabulary of so fundamental a word. The old woman spoke no English, and how much she was aware at all of where she was and what was going on around her Rosa was unable to decide. Sometimes, when Rosa was talking to the brothers, she would lie for hours with her eyes closed. But occasionally Rosa had found her watching her, with an intent and puzzled expression; perhaps she imagined that Rosa was someone else, a niece, or a friend from long ago whose name she could not recall. On the other hand, perhaps she knew very well indeed what was going on. Rosa wondered, and when she knew the brothers a little better she asked them, but they were short on the subject. 'She think it is still in Poland,' said Jan. 'She never know that it is not.'

'Never,' said Stefan. They stood looking down at her. Their mother seemed to fill them with a mixture of tenderness, irritation, and savagery. When Rosa, who was rather shocked at the way in which the old woman was stored there in the corner of the room, had offered to help them to make her more comfortable, they had refused all her suggestions almost with anger. They would not even let Rosa approach near to the place where she lay. 'She is our mother,' said Stefan. 'It is enough.'

When Rosa had realized that the brothers had a mother, her first reaction had been one of uneasiness, almost of jealousy. She thought of her at once as a being to be reckoned with, someone to be coaxed, cajoled, humoured, satisfied, and handled. Soon, however, although the old woman never ceased to inspire in her a kind of awe which nearly amounted to terror, she fell into paying her no more attention, for practical purposes, than if she had been another quaint piece of furniture. When, as sometimes happened, they were alone together in the room, Rosa would keep her distance, but would settle down to study the face of the old idol without embarrassment.

It was indeed like being in the presence of a native god, in which one does not believe but which can terrify one all the same. The mother was yellow in colour and her skin resembled leather. On her face and neck it was crossed with innumerable deep wrinkles until it was almost impossible to descry her features, so many other dark lines distracted the eye. Her cheeks were furrowed with deep cracks, like a vessel that had been broken and stuck roughly together again. The lower part of her face had fallen in, so that her mouth and chin hung like a flabby bag from the bony protuberances above. Only her plentiful grey hair still seemed to be alive, and her eyes, which were

45

large and dark and moist, and lived in their jagged caves like a pair of jellyfish, their wet and lustrous surface contrasting oddly with the extreme aridity of their surroundings. She always lay propped up on three pillows, and slept so at night too, as far as Rosa could see. She spoke seldom, but when she did address one or other of her children in Polish her voice sounded quite strong and not at all like the babble of someone who was senile. Once or twice when they were alone together Rosa had addressed her in English, but she had made no response of any kind beyond continuing to stare with her large wet eyes. So Rosa would sit contemplating her and she would contemplate Rosa, with as little relationship between them as if they had belonged to two different historical epochs.

Rosa was surprised to find that she was not disposed to pity the old woman, and that she was soon able to take her cue from the brothers, who mostly ignored their mother altogether. They very seldom addressed a remark to her when Rosa was there. At times, however, the presence of the mother seemed to induce in them a strange frenzy of excitement. Then they would stand staring at her with a kind of astonishment. Rosa learnt to know this mood, which would begin with both the brothers tense and quivering, and would rise rapidly to an orgiastic climax, like some native festival.

'She is earth, earth,' Stefan would say in solemn tones to Rosa. 'She is our own earth.'

'She is our land,' said Jan. 'Sometimes we dance on top of her, we do the dance of our land. Eh, old woman!' he shouted suddenly, prodding her with his foot. The mother would smile up at them toothlessly and then continue to stare with her mouth open.

'She decay inside,' said Stefan. 'All is decay. I cannot explain. You smell it soon.'

'One day we burn her up,' said Jan. 'If we insure her we burn her up long time ago. She so dry now, like straw, she burn in a moment. One big flame and all gone.'

'We burn you, yes, you old woman, we put fires in your hair!' Stefan would shout, and the old mother would smile again and her eyes would begin to glow feverishly as she looked up at her tall sons.

'You old rubbish! You old sack!' cried Jan. 'We soon kill you, we put you under floorboards, you not stink there worse than

46

here! We kill you! We kill you!' And the pair of them would begin to dance about the room, shouting things out in Polish, and the old mother would arch herself up on the pillows as if at any moment she might get up and join in the dance.

Then quite suddenly the excitement would be over, and the two brothers would sit down one on each side of the bed frame and mop their brows. This performance alarmed Rosa very much on the first occasion, but she soon got used to it.

'How old is your mother?' she asked them once, after they had danced themselves to a standstill.

'A hundred,' said Jan.

'He mean, very old,' said Stefan. 'Very, very old. She soon forget Polish language too. She forget all. When is so old, past is nothing, future nothing. Only is present — so big.' He approached his two hands towards each other until there was only a fraction of an inch between them.

'It is so,' said Jan. They both sighed deeply.

After their capering and shouting, a profound sadness would seem to fall upon them and they would begin to sing, in lugubrious voices, their repertoire of Polish songs, concluding always with a rendering of *Gaudeamus igitur*, which they sang like a dirge, to a slow rhythm, swaying solemnly to and fro, shoulder to shoulder.

'That is student song,' Jan would always explain. 'In Poland we are students of technic, but we have no time to make our doctor.'

'Now we drink,' Stefan would say. A bottle of British sherry would be produced, and a toast drunk out of tea-cups.

'Our mother!' said Jan gravely.

'See, we are patriotic for our new country too,' said Stefan. 'We drink the horrible wines of our new country!' Then there would be uproarious laughter, in which Rosa would join.

Rosa had been discouraged at first by the excessive deference with which the brothers treated her. She had wished to be friends with them; but they had made for her a role which was half lady of the manor and half social worker. After she had at last persuaded them to call her 'Rosa', a word which they would utter awkwardly, with blushes, hesitations, and smiles, she set about wooing them in every way possible. Their deference, their helplessness, their timidity called up in Rosa a perfect frenzy of protective tenderness. She felt as if she were warming back to life a couple of small birds who had been battered and frozen almost to extinction. Every day brought her an advance, a triumph, a surprise. During this time she was made very happy indeed by the Lusiewicz brothers.

It gave her a particular joy to teach them English. At first their communication had been by means of pantomime and the astonishingly small number of words which the brothers had brought with them. But gradually, and with increasing speed, the area of communication grew wider, the intercourse between them richer and more subtle – and Rosa would continually have occasion to congratulate herself upon the instinct which had led her to adopt these two strange and helpless children. She felt like the princess whose strong faith releases the prince from an enchanted sleep, or from the transfigured form of a beast. As her pair of princes awoke into the English tongue and as they were able more and more to reveal themselves to her, she found in them a hundred-fold the intelligence, the humour and the joy at which she had at first only guessed. Though even then there were moments when, like the princess who remembers with a strange nostalgia the furry snout and fearful eyes which are now gone forever, she wished to have back some particularly moving moment in the metamorphosis. Indeed, if she could she would have slowed the process down, so delightful did she find it.

The lessons would take place in the room in Pimlico, with the three of them sitting cross-legged on the floor inside the frame of the bedstead. In the centre were the grammar books and dictionaries. At first the brothers talked a great deal to each other in Polish, and could barely be persuaded to stammer out an exercise with Rosa's help. Then they discovered how to make simple remarks in English. Rosa banned the talk in Polish, and they would take a special pleasure in showing off to each other or taunting each other for mistakes.

'You are like peasant!' Stefan would say to Jan. 'Only so talk peasants in England!'

'You not even like peasant!' Jan would answer. 'Rosa not understand you at all. I talk like peasant, but you talk like pig!'

Sometimes they would make Rosa laugh so much that the tears would stream down her face; and then suddenly she would find that these tears were not to be checked, and they would flow and flow until she was sobbing to relieve a pain that

48

She moved, and fell upon one knee beside him, looking into his face. In a moment he grasped her by the shoulder and pulled her down towards him. Rosa lay stiffly in his arms. As she lay she was looking straight into the eyes of the old woman, who watched them without any change of expression.

'We make love now, Rosa. It is time,' said Stefan, in a matter-of-fact tone.

'It's impossible,' said Rosa, in an equally matter-of-fact tone, 'because of Jan.' She was not able to think, and she could not say anything more explicit than that.

'Jan is nothing here,' said Stefan. 'Now is me, not Jan. Come.' He rose to his feet, pulling Rosa with him.

'Your mother!' said Rosa.

'She not see, not hear,' said Stefan.

Involuntarily Rosa stepped back so as to be out of sight of the old woman round the angle of the room, and as she moved Stefan caught her off her balance and threw her full length on to the mattress. He fell on top of her, and they lay there panting. After a few minutes he was making love to her savagely.

On the following day Rosa began to wonder what on earth she was to do. The first shock of her despair was over. She thought of every possibility, including that of giving in her notice and leaving London. It was impossible to divide Jan and Stefan; for her they were one being. Yet the idea of losing the brothers seared her with such pain, the notion of life without them was now so purely agonizing that she soon veered back towards other even less practicable but less painful plans of action. If it was impossible to part the brothers, it seemed equally impossible to part from them. In fact, Rosa could decide nothing because of a profound and disquieting vagueness in her conception of the whole situation. She knew neither what had happened nor where she stood. There was nothing which she could decide to do but wait; and she found herself secretly hoping that in some way the brothers would take over the situation and make all the necessary decisions for her.

That evening she was expected at Pimlico again, according to their usual arrangement. Normally on that day she made the walk across the river at the end of the shift with both brothers, but when the time came to leave the factory she could find neither of them. Eventually Rosa set out alone, and as she walked the tears fell down in a slow stream, steadily and endlessly as winter rain. These were bitter and distressful tears, not the warm tears that brought solace to the nameless grief. Perhaps there would never be such tears ever again.

She climbed the stairs and entered the room. Jan was there, sitting on the edge of the bed frame, pretending to read a book. There was no sign of Stefan. Jan stood up as she came in, and said, 'Ah, Rosa!'

'Where is Stefan?' asked Rosa.

'He has gone with friends,' said Jan. 'He asks for excuse.' Jan was looking radiant.

'I see!' said Rosa.

They had supper in silence. After supper they smoked a cigarette, sitting inside the bed frame opposite to each other, leaning back against the iron bars. Rosa looked at Jan, and it seemed to her that she saw him through such a thick cloud of melancholy that he was scarcely visible at all. He looked back at her, not with sternness but with a strong fierce expression.

'Now, Rosa!' he said and got up.

'Now *what*?' said Rosa, with all the sudden irritation of deep misery.

'Now we make love,' said Jan.

'O God!' said Rosa. Then she added, 'That is not possible, Jan.'

Jan looked down at her with a look of surly incomprehension. 'How, not possible?' he said. 'For Stefan, but not for me? So is *not*! Get up.'

Rosa got up. They were standing very close to each other. Jan was immobile, his face stony. Rosa was trembling between anger and the grief of despair.

'You know about Stefan?' she said.

'Of course,' said Jan. 'And now is me. Come.'

Rosa's knees gave way and she sank down on to the mattress.

After that day Rosa was completely at a loss. The initiative had passed, as she had obscurely wished, into the hands of the brothers. It was soon clear to her that everything that had occurred had been arranged between them beforehand. She made this discovery with a mixture of relief, horror, and grotesque amusement. She saw them as frequently as before; and was grateful to them for the gentle tact with which they made plain to her the rules of the new régime. The English lessons continued, and the late suppers which they ate all three together; only now sometimes after supper one or other of the brothers would get up, stretch himself, and say that he needed a breath of fresh air. He would then absent himself for about two hours, and reappear in time for the pair of them to see Rosa to the station.

Rosa was surprised at the speed with which she accustomed herself to the new situation. As soon as it became clear to her that the loss of the brothers could be avoided – and this was clear as soon as she realized their collusion – the sharp pain left her and was succeeded by a cloudy fatalism in which disgust and despair lay uneasily asleep. The brothers had decided, and there was little now that she could do about it. The only thing which troubled her in an immediate way was the old mother, whose presence in the room during the love-making horrified and frightened Rosa in a way that she could not get over, and whose very existence hung upon her like a threatening cloud beneath whose menace she felt herself to be guilty of a fearful crime. And all the while, behind that fatalism and this distress, there grew in Rosa a more profound uneasiness. The power had left her now. The mastery had passed to the brothers. They were as gentle and as respectful as ever – but their eyes were the eyes of conquerors. In the deep heart of her which they themselves had laid open Rosa resented this; and as the days passed she began to fear them.

FIVE

Annette was lying on her bed with her legs in the air. She was admiring the extraordinary slimness of her ankles. Both her wrists and ankles were narrow, almost, as Nicholas would declare, to the point of absurdity; but Annette was pleased with them. When she saw the delicate bones there moving under the skin, she became conscious of her whole body as a sort of exquisite machine. She twisted one foot slowly to and fro, watching the stretching of the white skin over the bone. Then she lowered her legs slowly, placing her hands on her hips and tensing her stomach muscles. She lay limp and drew in a deep breath, her lips relaxing gently as if she were breathing in a smile at the same time. She lay there with her eyes open, and as she did so she saw herself lying there like a beautiful corpse. Her body was long and supple, her waist was narrow, her head was small and neat like a cat's. She had large luminous brown eyes and a very thin and slightly *retroussé* nose. 'Annette's nose is like a piece of paper,' Nicholas used to say. 'It's so thin you can almost see through it.'

Annette was waiting for Rosa to come home. Annette, who was never very sure what Rosa's reaction to anything would be, wondered what she would say to her latest exploit. But while she waited, she did not worry. Nicholas had said to her long ago, 'Live in the present, Sis. And remember, you're the person who decides how long the present is.' Annette, who always tried to follow her brother's advice, was glad to find that in this case she seemed to have a natural aptitude for doing as he suggested. She lay now, without a thought in her head, in a happy coma, enjoying the silence and the slim feeling of her body.

Annette's life had always been full of agitation and clatter: engines and dance bands and *badinage* in four languages. If she crossed a continent it was always at the maximum speed which the age could muster, and if she walked down a road it was always in the company of several people who were usually singing. She had rarely stayed in one place for long. 'Don't worry, we'll soon be off!' was what her father used to say to comfort her when she was small for any distressing thing, whether it was the hostility of the chambermaid or the unexplained knocking which she heard at night. But this was just what did worry her. It was because of these things that there was a mystery which had never been revealed. She remembered how, very long ago, she had seen a rose in bud in a garden in Brittany, and had said to her nanny that she didn't want to go to bed yet, because she wanted to stay and see the flower open. Her nanny had told her not to be silly, and her father had laughed and said that by the time the flower had opened she would be three hundred miles away. 'People like us can't have a normal childhood,' Nicholas had told her when she was ten and he was twelve. 'We'll cop it when we're forty-five!'

Annette felt always that she was travelling at a speed which was not her own. Going to or from her parents on one of her innumerable journeys, her train would stop sometimes between stations, revealing suddenly the silence of the mountains. Then Annette would look at the grass beside the railway and see its green detail as it swayed in the breeze. In the silence the grass would seem very close to her; and she would stun herself with the thought that the grass was really there, a few feet away, and that it was possible for her to step out, and to lie down in it, and let the train go on without her. Or else, travelling towards evening, as the lights were coming on in the houses, she would see the cyclist at the level-crossing, his face preoccupied and remote, and think that when the train had passed and the gates opened he would go on his way and by the time he reached his house he would be passing another frontier. But she never got off the train to lie down in the grass, nor did she ever leave it, high up in the mountains, at the small station that was not mentioned in the time-table, where the train unexpectedly halted and where the little hotel, whose name she could read so plainly, waited with its doors open. She could not break the spell and cross the barrier into what seemed to her at such moments to be her own world. She stayed on the train until it reached the terminus, and the chauffeur came to take her luggage to the car and Nicholas came bounding into the carriage, filling her with both sadness and relief at the ending of the journey. But the world of the chambermaid and the cyclist and the little strange hotel continued to exist, haunting and puzzling her with a dream of something slow and quiet from which she was forever shut away.

The idea of growing up had always been for Annette the idea of being able to live at her own pace. It had been no better when Nicholas was old enough to act as her chaperon. This had occurred at an early age, since Annette's parents, christened by Nicholas 'the Olympians', held that children ought to be independent, which meant that they ought to grow up as quickly as possible and fit intelligently into the adult world, which after all was the world in which they lived. Nicholas, who had hated his public school almost as much as Annette had hated Ringenhall, had soon decided that Paris, where he was now completing his studies at the Sorbonne, was his spiritual home. Annette had had to spend many evenings there in the company of Nicholas and his friends, listening to endless conversations which went on into the morning hours until the air was so thick with abstractions that she fell, half stifled, into a comfortless sleep. The very general nature of the subjects and the very finished quality of the remarks seemed to make it impossible for Annette to enter these conversations, though she was never sure whether it was herself or her brother's friends, or the French language that was to blame. '*Moi, j'aime le concret!*' she had cried out, waking up suddenly at the end of one of these sessions. '*Le concret! C'est ce qu'il y a de plus abstrait!*' her brother had replied smartly. Everyone laughed and Annette burst into tears.

To the young women at Ringenhall Annette had said, 'I have no homeland and no mother tongue. I speak four languages fluently, but none correctly.' This was untrue. Her French and English were perfect. But Annette liked to think of herself as a waif. Even her appearance suggested it, she noted with satisfaction. She would sit sometimes looking into the glass and trying to catch in the depths of her large restless eyes the flicker of a tragic discontent. Annette had never been in love, although she was not without experience. She had been deflowered at seventeen by a friend of her brother on the suggestion of the latter. Nicholas would have arranged it when she was sixteen, only he needed her just then for a black mass.

56

'You must be rational about these things, Sis,' he told her. 'Don't build up an atmosphere of mystery and expectation, it'll only make you neurotic.' Since that time Annette had had a number of adventures, attended by neither delight nor grief. But if Nicholas had hoped by this training to dispel for her that mystery which seemed to him so far from hygienic, he had certainly not succeeded in his aim. The mystery was displaced, but it remained suspended in Annette's vision of the future, an opaque cloud, luminous with lightning.

Annette got up swiftly. She had decided to change her clothes. She kicked off her skirt and petticoats, drew on a tight pair of black trousers, and admired herself in the glass. She was pleased with the figure she cut in male attire, looking like a very young dandy just starting out on a career of dice and women and champagne. She had silk shirts of every colour with silk handkerchiefs to match. There were times when Annette felt that nothing really interested her except clothes: clothes, and her jewels. Annette had taken it into her head at an early age to collect unset precious stones: and this expensive hobby had been, in the opinion of some people, shockingly, indulged by wealthy relatives and diplomatic acquaintances in various parts of the world. She now had a remarkable collection, which to the despair of her father and the insurance company she insisted on keeping not only with her, instead of as her more sober advisers urged in the bank, but even exposed to view upon a blue velvet cloth which she had spread out at present on top of her chest of drawers. Annette's mother, Marcia Cockeyne, appealed to in the controversy of Annette's jewels, had laughed and said that the only justification for spending so much money on precious stones rather than investing it in railway shares was that precious stones gave to some people a very special kind of pleasure, and that she would have been disappointed in her daughter had she been willing to have such possessions and to keep them in the bank. That closed the matter.

Annette did not keep her whole collection exposed, but only a selection from it which she altered from time to time. The stones which were on view she rearranged every day, sometimes putting them in symmetrical pattern, sometimes laying them out in constellations, and sometimes just scattering them at random over the cloth. Annette's most valuable stone was a ruby, which had been given to her when she was twelve by an Indian prince who was in love with her mother. But this was not her favourite. The stone which she liked best was a white sapphire which had been given to her when she was fourteen by an aeroplane manufacturer who was in love with her brother. She held this stone now in the palm of her hand and looked into it as into a crystal. Its radiance was not white or blue but golden, a golden lustre refined almost into a transparent light. The present moment was narrowed down into a single point of fire. She looked into the heart of it.

'Annette!' said Rosa. Annette jumped and nearly dropped the sapphire. She replaced it hastily. Rosa disapproved of her jewels. Rosa looked tired, and her hands hung down, as she stood framed in the doorway, like the big hands of a statue. At such times her flesh hung upon her heavily in a way which inspired in Annette a mixture of pity and aversion. Rosa had arrived back from the factory to be met by Hunter with the story of Annette's decision to leave Ringenhall and her encounter with Calvin Blick. Rosa, who was expected later that evening at Pimlico, was full enough of her own troubles. 'So she's left school,' said Rosa. 'Now the balloon will go up!'

'Just what I thought!' said Hunter, relieved that her anger was not falling on him.

Rosa had been very fond of Marcia Cockeyne when they had been at school together in Switzerland, and later when they had shared a flat in London, and she did her best to be fond of Annette, not without some success. This was the easier, since Annette had never yet occupied very much of Rosa's attention. Rosa, who was half charmed, half irritated by her kittenish ways, could not but compare her unfavourably with her memories of herself at that age. But such criticisms as she found herself obscurely tending to make of Annette's deportment had never yet been formulated, and she had not troubled to ask herself whether they were just and reasonable or not perhaps the expression of a sort of envy of a younger and in some ways luckier woman such as Rosa knew herself to be well capable of feeling. She often enjoyed Annette's company, yet the child made her nervous. She knew that Annette feared her sarcasm, and this made her but the more inclined to prick and bite her.

She sat down now on Annette's divan, not to be friendly but because she was tired out.

'I hear you've decided to leave school,' she said to Annette.

'Yes,' said Annette, standing rigid. 'Rosa, do you mind?'

Rosa stretched out her hand towards her, noticed how dirty it was, and withdrew it just as Annette was about to clasp it. 'No, of course not!' said Rosa. 'And if I did, it wouldn't matter.'

She lifted her legs on to the bed, keeping her feet dangling clear and clasping her hands carefully together so as not to soil the counterpane. She lay there awkwardly, half turned towards Annette. 'I never thought much of Ringenhall anyway. What are you going to do with your time now?'

'I was learning nothing there,' said Annette. 'I have decided that from now on I shall educate myself.'

'I asked what you were going to do with your time,' said Rosa.

'There are a lot of things I want to find out,' said Annette vaguely. 'I shall make a plan.'

Lying on the bed, Rosa suddenly forgot all about Annette. A cloud of tiredness and depression came down and covered her like a bell.

'May I unpin your hair?' said Annette's voice from a distance. She was crouched on the bed now beside Rosa's shoulder.

'Yes, if you like,' said Rosa. This was a customary ritual, and Rosa had no strength to move. She lifted her head, and in a moment her hair fell in a heavy dark cascade. Annette drew it away into her lap and caressed it; it was not quite like touching Rosa.

'How beautiful it is!' said Annette. 'I tried to grow my hair once, but it got down to my shoulder blades and then stopped.'

Annette's hair was brown and extremely short and curly. The curls were the creation of her hairdresser. Her brother's hair, which lacked this attention, was thick and very straight, and fell in such a neat circle from the crown of his head that some people thought that he wore a wig. If Annette had worn her hair in this way, her resemblance to him would have been striking.

'You mean you got tired of it and cut it off,' said Rosa, thinking hard about something else.

'Lie and rest now,' said Annette. 'Put your feet up properly.'

Gently she pulled Rosa's feet on to the bed and unclasped

her hands. Rosa lay limp, smiling a little ironically, while Annette leaned over her, scrutinizing her like a lover.

'You are a picture by Renoir,' said Annette. 'You have those very bright dark eyes.'

Rosa, who knew that the brightness of her eyes was due to the proximity of tears, turned her head away.

'What's that?' asked Annette, pointing to a round scar on Rosa's arm.

'It's a vaccination mark,' said Rosa. 'You've probably got one too.'

'I don't think so,' said Annette. 'I was vaccinated, but it didn't leave a mark.' She rolled up both her silk sleeves to the shoulder. It was true. There was no mark.

'I'm glad of that,' said Annette. 'I'd hate to have any mark on my body that was there forever, or to lose anything that wouldn't come again. I'm glad I've never had a tooth out. And I've never had my ears pierced.'

'You don't *lose* any flesh when your ears are pierced,' said Rosa. 'The flesh is parted, but nothing is taken away.'

'I know,' said Annette, 'but it would make a difference to my body and it would never be the same again. It would make me feel that it was getting used up and that there was no going back.'

'It *is* getting used up and there *is* no going back,' said Rosa. 'What about wrinkles? Those are marks that come and are never rubbed out. Even you have some.'

'No!' said Annette. She unlaced herself from Rosa and ran to study her face in the mirror. Rosa studied it too. It was perfectly smooth and the skin was pale and transparent with the bloom of extreme youth.

'There you are!' cried Annette. She turned to Rosa, holding out her face as if for a kiss.

'Yes,' said Rosa, 'you are like a little fish. You are completely smooth. You should have been a mermaid.'

Annette drew a hand down each of her smooth arms and held it out for display as if it were a priceless embroidery. Then she began to caper about the room doing high kicks and singing, 'I am like a li – ttle fish, I should have been a mer – maid!'

Lying now completely relaxed and entangled in her hair, Rosa had once again forgotten all about her.

60

SIX

Rosa came through the front door of the house in Pimlico. It was always unlatched. She hurried up the stairs and entered the brothers' room without knocking.

Jan was lying flat, balancing himself on one of the iron bars of the bed frame. 'So do fakirs,' he said, 'like this. For years perhaps they lie so. Is it not? Then they know God.'

'I don't believe it,' said Rosa. 'I mean, that they know God.'

She cast a glance towards the alcove. The old lady was propped up as usual, and her eyes turned to Rosa were like the eyes of a statue. 'Good evening,' said Rosa, a greeting which she always gave and to which she never received any response.

At the far end of the room Stefan was fiddling with a curious machine made of straps and springs.

'Whatever is that?' said Rosa.

'It is exercise machine,' said Stefan. 'We make it ourselves. We see one in shop and pretend we buy it. We look at it long time and then we make one the same. We take the pieces from factory. It is clever, no?' He sat down on it, enlaced himself in the straps, and began strenuously to shoot himself to and fro, bending down and straightening out with a kind of rowing motion.

Rosa went into a peal of laughter. 'You're mad!' she said.

'But so we get strong,' said Stefan, getting up. 'We get strong, until we are stronger than anyone else. If one of us is so, we are king. If both of us together, we are emperor.'

'In Poland we make much sport,' said Jan. 'Stefan was champion boxer.'

'And Jan champion cyclist,' said Stefan.

At this they both started madly to leap about the room, Stefan sparring and Jan agitating his legs in a cycling motion and bending over imaginary handle-bars. The din was tremendous. Someone in the room above began to bang on the ceiling.

Rosa sat down on the bed frame, laughing till she wept. 'Oh, do stop!' she said, 'I'm so tired already. I can't bear it! I can't bear it!'

The brothers became quiet and approached her attentively. Their smiles hovered over her like two angels.

'We give you supper now, you poor thing,' said Stefan. 'Come and sit here.'

They sat her on the mattress and spread out the things for supper. Rosa leaned back against the wall. She felt an immediate contentment in their presence which drove away all other troubles. Stefan was stirring something over the gas-ring. Jan stood looking down at her fondly.

He touched her with his foot. 'You are our sister,' he said. 'You belong to both.' The brothers often said this. They repeated it every time she came, like a charm.

'Wife is nothing,' said Jan. 'Where is *this* thing is wife. But mother is much and brother is much. Always can be made a new wife. But brother is only one. And sister too. You belong to both of us. It is enough.'

Rosa looked up at him quietly, allowing herself to be spellbound. His words seemed to come more and more softly, as if he were trying to make her fall asleep.

'Tonight we tell you a story of our village,' said Jan. 'The story of the first woman!'

On most evenings when they met, one or other of the brothers would tell a story about Poland. The stories would always begin with the words. 'In our village . . .' Rosa never tired of hearing these stories. What they conjured up for her was something very remote yet crystal clear, like a vision procured in a fairy-tale. She could see it all, down to the blades of grass and the door handles and the shine on the windows; and she could see the brothers passing along the street, now small children, now growing towards manhood. It was very detailed yet very delicate and frail, and she found that she never wished to ask herself whether it was true.

Once she begged the brothers to show her on a map where their village was; but when the map was before them they differed so much about its position and became so angry with each other that Rosa had never asked again and contented herself with the image which their stories had conjured up.

Another time she had said, dreaming aloud, 'I wonder if you will ever go back there.'

And Jan had replied, 'Why we go back? They are stupid in our village. They not know even what is university. They think it is mechanic school. They know only of school of mechanic. When Jan and I make our semesters they think it is that. They are peasants.'

'Also,' said Stefan, as a kind of afterthought, 'it is no more. Hitler break it. Shoot at it, then burn it. Nothing left. Perhaps we not find it, not remember where it is. All is flat land now.'

When supper was done, Stefan began the story. 'In our village,' said Stefan, 'there was school. Not proper school, like in England, but peasant school. All children come there together in big room, big children and little children all together. Was much noise. Children sit in groups and teacher go round, so that some get lesson while others do work for themselves. It was so. Jan and I, we go to that school since we are seven. We not have to go, but we want to go. I say to Jan when we are little, we learn much, read, write, so we become strong, not like peasants. So we go. At first was schoolmaster with long beard, so. Very old, and big fool too. I say to Jan, "We stay a while. He soon die." We learn to read, write a little. Then schoolmaster die. We wonder, what is now? In Poland is not like in England. Not everyone is schoolmaster. The village ask, what is now?

'Then from town comes schoolmistress to our village. Never is before schoolmistress. At first all are surprised, suspicious. She is young, pretty girl. Can such pretty girl be schoolmistress? We laugh. First day, all village come to school to watch. All children go in, then all village is outside, at doors, at windows, watching. Schoolmistress is there, very red, very pretty. We all laugh. But soon we see she is really schoolmistress. She know all, cannot be joked at. We see our mothers, fathers, at doors looking in, and we want to laugh and play. But she make us be silent. She take off her shoe and bang it on desk, so, *rat tat,* and we are silent. She wear town shoes with long heels. Suddenly we all feel afraid. Then she turn to door where is our mothers, fathers, looking in to see if so pretty girl can be schoolmistress. She say, "If you want lesson, come in, if you not want lesson go away from here." Now is their turn to be red. They go away, so, creeping foolishly. After that no one make joke at schoolmistress, not in school, not in village.

'We stay at that school and we learn much things. We are

best pupils, far far best. We are big boys now, Jan and Stefan. Our family have much money, so we not work in fields. Schoolmistress is pleased with us, teach us much, more than to the others. She want that we go to university when we grow up. We think so too. But one day she make big mistake with us. We are thirteen years, or I thirteen and Jan is twelve. She strike us, so, upon the face. Why she strike us I not remember nor Jan remember. But she strike us both, first Stefan, then Jan, and all children see and laugh. In Poland, in village people do not so to strike in that way. Is not to be forgiven, such a blow. I am silent and Jan is silent — but each of us think then in his heart, we never forget this, and when we are big we have that woman, and so we revenge on her. Each of us he think this, but he not say to the other.

'After that day, in the class, we are silent, always silent. Before, we talk much, answer and ask questions. Now we are silent. We sit so and look at her, all time we stare at her. If she asks us something we answer very short, and all time we stare and stare. She soon become miserable. She say, "Why you never talk now, you two, what is with you, are you sick?" But she know very well what is with us. We say nothing. We make her very unhappy. All time we stare, we lean so with our heads in our hands, and stare. So passes a year, two years. We learn much, but now we learn for ourselves, out of books. Soon we know many things, more than the schoolmistress. We still come to school, but only to stare at her, and sometimes now if she say something wrong we correct her. She very unhappy now when she see us there. She begin to be afraid of us. And all time, each of us in his heart is saying, it is not long now, it is soon now. But still we not speak to each other. Each one keeps plan in his own heart, secret. We wait to be big, tall, strong. Now every day we are looking in glass to see if we are like men. We see how we become tall, fine, like soldiers. Is much beard coming at last. Every day I look so in glass and admire, and everyday I see is Jan doing the same, how he measure himself on wall, look in glass, throw shoulders back, so, and clench fist. But I not know what he think and he not know what I think.

'Then one time our mother go away from village. She begin then to be ill and she go where is sister in other village. I think to myself: it is now. Jan he think so also to himself: it is now. It is same day. But we still not speak. We both go into school, and we sit as we do before and stare, and schoolmistress is red and unhappy when she see us there, as she is before. The lesson is done. Then each of us pass her a note, but we still not see what is doing the other. I, Stefan, I put the note into her book. Jan he put his note into her hat. Then we go home, very pleased, very excited. But we still not tell each other. In my note to schoolmistress I say: *I love you. Meet me tonight at nine beside well.* In Jan's note to schoolmistress he say: *I love you. Meet me tonight at nine beside oak tree.* All afternoon we laugh very much, we wait for the evening. Still each does not know what has done the other.

'At last is evening. I, Stefan, go and stand by well. Jan he go and stand by oak tree. Well is near end of village street, but on north side of village. Oak tree is near same end of village street, but on south side of village. In between at end of street is a fountain. When I come to well it is only a little dark, and I look about. I see not schoolmistress, but I see Jan sitting under oak tree. And Jan see me. We both curse, and then we pretend we have not seen. I sit down too. Between us is not far, is perhaps two hundred metres. So we wait. Is twilight, very quiet, very beautiful. I think to myself: if only is not Jan. What can he be doing under oak tree? Jan think to himself: if only is not Stefan. What can he be doing beside well?

'Then suddenly is schoolmistress, in white dress, like bride, coming down village street. She show very clear in twilight. We both see her. She come to end of street. She look to right and see me. She look to left and she see Jan. She stand so for a moment. Then she sit down beside fountain and arrange her skirt. She look up at sky. She put her hand into fountain. Is silence. The minutes go by. I say to myself, she see Jan there, and she wait for him to go away, then she come to me. Jan say to himself, she see Stefan there, and she wait for him to go away, then she come to me. So we wait all three. Evening is so blue, so warm. It is darker and the stars come out, one star, two, then very many. There is a bird sings in the wood, perhaps a nightingale. And all time we see schoolmistress sitting there, very still, with the head back, so, and the hand in fountain. We see her always, even when it is dark, because she wears so white dress.

'I am becoming mad. I want now desperately this woman. I feel water on my brow, I tremble; but always I see Jan there under oak tree, even when is dark I see his face there, very pale. And while is Jan there I cannot move, I am like man in chains. Village street ends at fountain, but then is path that leads on to church. Suddenly now are coming the people from church and coming towards the fountain. It is time just before Easter, the service of the evening. First comes old lady who is schoolmistress's mother — and now she take schoolmistress by arm and lead her away. And now is all voices in the air, and nightingale go away, and night is very dark. I sit still by well and I begin to cry. Jan tell me later that he cry too, sitting by oak tree. Then we both go away alone through woods, long way, with many tears, and we hit trees with our hands and lie among leaves and plants. Very late we come home. We say nothing to each other, not a word, and we sleep.

'Next day we not go into the school. We take books and go far away over hill. I, Stefan, go north, and Jan go south. And so we wait for it to be evening. When is evening we both come back, and at nine o'clock I am again at well and Jan is at oak tree. So we wait. Then all is as before. Schoolmistress come in white dress as before, and sit beside fountain. Stars, one, two, three, many come out in blue sky. Now is so silent we can hear fountain falling. Then there is again nightingale. I sit beside well, and is water running down my chest. I tear my shirt, so, at the neck. I cannot breathe. I am mad for this woman, but while is Jan there I am like dead, I sit like corpse, I cannot move scarcely my hand. I pant, and then I groan, but very softly, and I rock a little to and fro, so, and all my body is in pain. Then is all as before. Suddenly, are coming the people from church, and first of all is the mother, who takes schoolmistress away, like on the night before. Then I lie on my face beside well. I lie like a man dead. No longer can I even groan; so I lie for an hour. Then I go home and sleep. Jan he come back much later.

'In morning we look at each other. Each of us we are white like ghosts. But still we say nothing. We eat together, but we say nothing. We not speak now of anything, each talk only in his heart. I think to myself then that I will kill Jan. I tremble all through when I think this thought. I have bread in my hand, and I put it down. I get up from table. I am trembling and can hardly walk. I have to hold on to door as I pass or I fall down. I go out into shed, to look for axe. At same moment Jan has got up and gone into bedroom. I find axe and I come back. Then I see is Jan at door of bedroom holding long hunting-knife. We stand so for a long time, a very long time, perhaps ten, fifteen minutes, and we look at each other. Jan leans on bedroom door and I lean on door to yard. Then we both turn and put those things away. I go out into field then and am sick. Then I go away over hill as the day before.

'At evening I come back to village, and at nine o'clock I am at well. I look and I see Jan under oak tree as on nights before. All is then the same. Schoolmistress is come in white dress and is sitting by fountain. It is warm and with many stars. I hear sound of fountain and sound of nightingale. I not sit down this time, but stand, with foot on edge of well. I wait ten minutes. I am trembling, and I breathe very fast, but I am not weak now like night before. I feel not in chains. I look at Jan. I look at schoolmistress, I look towards church. And I think, but not again, the mother! Then I start to walk very slowly down hill towards fountain. I walk so slowly, I glide like ghost. I hope almost I am invisible like ghost. Is now very dark. I see white dress of schoolmistress. But at same time has Jan started too to walk down hill from oak tree. When I see this I walk faster, and Jan he walk faster too. Then I run, and Jan runs, and we both reach to fountain where is schoolmistress.

'Schoolmistress stand up. She say nothing. We say nothing. Then we take her, one arm each, and we march her back to our house. We take her round by fields so that village not see. We take her into house. Then we undress her and we have her, first one and then the other.'

Stefan paused. 'Which was first?' asked Rosa, after a moment's silence.

'I,' said Stefan, 'because I am eldest. In Poland, eldest, that means much. Eldest is king. Between us is no king. But as we cannot love her together, even we, we take turn, I first.'

'Since then,' said Jan, 'we share our women always. It is meant so.'

'Yes,' said Stefan. 'When we think to have her and not tell the other we do wrong so. Always a brother must tell all things to the other. It was a sign.' They both nodded gravely.

'Did you love her again,' asked Rosa, 'or only on that night?'

'Only that night,' said Jan. 'After that we love many girls in village, many many girls, all pretty girls in village we love, but not her again.'

'Why not?' asked Rosa.

'I don't know,' said Jan. 'We not like her. She tell lies. She say she is virgin, but is not so.'

'All girls in Poland say they are virgin,' said Stefan.

'Anyhow, we hate her,' said Jan. 'We not forget the blow. Why we make her pleasure? Is for her enough honour that she is the first.'

'We make her much pain then,' said Stefan. 'In days after, we not go into school. We not go there ever again. She look at us in street, she wait for us. Sometimes she wait again by fountain. We watch her. But we do nothing. We not know her, not greet her. All is as if she is stranger. We make her much pain.'

'Poor thing!' said Rosa. She felt close to tears. 'Poor thing! Was she beautiful?'

'Yes,' said Jan. 'She was beautiful, as such women are. She comes from town, but she is peasant woman, not lady, like you. She have long, very long black hair, almost is two metres long, her hair, and like tail of a horse. Is not silk, like yours, but so strong, she almost embrace you with her hair. And eyes, very big, on side of face like animal, and going up, so.'

'And she wear always four black petticoats,' said Stefan.

'What happened to her?' asked Rosa.

'Funny thing, she fall down a well,' said Stefan.

'The well in the village?' asked Rosa. 'The one where you waited?'

'Yes,' said Stefan. 'She not fall by accident. She jump down herself.'

'Why?' asked Rosa.

'Because Hitler,' said Stefan.

'Was she Jewish?' asked Rosa.

Stefan shrugged his shoulders. 'Perhaps was Jewish, perhaps Socialist, I don't know.'

'I think she was gipsy,' said Jan. 'Hitler not like gipsies either, he kill gipsies too, so they say in Poland.'

'Was funny thing about that,' said Stefan. 'When she fall in the well, she not do it properly, but catch her foot in well rope, and hang upside down half-way in well.'

'What happened?' asked Rosa.

68

'Someone of our village come past,' said Stefan. 'Who was it, Jan, who come past?'

'Nikolai the carpenter,' said Jan.

'Nikolai come past,' said Stefan, 'and see her there down well. All he see is her black petticoats. And he ask her, "You want to come up or to go down?" She say "Down", so he shake well rope, and she fall into well and drown for good. That was funny, wasn't it? "You want to come up or to go down"!'

'So say Nikolai,' said Jan, 'but he was always great liar, Nikolai.'

'Funny thing too about that well,' said Stefan. 'Always there were fish in that well. We pull them out with long net, but always come more fish. Where they come from, those fish?'

Rosa got up abruptly. She stepped over the bed frame and looked down at the brothers. They sat shoulder to shoulder inside their enchanted enclosure, looking up at Rosa. Then very softly they began to sing, swaying to and fro in an identical rhythm, as if their bodies were joined together.

> Gaudeamus igitur,
> Iuvenes dum sumus;
> Post iucundam inventutem
> Post molestam senectutem,
> Nos habebit humus,
> Nos habebit humus.
>
> Vita nostra brevis est,
> Brevi finietur,
> Venit mors velociter,
> Rapit nos atrociter,
> Nemini parcetur,
> Nemini parcetur.

Rosa sat down on the mattress and closed her eyes. She stiffened her body and crushed down out of her consciousness something that was crying out in horror. It was nearly gone, it was gone; and now as she sat rigid, like a stone goddess, and as she felt herself to be there, empty of thoughts and feelings, she experienced a kind of triumph.

The brothers finished their song, and then they got up slowly, uncurling their long legs. They both came and stood

69

looking down at Rosa. She heard them come, as she sat there still with her eyes closed, and felt their proximity in a vibration through her whole body. Then Stefan knelt beside her, and Jan lay down on her other side.

There was a ritual whereby the two brothers together would undo her hair, and sit by her for a while before one of them would move to go away. Stefan began now to remove the pins. Rosa opened her eyes.

Jan was lying with his head in her lap. He looked up at her, and his eyes upside down were the eyes of a demon. 'How many kisses you have for me?' he said. 'I want many, many. You give always more to Stefan than to me.'

She saw his teeth gleam in what must be a smile. She looked down at him sadly and touched his brow. She never replied to any love speeches made to her by one of the brothers in the presence of the other, nor did the brothers expect her to reply. Stefan undid her hair and let it fall over on to her breast. Jan caught it in his two hands and drew it down to imprison it under his arm. Stefan was leaning against her back, his lips very close to her neck. All three closed their eyes and a kind of slumber seemed to fall upon them. They rested so, breathing very softly.

Then suddenly something very strange happened. The old woman, who was out of sight in the alcove, gave a loud cry, and at the same moment the room was illuminated by a very bright bluish flash. In a second the brothers had leapt to their feet, and Rosa found herself crying out in alarm. She sprang up too, and for a moment they stood there dazed. Then Jan ran to his mother. The old woman was sitting up in bed and talking rapidly in Polish. Stefan followed, and both the brothers stood listening to her. They spoke to each other in Polish, and then Stefan left the room for a moment, only to come back shaking his head. They were both pale and tense with alarm.

'What is it? What is it?' Rosa kept asking.

Jan turned to her and put his hand on her arm. Then he embraced her. 'It is nothing, Rosa,' he said. 'It is something with the electricity. We see the landlord about it tomorrow.' And they would say no more.

Stefan produced the bottle and they all three had a stiff drink. Rosa was shivering and looking anxiously from one to the other. Soon afterwards she said that she must go home, and they did not dispute this. They saw her to the station in silence. And all the way home she kept remembering every detail of the scene as if it were something potent with the most terrible menace, but she could not bring herself to understand either what had happened or what it was that she feared.

SEVEN

Nina the dressmaker lived in a very tall house in Chelsea. Annette was on the way to visit her; it was the morning of the next day. As it was such clear bright spring weather, Annette had decided to walk all the way from Campden Hill Square, and by now she had almost reached Nina's house. Annette walked quickly, taking long strides and breaking now and then into a run. She swung her arms about a lot as she walked, occasionally cuffing passers-by. She felt herself to be tall and slim and fresh, and she read this again in the faces of the people who eyed her as she approached and turned to stare after her when she had passed. As she went, her breast was filled to bursting with a vague expectancy of bliss, the force of which, rising in her sometimes almost intolerably, made her catch her breath and close her eyes.

Nina was a good dressmaker and not too expensive. When Annette had been about to leave for England, her mother, who did not conceive of life without a dressmaker, had said to her: 'Find yourself a good dressmaker, but not too expensive. For me, it is right to spend much on my clothes, but for you, a *jeune fille*, no. Ask Rosa to advise you.' Rosa had suggested Nina, and Annette had been well pleased. Nina was patient, good-tempered, humble, discreet, fast, an exquisite worker, and where clothes were concerned inexhaustibly imaginative. Annette had once had the idea that she might make of Nina some superior sort of lady's maid. She had visions of herself in later years sweeping about Europe followed by Nina in the role of a confidential servant. These ideas, however, although they never left her, remained in the embryonic stage, as Annette could never quite make Nina out. Although the little dressmaker behaved to her impeccably, there were moments when Annette suspected that really Nina detested her heartily.

Nina was what Annette classified as 'some sort of refugee'.

72

She spoke with a charming and quite undiagnosable foreign accent. Annette had attempted, to begin with, to talk to her in German or French, but Nina had always politely but firmly replied in English, and made no further comment. Nina was a small woman, with a brown complexion and dark straight hair which she dyed blonde. Her arms were covered with long downy hairs which she also dyed blonde, so that she gave the impression of a small artificial animal. Annette always felt that she wanted to stroke her. Concerning Nina's age, Annette was also in the dark. It was still necessary to Annette to know people's ages exactly, in order to place them in relation to herself. About Nina she was never sure; she thought she might be about twenty-nine. And this uncertainty blended with her other doubts to make her relations with Nina, though cordial, always a little uneasy. In her heart, Annette felt towards Nina a mixture of possessiveness, nervousness, and contempt. She could not help feeling that Nina's small stature was the mark of a small nature. She surprised herself with this thought, which she knew to be unreasonable. She had never had such a thought before in relation to other people, but she could not rid herself of it.

Annette liked to believe that Nina was always working for her. Annette had a mystical feeling about her clothes. It was as if the task of clothing her must never come to an end. She must be like a princess for whom all over her realm people toiled day and night to make her trousseau. There was no feeling Annette liked so much as the feeling that someone else was making or doing something for her the fruit of which she would soon enjoy. This feeling was perhaps for her the essence of freedom. Annette hated the notion that things should ever be complete and that she should have to live on what she had. She had disliked desert island stories when she was a small girl for just that reason. She had quarrelled with Nicholas about this, for he was always fascinated by the idea, which was hateful to Annette, of being isolated and living on one's wits with a few given resources. Certainly where clothes were concerned she abhorred completion, and however big her wardrobe, and it was already colossal, it would have been torture to her to have to make do with what was there.

Nina lived in a large light room on the top storey and Annette arrived at the door panting. The door opened into a forest of clothes. The room was criss-crossed with a number of steel rods, fixed near to the ceiling, from which hung garments in various stages of completion. As Annette entered, the draught made a rustle of silks and a murmur of velvets that swept like a sigh along the hanging rows of garments towards the mirror, which was fixed to the wall at the far end. The mirror was very tall and luminous, and in the light that fell from it were grouped the white full-breasted dummies, some clothed and some unclothed, between whom Annette, her eyes big with anticipation, now as she entered saw her own reflection. Nina's room was mysterious to Annette. She was not sure whether or not Nina lived there. Apart from the clothes and Nina's big treadle sewing-machine there was very little furniture and only a few objects of any personal significance. The most notable of these was a finely carved wooden crucifix which hung over the doorway. This thing embarrassed Annette. Her parents had always been indifferent to religion, but she herself had picked up a certain number of superstitions at a convent school which she had once attended for a short time. She had even for a while said nightly prayers, until she noted that a strangely sneering tone was creeping into these utterances – and she had discontinued them through fear. Shortly after that Nicholas had demonstrated to her satisfaction that the concept of God was contradictory. All the same, the presence of the crucifix upset her, and she found something strangely disagreeable in the thought that Nina believed in God.

Annette shut the door, and Nina came towards her, zigzagging soft-footed through the lines of clothes.

'Miss Cockeyne!' said Nina smiling. 'I was just thinking about you. The short evening-dress is ready for fitting.'

'Thank you, Nina, so much,' said Annette. 'May I try it now? I'm sorry I didn't let you know I was coming.'

Nina pushed the clothes away to each side along the rails and made a wider lane in the centre of the room down which Annette walked towards the mirror. Nina followed behind her. Looking into the mirror, Annette could see the top of Nina's head just appearing above her shoulder.

One of Nina's dummies was wearing Annette's evening-dress. It was a low-necked dress made of a stiff sea-green brocade. When Annette saw it, every other idea went out of her head and she exclaimed with joy. Her eyes glistened with admiration for the dress, and for herself.

'Quick!' she said to Nina. 'Let me put it on!'

'It will need some adjusting,' said Nina. 'I've left it quite free at the waist. None of my dummies are as slim as you, Miss Cockeyne. It will look even better on.' Nina always flattered Annette.

Annette had already jumped out of her skirt, revealing a red-and-white check silk petticoat, and was tearing off her blouse and her scarlet scarf with the sort of haste she had used when going swimming as a child. 'Quick!' said Annette. 'Quick! Quick!'

Nina was carefully unpinning the dress from the dummy. It came apart into apparently shapeless pieces and Nina carried them over her arm to where Annette stood before the mirror, braced, one foot before the other and arms hanging free, like a circus dancer before a leap. Nina began to help her into the dress, and as she felt the cold smooth material slipping along her flesh, Annette closed her eyes with sheer joy. When she opened them again she was transformed. The dress was a triumph. The stiff material cascaded outward from Annette's narrow waist to a wide hem, an inch or two above her ankle, and the deep oval neckline swept inward to a high collar behind Annette's long neck. Her white bosom, revealed in the shape of a tear, lying between the formal complication of the tightly buttoned bodice and of the lofty collar, gave the strange impression as of a woman both elegantly dressed and naked at the same time. This was exactly what Annette had wanted.

'It's marvellous!' she said to Nina. 'It's what I dreamed of! I felt I would die for such a dress!'

Nina looked critically at the dress. She was pleased with it too. For the moment, Annette had faded away. Annette was merely another dummy. Annette was nothing more than the dress. 'Yes,' said Nina, 'it will do.'

She took a mouthful of pins and began to pull the material more tightly in at the waist and to deepen the darts in the bodice. As Annette felt the dress clinging more and more closely to her, and her two breasts lifting like a ship lifted by the tide, she thought that she loved Nina. Nina stood back for a moment, the pins still in her mouth, to survey her work in the glass. It was then that Annette realized that someone else had

75

entered the room. A man had come in and was standing by the door at the far end of the lane of clothes. Annette could see him in the mirror. She could see their three heads, her own bright and close, Nina's below her, a little in shadow, and the man's head, far back over her shoulder, and quite darkened. Yet she knew that he was looking into her eyes. A second later Nina, as she looked into the mirror, also saw him; and before Nina turned round Annette caught in her face a look which might have been anger or fear, or both.

As Nina turned about, the man began to walk towards them down the room. Annette felt like a queen in her green dress, and it did not occur to her to turn to face him. She merely watched his reflection curiously as he approached. Nina had stood aside, pressing herself back into the thick bank of clothes. The man stopped level with her, gave her a nod, and then stared directly at Annette in the mirror. She saw him clearly now. He was a stranger to her; and the most striking characteristic of his face was noticeable immediately, making everything else about him for the moment invisible. He had one blue eye and one brown eye.

Annette turned round slowly, lifting her heavy skirt slightly with one hand. She looked at Nina, and then back at the man, who was standing close to her and scrutinizing her without embarrassment. He was a slight man of medium height, with soft brown hair and a small moustache and a long tenderly curving mouth. But Annette could not help staring at his eyes. The blue one was not brownish, nor was the brown one bluish. Each one was its own clear unflecked colour. There was thus a brown profile and a blue profile, giving the impression of two faces superimposed.

'You must introduce us, Nina,' said the individual with the eyes.

'Miss Cockeyne,' said Nina, 'may I introduce Mr. Fox.' She mumbled the words in a tone of exasperation, and as she spoke she drew her hand across her mouth and took it away marked with blood; in her surprise at seeing the newcomer she must have cut her lip on the pins. Annette, who heard thousands of names mentioned every year, and had a deplorable memory, could recall having heard the name of Fox in connection with something or other, but could not remember exactly what.

'How do you do?' she said, stretching out her hand. She was still fascinated by the eyes, and rather wishing that hers were like that. At any rate it would make one memorable.

The man kissed her hand with a quick graceful movement and stepped back. 'You resemble your mother,' he said. He spoke without any accent, but with a sort of precision which marked him as foreign.

Annette, who had heard this remark repeated *ad nauseam*, placed him roughly as an admirer of her mother and felt a corresponding decrease of interest. 'Ah, yes, how nice,' she said vaguely.

Fox had stepped back now into the shadow of the hanging clothes and stood there like a man on the edge of a forest.

'Might I have a chair?' he said to Nina. She brought him one, and he sat down where he was and crossed his legs. 'Don't let me interrupt you,' he said.

Nina stood stiffly for a moment, as if she were about to cry out. Then she moved back towards the mirror, spun Annette round as if she had been a dummy, and began to attend once more to her dress. Suddenly now Annette felt helpless. Nina was moving her arms and her head about as if she were made of wood. She felt like a puppet. She tried, by staring into the glass, to see what the expression was on the man's face, but his face was in shadow again: and in a moment Nina had turned her head in the other direction, taking hold of it firmly as if it had been a ball and swinging it round as if what she would really have liked would have been to send it spinning into the far corner of the room. Now Nina had hold of Annette's left arm and had raised it straight up to point at the ceiling, now she took her right arm and bent it vigorously at the elbow, and all the time her hands fled about here and there over Annette's body, nipping in the material. Annette could feel the pins pricking her flesh. She saw herself in the glass with her arms lifted stiffly like a doll and thought that she looked ludicrous. She began to feel the need to be unpleasant to somebody.

With an inspiration of memory she said suddenly, 'Are you the person they call Mischa Fox?'

'Yes,' said the man behind her. She saw his teeth flash, but he said no more.

'I believe you're famous for something or other,' said

77

Annette, 'but I'm afraid I can't remember what it is. I have a very bad memory.'

'I am not surprised that you do not remember,' said Mischa Fox, 'for in fact I am not famous for anything in particular. I am just famous.'

'I see,' said Annette. 'I hope I shall manage that too. As I shall certainly never be famous for anything in particular, the best I can hope is to be just famous.' She felt that she was being impertinent, and this gave her a pleasure mixed of exhilaration and shame.

Mischa Fox said, 'It is not difficult.' He smiled again. There was something lazy and relaxed about his attitude which annoyed Annette. He was clearly not exerting himself. He was simply watching her, as one might watch a bird.

Then Annette realized that Nina was beginning to unpin the dress. She lowered her arms and instinctively held the material together at her bosom.

'Keep still, Miss Cockeyne, or I shall go wrong,' said Nina tonelessly. She bent both Annette's arms at the elbow and stretched the forearms out to point towards the mirror, so that she looked like a person preparing for a dive. Annette stood rigid. Nina undid a pin, and in a moment the heavy skirt had fallen to the floor. Then Nina began carefully to unfasten the bodice. Annette stared at her own image in the mirror. Like someone upon a high place who is only saved from vertigo by looking straight ahead, she looked into her own eyes. She held her breath, and for a second the other two ceased to exist. Gently manipulating Annette's arms, Nina had removed the bodice. Then she picked up Annette's blouse and skirt from the place where they had been carelessly left on the floor and thrust them at her with a gesture of violence. Annette sprang to life, and in a moment she had slipped them on. She felt that she had been defeated. She was blushing violently.

'Nina,' said Mischa Fox, 'I wonder if you would mind making a cup of tea for Annette and myself?'

Nina turned, and without looking at either Annette or Mischa, left the room. He was still sitting in an idle way upon the chair, with one leg tucked under him in a posture which was more feminine than masculine. He got up slowly, in the graceful loose-limbed manner of an animal rising, and came out into the bright light beside the mirror. Annette noticed the long and gently curving line of his mouth. She looked upon him with nervousness and surprise. Mischa Fox was studying her face meanwhile. Then he smiled at her. Then he reached out a long arm, and taking her by the shoulder turned her round so that more light fell upon her face.

Annette sprang back. 'Don't touch me!' she said. This cry brought them closer together than any physical contact.

'I'm sorry,' said Mischa Fox. 'I simply wanted to see your face.'

They stood facing each other, a few feet apart. Annette could feel her shoulder burning where Mischa had touched it. He was unsmiling. She could see his blue eye. His brown eye was in shadow.

'Oh!' said Annette with a kind of moan. She raised her hand to her head.

Nina came in with the tea. Mischa Fox turned to her and began saying polite things. Annette stepped away from them. A velvet hem was brushing her cheek and some sort of gauze hung before her eyes. She would have liked to have plunged deep into the forest of hanging clothes. She suddenly did not know what to do with her body. She picked up her scarf and her handbag and began to rummage inside the bag, partly to give herself something to do and partly in the hope of finding some charm against the incomprehensible pain of the present moment. She found her powder compact and began to powder her nose. Then Nina was pressing a cup and saucer against her wrist, and she had to lay the handbag down on the floor.

'I've stayed too long!' Annette said suddenly.

The other two turned to look at her. Annette gave Mischa Fox a firm fierce stare. 'I'm late,' she said. 'Will you take me in your car to my next appointment?'

Mischa Fox smiled his lazy tender smile. 'Alas,' he said, 'I came here on foot. Otherwise I should have been delighted. May I telephone for a taxi?'

'No,' said Annette. 'Don't trouble yourself. I shall just run away. Good-bye.' As she said these words she darted away down the lane of clothes and out of the room.

After the door had shut, the dresses rocked gently and came to rest in a subsiding murmur of silk and velvet and nylon. Mischa Fox continued to sip his tea, and his glance wandered about, from the crucifix to the sewing-machine, and from the sewing-machine to the pale heavy-breasted dummies. At last his eyes came to rest upon Nina, who was looking expression-lessly into her tea-cup. It was a long time before she would consent to return his gaze.

EIGHT

John Rainborough was sitting in his office. His legs were stretched out rigidly under his desk. The heels of his shoes bit deep into the carpet and the soles of his shoes rose therefrom at an angle of approximately eighty degrees. He held his hands lightly together, meeting at the finger-tips. He looked down at the blank sheet of paper before him, and his eyes had a soft penetrating look, as if he could see right through the paper into a subterranean cavern. He was absorbed in the problem of Miss Casement.

Miss Casement was Rainborough's personal assistant. She had been appointed by one of Rainborough's predecessors, and he had inherited her together with his office and the files. In those days Miss Casement had been a typist. There are certain human species whose members appear to be indistinguishable one from the other. What these species are will vary with the observer. Some people find it impossible to distinguish under-graduates. Rainborough had never been able to distinguish typists. They all looked to him exactly alike. He could see their smile, but no other features. So it was that, without giving the matter a second thought, he had taken over his new post, and with it Miss Casement's clicking typewriter and her radiant grin.

Very soon, however, Rainborough discovered that there was a great deal more to Miss Casement than her smile. Miss Casement's appointment had been a special one, made personally by the then head of the department and not routed through Establishments. Such appointments, though officially frowned upon, were not uncommon in the office of SELIB; and notwith-standing the slight irregularity attaching to her advent, Miss Casement seemed to be on the best of terms with Establish-ments, since she received a considerable increase in salary during the first weeks of the Rainborough régime. Shortly after that, Miss Casement was upgraded from the position of typist to that of Organizing Officer grade II. These happy events occurred without any recommendation having been made by Rainborough, and indeed without his having been officially informed. On both occasions, since Miss Casement modestly refrained from enlightening him, he found out only by accident.

It was a peculiarity of SELIB that promotions were made upon some obscure system known only to Establishments and which dispensed with such traditional features as testimonials from superior officers. This system, which was described by a member of Establishments as 'thoroughly democratic', had as one of its results that it would often happen that a sectional or departmental head, when giving orders to someone whom he took to be his junior, would be shyly informed by that individual that a recent promotion had reversed their relative positions. Thus the staff of SELIB were kept in continual and irregular motion, jerking past each other like wooden horses racing at a fair, all involved in the movement, which though governed by mysterious forces continued to operate in the long run to the satisfaction of all, towards the upper ranges of the hierarchy and the higher income levels. The only difficulty about this liberal, and on the whole uninvidious, system was that it was hard to see what would happen when all members of the staff had achieved the maximum promotion and, as it were, all pawns had become queens. This happy millennium, in which all differences would be forgotten and all officers would be united in blissful union at the highest salary range, though not unimaginably distant provided the present speed of promotions was maintained, had, however, not yet arrived; and meanwhile the happy ferment continued at all levels of the organization, providing continual employment for Establishments and for the rest of the staff a daily interest with which it was as well to provide them, since they certainly took none in their work.

Rainborough had been with SELIB now for more than a year and had not succeeded in getting used to it. In order to take up his present post as a head of the Finance Department he had abandoned a safe and peaceful position in the Home Office, and had been regretting the change ever since. Surveying the scene which now confronted him, he felt somewhat of the emotions of a man catapulted from the security of the feudal system into a brisk expanding society where the doctrines of *laisser-faire* were just beginning to pay dividends to enterprising individuals. Rainborough was not an enterprising individual and had no intention of starting, at this time of life, upon the task of becoming self-made. He considered that the efforts which he had put into his education at school and at the university should be enough to carry him by their inertia, with only a small expenditure of further energy, through a reasonable career as a public servant, and even earn him in the end the title of a distinguished man.

Rainborough had left the Civil Service in a moment of divine discontent. Such moments were rare in his life, and the mood which inspired them was ephemeral. How ephemeral he now had ample time to realize as he looked with distaste upon his surroundings and wondered if he would ever have occasion in the future to put to use the self-knowledge which he had bought at so high a price. When Rainborough had started on his career as an administrator, being then a young Assistant Principal in the Treasury, one of his superior officers had remarked about him, 'Young Rainborough produces highly intelligent and polished stuff – but somehow it's always entirely useless.' This saying was reported to Rainborough, who heard it without surprise and fell forthwith into a senile resignation from which he had never since recovered. This resignation had, in the course of the years, developed into a quiet melancholy, and it was in order to escape from this melancholy, which for a moment had seemed excessive, that Rainborough had so rashly leapt from the frying-pan into the fire.

As head of the Finance Department, Rainborough held what was potentially a key position in SELIB. This fact had been pointed out to him in a fatherly way, when he had joined the organization, by the Director, Sir Edward Guest, an elderly public servant who had been exhumed from retirement to decorate SELIB's summit with his well-known name and his presumed experience. 'As you'll know from your time in the Treasury, my dear fellow,' said Sir Edward, 'the man who controls purse-strings controls policies. Financial matters are matters which admit of a wide interpretation, especially in a young organization such as this one. We shall be looking to you for a lead.' Rainborough had harkened seriously to these words, and they had conjured up for him a vision of power, the sense of whose delicious temptations, absent for so long from his resigned spirit, he had almost forgotten.

But the vision faded soon. Rainborough very quickly realized that the situation presented by SELIB was one which was completely beyond him. There were times when he felt that SELIB had got so totally out of hand that it was beyond the power of any human being to control it. There were other times when he suspected that an administrator of genius might perhaps in time have reduced it to order. But he never wavered in his certainty that there was nothing whatever which he, Rainborough, could do about it. As he liked to point out to his colleagues, the realm represented by the Board resembled Renaissance Italy in its profusion of lively independent centres, while being unlike it in the quality of the results produced. Each department showed a vigorous sense of its own autonomy, which it often carried to the point of ignoring completely the existence of the other departments. The only power which was recognized by all was that of Establishments, whose beneficent activity was naturally a matter of general interest.

Sometimes in a mood of curiosity Rainborough would roam about the building. His arrival in distant departments passed unmarked and caused no uneasiness, since no one had the faintest idea who he was. He would wander along far-flung corridors, glancing into rooms where from behind trestle tables piled with dusty files came the merry laughter of girls and the clatter of tea-cups. Here and there, however, Rainborough would happen upon some earnest worker, some swot, mocked at by his companions, who was busy, surrounded by documents and works of reference, investigating the history of Polish agriculture or the incidence of unemployment in cities in Bavaria. The labour of these scholars was, however, rendered void by an entire lack of liaison between one department and another, which brought it about that while on the one hand much research was often devoted to the discovery of matters which, elsewhere in the office, were already well known, on the other hand, even when the assembled data would have been of some value to someone in SELIB, it rarely found its way to the right place.

All this Rainborough saw and deplored; and at times he dreamt of sweeping through the office like a cyclone and setting all to rights. But he knew in his heart that the task was beyond him. In any case, to achieve it he would have had first to conquer more power for himself; and the conquest of power in any form was something for which Rainborough knew himself to be unfitted. He looked back with nostalgia to the Civil Service, where an age-old hierarchy, ancient values, and hallowed modes of procedure reduced to a minimum the naked conflict of personalities. Concerning these things he would often discourse at length to the only other person in SELIB whom he took to be his equal, one G. D. F. Evans, a Cambridge man and also an erstwhile Civil Servant, who was head of the so-called 'Social Services' Department.

Rainborough had regarded Evans, to begin with, with a certain amount of suspicion. What he suspected was that Evans might in fact turn out to be what he himself ought to be, the power that would cleanse SELIB, making all things new. So Rainborough would devise all sorts of testing questions relating to their work, to which Evans would invariably return the satisfactory reply. 'Got me there, old man! I'm afraid I haven't done my prep on that one!'; or else Rainborough would come bounding unexpectedly in Evans' room at all hours of the day, only to find him either absent or reading Proust. For some time this did not quite reassure him that Evans might not perhaps be working secretly; but in the end he decided that Evans was harmless, and was able to relax in the knowledge that no one in the office was being less idle than himself.

It was Evans who had first pointed out to Rainborough, on a long afternoon when they had been drinking tea together and surveying the office with the calm objectivity of historians, that a new social phenomenon had made its appearance. This was the rise to power of the grade of Organizing Officer. This grade, originally sparsely staffed, had been invented to give positions of some small dignity to various nondescript 'experts' who had been recruited by SELIB to give advice on problems ranging from publicity techniques in Balkan countries to the teaching of English by the direct method. Very soon, however, the grade had been invaded by an army of young women who, appointed initially as typists, had rapidly set about bettering themselves, and having once got a foothold in this new territory advanced with formidable speed, leaving behind a trail of repercussions and precedents of which their successors were not slow to take advantage. The key idea in this social change was the idea of the Personal Assistant; and the ambition of these young women, intoxicated by the absence of any insuperable barrier to their advance to higher levels of income and prestige, combined with the lethargy of their chiefs, who had no further possibilities of promotion for themselves, produced a real shift of power. It was rapidly becoming the case that these energetic young women were in fact the only people who understood the working of SELIB and really knew what was going on.

Prominent in this band of beautiful adventurers were Miss Perkins, the Personal Assistant of Evans, and Rainborough's Miss Casement, who had recently received a further promotion to the position of Organizing Officer grade I. Evans was laughingly pointing out that these young women and their friends would soon be able to run the entire office themselves. 'Then we can just stay at home and draw our salaries!' said Evans. Rainborough, who found this cynicism in bad taste, was far from being amused at the social change to which Evans had drawn his attention. He felt, in a way which he suspected to be a little absurd, if anything rather nervous at the thought of the pretensions of this group of young vigorous females whose lust for advancement recognized no ancient laws concerning the natural superiority of university graduates, members of the other sex, or persons seconded from administrative posts in the Civil Service. It was with something of a shock, too, that he had realized that the first and foremost of these harpies was his own Miss Casement. This, too, had been pointed out to him by Evans. 'Your P.A. is the Queen Bee, you know,' Evans had told him, with a note of envy in his voice.

It was in fact some time before this that Rainborough had started to pay attention to Miss Casement. He had been struck first by her extraordinary industry. She was to be found at all hours of the day employing her spare time, which was considerable, in reading through the entire files of the Finance Department. These files were confused and voluminous, consisting partly of papers which SELIB had taken over on its creation from other international voluntary organizations. Over these complicated documents Miss Casement pored for long hours, taking notes. She called this 'familiarizing herself with the background'. Rainborough admired her thoroughness. He had intended, on his appointment, to do precisely this himself; but the files of the SELIB Finance Department presented such a horrible contrast to the orderly and intelligent files of the Home Office that he had become discouraged and decided it was not worth the trouble.

Also, Miss Casement was pretty. So, in point of fact, were most of the other O.O.s. But there was little doubt that Miss Casement was the prettiest. Rainborough pointed this out to Evans with some pride. Miss Casement had a very highly finished complexion, a small mouth of the type much favoured in the early nineteenth century, and an abundance of dark hair which, laid out by her hairdresser in regions like an elaborate garden, managed, in spite of the variety of curls, rolls, fringes, and pinnacles into which it was extended, to remain always exquisitely tidy. Beneath this hair there was, at the back, an expanse of smooth, slightly-lemon-coloured neck, which had of late been particularly engaging Rainborough's interest, and, in front, the smile before mentioned which, although small in area for the reason given, was in intensity and brightness a considerable event. Miss Casement's eyes were not her best feature, being inclined to narrowness, but her eyelashes, whether endowed by nature or contrived by art Rainborough could never decide, were long and sweeping; and out of this alluring boskage Miss Casement's gaze, when not directed to her typewriter or to the departmental files, now tended more and more to rest upon Rainborough.

It was through Miss Casement that Rainborough began gradually to be aware of an entirely new range and type of feminine charms. He noticed, for instance, that when she sat down, Miss Casement hitched her skirt up so that the whole of her legs from the silken knees downward were plainly visible, together with an inkling of underclothes. This gesture, which Rainborough had imagined was affected only by film stars when being photographed for the evening papers, infuriated and delighted him. He then observed that it was in daily use by all the girls in the office. So it was that Rainborough, who had been used, when he admired a woman, to confine his attention to her head, her conversation and the simpler bodily curves, started to become a connoisseur in such matters as perfume, lipstick, shoes, stockings, bracelets, ear-rings, and nail varnish; and always it would happen in this way, that Rainborough would be struck by some new and delightful aspect of his junior, and would then find the same note repeated, like a fading tinkling echo, through the whole office, until gradually, in his imagination, SELIB became peopled by a host of women, terrible and desirable by reason of their artificiality.

When it had occurred to Rainborough that he was interested in Miss Casement, he had decided to find out something about her and had sent to Establishments to ask to see her personal file. This request had been refused by Establishments, who seemed to regard it as in rather bad taste. The qualifications and past histories of officers of SELIB were, in the view of Establishments, sacred and mystical secrets which were not to be divulged to any but members of their own priestly caste. This discretion, which was an obvious corollary of the unsettled social hierarchy of SELIB, was respected by Rainborough, whose sense of historical necessity was strong. He therefore had to have recourse to other methods. He had begun by asking Miss Casement a few direct questions; but these had been badly received. He asked her once about her education, to which she replied shortly that she had 'attended college': a phrase which Rainborough found repellent and which filled him with suspicion. Because of certain peculiarities in Miss Casement's vocabulary, Rainborough was certain that she had once been in the Civil Service, but although she admitted to having worked 'in connection with the Ministry of Labour', he was unable to discover what her tasks had been. However, he soon abandoned these more abstruse researches and began to concentrate on simpler matters, such as discovering her Christian name.

This had proved surprisingly difficult. When Miss Casement had occasion to sign any document for him, she did so with an indecipherable scrawl of initials. It was only when, driven to desperation, he had looked in her handbag just before she was due to go on her summer holiday, that he had discovered from her passport that her name was Agnes May Casement. This discovery but drove Rainborough into a deeper frenzy. Which of these lovely sounds was the one to which Miss Casement most commonly answered? Every day at eleven and at four there occurred meetings of the O.O.s, called respectively the coffee-meeting and the tea-meeting, and presided over by Miss Casement and Miss Perkins, where 'the cuties', as Evans called them, gathered together to discuss matters of office procedure and feminine interest. Rainborough tried once or twice, by listening at the door of these gatherings, to find out what he wanted to know; but so far as he could find out by this method, which he abandoned when he was surprised by a latecomer in a listening attitude, the young women without exception addressed each other as 'Miss So-and-so'. This discovery increased his awe of them considerably.

It was in the end the office messenger Stogdon who revealed to Rainborough that Miss Casement was most properly addressed as 'Agnes'. This revelation occurred when Rainborough once surprised Stogdon chatting with Miss Casement and addressing her in this way: a degree of familiarity which, it soon appeared, he had achieved with all the young women in a remarkably short time. They in turn doted on him and called him 'Stoggers'. This man was a continual source of pain to Rainborough, whom he treated with a sort of hideous friendliness and complicity. 'Them young ones, they're real smarties,' he would exclaim, concerning the O.O.'s, and something in his manner would associate Rainborough with himself as belonging among 'the old ones'. 'They'll make things hum before they're much older!' Stogdon would say, with a leer which Rainborough interpreted as a threat to himself. Stogdon's evident assumption that most decisions in the office were now taken by Miss Casement and her friends maddened Rainborough the more as there was some slight element of truth in it. 'Sir Edward Guest is the director of the Board,' he once said coldly to Stogdon, 'not Miss Casement.' But Stogdon had only replied by winking, as if to say, 'You and I, we know better!' On another occasion Stogdon said to Rainborough with a sigh, 'Ah, them young girls, they got all their lives before them. What it is to have your life before you, eh?' This 'eh' with which Stogdon ended so many of his sentences enraged Rainborough as much as the sentiment expressed. He wanted to point out that he too had his life before him, and such as they were, his prospects were certainly brighter than Stogdon's. The man doesn't realize who I am, Rainborough thought, with the desperation of one who knows that he is confronted with a nature against which he has no way of asserting himself. He was without the means to impress Stogdon. And then the thought, with all its melancholy, would follow: Well, who am I, anyway?

During the earlier stages of what Rainborough and Evans called her 'campaign' Miss Casement had quietly continued to perform her duties as a typist, which took up in fact remarkably little time, in the intervals of her other activities. Later on, however, as she took over more and more of Rainborough's work, and as she passed from the stage of accompanying him to conferences to the stage of representing him at conferences, she began to be restive. At last she said firmly, 'We must have a typist.'

'I thought we had one!' said Rainborough, who was in a bad temper that day.

Miss Casement ignored this, and said, 'We only have to ask Establishments.' This kindly body was indeed ready to provide staff of any description in response to a department's lightest wish.

'Well, you fix it,' said Rainborough, and went away for the week-end.

When he returned he found that the office had been re-arranged. Previously he had occupied the larger room, which gave on to the corridor, while Miss Casement occupied a smaller inner room which gave only on to his room. He now found that his desk had been moved into the inner room, while Miss Casement and the typist were installed in the other one.

'I thought you'd probably rather have the single room,' Miss Casement explained vaguely. Rainborough had made no comment; in a way, the arrangement suited him quite well, and he was able to lead an even more peaceful existence. Most of the business which found its way towards him through the door from the corridor came no farther than Miss Casement.

The typist attracted Rainborough's interest for a short while. He suspected that Miss Casement had not in fact acquired the girl from Establishments, but had selected her privately herself. From one or two things that were said, Rainborough thought it possible that the typist had been at school with Miss Casement, but in a lower form. The girl was, in any case, Miss Casement's slave. She was a dowdy, fluffy girl, off whom pieces continually fell as off a moulting bird; and Miss Casement, who had, Rainborough suspected, chosen her carefully for just these qualities, proceeded to make her life a misery. This process was so painful to hear that Rainborough often had to shut the door so as not to hear it. The girl, whom Miss Casement always referred to, and Rainborough soon found himself following her example, as 'the little typist', was very often to be found in tears.

With the arrival of the typist, Miss Casement became even more confident. Rainborough, who had always behaved to her with the utmost formality, suddenly began to find himself being driven more mad than usual by her perfume, the lemon-coloured expanse of her neck, and the red-rimmed cigarette ends which she would leave behind in the tray on his desk. He at first attributed this disturbance to the cumulative effect of living in the proximity of so many provocative harpies; but later he realized that it was perhaps rather the result of some subtle change of tactics on the part of Miss Casement. He noticed then how she would linger a little longer than before at the door of his room, swaying her long body to and fro, or how she would bring him the most unnecessary files, which they would then have to pore over together, Miss Casement's powdery cheek almost brushing his. And then one day she electrified him by calling him 'John'.

This move was not, so far as Rainborough could see, correlated with any other real alteration in their relations, and could not but be interpreted as an unprovoked frontal attack which he was at a loss to counter. He made, of course, no comment upon the now fairly frequent incidence of this monosyllable. He was only grateful that, so far, Miss Casement had refrained from making use of it in the presence of a third person. What he could not bring himself to do was to respond by calling her 'Agnes'. Do what he would, he could not think of her except as Miss Casement; and as it was now impossible for him to address her in this way, since she had elected to address him less formally, he was forced to attract her attention by other devices such as coughing, dropping books, or cries of 'Oh, er, I say!' The state of misery and embarrassment to which his situation reduced the nervous Rainborough seemed to touch Miss Casement not at all. She tripped about the office with a gay and dainty demeanour, more neat and freshly laundered than ever, and her repeated utterance of Rainborough's Christian name rang in his ears like the monotonous cooing of a dove.

Rainborough had been saying to himself for some time, 'It can't last much longer,' without having much of an idea in his head about how it was likely to finish. He was by now very much concerned about Miss Casement, and during office hours he thought about little else. She became in fact a subject for both contemplation and research; and Rainborough reflected bitterly, as he settled down to these studies, that after all what he was doing was no more pointless than what was going on at that moment in most of the other rooms in the SELIB building. His latest craze was to discover her age, which he cursed himself for not having observed when he had her passport in his hands. He proposed to do this by an elaborately prepared scheme of questions which would be asked at intervals over a certain period, in such a way that the answers would, when pieced together, provide the required information. The starting-point of this scheme was the datum that Miss Casement's brother was three years her senior. Surreptitiously to discover her brother's age was the aim of the subtle plan which Rainborough, reaching for his pen, was now about to commit to paper.

There was a knock on the door. Miss Casement and the typist, it appeared, had gone to tea, and someone had penetrated as far as the door of Rainborough's room. He put down his pen with irritation and called 'Come in?'

It was Hunter Keepe. Rainborough looked at him with surprise and annoyance. 'How very nice to see you!' he said.

'Hello,' said Hunter. The boy seemed agitated and embarrassed. He looked round for somewhere to sit, and settled himself quickly on a seat with the ungraceful haste of a player of the game of Musical Chairs.

Rainborough leaned back and regarded him with a puzzled frown. Hunter's arrival put him completely at his ease, so calmly superior did he feel to Rosa's not very mature and not very successful younger brother. The sight of Hunter, however, also reminded him of Rosa, and he felt a tiny pang of guilt at the juxtaposition in his mind of the images of Rosa and Miss Casement. It was axiomatic to Rainborough that Rosa was above all other women; and he would have told himself quite simply that Rosa was a matter of the spirit while Miss Casement was a matter of the flesh, had he not been honest enough to suspect that his interest in Miss Casement had become complex enough to deserve a better name. For this fact, when he thought of Rosa, he despised himself.

Rainborough felt, if anything, a certain dislike for Hunter. He knew that Hunter was aware of, and even perhaps over-estimated, his, Rainborough's, interest in his sister. He knew, too, that Hunter was notoriously hostile to anyone who was sweet on Rosa. This led Rainborough to expect, and then very easily to find, Hunter's behaviour to be studded with small acts of aggression. He looked at him now with impatience as he sat on the edge of the chair, blushing like an undergraduate. What on earth can he want? Rainborough wondered.

'What do you want?' he asked Hunter. 'I mean, what can I do for you?' And as he spoke he thought to himself, it's probably something to do with Mischa Fox.

Hunter was in no hurry to explain. He began by looking about the room as if he expected to see some strange animal roosting in a corner. Then he said to Rainborough, 'I expect you're pretty busy.'

Rainborough, who was not sure whether or not this was sarcastic, replied vaguely, 'Oh, it comes and it goes, you know.'

'I was passing,' said Hunter, 'and I just thought I'd drop in for a chat.' This was so transparently false that Rainborough was silenced.

Hunter continued, 'I hear Rosa saw you the other day with Dr. Saward.'

'That is true,' said Rainborough.

'What a nice man Dr. Saward is,' said Hunter; 'really almost a saint.'

'He's a good man,' said Rainborough, 'but he'd be the first to tell you not to mistake a scholar for a true ascetic.'

'Of course,' said Hunter. 'And then there's his health.'

Rainborough was wondering whether he hadn't better make some thoroughly nice remark about his friend, when Hunter went on, 'Dr. Saward saw Mischa Fox last week.'

'So I believe,' said Rainborough. He was interested to see just what the information was that Hunter wanted.

'Have you seen him?' Hunter asked.

'Who?' asked Rainborough, simply to annoy.

'Mischa Fox.'

Rainborough did not like to admit that he had not seen Mischa, so he said, 'Yes, I saw him a few days ago, but very briefly. I've been rather busy.'

'Did he say anything special?' asked Hunter.

'No,' said Rainborough, 'nothing special.' It occurred to him that people were always impelled to ask this question about Mischa, although they always got the same discreet reply.

'Oh,' said Hunter. He began once more to look round the office with simulated interest. Rainborough, watching him, felt irritation at his simplicity and envy for his copious head of hair.

'It must be interesting, this work of yours,' said Hunter. 'Tell me now,' he said, 'when people immigrate under your scheme, do they have only temporary leave to work here, or can they stay for good?'

He's being polite, thought Rainborough. 'In effect,' he said, 'unless there's some special reason to chuck them out, they can stay for good. For the first five years they hold a special SELIB permit. After that they can apply for an ordinary Ministry of Labour permit, or else ask for naturalization.'

'I see,' said Hunter. 'I imagined they were somehow on probation.'

'Only in the sense,' said Rainborough, 'that their permission to be here at all depends on their work permit. But in fact, once they're here, no one is going to bother their heads about them, and provided they behave normally there's nothing to stop them being here forever.'

'I see,' said Hunter rather gloomily. 'Forever.'

'Of course,' said Rainborough, who was suddenly beginning to feel interested in the subject, 'the whole thing is absurd in a way. Technically speaking, half these workers oughtn't to be here at all.'

'How is that?' asked Hunter.

'Well, you know we're a hybrid organization,' said Rainborough, 'half State-aided and half voluntary. Most of the voluntary contributions come from America. When we accepted this money originally we made an agreement that we would only use it for the benefit of people born west of a certain line.'

'People *born* west of a certain line?' asked Hunter.

'Yes,' said Rainborough. 'It sounds crazy and arbitrary, doesn't it? But we had to adopt some sort of rough and ready distinction. You see the point, of course, of some such arrangement. An international organization like this one has a tricky course to steer. We're likely to be accused by one party of enticement and by the other of using their money for political purposes. Not that some Americans would mind about that. But our benefactors are mainly liberal organizations, Quakers and so on, and they were very correct about the way the money

94

should be tied up. In our foundation charter there's a lot of stuff about our purpose being to assist people who want to emigrate because of purely economic hardship. It's very artificial, of course. Who's going to define economic hardship? Every conference we have, someone harks back to that. But one just has to make a distinction and stick to it. That's administration. That's what that line was invented for. Here it is.'

Rainborough got up and turned to a large map which was hanging behind him. He pointed to an irregular red line which ran through Europe from north to south. 'We call it the FPE,' said Rainborough. 'That means Farthest Point East.'

'But, in fact,' said Hunter, 'if I understood you, a lot of people who immigrate under SELIB were really born east of the line?'

'Yes,' said Rainborough, 'but we just keep quiet about that. Like so many things in England, it's known unofficially in high quarters, but so long as it's not known officially there'll be no trouble.'

'What would make it known officially?' asked Hunter.

'Well,' said Rainborough, 'if someone were to write to *The Times*, or to ask a question in Parliament, or if some minister were to take it up, then obviously it couldn't be ignored. But, in fact, it's to no one's advantage to raise the matter.'

'To no one's advantage?' asked Hunter.

'No,' said Rainborough, 'neither the Government of the day nor the Opposition has any interest in making a stink about it. Why should they? It would merely expose Great Britain to attacks from both sides.' Rainborough was beginning to put on what his friends called his 'Royal Commission manner'; he liked explaining this sort of point.

'How do you know where your people were born, anyway?' asked Hunter.

'Well, in some cases, when documents have been lost,' said Rainborough, 'it's hard to tell. A lot of these lads hold passports that are obviously forged.' He went to a huge filing-cabinet in the corner, unlocked it, and pulled out a few drawers. 'We hold all their identity documents here. Look at that,' he said, holding out a greenish booklet to Hunter, 'obviously a crude forgery. We just wink the eye at that. But in some cases there isn't even concealment. Their papers show quite clearly that they were born to the east.'

'It would be a sad thing for a man,' said Hunter, 'to have his fate decided by where he was born. He didn't choose where he was born.'

'Yes, it's not a pleasant way to have to discriminate between human beings,' said Rainborough, 'but you have to deal with the situation that you have, and we didn't make this one. Anyhow, life is full of that sort of injustice. We have to be things that we didn't choose.' Rainborough looked at Hunter's hair.

'Supposing there *were* a scandal,' asked Hunter, 'what would happen to the people born east of FPE who were already working in this country?'

There was a knock on the door.

'I don't know,' said Rainborough. 'I suppose they'd be deported. Come in!'

Evans put his head round the door. 'So sorry,' said Evans, 'I didn't know you were busy. It's just about the usual.' The usual was *The Times* crossword, concerning which Rainborough and Evans normally exchanged information at this hour in the day.

Rainborough, who did not want this matter mentioned in Hunter's presence, said, 'I'll come along to your room in a moment.' Evans went away. 'You must excuse me,' Rainborough told Hunter, 'a routine check-up. I won't be long.'

As soon as the door closed behind Rainborough, Hunter sprang from his chair and ran to the filing-cabinet. Suddenly he was trembling and breathing hard. He drew a shaking hand along the top of the files. It was not long before he found what he wanted, and he studied it carefully for some minutes. Then he left the cabinet as he had found it and turned his attention to the map.

When Rainborough returned, Hunter was still studying the map. He seemed absorbed in it.

'It's a good map,' said Rainborough. 'Even the smallest places are marked. Looking for anything special?'

'No,' said Hunter. He was drawing his finger slowly across eastern Poland. At last he sighed deeply and turned away with a smile. 'I'm afraid I must be off now,' he said to Rainborough.

Rainborough felt quite sorry. He would have liked to tell him more things. 'Ah, well,' said Rainborough, 'drop in again some time. How's Rosa?'

Hunter's face closed up. 'Rosa's fine,' he said.

'Very tied up at the factory, I suppose,' said Rainborough.

'Yes,' said Hunter, 'she's fine. Good-bye, and thanks for the talk.' He went away.

Rainborough sat down again and looked at his watch. Nearly time to go home. Silly puppy, he thought; what did he want, I wonder? His thoughts reverted to Miss Casement.

NINE

Rosa was very unhappy indeed. She felt that her relation with the Lusiewicz brothers was drawing nearer and nearer to the brink of some disaster. She also knew that she was passing through a period to which she would look back later to marvel at her inertia. There was still some possibility of action. She had not yet entirely lost the initiative. Very soon she would be powerless. But she was not yet powerless; not quite yet. This was the most painful thought of all.

She was worried, too, about Hunter. It was obvious that Hunter needed help. He was in a torment of indecision about the *Artemis* and badly wanting Rosa to give him a lead. Rosa loved her brother, and to have to withhold this help from him caused her continual distress. But so far she had felt herself unable to make any move. Neither she nor Hunter spoke of the matter, and as this silence made them incapable of talking about anything else, they had hardly exchanged a word for days. Only Hunter's eyes, reproachful and sad, continually reminded Rosa that she herself had brought upon him the griefs in the midst of which she now refused to give him her good counsel.

Rosa had no special affection for the *Artemis*. She had imagined once that she might edit it herself and make it into a great pure-hearted periodical; but her time in Fleet Street had taught her both how hard it is to sell pure-hearted periodicals and how little she herself had the temperament of an editor. If she had had a sum of money to put behind the magazine, it might have been different. As it was, she had left it to struggle on, and the best that she hoped from it was that before it finally perished it might afford some useful experience to Hunter and help to qualify him for a more lucrative occupation. If at any time Hunter had received from anyone else such an advantageous offer as he had now received from Mischa Fox, Rosa, who felt herself to be responsible for her

98

brother's poverty, would have counselled him to accept. She knew that the idea of buying *Artemis* had come up more than once in highly reputable quarters, and she had always been disappointed when she had heard no more about it.

There was no doubt in Rosa's mind that Mischa Fox's offer was carefully timed. It was also clear to her that what Mischa wanted was not so much the *Artemis* as to put Hunter and herself into a certain kind of dilemma. This was typical of him. Further than this she could not see; and she was still unsure whether Mischa's move was to be thought of as an attempt to reopen negotiations and not rather as an act of revenge. Mischa was quite capable of taking, after ten years, a carefully-thought-out reprisal. As Rosa sat wondering about this, she was tortured by her lack of knowledge. She could hardly think of anything she would not have given to know Mischa Fox's mind at that moment. What terrified her most was that she found deep in her heart a strong wish that Mischa might indeed want to reopen negotiations. This discovery alarmed her for many reasons. She had decided ten years earlier that any relation with Mischa could only do her harm, and she had not had occasion to change her mind. But to find herself still, however partially and however obscurely, fascinated by the idea of Mischa was alarming, not so much because this fascination might ever come definitively to tempt her, as because of the endless variety of torments which such a situation could promise.

When Rosa began to feel how strong, after so long a time, her interest still was in Mischa, her position with the Lusiewicz brothers began to seem unendurable. She found herself aching with the desire to be free of them, partly because of a simple wish to be able to indulge, without any further complication, her hopeless and half-guilty thoughts about Mischa Fox, and partly because, and this was perhaps what bit most deeply into her, she was sick with fear at the thought that Mischa might find out about the brothers. So far, Rosa was very certain that the secret of her association with them had been well kept. They had their own motives for silence. As for herself, she had not mentioned their name to anyone for many months, and there was no one, except Hunter, who was in any position to follow her movements; and whatever Hunter suspected, he would be but too anxious to keep to himself. But if Mischa Fox should find out, then the discovery would be likely both to make up his mind in favour of revenge rather than negotiations and to put him at the same moment in possession of a weapon against Rosa of such power that she grew pale at the thought of any person even possessing it, let alone using it.

Rosa knew this; and she knew, too, that she had not got the strength to escape from the power of the brothers. It was profitless to ask now whether the bond that tied her to them was love. The darkness in which those two held her was profound beyond the reach of names. She could not of her own will break the spell. And then she would ask herself – and why should I break it? What do I care about other people! Why should I sacrifice this true love? The brothers, after all, had committed no fault beyond that of loving her. They were poor and helpless, they were her children. In reason, she had nothing to hold against them. Whereas of Mischa she knew much ill and suspected more, so that he became for her at moments the very figure of evil. These things Rosa said to herself. But they were not the things which she was really thinking.

Rosa was aware that Hunter had never forgiven her for refusing to marry Mischa; and that inevitably the boy must be dreaming something, hoping something, in the present situation. Sometimes it seemed likely to Rosa that to sell himself into Mischa's power was precisely Hunter's profoundest wish – though it was not necessarily the one on which he would have acted, even had the complication concerning his sister been absent from the scene. As it was, Hunter was in the dark, even concerning the degree of Rosa's attachment to the *Artemis*, let alone concerning the possible existence of any remnant of her attachment to Mischa. He could only make guesses about her attitude; and his sharpest temptation would be to imagine that perhaps what Rosa really wanted, only she didn't like to say it to him openly, was that he should sell the periodical and so in some sense let them both be drawn back into the orbit of Mischa Fox. This was how Rosa saw the situation. Her prediction was that, failing any lead from herself, Hunter would refuse to sell the *Artemis*, influenced partly by ideals of independence but chiefly by the fear of offending his sister, should it be the case, as after all the available evidence suggested, that

100

she wished to have no further dealings of any kind with Mischa Fox.

The annual meeting of the shareholders of *Artemis* was due to occur in about a week's time. If Hunter should decide to sell, the matter could most conveniently be raised then, and indeed, technically speaking, settled at once. It was a part of the constitution of *Artemis* that decisions taken at an appropriately publicized meeting of shareholders required no quorum. The energetic women who had founded the periodical and who had felt their love for it to be eternal had argued that if ever a time came when shareholders were too indifferent to attend meetings the thing should be left to its fate. That time, which they had been unable to imagine, had come; and now each year, as they dozed by their firesides, Hunter read out the annual report to an empty room and took whatever policy decisions were necessary with the assistance of Rosa, who was very often the only shareholder present. The sale, therefore, could very easily be put through; and when Rosa reflected upon how, from so many mundane points of view, attractive the idea must seem, she felt that she was putting an intolerable strain upon Hunter. But in so far as to help him she would have to make up her own mind about a number of matters which she could scarcely bear even to think about, let alone to make definite, she felt herself to be incapable of doing so.

Suddenly, however, Rosa did think of a project which held some promise of at least lightening the tension – and, passionately desiring action of some kind, and quite incapable of the action which was most gravely needed, she seized upon the idea with joy. It was an idea which had been suggested to her by John Rainborough when she had last met him with Peter Saward and which had indeed occurred to her very much earlier but had been rejected for a variety of reasons: namely, to appeal for funds to one of the shareholders. Rosa and Hunter had discussed this possibility long ago, but they had decided against it then. As Hunter put it, 'If we go stirring up those old girls, they'll start to interfere'; and Rosa herself had felt too proud to ask for contributions from elderly and wealthy women who had been the admirers and followers of her mother, and who, she felt, ought to be coming forward now of their own accord to give assistance to *Artemis*.

101

When this idea came afresh to Rosa in the midst of her troubles, it seemed to her a very good one. If some large sum of money were suddenly forthcoming for *Artemis* from another source, this would simplify, though it would hardly solve, the situation *vis-à-vis* Mischa Fox. Rosa told herself that as things stood at the moment she could never be sure how much in her own attitude was a genuine concern for Hunter's welfare. If this item could be looked after by some means quite external to the situation, then, Rosa felt, she might be able to see more clearly just what was at stake. To bring the *Artemis* financially speaking out of danger would so enormously relieve her mind and Hunter's that she could believe them both capable of miracles of clear thinking and decisive action once that was achieved. If the sum of money available were large enough, she might even think in terms of a regular salary for Hunter and a new lease of life for the periodical; and although Rosa was not optimistic enough to imagine that money was really the solution to all her difficulties, she was certainly overjoyed at finding at last a field in which she was free to move – and the notion that she could, on her own initiative and in however small a way, alter the situation in which Mischa Fox had placed her, made her feel already half-way towards winning back her freedom.

When she got home from the factory that night she took the book of shareholders and carried it off to her own room. She said nothing to Hunter about her plan. As she studied the book, it seemed to her that there were two people whom she might approach, one a Mrs Carrington-Morris, who had been and still was, a prominent Methodist, and the other Mrs Camilla Wingfield, the eccentric lady who had been mentioned by Rainborough. Rosa debated for some time between these two and decided finally in favour of Mrs Wingfield. It might turn out that Mrs Wingfield was too crazy, but it was even more likely to turn out that Mrs Carrington-Morris was too sane; and Rosa decided to bet first upon the generosity of Mrs Wingfield, which might be non-existent but might equally be extravagant. Rosa could also remember having met both ladies some thirty years ago and having felt a marked preference for Mrs Wingfield. It was her name, therefore, which she now looked up in the London telephone directory, to discover to her surprise that Mrs Wingfield also lived in Campden Hill Square, in a house on the opposite side which could be seen out of the window. Rosa took this to be a good omen.

Rosa decided to open her campaign by a personal visit, rather than by a letter, and to rely upon the effects of surprise together with her mother's name and her own physical resemblance to that lady to bring about an immediate capitulation. So it was that on the following day, which was a Saturday, Rosa was knocking on Mrs Wingfield's door at about four o'clock. She had calculated that it was wisest to call at tea-time, when any embarrassment caused by her arrival could be rapidly dispelled amid the dispensing of cups of tea.

Rosa knocked several times without getting any answer and had stepped back on to the pavement to look up at the closely curtained windows when the door opened very quietly to a gap of a few inches and a pale face peered out. Rosa sprang forward with such alacrity that the owner of the face immediately shut the door again, and Rosa could hear the chain being fixed. With this additional safeguard the door opened once more to a narrow slit and Rosa could see one pale blue eye looking out at her.

'Excuse me,' said Rosa, made thoroughly nervous by this reception, 'I am anxious to see Mrs Camilla Wingfield. I wonder if you could tell me whether she is at home?'

At this the door closed again, and Rosa was about to go away in despair when she heard the chain being removed, and a moment later the door was thrown wide open to reveal a fuzzy-headed woman dressed in an overall.

'Oh, I *am* so sorry!' said this personage, beaming at Rosa. 'I took you for a gipsy. You must forgive me. There are so many around at this time of year. They work with the circuses in the winter, you know, and in the summer they do farm work, and about this time of year, which is an inbetween time, they go about in the towns and try to sell things. One came last week and was *so* unpleasant. She put her foot in the door and wouldn't go away. In the end I had to buy some heather off her to make her go. You wouldn't mind if they sold useful things like brushes, but selling heather at that price, it's just daylight robbery. You must excuse me for having thought you were a gipsy. As soon as you spoke, of course, I knew you weren't one. But at first I just saw your black hair, and it gave me a turn. I can see now from your appearance, too, that you're not a gipsy.

It was just seeing you for a moment I made a mistake. It's so unusual for a lady these days to wear her hair so long. *They* all do, of course, I mean the gipsies. But your hair is very beautiful, if I may say so, and very becoming the way you wear it. I wish more young girls would wear their hair long. But they can't be bothered, can they, they're always in such a rush, the poor things, bless their hearts.'

During this speech Rosa relaxed completely and began to smile. She liked the speaker, whose social class she still felt unable to guess. Rosa prided herself on being able to place the people she met, considered as social phenomena, very rapidly: a capacity she had picked up from her mother. That distinguished Socialist had possessed an almost uncanny sensitivity to social differences. Rosa decided that what confronted her was, in spite of the overall and the woollen stockings sagging towards the ankle, Mrs Wingfield's lady companion. But the age of this person remained uncertain. Her large eyes were of a blue so pale as to be almost white, like a washed-out garment, and the flesh of her face and neck, which was of a light greyish colour, was covered all over with a criss-cross of tiny wrinkles of anxiety and good nature which destroyed the lines of the features, so that the eyes looked at Rosa out of a flabby expanse of flesh which reached with no other interruption from the wig-like hair, which resembled the interior of a mattress, to the round-necked lace of the ancient dress which announced the beginning of the body.

'I am Miss Foy,' said this person, with the air of one uttering a famous name. The dry skin undulated as she spoke, like the skin of an alligator.

'Ah!' said Rosa, with what she hoped was the appropriate intonation.

'Yes!' said Miss Foy triumphantly. She laid the dishcloth which she was holding over her arm. 'I'm doing the wash-up,' she said.

'I was wanting to speak to Mrs Wingfield,' said Rosa. 'I wonder if that's convenient?'

'She doesn't expect you,' said Miss Foy reproachfully.

'I'm sorry,' said Rosa. 'If it would be easier, I could go away and come again.' She cursed herself for not having thought to bring a visiting-card.

'Oh, it doesn't matter!' said Miss Foy cheerfully. 'She'll be amused to see you. You'd better go straight up. Come in, my dear; that's right.'

Miss Foy ushered Rosa in, and as the door closed behind her they were plunged into almost complete darkness. Rosa could descry various very large objects clustered round the walls, while overhead there appeared to be a number of plants which leaned over the scene, rustling and breathing. In the background there was a curious moaning sound, as if some sort of machine were working.

'You must forgive me if I don't announce you,' said Miss Foy. 'She hates to see me when I'm washing up. The drawing-room is in the front on the first floor. You'll probably hear her singing, and that will guide you. Don't be nervous, my dear. And,' Miss Foy drew Rosa close to her and lowered her voice, 'don't mind the funny things she says, will you, she only says them to shock people, and she doesn't really mean them, you know.'

With that, Miss Foy abruptly vanished into the darkness, leaving Rosa to find her way upstairs. She began to mount; and as she went, she became aware that the curious sound which had met her as she entered and which had continued throughout her conversation with Miss Foy was in fact made by a human voice. This sound, as Rosa approached it, revealed itself as a deep and not unpleasant voice, which was singing in an oddly monotonous manner. Filled with curiosity about what she was going to see, Rosa knocked on the drawing-room door. There was no reply, and the singing continued. So she knocked again, more loudly, and then walked in.

She found herself in a large, bright, untidy, over-furnished drawing-room, amid whose litter of objects her dazzled eyes could at first descry no human form. Then she became aware of a pair of stout masculine-looking shoes, whose soles, high upon the arm of an enormous sofa, were pointing towards her. The owner of the shoes and the voice, which continued to sing, evidently lay out of sight upon the sofa. Rosa walked round until she was broadside on to the sofa, and there was revealed a tall grey-haired woman, dressed in a tweed jacket and corduroy trousers, who lay prostrate with her feet raised well above her head, while beside her upon the floor stood a champagne bottle and a glass. As Rosa came into sight, the owner of the shoes turned upon her a face of considerable power, from

105

whose very dry, heavily powdered and apparently unwrinkled expanse two dark brown eyes looked serenely out.

'You're just in time for the row in the hall,' said Mrs Wingfield.

'I beg your pardon?' said Rosa.

'I said you're just in time for the row in the hall,' said Mrs Wingfield. 'It's simply an expression. Before your day, I expect. Fashions in idiom change so rapidly.' Mrs Wingfield spoke in a deep lazy voice, which was not the voice of a very old woman.

'I'm so sorry to walk in unannounced,' said Rosa, and then regretted this remark, which seemed to reflect on Miss Foy.

'I suppose the old trout let you in,' said Mrs Wingfield. 'That's all right. She's washing up. Have some champagne. It's the only thing I can drink now that doesn't upset my stomach. Sorry there's only one glass.'

With surprising energy she swung her legs down and poured out some champagne, which she handed to Rosa. Then she swung her legs back into their original position and began to drone, '*In the twi – twi – twilight, out in the beau – ti – ful twilight.* I've never forgotten a song that I heard before 1910 and never remembered one that I heard since,' she explained to Rosa.

'You have not, in my view, missed much,' said Rosa politely. She had not yet got the wavelength of Mrs Wingfield, and was trying to move carefully.

'Who the hell are you, anyway?' said Mrs Wingfield. 'This is just like this bloody age. People walk into your drawing-room without any by-your-leave, and before you know where you are they're drinking your champagne, and you don't know them from Adam.'

Rosa was about to announce her identity when Mrs Wingfield cried out, 'Don't tell me! Let me guess!' She turned her head towards Rosa, and her two dark eyes, which appeared vertically one over the other above the plump cushions of the sofa, surveyed her critically.

'Would you mind showing me your profile?' said Mrs Wingfield. 'Thank you. Yes, I thought so. You are Miss Keepe, Margaret Richardson's daughter, and you live on the other side of the square.'

'That's right,' said Rosa. 'We met once, a long time ago, when I was a child. You've probably forgotten.'

'I haven't forgotten at all,' said Mrs Wingfield. 'Sorry to disappoint you, but I'm not as senile as you evidently imagine. We met at Wimbledon. You must have been about eight, and your manners were shocking, even then. But I'm damned if I can recall your Christian name.'

'Rosa.'

'Ah, yes,' said Mrs Wingfield. 'Your mother was an absolute bolshy. But she'd have had her bellyful of it by now if she'd lived.'

Rosa flushed with annoyance and was about to reply when Mrs Wingfield cried, 'Don't be angry! I adored your mother. I probably appreciated her far better than you did. I must say I wondered when you'd have the courtesy to call on me. I suppose you want some money, though; that's the only reason why anyone calls on me nowadays. Well, you can't have any. Hasn't anyone told you? I'm an old skinflint. But you can stay and talk to me till I go to bed. You may have precious few manners, but you can't walk out as soon as you've come, and now I've got you here I'm going to keep you. What do I care if you never come again? Have some champagne.'

Rosa, who was poised between annoyance, amusement, and despair, said 'Thank you,' and held out the glass.

'Oh, you want some *more*, do you?' said Mrs Wingfield. 'Well, give me back the glass. You can drink it out of a cup. There's one left over there, I think, in the cabinet.'

Rosa went over to the cabinet, picking her way between the poufs, hassocks, cushions, footstools, and occasional tables with which the floor was strewn in the interstices of the larger pieces of furniture. She took down a very beautiful Dresden cup and brought it back to Mrs Wingfield. The latter had meanwhile filled and emptied the champagne glass with startling rapidity and was filling it for herself once again, her head dangling awkwardly over the edge of the sofa.

'You'd better wipe it with your hanky,' she said, as Rosa held out the cup. 'It hasn't been dusted for two or three reigns.' This appeared to be true. Rosa rubbed her handkerchief over it, and Mrs Wingfield poured in the remnants of the champagne.

'Not much left, I'm afraid,' she said, 'and this is the last bottle. Well, I'm a liar, it's not the last bottle, I only mean it's the last you'll get.'

'It's a beautiful cup,' said Rosa politely.

'Yes, it's sweet, isn't it,' said Mrs Wingfield. 'I've got some lovely stuff here, only you can't see it, there's such a mess. I must get the old trout to show you round some time. Just now she's washing up. I only let her wash up once in three weeks. It takes that long for us to work through all our china. I hate Foy dashing away after a meal to wash up, it destroys my digestion. So we wait till there's no china left and then Foy makes a day of it.'

'I see. What a sensible arrangement,' said Rosa.

'It's not a sensible arrangement,' said Mrs Wingfield, 'but it's the arrangement we've adopted.'

At that moment Miss Foy came into the room carrying a champagne glass. 'I thought you might want another glass,' she said.

'You thought right,' said Mrs Wingfield, 'but a bit late in the day, as usual. Don't go away, you fool. Leave the glass, now you've brought it. You can take that cup down, I don't know how we overlooked it. Have you got any drink left, girl? Well, pour it into the glass, and give Foy the cup to take away. That's right.'

Miss Foy turned to go. 'By the way, Foy,' Mrs Wingfield shouted after her, 'this is Rosa Keepe.'

Miss Foy came running back, her pale eyes glistening with excitement. 'Why, Miss Rosa,' she cried, 'what a pleasure this is, and what an honour!'

'Honour my foot,' said Mrs Wingfield. 'It's Miss Keepe, not her mother.'

'I remember your mother well,' said Miss Foy. 'I often heard her speak in the halls around Holborn and Kingsway. What a speaker she was! Of course, I was very young then.'

'Not so damn young,' said Mrs Wingfield. 'How old do you think Foy is?' she asked Rosa.

Rosa looked embarrassed. 'I'm not very clever at guessing people's ages,' she said coldly.

'Look at her!' said Mrs Wingfield, 'she's putting me in my place! Well, make a guess. But take a good look first. She's like an old mop, isn't she? Have you ever seen a human being look more like an old mop? And look at her legs. Lift your skirt up, Foy. They've got no shape at all. They're like two posts. Have you ever seen anyone with legs more like a couple of posts?'

'Don't you mind her, Miss Rosa,' said Miss Foy, who appeared to be fairly used to this. 'She doesn't mean it.'

'Don't I just mean it!' cried Mrs Wingfield with passion. She swung her legs down again with the same energetic gesture and sat pointing at Miss Foy, who now turned a shade paler under her grey. 'Look at her hair. Did you ever see such a frizz? It shows one of her attacks is coming on. Mad people's hair always stands up like that. They say a lunatic is a lunatic to his fingers' ends.'

'Don't!' said Miss Foy. 'Please stop it! You're giving me the creeps.' She turned and fled from the room.

'What a frump!' said Mrs Wingfield. 'She thinks I'm serious. I was much jollier before I met Foy. All the same, if it wasn't for her I'd be sunning myself in the porch of some damned hotel. Would you say old Foy was a virgin?'

'I have absolutely no opinion on the subject,' said Rosa savagely, who was very much disapproving of this persecution of Miss Foy. She had by now decided that Mrs Wingfield was by no means mad.

'What do you mean, you've no opinion?' said Mrs Wingfield. 'You must think *something* about it, one way or the other!'

'I mean,' said Rosa, 'that I think you've been very rude to Miss Foy.'

'Well, why the hell don't you say what you mean?' said Mrs Wingfield. 'I'm not a thought-reader. I'll tell you something. Of course you think she's a virgin. Everyone does. And I'll tell you something else. She isn't! You'd be surprised. But I'll tell you all that some other time. Could you go to that cupboard and get out another bottle of champagne? That's right. Do you know how to open a bottle of champagne? Well, open that one, and don't let it spurt all over the furniture.'

Mrs Wingfield was sitting up now, her trousered legs sturdily apart, leaning back against the cushions of the sofa. As Rosa poured her out a glass of champagne, she was struck by the extraordinary dry texture of her face, which seen at close quarters had an alarmingly artificial appearance. The surface was more like smooth slightly dusty cardboard than like skin. In the midst of this desert the two eyes gleamed alarmingly, like weedy pools. Rosa felt almost terror at the thought that if those eyes were ever to spill a tear it would surely cut a strange furrow in the dry powdery surface, revealing heaven knew what beneath. There was a sweet dusty smell, as of old linen preserved in lavender.

'You're thinking,' said Mrs Wingfield, 'that I'm a fine one to talk about age. I make no secret of my age. I'm eighty-three. You think I've got an enamelled face, like Queen What's-her-name. Would you like to see a picture of me when I was twenty? Pass me that album.' Rosa passed over a thick book with a red velvet cover which lay amid a miscellany of vases and brass animals on top of a nearby piano.

'There I am,' said Mrs Wingfield.

Rosa looked at the picture of a proud sweet-faced girl with a cloud of dark hair and glowing dark eyes under an enormous hat. 'You were beautiful,' said Rosa. 'You're not terribly unlike this now,' she said seriously. She suddenly saw, as in a vision, the young face looking through Mrs Wingfield's old one. It was startling.

'You're a little flatterer,' said Mrs Wingfield, 'and a flatterer is a liar. That's not like your mother. She would never have flattered anybody. But then, of course, you want to get something out of me. There's me again a bit later.'

She turned the page, and Rosa saw a confused picture of a tall woman in an ankle-length skirt standing with her arms held out in an unnatural position, with a crowd gathered round her. 'That was when I chained myself to the railings at Wellington Barracks. I've still got a mark on my wrist from that day.' She showed Rosa a small red mark on her left wrist.

'Really!' said Rosa.

'Do you believe me?' asked Mrs Wingfield, and then laughed fiendishly. 'Never mind! Look, here I am arrested at Ascot. I got those photos from the newspapers. They always sent a polite man round next day to ask if we wanted pictures. Your mother must have had quite a collection.'

'Yes, she had,' said Rosa. 'I remember one of her and you throwing leaflets about in a theatre.'

'That's right!' said Mrs Wingfield, her eyes kindling. 'It was Covent Garden. *Il Trovatore*. Royalty was present. You clever little thing, you're working hard for whatever it is you want!' She turned the page again. 'There's a picture of me talking to Bernard Shaw.'

Rosa studied the picture respectfully. 'Old Wingfield was jealous about me and Bernard,' said Mrs Wingfield. 'That was before I crowned the old blighter – old Wingfield I mean. I killed him with an axe, you know. He needn't have minded about Bernard. *Him* I despised, the conceited ass. Left his money to Spelling Reform! And now you're wondering,' Mrs Wingfield went on, 'what I'm going to leave *my* money to! Well, I shan't tell you. Old Foy thinks she's going to get it, but I haven't left her a penny!' Mrs Wingfield cackled and threw herself sideways among the cushions.

Rosa backed away slightly and found herself a chair. She didn't want the situation to get out of hand.

'And don't you say to me,' Mrs Wingfield went on rather breathlessly, 'that I needn't care what happens to my money when I'm gone. I won't care then, but I care now. After all, we all live in the future, even if it's a future where we aren't to be found anywhere upon the earth. We all live in the future, so long as we live at all, which in my case won't be much longer. Another few months and they'll be digging in the bureau looking for the will. Did you believe what I said just now?'

'What?' asked Rosa. She felt a growing distress for Mrs Wingfield, who was beginning to look a little wild-eyed.

'About how I coshed old codger Wingfield with an axe!'

'No!' said Rosa.

'How right you were!' cried Mrs Wingfield, beginning to laugh and cough. 'When people are as old as I am they get to be terrible liars! I didn't cosh him with an axe, I broke his head open with a flat-iron!' She nearly choked herself laughing.

'Mrs Wingfield, please!' said Rosa. 'Please be calm.'

'I'm perfectly calm,' said Mrs Wingfield. 'And as for what you think of me, do you imagine I care? Lust and rage! Lust and rage, as the poet says! When you're as old as me you begin to lose your identity. What's the difference between me and an old soak in the Bayswater Road, except the memories that we trail behind us? And what are they? Old tales that nobody wants to hear and we scarcely believe in ourselves. Old stories and photographs. And don't tell me the old soak is a better woman. That's what your mother would have said. I haven't forgotten what a bolshy she was!'

'Please, Mrs Wingfield,' said Rosa, who felt that she had indeed let the situation get out of hand. 'I'm sorry, perhaps I've stayed too long, and —'

'You certainly have!' said Mrs Wingfield. 'You've been here

111

for an hour and you haven't even had enough spunk to say why you've come. Out with it!'

'I came to consult you on a matter of business,' Rosa began.

'I knew it was money!' said Mrs Wingfield. 'Well, I've told you, you can't have any. And now you can go. I'm tired.'

'I'm sorry!' said Rosa. She was red with mingled distress and annoyance. She picked up her coat. 'I'll come back if I may another day.'

'You'll do nothing of the sort!' said Mrs Wingfield. 'Another day I may be underground. I'm dying with curiosity to know what you want. I shan't sleep tonight unless you tell me. Sit down, girl, and relax. I'm not as mad as I seem.'

Rosa sat down again and looked doubtfully at her hostess. 'It's about the *Artemis*,' she said. She was feeling tired too.

'The *what*?' asked Mrs Wingfield.

'The *Artemis*,' said Rosa. 'It's a periodical.'

'Oh, you mean the *Artemis*,' said Mrs Wingfield. 'Of course. You pronounce it so oddly. Well, what about it?'

'It needs money,' said Rosa. She thought she had better be simple. 'Unless we get some financial help, we shall have to close down. I thought you might perhaps be willing to make a contribution. You are one of the major shareholders.'

'I know *that*,' said Mrs Wingfield. 'Don't treat me as if I were something out of the Pyramids. I suppose you run the thing yourself?'

'Well, not exactly,' said Rosa. 'In fact, my young brother runs it.'

'Your young brother!' said Mrs Wingfield. 'A fair-haired ninny, if I remember. Resembled your father. Why Maggie ever married *him* was beyond us all. I saw your brother a few years ago at Oxford. Yes, I got as far as Oxford. I went to a college play. Someone pointed him out to me. He was acting. He was supposed to be some sort of gentleman. It was Shakespeare. He had three lines to say, and even then he forgot one of them. So you want me to rescue the *Artemis* to be a play-thing for your brother? You're going to be disappointed, Miss Keepe.'

'My brother is a perfectly competent editor,' said Rosa. 'All he lacks is funds. But in any case that isn't the point. What is urgent is to prevent the *Artemis* from going bankrupt.'

'Well, why come to me?' asked Mrs Wingfield. 'Why don't you auction it in Fleet Street?'

It was abundantly clear to Rosa that Mrs Wingfield was indeed not something out of the Pyramids. She smiled faintly. 'No one in Fleet Street wants to buy it just now,' she said; 'at least not anyone to whom we wish to sell it.'

'So you've had an offer?' said Mrs Wingfield. She was leaning forward, her bright liquid eyes popping out slightly as she stared at Rosa. 'Cards on the table!'

'Yes,' said Rosa, 'we've had an offer from Mischa Fox. But we don't want to have to accept it. We would prefer the *Artemis* to remain independent. That would be better than selling out to *anyone*. But if we sell to Fox he will change the character of the magazine completely.'

'Your brother's probably changed it already, for all I know,' said Mrs Wingfield.

'You receive a free copy every month,' said Rosa coldly.

'Do I?' said Mrs. Wingfield. 'I wonder what happens to it. Foy must scoff it up in her room. Well, why come to me with this tale of woe? Do you imagine I care whether this Fox or the Devil himself buys the *Artemis*? Why don't you try Ada Carrington-Morris? She still has ideals. I'm too old. Lust and rage, lust and rage, Miss Keepe!'

Rosa could see that Mrs Wingfield was saying this simply to see how she would react. 'We don't want to be helped by Mrs. Carrington-Morris,' she said coolly. 'We want to be helped by you.'

'More flattery!' said Mrs Wingfield. 'Here, have some champagne, I quite forgot to offer you any, or would you rather have some tea?'

'Don't bother about the tea,' said Rosa. 'I'll drink champagne.'

'She says don't bother about the tea, she'll drink champagne!' cried Mrs Wingfield. 'Do you realize how much this champagne costs a bottle? And the tea we use is elevenpence a quarter. Ring for Foy and ask for tea! I told you I was a skinflint!'

'All I mean,' said Rosa desperately, 'is please don't bother. I don't really want either tea or champagne.'

'So you've been drinking my champagne without really wanting it, have you!' cried Mrs Wingfield.

'I do beg you,' said Rosa, 'to consider this matter of the *Artemis*. There's a shareholders' meeting in a week's time and a decision ought to be reached before then. My brother has given a great deal of work to the periodical. He receives no salary, and in fact he's put savings of his own into keeping it alive. Unless we can get a substantial sum of money from somewhere, I can't honestly advise him against selling out to Fox. The *Artemis* is deeply in debt.'

'I thought it was a matter of closing down, not of selling out,' said Mrs Wingfield.

'Whichever it is,' said Rosa, 'it means the end of the *Artemis* as we know it, the periodical that was founded by my mother and yourself.'

'Flattery!' said Mrs Wingfield. 'Soft soap! Why should it gratify me now to be associated with that bolshy? I can see you want to look after your brother. A natural reaction. Even animals have it. As for this man Fox, is he a friend of yours?'

Rosa looked sharply into Mrs Wingfield's dewy intelligent eyes. 'No,' she said.

'I've heard of him,' said Mrs Wingfield. 'He's a bit of a press lord and general mischief-maker, isn't he?'

'Yes,' said Rosa.

'There are too many men in this story,' said Mrs Wingfield 'The *Artemis* as I knew it was a women's periodical. And now it's my bedtime. I get around a lot during the day. If I lay down now I'd never get up again. But it means I have to go to bed early. Could you call that wig-face as you go out?'

Rosa stood up and prepared to go. 'We should be very grateful,' she said, 'if you would consider helping us.'

'Of course, you realize that I could rescue you with my little finger,' said Mrs Wingfield. 'I'm as rich as a Jew!' She leaned back into the sofa cushions and swung her legs up on to the arm. 'Whether I *will* or not is quite another matter.'

'May I hope —' said Rosa.

'Oh, you may *hope*,' said Mrs Wingfield; 'that doesn't cost me anything! But not a word to your blond brother.' She closed her eyes and folded her hands on her stomach.

Rosa saw that it had become quite dark in the room. She picked her way around the various obstacles to the door. As she opened it, she said, 'Good afternoon.' Mrs Wingfield did not reply or open her eyes, and Rosa left the room on tiptoe.

TEN

John Rainborough was standing in his garden. It was Sunday afternoon, and the sun, which had been shining now for several hours, was beginning to warm the earth. Rainborough had always made a serious effort, so far successfully, not to think about SELIB when he was at home. His home was a safe stronghold; it had been the home of his childhood, and it was full of myths and spirits from the past, whose beneficent murmur could be heard as soon as he had stilled his mind and put away the irritations of his day at the office. Then these spirits would come flocking about him, comforting him and brushing against him with their soft substance until he was lulled into a contentment and a sense of knowledge deeper than any thought. It was many years now since Rainborough had put it to himself that the only matter which really concerned him was the achievement of wisdom. Sometimes he called this: the achievement of goodness; but just now, for various reasons, he preferred the other title.

It was true that since the phenomenon of Miss Casement had made its appearance in Rainborough's life he had found it more difficult to observe the rule about forgetting the office when he came home. Today it seemed likely to be especially hard. On the previous day, Miss Casement had startled him by suddenly producing a long report which she had been writing about the reorganization of SELIB. This report, which was clearly the fruit of researches not only into the files of the Finance Department but into the files of the other departments as well, was extremely detailed and thorough. It opened with a clear survey of SELIB's present staff and activities, it proceeded to an analysis of SELIB's functions, including a history of their development, and it went on, through a section on the international significance of SELIB, to a number of concrete proposals for streamlining the organization of the office and producing a greater efficiency at a smaller cost. These proposals involved the virtual abolition of several departments and the curtailment of others; and Rainborough noticed at once that in the new régime, as envisaged by Miss Casement, the Finance Department would occupy that leading position which he had himself so often felt it should occupy, but which he had so far failed to capture.

This report had been presented to him by Miss Casement in a submissive and modest manner. She had produced it with a show of reluctance and misgivings, saying that it was just something which she had written in her spare time, to clear her own mind, and that it might perhaps be useful to him as a rough draft when he made proposals to Sir Edward about reorganizing the office. Rainborough was not aware that he had at any time suggested to Miss Casement that he was likely to make such proposals, though he might possibly have dropped some remark which could be so interpreted in the early days of his appointment. Rainborough accepted the document with vague thanks and read it with curiosity.

He discovered to his extreme chagrin that it was very good indeed. Apart from one or two inelegancies of style, he would have been proud to have written it himself. It was in fact precisely the document which he had dreamed of producing when he first arrived in SELIB. It combined an accurate and detailed knowledge of the Board's organization with an imaginative interpretation of its essential functions. The section on SELIB and the international scene was positively statesman-like. The only thing which could be said against Miss Casement's report was that, if carried into effect, it would damage a great many existing interests. Rainborough noticed, for instance, that in the proposed new office the department of Evans would disappear altogether.

Rainborough was well aware that if he were to sign his name under Miss Casement's report and send it to Sir Edward he would be ushering in an era of wars and revolutions of whose savagery he quailed even to think; and who knew how he himself would fare in such a struggle? He could think of a number of individuals whose position was attacked by the report who would certainly not hesitate to take reprisals. In short, Rainborough felt that in sponsoring the report he would be both offending against a certain subtle gentleman's agreement which existed in SELIB concerning mutual abstention from criticism and laying himself open to counter-attacks to which he knew he was more than a little vulnerable. He made to himself a display of dubiety; but he knew in his heart that he was determined to kill Miss Casement's report, and he decided that he had better start breaking this news to her as soon as possible. He had already stored up a number of phrases about 'youthful enthusiasm', 'sleeping dogs', and so on. The only thing about which he was unsure, and this caused him a certain uneasiness, was how Miss Casement would react to the prospect of her report being filed away *sine die*. He wondered if she knew how good it was. He had an uneasy suspicion that she did.

Such thoughts had been intruding upon the peace of Rainborough's week-end. By now, however, they had almost completely faded away, leaving behind only a sort of resentment which mingling itself somehow with memories of Miss Casement's perfume and her red-rimmed cigarette ends faded at last into a tiny cloud of desire. As Rainborough stood now in his garden, with the spring sun perceptibly warm upon his neck, other sorrowful matters were in the forefront of his mind. Rainborough occupied a large house just off Eaton Square which had been the home of his parents, and which had attached to it a garden, large by London standards, surrounded by a tall grey stone wall. Along this wall, opposite to the French windows of Rainborough's drawing-room, a dreamy wistaria had been growing for several scores of years, extending its gnarled and golden-brown trunk in a series of grotesque and romantic curves and lifting its dusty blue blossoms above the herbaceous border. This wistaria was connected in Rainborough's mind not only with his childhood but with what he regarded as all his deepest thoughts: those phantoms through whose nebulous forms, as through the bodies of ghosts, he had seen, sitting for hours on end at the drawing-room window, the knotted branches and the feathery leaves, until the outer world had disappeared altogether, mingled with thought and transformed into an inner substance.

Behind the wall upon which the wistaria grew were the premises of a hospital; and some six months ago Rainborough had turned cold with horror on receiving a polite and regretful notification from the local council to the effect that, in order to complete a plan for building a much-needed X-ray department,

117

it would be necessary to confiscate a plot of land some five feet wide and sixty-five feet long which lay at the bottom of his garden. The council pointed out that this territorial requirement had been kept to a minimum, and that the removal of this very narrow strip would not noticeably diminish the size of his garden. They themselves would of course bear the cost of pulling down the existing stone wall, which they noted to be in any case in a bad state of repair, and erecting in its place, along the line agreed upon, a new brick wall of the best type. He would of course receive compensation for his land at the rate fixed in the statutes for such cases of compulsory confiscation.

When Rainborough received this news he was made so miserable by it that he was not sure that he could survive. The confiscation seemed to him to be an act of sheer gratuitous cruelty and injustice such as he had never suffered before. At first he was completely stunned. Then, for about a week, he ran about complaining in every quarter in which help could possibly lie. He wrote to his M.P., he even wrote to *The Times*, who failed to print his letter. But he met with no success, and not even with any encouragement. After that he fell into a lethargic melancholy about the whole matter and forbade his friends ever to refer to it.

The time fixed for the destruction of the wall was now about two weeks away. As it drew nearer, the hospital authorities had attempted to establish human relations with the victims of the confiscation, who inhabited some half a dozen houses on either side of Rainborough, by inviting them to look over the hospital, examine the blueprint of the X-ray department, and inspect the present inadequate accommodation. Rainborough had refused to go. He had no intention of trying to be charitable about the matter; and when a well-meaning lady next door exclaimed to him that really, when you saw how much they needed the space, poor things, you couldn't be resentful any more, he replied with positive rudeness. He felt very bitter indeed.

Rainborough knew very well that this ought not to be so, ought in fact to be far otherwise. He quietly deplored his attitude, but left it to take its place in that ensemble of realities, a clear-sighted vision of which had lately come to serve him in the lieu of virtue. Self-knowledge, after all, was his ideal; and could not knowledge, by its own pure light, transform the meanest of its discoveries? Rainborough did not feel that he was called upon, at his time of life, to put any more work into the development of his character than was required to provide a fairly minute commentary on how that development was in fact progressing. Actually to interfere with it did not enter his head. In moral matters, as in intellectual matters, Rainborough took the view that to be mature was to realize that most human effort inevitably ends in mediocrity and that all our admirations lead us at the last to the dreary knowledge that, such as we are, we ourselves represent the *élite*. The dreariness of this knowledge is only diminished by the fact that it is, after all, knowledge.

The warmth of the garden was joining with the silence to make an image of summer. For the first time that year Rainborough could feel the sun on his neck, stirring memories of other summers; and through his reflections he began at last to see the flowers. Hyancinths, narcissi, primulas, and daffodils stood before him, rigid with life and crested with stamens, tight in circles, or expanding into stars. He looked down into their black and golden hearts; and as he looked the flower-bed seemed to become very large and close and detailed. He began to see the little hairs upon the stems of the flowers and the yellow grains of pollen, and where a small snail, still almost transparent with extreme youth, was slowly putting out its horns upon a leaf. Near to his foot an army of ants had made a two-way track across the path. He watched the ants. Each one knows what it is doing, he thought. He looked at the snail. Can it see me? he wondered. Then he felt, how little I know, and how little it is possible to know; and with this thought he experienced a moment of joy.

Rainborough became suddenly aware that there was someone else in the garden. He lifted his head quickly and saw Annette Cockeyne standing just outside the drawing-room windows. He recognized her at once. He looked down again at the ants. But now they seemed very tiny and very remote. He sighed, and turned towards Annette, only a faint glimmering of interest mingling with his annoyance at being disturbed. She looked to him much the same child as he had met six years ago, only now, he saw at a second look, she was also a woman. It was absurd.

'Miss Cockeyne!' said Rainborough, and contrived to express surprise, pleasure, and obeisance in the way he said her name.

'Oh, good,' said Annette vaguely, Rainborough was not sure in reference to what. She held out her hand. 'We've met before,' she said.

'As if I could forget you!' said Rainborough, casting his mind back to the tantrum Annette had been in when he had last seen her. 'This is an unexpected pleasure!' What does the little devil want, he wondered. Then he decided, still half-irritated, to make the best of the matter and at least to derive some entertainment from Annette's visit. He felt, in proportion to his annoyance, irresponsible. 'Come in and have a drink.' Annette stepped back into the drawing-room.

While Rainborough poured out some sherry, she stood awkwardly, her feet crossed, looking round the room with an air both of being curious and of noticing nothing.

'Do sit down, Annette,' said Rainborough. 'You don't mind if I call you Annette? I feel I've known you since you were a child.'

'Indeed, please!' said Annette. She dropped her coat on the floor and drank some sherry quickly. She seemed neither embarrassed nor at ease.

Rainborough sat down opposite to her and studied her. He noticed at once the feathery summery air of her clothing. She wore a light cotton blouse and a linen skirt and a scarlet silk scarf about her neck which she now undid and twisted in her hands. Her extreme slimness seemed to emphasize the scantiness of her clothes. The blouse hung upon her breasts like a cloud. Rainborough was suddenly and irresistibly reminded of the snail – and he smiled.

'How is Rosa?' he asked Annette.

'Cross with me!' said Annette, making a face.

'Why?'

'I'm not sure,' said Annette. 'I think it's because I left school; I'm not sure.'

'You left school?' said Rainborough.

'Yes,' said Annette. 'I was at Ringenhall College, you know, but I decided I would prefer to educate myself.'

'And what will you study?' asked Rainborough.

'Well, I don't know,' said Annette. 'At the moment, I'm just going round visiting.'

'I see,' said Rainborough; 'to find out who can help you with your education.'

Annette looked at him suspiciously. 'I've had so little time since I came to England,' she explained. 'I wanted to call on you before.'

'Did Rosa discourage you?' asked Rainborough; 'from visiting, I mean.'

'A bit,' said Annette.

'Rosa must be a difficult person to live with,' said Rainborough. He would have liked to draw Annette on to criticize Rosa.

But Annette replied, 'No, I love her.'

So you imagine, thought Rainborough to himself, but it isn't true. Then it occurred to him that he had really been thoroughly bored all the afternoon, and now was bored no longer. He refilled Annette's glass and his own.

'You're a friend of Mr Fox aren't you?' asked Annette.

So that's it! thought Rainborough. 'Yes,' he said, 'are you?'

'I met him once,' said Annette. 'He's an odd man, isn't he?'

Although it happened to him so many times, Rainborough could never resign himself to the idea that people should visit him simply in order to find out all that he knew about Mischa Fox. He ground his teeth together.

'What's odd about him?' he asked.

'Oh, I don't know,' said Annette. 'He's so – er –'

'I don't find him odd,' said Rainborough, after waiting in vain for the epithet. 'There's only one thing that's exceptional about Mischa, apart from his eyes, and that's his patience. He always has a hundred schemes on hand, and he's the only man I know who will wait literally for years for even a trivial plan to mature.' Rainborough looked at Annette with hostility.

'Is it true that he cries over things he reads in the newspapers?' asked Annette.

'I should think it most improbable!' said Rainborough. Annette's eyes were very wide, and as he looked into them and saw how little effect his abruptness was having upon her mood, he felt with a shiver the reality of the image which was at that moment obsessing her.

'How old is he?' asked Annette.

'I've no idea,' said Rainborough, 'and neither has anyone else.' He felt an irritation he could hardly conceal at the

121

prospect of discussing Mischa Fox any further with Annette. He changed the subject abruptly.

'What are you going to do for your living?' he asked, deliberately making the question sound brutal.

'I don't know,' said Annette. 'I'm not much good at anything.' She smiled in a helpless feminine way about which Rainborough could not decide whether it was natural or the effect of art. Women pick up these conventions at such an early age, he thought, they're almost bred in them.

'You work in an office, don't you?' said Annette. Without intending it, she made the question sound slightly contemptuous.

'I work in an office, and I do other work as well.'

'What other work?'

'Thinking,' said Rainborough.

'I think it must be difficult to think,' said Annette seriously. 'Whenever I try to think I just day-dream.'

Rainborough shifted his chair. The atmosphere seemed oppressive. How can anyone who has travelled so much be so appallingly juvenile, he wondered. Annette was sitting opposite to him, and her extremely small right hand, which had just released the sherry glass, lay limply upon the table, while her left hand fidgeted with the scarf. Rainborough looked at her hand and at her very bony wrist. The sleeves of her blouse were rolled up to the elbow. He picked up the sherry decanter and filled her glass again, standing over her. Then he resumed his seat. Neither of them had spoken for a minute. Then Annette said something which Rainborough didn't hear.

'I beg your pardon,' he said.

'I said what a beautiful black-and-white moth,' said Annette. She pointed to a large moth which was perched half-way up the wall behind Rainborough's head. He cast a glance back at it, and thought that he saw the dust of its wings and the furry texture of its head. He even imagined that he caught its eye.

'It's a wood leopard,' he said. 'You don't often see them around so early in the year.'

'I'd like an evening-dress like that,' said Annette.

Rainborough was frowning and breathing slightly faster, like a man with a deep problem. He seemed almost unaware of Annette's presence. His problem was this. He had realized within the last half minute that the curious and uneasy sensation which was oppressing him was a very powerful desire to reach out and take Annette's hand. The problem was, if he were to do this, what would be the result and would he like it? Rainborough wished that there was some way of becoming intimate with a woman which did not involve these agonizing moments of irrevocable decision. It was like hunting fish with an underwater gun, a sport which he had once been foolish enough to try. At one moment there is the fish – graceful, mysterious, desirable and free – and the next moment there is nothing but struggling and blood and confusion. If only, he thought, it were possible to combine the joys of contemplation and of possession.

As he completed this thought he reached out and took hold of Annette's hand, covering it with his and pinning her wrist with his fingers as if he were trying to feel her pulse. As this involved his leaning considerably forward, he awkwardly pulled his chair after him with the other hand, but without relaxing his hold. He did not look at her, but studied her hand and arm closely as if they had been detached from her body.

Annette, who had had her tiny hand imprisoned more times than Rainborough realized, made no movement, but fixed her eyes with intensity upon his forehead.

Rainborough, with the patient gentle air of the man who raises his head to say 'Here endeth the first lesson', lifted his gaze. He felt so far an extraordinary and most satisfactory calm. He smiled at Annette. Then he began to study her face.

'I'm afraid I can't recall your Christian name,' said Annette.

The coolness with which she said this shocked Rainborough for a moment. 'John,' he said.

'John,' said Annette.

Rainborough thought that there was a very faint gleam of amusement in her eye. This shocked him too. He might be amused, but she ought to be trembling. Was it amusement or was it just the gratification of a sense of power? the little demon! he thought to himself, and for a moment the image of Miss Casement was superimposed upon that of Annette.

At that moment Annette, dropping her scarf upon the floor, reached her left hand across and picked up her glass of sherry. Pensively she drank what remained in the glass, while her right hand lay inert in Rainborough's grip. This was too much for him. Rainborough took the glass from her and threw it across the room, where it rolled without breaking into a corner. Then he slid his hand gently inside her blouse. He was pleased to feel the quickness of her heartbeats and the involuntary gesture with which she now put her hand defensively upon his arm. Her other hand began to flutter feebly. Rainborough hastened to kiss her rather awkwardly upon the cheek.

'John, please!' said Annette.

'Don't imagine that you can convince me,' said Rainborough, 'if you speak in that tone of voice!'

He sank from his chair and with a sweeping movement took her with him on to the floor. He began to unbutton her blouse. As he suspected, she was wearing nothing underneath. He then began to force one of her arms back so as to take the garment off. Annette, neither helping nor hindering him, lay doll-like, except that her gaze was extremely intent and bright. As he met it now, Rainborough could have sworn that it was indeed amusement, and not the delight of power, that lit the point of fire in her eyes.

'Do you often do this?' asked Annette.

'About once in ten years,' said Rainborough. This was true, and he would have paused to meditate on this sad confession if he had not been otherwise engaged. Also, he was nettled by her glance and by the detachment of her tone.

'Annette,' he said, 'you're a grown woman now. Don't pretend that you're not making this scene just as much as I am. Give me, at least, that pleasure.' It was a long time since Rainborough had addressed such a serious speech to a woman.

The effect was instantaneous. Annette's eyes suddenly clouded over with a look of hurt indignation. 'Oh!' she said, 'How can you be so —', and then with a violence which took Rainborough by surprise she began to struggle.

When he felt Annette struggling Rainborough automatically tightened his hold, and for a moment they rolled madly to and fro upon the floor. While this was happening, Annette's blouse, which had been half off when the fight started, came off completely, and Rainborough felt her twisting and turning in his grip like a powerful fish. Remembering the incident later, he could recall only a confused impression of the pliancy of her body, the thinness of her arms, the smallness of her breasts, and the enormous furious surface of her eyes which in memory seemed to grow and grow until they filled nearly the whole picture. Rainborough had risen to one knee and was pressing her fiercely down on to the ground when the front door bell rang – and immediately after came the sound of someone walking into the hall.

As if touched by a wand, Annette and Rainborough froze into a silent immobility, arrested in the wild gestures of the struggle. For an instant they stared terror-stricken into each other's eyes. Then Annette sat up. She was naked to the waist. Of course, thought Rainborough, I left the front door open. The girl came in that way. Without drawing another breath, he regained his feet, pulled Annette up by her shoulder, and opened the door of a china-cupboard which was just behind her. He threw her in and threw her clothes and her handbag after her. There was just room inside for her to stand upright. Then he closed the door on her. The footsteps were coming across the hall. Rainborough straightened his tie and set the rugs to rights.

Someone knocked on the drawing-room door and then entered. It was Mischa Fox. Rainborough stared at him open-mouthed. At any other time he would have felt joy, even triumph, at having Mischa in his house; but now the sight of him afflicted Rainborough with an emotion of pure terror. He recovered himself instantly.

'Mischa! How splendid!' he cried, and as he rushed forward to usher him in he deftly pushed Annette's sherry glass, which was lying inconspicuously upon the floor, in under one of the armchairs with his foot.

'How good to see you, Mischa!' Rainborough continued, and shepherded his friend along, one eye nervously upon the china-cupboard door.

Mischa stood politely in the middle of the room, smiling. If only I can get him out into the garden, Rainborough thought, the girl may have the sense to slip away, or I might come back myself on some pretext and put her out of the house. He felt that somehow if he could only get Annette right out of the house, never to return, everything would be all right – and if he could have shrivelled her to nothing at that moment by the sheer power of his thought he would have done so. As it was, he felt her bodily presence a few feet behind him, weighty, inexorable and accusing.

'Come and see my garden, Mischa,' cried Rainborough, 'I've got some new rock plants that would interest you!'

'Thanks, John,' said Mischa. 'I think I'll just sit here for the moment and see it through the windows.'

He made for the armchair which Annette had been occupying, opposite to the door of the china-cupboard, and settled himself in it comfortably, crossing his legs. Rainborough groaned inwardly. He walked uncertainly to the other chair and sat down. He hoped he was behaving naturally. In order to make things more normal he said, 'Have a drink?'

'Please,' said Mischa.

Then it occurred to Rainborough with a further jolt that the only glasses in the house were in the china-cupboard with Annette. He thought at breakneck speed, and then poured some sherry into his own glass, which was still on the table, and handed it to Mischa.

'Thank you,' said Mischa, and added after a moment, 'Aren't you drinking, John?'

'No,' said Rainborough desperately, 'I've given it up. I mean, I've got a bad stomach these days, the doctor says I'd better cut down on alcohol.'

'I'm sorry to hear that, John,' said Mischa. His eye dwelt upon the sherry decanter. 'Then you were expecting company?'

'No, yes,' said Rainborough. 'I thought a man from the office might drop in, but now it's too late. I'm sure he won't come now.' After saying this, he cursed himself for not having said the opposite, so that he might have used the expected guest as a lever to get rid of Mischa. A thousand plausible fictions, now all spoilt, crowded into his head.

'Well, I shall be selfish and say that's excellent!' said Mischa. 'We shan't be disturbed. We can have a good long talk.'

Rainborough looked at him hollow-eyed. He was beginning passionately to want a drink. If he could only have a drink to steady his nerves, he felt, he could carry anything off. In torment he watched Mischa Fox, who was sipping his sherry like a cat.

'I saw a sad thing as I was coming along,' said Mischa.

'What was that?' asked Rainborough.

'A bird with only one foot,' said Mischa. 'How would it manage with only one foot to hold on to a branch in a storm?'

Rainborough neither knew nor cared. He was beginning

already to have the uncanny feeling which he remembered having had so often in the past during conversations with Mischa. He never knew how to take Mischa's remarks. It was as if Mischa were deliberately reducing him to a state of hypersensitivity and confusion. It also appeared to him, but doubtless he was imagining it, that Mischa was staring hard at the door of the china-cupboard – and then he recalled that the door didn't fasten very well and sometimes came ajar even after it had been firmly shut. He had a terrible vision of the door opening slowly and revealing to Mischa the semi-nude figure of Annette. He could not prevent himself from looking round. The door was fast shut. Rainborough got up and fetched the cigarette-box, which he offered to Mischa, and then as he returned to sit down he moved his chair back so that it pressed hard against the door of the cupboard. He seemed to feel something yielding inside. He sat down vigorously and lighted a cigarette with trembling hands.

'How peaceful it is here!' said Mischa, who evidently did not feel sufficiently encouraged to pursue the topic of the bird with one foot. 'How quietly you live, John. I love the silence of this room and garden. One would hardly believe it was London.'

'Yes, it's very peaceful,' said Rainborough, casting a cautious eye about to see that nothing else had been displaced or broken in the course of the struggle.

'And what a beautiful moth there is over there on the wall,' said Mischa. 'Have you seen it, John?'

'Yes, I saw it,' said Rainborough without looking round. 'It's a wood leopard. You don't often see them around so early in the year.'

'You're looking tired and strained though,' said Mischa. 'How are things at SELIB?'

'Oh, hellish!' said Rainborough, glad to find a topic on which he could let fly some of his suppressed fear, anguish and fury. 'Beastly! Intolerable! Nauseating!'

'But why?' asked Mischa.

'It's the women,' said Rainborough. It hadn't occurred to him quite like this before, but suddenly he saw it. A vast legion of clever and provoking females, each one looking like a combination of Annette and Miss Casement, spread across his inner field of vision. They infested everything. They made life at the

127

office impossible. Now they were even pursuing him to his house. He felt a deep need to explain this to Mischa.

'What are these women?' asked Mischa.

'They're furies masquerading as secretaries and so on,' said Rainborough, 'and things called Organizing Officers. There are dozens of them, dozens and dozens. They take one's work away. It's not that *they* do any work, they just make the place pointless by being there.' He knew that he was talking wildly, but Mischa seemed to understand and was nodding his head encouragingly.

'And I suppose they're pretty girls?' said Mischa. 'It is the beautiful birds that have the sharpest beaks.'

'Ravishing girls,' said Rainborough. 'Exquisite and hard as iron, with cruel eyes.'

'Such beings can fascinate all the same,' said Mischa.

'Fascinate, yes,' said Rainborough. 'They'd enslave one if they could, they'd eat one.'

'But, of course, you struggle against the fascination?' said Mischa.

'I struggle,' said Rainborough, 'but what's the use? I can't *get away* by struggling. I'm alive with the things. What can I do?' I'm raving, he thought to himself, but without caring much. He felt a strange relief in talking like this to Mischa.

'It depends,' said Mischa, who seemed to have taken his last question very seriously. 'Not every woman is worth struggling with. Only a woman with some complexity of structure is worth struggling with.'

Rainborough wondered to himself, had Miss Casement got complexity of structure? He wasn't sure.

'Many women,' said Mischa, 'have no form at all. They are like the embryos in biological experiments, any organ will grow anywhere. Place a leg where the eye should be and it will grow into an eye, and the eye will grow into a leg. At best they are formless, at worst monsters.' Rainborough shuddered.

'On the other hand,' said Mischa, 'take a young girl, a child of nineteen or so —'

Rainborough crushed his chair savagely against the cupboard door. He suddenly felt afraid that Annette would break out with a wail like an affronted ghost.

'Take a very young girl,' said Mischa. 'With such it is not

128

worth struggling either. A woman does not exist until she is twenty-five, even thirty perhaps.'

'Not worth struggling with. No, I'm sure you're right,' said Rainborough.

'Young girls are full of dreams,' said Mischa. 'That is what makes them so touching and so dangerous. Every young girl dreams of dominating the forces of evil. She thinks she has that virtue in her that can conquer anything. Such a girl may be virgin in soul even after much experience and still believe in the legend of virginity. This is what leads her to the dragon, imagining that she will be protected.'

'And what happens then?' said Rainborough.

'The poor dragon has to eat her up,' said Mischa, 'and that's how dragons get a bad name. But that's not the end of her.'

'Isn't it?' said Rainborough. He felt a cold sweat coming on his brow and a frantic desire for a drink.

'After the unicorn girl,' said Mischa, 'comes the siren, the destructive woman. She realizes that men have found her out, that she cannot save men, she has not that virtue in her. So she will destroy them instead. She is dry, a bird with a woman's head. Such women are dangerous too, in a different way.'

'Are they worth struggling with?' asked Rainborough. He had noticed that Mischa's sherry was standing in front of him practically untasted. He lit another cigarette.

'It depends,' said Mischa. He was leaning back reflectively and taking his time. 'Women are Protean beings. One may develop through many stages before becoming stabilized; and in such a case you may transform a woman by struggling. Others remain all their lives in a first or second stage. There are perpetual virgins as there are perpetual sirens.'

Rainborough wondered what Miss Casement would be transformed into if he struggled with her. He reflected that his last state might very well be worse than his first.

'But if a woman is a siren by nature,' said Mischa, 'it is better to leave her alone. You cannot conquer such a woman, you can only wound her, and then she will poison you, like the toad whose skin exudes venom when attacked.'

'And if in doubt —?' asked Rainborough. He wondered if he dared go out to the kitchen and have a quick drink from one of the bottles in the larder. But he was afraid to leave Mischa alone with the contents of the cupboard. He felt that unless he positively kept his chair braced against the door Annette's nerve would fail her.

'Perhaps one should always fight,' said Mischa. 'The way to overcome Proteus was to hold on to him until he finally took on his real form. You must tire a woman out, even if it takes years. Then you will see what she is.'

Rainborough noticed that the sun had gone in and it was becoming chilly and a little dark in the room. Mischa's voice continued monotonously like the pale dreaming voice of a priest. Is he mocking me, Rainborough asked himself, or is he mad, perhaps? Then he remembered how often he had wondered in this way inconclusively about Mischa in the past.

'Has it ever struck you that women are like fish?' Mischa was saying. 'The female equivalent of Pan is the sleek mermaid. Their bodies are streamlined. They are proud of this, not ashamed as the psychologists say. A real woman is proud of this.'

'A real woman,' said Rainborough. 'Where is that to be found?'

'There is a kind of wise woman,' said Mischa; 'one in whom a destruction, a cataclysm has at some time taken place. All structures have been broken down and there is nothing left but the husk, the earth, the wisdom of the flesh. One can create such a woman sometimes by breaking her —'

Rainborough felt that Mischa was watching him closely as he spoke. He looked up quickly, but it was already too dark to see Mischa's eyes. Rainborough felt his old fear of Mischa and a sort of disgust.

'Why are you talking this rubbish, Mischa,' he said, 'and making me talk it too? If what you say were true, women would be either poisonous or boring!'

'Ah,' said Mischa, and Rainborough could see his very white teeth flashing under his moustache, 'but there is always the possibility of finding a free woman.'

'What's that?' asked Rainborough. How can I get rid of the man, he wondered frantically.

'What must happen first,' said Mischa, 'is the destruction of the heart. Every woman believes so simply in the heart. A woman's love is not worth anything until it has been cleaned of all romanticism. And that is hardly possible. If she can survive

130

the destruction of the heart and still have the strength to love —'

With a desperate movement Rainborough reached out and raised the decanter. He tilted it back and poured a quantity of sherry partly into his mouth and partly over his face and neck.

'Poor John!' said Mischa kindly. 'I am evidently boring you to distraction.'

'Sorry,' said Rainborough, 'this twilight is getting on my nerves.' He leaned over and switched on an electric lamp.

Startled by the change of light, the wood leopard left its place on the wall, blundered once round the room, and then alighted upon the back of Mischa's hand. Rainborough stared for a moment at this strange portent and then made a gesture as if to protect the moth, for his immediate thought was that Mischa was going to crush it. Mischa, who understood the gesture, laughed and got up. 'Don't worry,' he said, 'I love all creatures.'

He walked through the french windows into the garden, which was still well lighted with a rich twilight which seemed to draw colour and perfume together out of the flowers in a powdery haze. Very gently Mischa persuaded the moth to walk off his hand on to a leaf. He stood for a moment in the doorway, his face and his hands caught in the lamplight. And then Rainborough noticed something appalling. He had been vaguely aware that Mischa, as he talked, was holding something in his hand, which Rainborough had taken to be a handkerchief. Looking at it now in the light of the lamp, he saw what it was. It was Annette's scarf.

Rainborough leaned against the door. 'Mischa, you must go now,' he said weakly. 'I have to go out and see someone.'

'Don't worry, John, I'm just going,' said Mischa. 'Do you mind if I let myself out by the garden gate? I did enjoy our talk. But don't believe a word I say. I love all creatures.' As he spoke he was going away down the path into the twilight. He was nearly at the gate. 'I love them all!' he called. Laughing as he spoke, and waving Annette's scarf, he disappeared through the gate, and for a moment Rainborough could hear his laughter in the street before it died away.

Rainborough turned back into the drawing-room – and it was a second or two before he remembered Annette. When he

131

remembered her he rapidly pulled the curtains, and said cautiously, 'All clear now!' He didn't imagine that Mischa would come back, but he didn't yet feel quite safe. There was no movement from the cupboard door. A terrible panic seized Rainborough. Supposing the girl had been suffocated? How would he ever explain it? He rushed forward and pulled the door open.

Annette fell stifly forward and Rainborough had to catch her in his arms to prevent her from crashing to the ground. He noticed, with an absurd surprise, that she was still half naked. He took her by the shoulder and shook her violently. She was certainly alive. She even had her eyes open, but she appeared to be in some kind of trance. Rainborough noticed that she had been crying, her face was stained with tears – and the idea that she had been crying silently in the cupboard during his conversation with Mischa struck him as disagreeable and almost uncanny. 'Annette!' he cried into her ear, 'Annette!'

He put his arms round her and pummelled her in an attempt to bring her back to consciousness. Her flesh felt cold and rather soft and flabby, like putty or uncooked pastry. She gave a moan and put her hand to her face.

'That's better!' said Rainborough. He opened the china-cupboard and pulled out a thick velvet tablecloth from a lower shelf and wrapped it round the girl. Then he turned on the electric fire and led Annette towards it. He came and put his arms round the bundle of Annette and the tablecloth. He remained for some time holding her like that, and it gave him an obscure comfort. Then he poured a good deal of sherry into Mischa's glass, drank some himself, and gave some to Annette.

She was by now sufficiently recovered to start crying again. She started hunting on the floor of the cupboard for her blouse, her tears dropping steadily in front of her feet. Rainborough found it and helped her into it, and then into her coat. She took her handbag and prepared to go. Rainborough was relieved that she did not ask for her scarf. She said nothing until, when Rainborough had conducted her to the front door, she said huskily, 'It wasn't your fault, John.'

'It was,' said Rainborough, 'but never mind.' He kissed her cold cheek. She went out and he closed the door at once behind her.

He turned back into the quiet house. He walked through the

drawing-room into the garden. In the last light he saw the flowers closing up; and he saw the wood leopard, which had left the leaf where Mischa had placed it and was walking on the path. Rainborough watched it for a moment or two and then he ground it under his heel.

ELEVEN

Nina the dressmaker was at her sewing-machine. It was a treadle machine of an old-fashioned design. She operated the treadle with both feet, and both her hands were free to guide the material as it came flying through. Nina had once tried to use an electric model, but she had soon given it up. It made her nervous and jumpy. The old machine was harder work, but she liked the way in which it demanded the rhythmical co-operation of her whole body and left her tired, with a satisfying tiredness like that which she remembered having had long ago in childhood after she had been working in the fields.

She was engaged in sewing an extremely long piece of cotton material. It was figured with some irregular pattern; but Nina was not looking at the pattern, she was absorbed in watching the steel jaws of the machine as they opened and shut with dazzling speed upon the stuff which was passing through them. The machine was looking more and more like some animal through whose rapacious mouth Nina was drawing the cotton, exerting a slight but steady pull to bring it through; and as she pulled it her feet upon the treadle moved at a corresponding pace.

Then Nina began to notice that the machine was not sewing properly. Perhaps the thread had run out or the needle had broken. The material still flowed towards her like a river and passed through the snapping mouth of the machine and out under her hand, but she could see no signs of stitching upon it. Nina knew that something had gone wrong, but she couldn't think what it was. She couldn't even remember now what she was trying to do with that piece of material, or where it had come from with its curious and unfamiliar pattern. The remedy for these doubts seemed to be to operate the treadle even faster. Nina's feet began to flash madly to and fro, and now the steel jaws were opening and shutting so rapidly that they appeared to be almost immobile. The rhythmical beat of the machine rose to a continuous hum, and the material came flowing through in an unending stream.

Then Nina realized that she was running through a dark wood. She was running with a desperate speed so that only once in every ten steps did her feet touch the ground. Always beside her ran the machine, and she could see its steel eye glistening in the darkness from time to time. As she ran, Nina was still pulling the cotton material towards her through the jaws of the machine. The creature kept opening and closing its mouth as it ran, emitting a high-pitched whining sound, and Nina was just able to pull the cotton through; but she was all the time in fear lest it should suddenly close its jaws fast. Unless she could go on pulling the stuff towards her, something terrible would happen. If only the material would come to an end, she thought, I could stop running. But there seemed no end to it, and Nina and the machine ran faster and faster and the wood became darker and darker. The darkness began now to be thick and full of impediments. Soft stuffs hanging down from the trees touched Nina's face with silk and velvet touches, and clawed gently at her arms and shoulders. The cotton stuff which flowed continuously through her hands seemed to be accumulating, however fast she ran, about her feet. It is binding my feet, she thought, I shall fall, and she turned to look at the beast beside her. As she turned she fell and the cotton suddenly billowed out, rising above her like a sail and descending to whirl itself round and round her limbs like a winding-sheet. Before it enveloped her she saw its pattern clearly at last; it was a map of all the countries of the world. At the same moment the creature began to savage the material, tearing it with its jaws, and then it sprang on top of Nina. She could feel its heavy paws upon her chest, and a deafening and continuous barking.

She woke up with a start and sat up in bed. Her heart was beating with a terrible violence. It was broad daylight. Someone was banging on the door. Nina got up quickly and put on a dressing-gown. She ran to the door. It was a telegram. She opened it with trembling fingers, although she already knew what it contained. It read: *Sorry can't come today*. It was unsigned, but she knew that it came from Mischa Fox.

Nina tore up the telegram and burnt the fragments, in accordance with Mischa Fox's instructions concerning all his communications, however anonymous. Then she got dressed slowly and tidied up her bed and pushed it away into the cupboard in the wall where it stayed during the day. She had overslept, but it was not important. She would have extra time to work that afternoon. She had put off an important client at short notice, and probably offended her, because Mischa had told her that he was coming; and now after all he was not coming. But nothing could be done about that, and Nina was not even troubled about it. It happened so often.

She moved now towards the window, pushing aside as she went the rows of hanging garments and letting the sunlight come down the room. The windows were tall, but high off the ground. Nina stood on a chair and pushed the sash up as far as it would go. Then she perched herself, as she so often did in the early morning, upon the edge of the window, sitting half upon the sill outside. But she could see neither the dizzy drop to the street below nor the green of the springtime plane trees which blurred the edges of the houses that lay between her and the river. The cool air blew suddenly into her face. But Nina, looking out with a glazed expression, knew at that moment only the darkness of her own heart. As she sat there stiffly, she looked like a blind girl.

Nina was thinking, today I will go to see Miss Keepe. I can't go on any longer. When she had decided this she felt a little relief. Nina knew very well how much she owed to Mischa Fox. When Mischa had first discovered her she had been working in a textile factory and was a dressmaker only in her spare time. Without his help she would never have been able to achieve an independent establishment and a clientele. He had found her this room, the rent of which he still paid, and had somehow brought it about that, without his own name being ever mentioned, a large number of people should hear of her. One client led to another, and soon Nina had as much work as she could deal with.

Nina had given up some time ago the attempt to define what her relation was to Mischa Fox. When Mischa had appeared in her life she could, from the first moment, have refused him nothing. He bore with him the signs of a great authority and carried in his indefinable foreignness a kind of oriental magic. She was ready from the first to be his slave, though it never occurred to her to think that she might take more than a very minor part in his life. She had been prepared to be neglected and even in the end abandoned. She had not been prepared for the curious role which she found herself in fact forced to play.

When Mischa had installed her in the room in Chelsea Nina had had, as she imagined, no illusions about his motives; and at that time she loved him with an intensity and an abjection which left her without misgivings. Time passed, however, and Nina began to find it harder and harder to make Mischa out. He came to see her at irregular intervals and asked her politely how she was getting on. Sometimes he would talk to her about something that was worrying him, a business deal, a friend in trouble, the organization of a journey — though always these stories had such an air of generality, such a lack of identifiable details, that Nina wondered whether they were true, while at the same time wondering why Mischa should tell them to her if they were not. At other times he would come and sit for long periods in her room in silence. On such occasions he would usually ask her to continue with her work, though without using the machine; and then Nina would busy herself with sewing seams and buttonholes, casting a cautious glance every now and then towards Mischa, who would be lying back in his chair with a far-away look, his lips moving from time to time. Twice it happened, when Mischa seemed more than usually troubled, that he asked Nina to come and sit near him and not to sew. On one of these occasions he took her hand, which he held rather abstractedly for ten minutes, while he seemed to think about something else. On the second occasion he pressed her hand against his forehead before he finally let it go. This was possibly the happiest moment of Nina's life. But nothing further ever happened.

That is, nothing happened of the things which Nina had expected or wanted to happen. But she soon became convinced, though what exactly the evidence was for this she would have been at a loss to say, that she was playing, in the strange economy of Mischa Fox's existence, some quite precise part — though what that part was she would perhaps never know. After a while he began to ask certain small favours of her. On a number of occasions she gave a night's lodging to certain individuals, both men and women, who came to her door very late bearing notes from Mischa. Mischa seemed to expect her to do this without complaining, just as he expected her to make herself available at any hour at which he chose to announce his own arrival; and she did not complain. At another time he suddenly asked her to put on her best clothes and accompany him in an open car which he then drove very fast as far as Richmond and very slowly round inside the Park, before bringing her straight home again. Nina was sure that this was a show put on for the benefit of someone else; but she asked no questions.

Were these things, she wondered, all that Mischa Fox required of her? She puzzled over this through long nights. At times she felt that he was waiting for her to understand something, to see some need which he would never speak of, and which she was simply failing to see. This thought tortured her. At other times, particularly after she had been present, silently, at one or two discussions of Mischa's character, she imagined that perhaps he was keeping her in reserve to play a part in some plot or conspiracy which had not yet matured, which might not mature for years. Time passed, and she came to no conclusion, nor did any opportunities come her way for making a closer study of Mischa. He never asked her to come to his house in London. Nina's thoughts dwelt a great deal upon this fabulous and much-discussed residence, but she had never dared even to go near it.

A little later again Mischa Fox suggested that he should pay her a monthly allowance, in addition to the rent of the room. When she demurred, he explained that what he called his 'inconvenient ways' were possibly damaging to her business, and it would relieve his mind if she would permit him to make this up to her. As Nina was incapable of opposing any will of her own to Mischa should he wish to define her position further in any way that he pleased, she simply agreed; nor was she at that time at all distressed at the thought that she was falling yet farther into Mischa's power. It was some time after that she first began to feel irked by her condition.

Nina was ambitious; she was also a good organizer and a good business woman. Her range of contacts was now very considerable, and it occurred to her that if she could have more space, and take on two or three girls to work for her, she could double her profits and set down the basis of a powerful enterprise. She spoke of this one day to Mischa Fox. It was apparent at once that the idea displeased him – and as soon as Nina had spoken she saw with a cold clarity that any plans of this kind would be likely to run counter to whatever Mischa Fox's mysterious purposes for her might be. It was important to him that she should be alone, that she should be available to speak with him privately at any hour, that she should be able to entertain his anonymous guests. In answer to her, Mischa said shortly, but without irritation, that he would prefer her not to carry out this plan — but that he would see that she was not financially a loser. Nina did not mention the matter again, but from that time her monthly allowance was considerably increased.

That she should be alone. After her first frenzy of love for Mischa had given place to an emotion more mixed with puzzlement and curiosity, this aspect of the matter became for Nina more and more a source of distress. The strange nature of her relations with Mischa effectively deprived her of any other private life. Although he visited her rarely, she had to be at all times available, and the iron discretion which Mischa, without explicitly enjoining, imposed upon her by his personality made it impossible for her to open her heart to anyone.

Then Nina began to realize — it became apparent to her in the manner of speech of her clients and acquaintances — that she was coming to be known, for all his and her secrecy, as one of Mischa Fox's creatures. This reputation would do her little good in her trade; but she was beyond caring about this. The title itself wounded her profoundly. She was aware, it was the current gossip, that Mischa Fox was supposed to have at his disposal dozens of enslaved beings of all kinds whom he controlled at his convenience. But it both shocked her and hurt her that she should be regarded as one of them. It was in her case, she felt, surely quite different. She loved Mischa. But on further reflection she wondered, was it so different? The régime which Mischa imposed upon her condemned that love to silence and deprived it of expression — until it was being transformed, Nina had to admit to herself, into a strange emotion which had in it more of terror and fascination than of tenderness. Once or twice Nina tried to nerve herself to speak frankly to Mischa. But the thought of all the help which she had accepted from him rose up to accuse her — and, more than this, she was too profoundly terrified of him to try to explain something which sounded so like sheer disloyalty.

Then an idea came to Nina. She had always been aware of the fact that the only way in which she could escape from

Mischa Fox would be to leave England — but she had never developed this notion, since it had not seemed to her that it was possible to leave England. She had come to England to get away from other places, and to get away from England there was nowhere left in the world to go to. But then, somehow or other, it occurred to her that this was not so. She might go to Australia. The more she thought of this, the more compelling the idea became. Nina had already rejected the notion of going to America, not so much because it might be hard to get in as because Mischa Fox was frequently to be heard of jumping on the plane for New York. Nina knew herself, and she knew that she could not oppose her will to that of Mischa in any direct combat, she could not propose even the mildest skirmish. Her only hope lay in flight; and once she fled she must be sure that she would never never see Mischa Fox again. America seemed to her, for this purpose, too small a place. Australia seemed to promise her some safety. She had never heard of Mischa going to Australia.

As soon as Nina became fully aware of this treacherous idea she became obsessed with the task of keeping it hidden from Mischa. She could hardly believe that he could not read her thoughts. It was partly because of this terror of being discovered that for a long time Nina made no move towards the execution of her plan. To begin with, her only indulgence was whenever possible to go to see Australian films, during which she would weep continuously. She pictured a life in Australia which would be in every way the reverse of her present life. There a rough and generous people would take her to their hearts. She would live in their midst a life of openness and gaiety, respected as a worker and loved as a woman.

At last she began to make a closer study of the matter. She read one or two books about Australia at the reference library. Greatly daring, she bought a map, which she kept in her room rolled up inside a bale of material and only consulted when she was sure that Mischa Fox was out of the country. She stood about, briefly and guiltily, outside Australia House in the Strand, looking at the pictures. The only thing she did not dare to do was to go inside and make some really businesslike inquiries. She was afraid that if she did so she would be asked to leave her name and address — and she had the refugee's horror of the power and hostility of all authorities and of their mysterious interconnection with each other. It seemed to her impossible that if she left her name at Australia House Mischa Fox should not be told of this within twenty-four hours.

What Nina needed if she was to carry her plan any further was a confidant and accomplice, someone, preferably an English person, who could advise her, make inquiries for her, and if necessary provide her with a reference; and it had for a long time been clear that there was only one person in the world whom she could trust in such a capacity, and that was Rosa Keepe. Nina had come to know Rosa in the way of business soon after she had come to Chelsea. She was not certain, but she thought it likely, that Rosa must have heard the rumours concerning her own dependence upon Mischa. Nina knew, as everyone did, though again, as everyone did, in rather general terms, of Rosa's former connection with Mischa — and her regard for Rosa was augmented by an astonished respect for a being who had once been under Mischa's spell and had freed herself without migrating to the Antipodes. For the austerity and rudeness of Rosa's character she felt a timid reverence, and for its generosity a timid affection — a sentiment which Rosa, who seemed indeed very scantily aware of Nina's existence, showed no particular sign of returning.

Although Nina had never achieved any extensive acquaintance with Rosa, her imagination had not been idle where the Englishwoman was concerned; and by this time Rosa figured in the mind of the dressmaker as a kind of archangel, a beneficent power, and in any case her only hope. The idea of telling all her troubles to Rosa had occurred to Nina much earlier, before the conception of the Australian plan; but fear, both of Mischa and of Rosa, had prevented her from acting. But the plan of escape, gradually growing in her mind, gave her strength; and now, with the terror of her nightmare still upon her, she said to herself, I can bear it no longer.

She climbed down from the window-sill, and walked slowly across the room. As she walked, the materials brushed her tenderly with their characteristic touches, and she paused to plunge her face into each and inhale its familiar smell, like one in a garden who moves from flower to flower. Comforted, she prepared to leave. She looked at her watch. It was nearly eleven. It was not too early to call on Miss Keepe.

It was eleven o'clock. Annette was still in bed. She had been awake for some time, lying there uncomfortably and trying to persuade herself that she felt ill. Unfortunately she did not feel ill, but only extremely miserable. As her gaze wandered about the room, lighting without consolation upon this or that familiar object, she wondered what she could do which would be extreme enough to give expression to the way she felt. She groaned intermittently and attempted to weep. It was most unsatisfactory. When she tired of this, she sat up in bed and began to pull on her dressing-gown.

She reached out for the picture of Nicholas which stood always on the table beside her bed and began to study it. Annette was always moved, both by the fact of her extraordinary resemblance to her brother and by the fact that, because of the difference of their hair, no one seemed to notice it. This made a kind of sweet secret between them, a secret written upon their flesh but covered by a cloud. Annette felt herself at times to be so close to Nicholas that she was sure they must be in telepathic communication. Nicholas had thought this too, at a time when he was interested in psychic phenomena, and had tried to establish it by experiment. Nothing sensational had come of this, however.

Annette looked into the face of her brother. It was a recent photograph, which she had taken herself last summer in Switzerland, which showed Nicholas in an open-necked shirt, with arms folded, looking very gravely into the camera. Behind him was the Lake of Geneva. He looked like a poet. Annette sighed. If Nicholas were only here, he would advise her. As he was not here, should she confide in Rosa? That was the question.

Annette was still staring into the photograph as into a mirror when there was a knock on the door. Annette imagined that it was probably Rosa, since today was a holiday at the factory, and she gave a guilty start and put the photograph down on the counterpane. She called 'Come in'. The door opened very slowly and a strange apparition presented itself. A very slim and tall young man, dressed in a red check shirt and flannel trousers, with a blue scarf knotted round his neck, leaned cautiously in through the doorway. His skin was very fine and pale and his eyes were very blue. He had brown hair and a rather bold expression. Annette was impressed by this figure, which she had never before set eyes on, and said to it,

'Hello!' The young man, after looking carefully at Annette, sidled in through the door and replied 'Hello!'

Annette, who felt that social initiative was at present beyond her, wrapped her dressing-gown closer about her and looked at her visitor with curiosity and said nothing. Jan Lusiewicz returned her look and then smiled. Annette found his smile charming.

'I come to look for Rosa,' he said, 'but I think she is *weg*, away.'

'I don't know,' said Annette. 'I haven't been up yet.'

'You are ill?' said Jan. 'Or you stay in bed always so late?'

'No,' said Annette. 'Who are you?' she asked, feeling that it was about time this was established.

'I am Janislav Lusiewicz,' said Jan. He pronounced his name with a flourish which made it incomprehensible to Annette. 'I work at factory with Rosa. I am engineer. Who are you?'

'I am Annette Cockeyne,' said Annette, and felt that she had nothing particular to add to this information.

'You are pretty girl,' said Jan. 'How old you are?'

'Nineteen,' said Annette. She spoke tonelessly to indicate her disapproval of this forwardness.

'So!' said Jan, 'we are just right ages, no?'

Annette was not quite sure what this meant, but felt it to be impertinent.

Jan suddenly reached out and picked up the photograph of Nicholas which was lying on the bed. 'This your boy friend?' he asked.

'No,' said Annette furiously, 'it is my brother! Give it back to me! I haven't got a boy friend.'

Jan returned the photo. 'So pretty girl not have boy friend,' he said, 'that is bad. But brother, that is good. I too have brother. You love your brother?'

'Yes,' said Annette.

'I too, I love my brother,' said Jan. 'Is not always so in England. In Poland all love their brothers, in England is not.'

'I'm not English,' said Annette savagely. 'I have no country. You can wait downstairs for Rosa, if you like.' She was clutching the photograph of Nicholas to her breast. She felt suddenly that she was going to cry.

'I go in a minute,' said Jan. 'Don't be afraid, I do nothing.' He turned and looked about her room. 'Nice room you have,' he said. 'I want always so nice room. But so is difficult when man comes poor to other country, foreigner always poor.'

'Not always,' said Annette.

'In Poland I am rich man, big gentleman,' said Jan, 'but now is all stolen.'

'Too bad,' said Annette. She realized with a sort of relief that she could postpone her tears no longer. When Annette wept, it was like a summer storm, a prodigious downpour without warning. Large tears welled suddenly from her eyes and coursed conspicuously down her cheeks.

Jan was amazed. 'I not frighten you, I hope,' he said. 'But I do nothing!'

Annette just wailed. Jan approached and stared down at her curiously. 'Stop crying,' he said. 'Look, I make you laugh. I make Polish dance, see!'

He posed for a moment, and then began to hurl himself violently about the room, uttering Slavonic whoops, his legs and arms flying out in improbable directions. Annette stopped crying. The room shook with the impact as Jan, leaving the ground at regular intervals, rejoined it without misgivings. The furniture was beginning to leap about in sympathy. The chest of drawers started to hop decorously. Annette stared. The whole room was dancing. The precious stones jumped lightly to and fro upon their blue cloth and then one after the other they began to spring to the floor. Diamonds, sapphires, emeralds, amethysts and rubies, the spoil of many continents, pattered to the ground between Jan's dancing feet. 'Stop!' cried Annette.

Jan stopped abruptly in a Slavonic attitude. 'Oh, pick them up!' she cried, and pointed to where they still rolled about on the dark boards, reflecting various lights. Open-mouthed, Jan obeyed, and when he could see no more of them he heaped them into Annette's open hands. She examined them carefully to see that none was lost, and then poured them into the pocket of her pyjamas.

Jan was regarding her with a mixture of doubt and respect. 'They are just glass,' he said, 'or real jewels?'

'Real jewels,' said Annette.

'So they are worth much money?'

'Very much money.'

'So you are rich girl?' said Jan.

There was a noise downstairs and a sound of voices. Jan turned abruptly and opened the door of Annette's room. He went out and leaned over the banisters and called 'Rosa!' Annette heard from below an exclamation of surprise, and then Rosa's feet on the stairs. But Jan, instead of going down the stairs to meet Rosa, turned back into the room and waited for her.

'I am here!' he called.

Rosa hesitated at the door. 'May I come in?' she said, and came in. She looked at Jan and she looked at Annette, who was still sitting up in bed. Some emotion which Annette could not decipher showed for a moment on her face, which immediately afterwards became expressionless.

'I just meet Annette,' said Jan. 'Perhaps we have some coffee now. No work, no hurry, isn't it?'

Rosa said 'Splendid!' and then said to Annette, 'Nina has just called. I met her at the door.' She left the room.

'You go and help Rosa make the coffee,' said Annette.

'I see Rosa plenty at factory,' said Jan. 'I see you never before, perhaps never again.'

Annette could not avoid his eyes, and found in them an expression of tender solemnity which was both absurd and touching. She smiled at him and they were silent. Rosa knocked and entered. She brought a tray with two cups upon it.

'You not take coffee with us?' asked Jan.

'No, I must look after my visitor,' said Rosa. She laid a book down on the dressing-table. 'You may need this too.'

As the door closed, Jan picked up the book. It was a Polish-English dictionary. He made a face. 'That mean she is angry,' he said, 'but I soon bring her back.' He sat down on the foot of Annette's bed.

Rosa went slowly down the stairs. She was feeling very shaken. It was the first time that one of the Lusiewicz brothers had dared to come uninvited to the house in Campden Hill Square. In the very early days, before Hunter's unaccountable spite against the brothers had developed, and before the arrival of Annette in the house, Rosa had brought them there once or twice. But since then, she had always met them elsewhere and had assumed it as an unwritten rule that they were never to visit her at Campden Hill Square. As she descended the stairs, she wondered why this seemed so imperative. She could not have the brothers visiting her at Campden Hill Square; and this was not just because of Hunter. She felt suddenly sick and afraid. Jan's unheralded appearance displayed a new boldness. It was a portent.

She found herself staring into the face of Nina, who had stood politely at the kitchen door while Rosa made the coffee, and who was now hovering about the hall, not sure whether she ought to go into the kitchen or into the drawing-room. Rosa tried to clear her brow. At that moment there was the postman's rat-tat on the door and a letter fell through the letter-box on to the mat. Nina, relieved that there was something that she could do, hastened to pick it up, and handed it to Rosa. As the letter changed hands, both the women noticed the superscription. It was addressed to Rosa in Mischa Fox's handwriting. They raised their eyes immediately to look at each other and then at once looked away. In that instant each surmised how much the other knew. Nina was white and Rosa blushing furiously. Rosa led the way back into the kitchen, putting the letter into her pocket.

'I am so sorry,' said Rosa, 'to keep you waiting like this. I'm being appallingly rude. Didn't I give you any coffee? Do sit down.' Nina sat down, and Rosa put the milk back on the stove.

'What can I do for you?' she asked Nina. The question sounded cruel. Nina was fathoming her inability to reply to it when there was another bang on the door.

'Excuse me,' said Rosa, and left the room. She opened the front door. It was Miss Foy.

'Oh, Miss Rosa,' said Miss Foy, 'I'm so sorry! Is this an inconvenient time to come?' Miss Foy was carrying a large brown-paper parcel and was wearing a small velvet hat which rested like a bird on top of her frizzy hair.

'Come in!' said Rosa, 'the more the merrier!' She led Miss Foy into the kitchen. The letter from Mischa was burning into her thigh. 'Sit down,' said Rosa. Just then the milk began to boil over furiously, Nina sprang up and took it off, and began to look round in a futile way for a cloth.

'Don't bother,' said Rosa, and she mopped it up with her handkerchief. 'I'm afraid that's the last of the milk, and it's quite burnt now. Do you mind having it black?' Neither Nina nor Miss Foy minded. 'Oh, do you know each other?' said Rosa, and introduced them. She was listening hard all the time for any sound of Jan Lusiewicz descending the stairs.

'I know a Mrs Carrington-Morris who I believe is a customer of yours,' said Miss Foy politely.

'Ah,' said Nina, 'how nice.'

'I always think dressmaking is *so* creative,' said Miss Foy.

Rosa looked at them both and concealed her exasperation. She wanted desperately to open Mischa's letter, but she wanted to be able to do so in complete peace. How could she decently dislodge them? 'Are you just going out shopping?' she asked Miss Foy.

'Well, no,' said Miss Foy, 'the fact is I was bringing a letter for you.' She handed Rosa an envelope. 'It's from Mrs Wingfield. I also took the liberty,' said Miss Foy, 'of bringing you a plum cake.' She set the brown-paper parcel on the table and opened it. An enormous brown cake was revealed.

'How very kind of you!' said Rosa. She put Mrs Wingfield's letter in the other pocket.

'It's from an old recipe my mother left me,' said Miss Foy. 'The secret of it is a little dash of cider, real country cider of course, not that fizzy stuff in bottles. I was born in the West Country, you know, not far from Tiverton. When I was a child my mother used to make cakes and send me out with them as presents to the neighbours. And the neighbours would give us presents too, and not only at Christmas time. Such a nice custom. In the towns nowadays you don't find it at all. But I'm told that on the Continent people still do that kind of thing. Perhaps in – er – your country, Miss er —'

There was a piercing cry from upstairs. Nina and Miss Foy sat petrified, and they both turned to look at Rosa. Rosa was staring at the cake and appeared not to have heard. She took a sharp knife out of the drawer and laid it on the table.

'I think,' said Nina, 'that someone called.'

'No, it was just something next door,' said Rosa. She sat down and crossed her legs. Then the cry came again, more urgently than before. It was somebody calling 'Rosa!'

'Really,' said Miss Foy, 'I think I must be getting on. I'm so sorry to have bothered you. I hope you'll like the cake.' She picked up her handbag nervously and made for the door.

'Oh, must you go?' said Rosa. 'Thank you so much for

calling.' As Miss Foy made off, Rosa went up the stairs two at a time.

She flung open the door of Annette's room. Annette and Jan were standing close together in the middle of the floor, both were dishevelled, and Annette was trying to draw her disordered dressing-gown closer about her. Rosa crossed the room in a stride, took Jan Lusiewicz by the wrist and thrust him away from Annette. As she did so, she struck him hard across the cheek with her other hand. For a moment the trio stood as if turned to stone. It would have been hard to know which of them was the most surprised.

Then Jan turned on his heel and left the room. He was as white as a sheet. His footsteps could be heard descending the stairs at a run. Without a glance at Annette, Rosa followed at a leisurely pace. As she reached the first landing she heard the front door close behind him with a bang.

Rosa went into the drawing-room and closed the door. She sat down. She felt an intense emotion in which pain and fear were mingled with exhilaration. Pain predominated. She held her forehead like someone in a crisis of drunkenness. The first blow had been struck, hostilities had opened. Remorse struggled with relief and was resolved into fear. I am lost, thought Rosa, but without yet knowing what she meant by this.

With a gesture as if of self-protection she took the two letters from her pocket. She laid Mischa's letter on the table and opened the one from Mrs Wingfield. On a torn sheet of paper in a rakish hand Mrs Wingfield had written, *Think I can help you perhaps. Call Monday. Not a word to anyone. C.W.* Rosa put the note away and then began to tear open Mischa's envelope. Her hand shook so much that she almost dropped it. She drew out the enclosure. It was a printed formal invitation to a party on the following Thursday. At the bottom Mischa had written, *Rosa, please come.* It was the first time in years that Mischa had taken any initiative towards seeing her. She closed her eyes.

There was a timid knock on the door. Rosa opened her eyes and called out. Nina appeared diffidently. 'Good heavens!' said Rosa, 'I'm so sorry! I'm afraid I'd forgotten all about you. How dreadful of me. It's been rather a difficult morning. I'm very sorry.'

'Don't worry, Miss Keepe, please,' said Nina. 'I'll come back another time. It was nothing important. Please don't worry.'

Rosa saw her to the door, and then returned to the drawing-room. Should she go to Mischa's party? She fell into a chair like a poled ox. As she lay there, the door opened again. It was Annette. Rosa hardly saw her. In all the conflict of emotions aroused by the portentous appearance of Jan in the house it had not occurred to Rosa to feel any irritation with Annette. She had forgotten her as completely as she had forgotten Nina. Annette, who was dressed now, was looking terrified. But before she could utter a word, Hunter came in. He was eating something.

'Hello there!' said Hunter, with his mouth full. 'What's that heavenly cake you've got in the kitchen?'

'A neighbour brought it,' said Rosa.

'It's got a most extraordinary and marvellous taste,' said Hunter.

'Yes,' said Rosa, 'it's cider, from Tiverton. Give Annette a piece.'

Then suddenly she began to laugh.

TWELVE

It was the day before the shareholders' meeting and Hunter still did not know what he was going to do about the *Artemis*. He was in the extremity of indecision and very wounded by Rosa's refusal to help him. She had even been avoiding him for the last few days. He longed to know what she wanted, but was afraid to ask. Helpful friends told him that Rosa had been heard to say that the *Artemis* was good for nothing but to be got rid of to the highest bidder. But Hunter did not imagine that his sister, who was not famous for saying what she really thought in public, was any more likely to have done so on this occasion. The responsibilities of his position became more tormenting as he began to realize their extent. There was no one who could help him, since there was no one to whom he could reveal the extraordinary conception of the situation which was gradually taking shape in his mind. He found himself unable to work, and spent the day sitting wretchedly in his office or else walking aimlessly round Kensington and Notting Hill; and each night he plunged into an uneasy sleep in which he would perpetually find himself required, by means which were either beyond his capacity or beyond his comprehension, to save his sister from some ill-defined catastrophe.

However, the very fact that he had decided nothing was by now beginning to amount to a decision. Hunter's desire to sell the *Artemis* had become very clear and very sharp. He had thoroughly rehearsed the advantages of doing so, and he wished profoundly to be through with the whole business and be free to start, as he put it to himself, on something entirely new — though what that new thing would be was not, when he interrogated himself further, quite so plain. Hunter felt that it would be wise to sell the *Artemis* — but he also felt that it would be scandalous. This aspect of the matter had not, in spite of much reflection, come out so clearly. Some sort, he was not sure what sort, of betrayal of trust seemed to be involved in selling the periodical. What Hunter needed in order to get over this uneasy feeling was a word from Rosa – and this was just what was not forthcoming. If Rosa had told him that his scruples were foolish, he would have been perfectly happy to sell. On the other hand, if Rosa had said that the *Artemis* must be saved at all costs, Hunter would have been equally happy to attempt that.

This degree of complication would have been bad enough. It was when Hunter tried to speculate about the intentions of the would-be purchaser that his head really began to reel. After a good deal of conjecturing, in the course of which he astonished himself by his capacity to conjure up the grotesque and the fantastic, he began to conclude that he had better not sell. Hunter said to himself, without a lead from Rosa, I can't do it. I've said No, and I'll stick to it. But he added to himself, even more secretly: Of course if Mischa Fox approaches me in person, that will be another matter.

It was some indeterminate time in the afternoon, and Hunter, who had had no lunch, was sloping along Kensington High Street. He noticed that he was feeling rather odd, and could not decide whether this odd feeling was hunger or whether it was the sensation of being followed, a sensation which Hunter had suffered from intermittently ever since his fourteenth year, and which had of late been much aggravated by frequent visits to detective films, a form of entertainment to which he was greatly addicted. He kept looking round quickly to see if he was perhaps really being followed, but although almost everyone within sight was looking sinister, he could see nobody to accuse. He dodged into Barker's and bought himself a veal-and-ham pie with the intention of eating it in Kensington Gardens, since it was quite a warm day. He emerged from the shop and then turned round to inspect his reflection in the glass door. He took a comb furtively from his pocket and dashed it two or three times through his hair. As he was about to replace the comb he saw something which chilled him with horror and made him pause and gape at his image in the glass.

His features had changed. Another face, a familiar and dreaded one, had come to take the place of his own. He was looking straight into the eyes of Calvin Blick. After the first shock, Hunter realized that what had happened was that Blick was standing inside the shop, on the other side of the glass door, and looking out at him through it. Hunter turned away abruptly and dashed across the road, narrowly missing a bus and two taxis. With mingled shame and fear he put the comb away and began to walk quickly in the direction of Kensington Gardens on the north side of the street. So I *was* being followed! thought Hunter. I'll soon shake him off!

After he had walked about fifty yards he slackened his pace and cast a quick glance to the right. He could see, a little way behind him, on the south side of the street, a figure which he took to be Calvin Blick proceeding in a leisurely way in the same direction as himself. What can he want? Hunter wondered, and he slackened his pace a little more. By the time he reached the first gate of Kensington Gardens Calvin was almost level with him on the other side of the road, walking at an even pace and showing no sign of being aware of Hunter's existence. Hunter did not turn into the Gardens, but kept walking along the pavement keeping an eye on Calvin. By now Calvin was if anything a little ahead of him. Blast the fellow, thought Hunter, what is he up to? He was consumed with curiosity.

At that moment Calvin turned to the right into Palace Gate, leaving the main road altogether, and disappeared. Hunter felt first astonishment and then frenzy. He stopped dead. An instant later he was plunging back across the street. He had to wait half-way across while hooting and infuriated traffic missed him by inches – and, when he reached the corner of Palace Gate, Calvin, who must have accelerated rapidly once he was round the corner, was a long way ahead. Hunter began to run. He caught up with Calvin just as the latter was about to turn into Canning Place.

'Look here, Blick,' said Hunter breathlessly.

Calvin stopped, turning round with a surprised expression. 'Why, my dear Mr Keepe!' he said, 'what a shock you gave me.'

'Look here —' said Hunter.

'You have all my attention!' said Calvin.

'You were following me,' said Hunter.

'I assure you,' said Calvin, 'you are mistaken, Mr Keepe. I was quite unaware until this moment that I had the privilege of sharing Kensington with you on this very bright and sunny afternoon.'

'Oh, stop it!' said Hunter. He was mad with embarrassment

and exasperation. 'You know you were following me. You want something. What is it?'

Calvin looked at him with delighted amusement. 'I am afraid you are suffering from delusions,' he said. 'If I were following you, why should you now be quite out of breath from running after me?'

Hunter was very red. He mumbled something inarticulate and then turned on his heel. Calvin let him go nearly ten yards and then called, 'Wait a minute!' Hunter stopped and looked round. He waited, and then as Calvin said nothing more and stood his ground, he came slowly back.

'What do you want?' said Hunter savagely.

'Don't be so angry with me, Mr Keepe,' said Calvin. 'It just occurs to me that since we *have* met, on this delightful afternoon, there is something that we might profitably discuss.'

'If it's the *Artemis*, the answer's No,' said Hunter.

'It's not exactly the *Artemis*,' said Calvin. 'There's something else which I should like to suggest to you. I know you're very busy, but have you got a moment?'

Hunter hesitated. He did not want to oblige Calvin – but he was very curious, and he thought it just possible that the new move might be to suggest a meeting between himself and Mischa Fox.

'All right,' he said, 'but make it snappy. I've got an important engagement at five.' This was untrue.

'How kind of you!' said Calvin. 'Would you mind walking along with me? I can't discuss business in the open air. In fact, I was just on the way to my studio. If you don't mind coming along, we could have a chat while I print a couple of photos.'

Calvin walked on briskly, and Hunter followed in silence. They walked the length of two streets and then turned into a rather dark mews, where it seemed to have been raining. Calvin produced a latch-key and opened a rickety door off which faded blue paint immediately fell in flakes. Inside the door was a dark hole of a corridor. Calvin went ahead and put on a light at the far end. Hunter stood undecidedly at the entrance. The electric light showed him a damp stone floor. 'Come in and close the door behind you,' said Calvin. His voice echoed.

Hunter came in and shut the door. The daylight disappeared. Calvin was standing under the lamp at the end of the corridor, his hair illuminated, but his face in shadow. Hunter came towards him. It was slimy underfoot.

'Some stairs here,' said Calvin. Hunter saw him vanishing down a twist of stone stairs. He followed, and as he reached the bottom step, the light above him went off.

'Stay still,' said Calvin's voice, 'till I find the switch.' Another light went on, revealing another corridor. It was, Hunter noticed, extremely cold. He put up the collar of his coat.

'This way,' said Calvin, 'and keep close behind me. These cellars go on for miles, you know. You could easily get lost. And the electric lights go out automatically after a minute.'

Calvin turned a corner and opened a door. 'This is my little studio,' he said.

Hunter stumbled in. An amber-coloured light was burning in the far corner, its face turned to the wall. There was a smell of science. Hunter stood still, taking in nothing, concentrated upon the task of showing no signs that he was feeling frightened.

'What a strange place!' he said. He began to look about him. The room, which was dimly lit only by the amber lamp, had walls of rough brick which had been whitewashed but were now gilded by the light. It was meticulously clean and neat. In the centre stood two tables. On the nearer one were piled a number of thick books, and on the farther one stood a tall black machine. Against the wall was what appeared to be an electric hot-plate, on which were ranged a number of dishes of liquid. Above this, attached to the wall, was a large clock, its face marked out in seconds. At the far end of the room, under the shelf where the lamp was standing, and set deep into the floor like a natural pool, was a large zinc bath. The place had something of the air of what Hunter imagined an operating-theatre to look like. An electric fire, which was fixed high upon the wall and which had been burning when they entered, made the room warm. But Hunter found that he was still shivering.

'Ever seen a photograph printed?' asked Calvin, who had put on a white overall and was busy collecting bottles, scissors, tongs and various implements which Hunter did not recognize from a drawer in one of the tables. 'No? Well, this may interest you. You can even help if you like.'

'Look here,' said Hunter, 'you were going to tell me something. What is it?'

'In a minute,' said Calvin. 'Don't be impatient. This little job won't take long, and then we can be free to talk. Would you mind turning that switch there beside you?'

Hunter turned the switch and the hand of the clock began to revolve round its sixty-divisioned face.

'I think the hot-plate is on, isn't it?' said Calvin. 'Just touch it would you? Yes. It's thermostatically controlled so that the developing solution stays at an even temperature. Chemistry and temperature go together, you know. Now I must see to the bath.'

He turned a tap, and the water began to murmur softly. 'That's ready to use,' said Calvin. 'The water-level is controlled by a funnel in the outlet pipe so that the water is quite deep and always in motion. That's for washing the photos after they've been developed and fixed.'

Hunter stood on the brink of the bath and saw below his feet the water swirling in a dark fountain. Then he turned back to stare at the huge face and the moving finger of the clock. He protested no more. He was fascinated; but he was also afraid. He began watching Calvin.

Calvin now had a camera in his hand and was fiddling with it. He drew forth a large crystalline object. 'This is my eye,' he said to Hunter. 'This is the truthful eye that sees and remembers. The lens of my camera. You couldn't buy an eye like this for five hundred pounds.'

He approached the black machine on the table and began to fit the lens into it. 'This is the enlarger,' said Calvin. He swung it round. The enlarger consisted of a big black metal head which was joined to a thick shaft by a parallelogram of adjustable steel arms. Calvin turned a switch and lights became visible inside the head. Beneath it was a wooden board upon which Calvin now began to fix a sheet of white paper.

'The camera is really like an eye,' said Calvin, 'in that it reverses the image. In the human eye the image is turned right way round again by the brain. In the case of a photograph this machine acts as a brain. What I am going to do now is to print from negatives.' He reached for one of the bulky books on the other table, and Hunter saw as he flipped the pages over that each page held half a dozen strips of tiny negatives, clipped firmly into place.

'Here's the one I want to print,' said Calvin. He drew out a strip of negatives and slipped it into an aperture in the head of the enlarger; and as he drew the black strip rapidly along, the light shining from above flashed first one and then another of the pictures on to the white sheet below.

'This is it,' said Calvin, and began to fix the negative into position. 'I haven't got the thing focused, so you can't see the picture properly yet.' A blurred rectangle, in various shades of grey, was projected on to the paper.

'Now you can help,' said Calvin. 'You see those three trays of liquid on the hot plate? The first contains the developing fluid, the middle one is plain water, and the third one is the fixer which prevents the print from being affected any further by exposure to light. In a moment I'm going to put this machine into action, and I want you to count for me twelve seconds on the clock. Then I shall give you the print and I want you to hold it in the developing fluid with these tongs, moving it gently to and fro, for one minute. I'll count that time for you. The picture ought to begin to appear after about thirty seconds. Then you remove it into the water, and then at once into the fixer. From the fixer it goes into the bath. All right?'

'All right,' said Hunter. He moved and spoke like an automaton. He could hear the soft continual murmur of the water and the ticking of the clock. The only other sound was the beating of his heart.

'We'll wait till the hand reaches one again,' said Calvin. They both stood watching the clock. '*Now*,' he said, and a switch on the enlarger clicked over. Hunter began to count aloud, 'One, two . . .' Out of the corner of his eye he could see that Calvin had placed his hand between the beam of light and the paper and was opening and closing his fingers above the left-hand side of the picture. His hand was very long and brightly illuminated, fire was flashing from his rings and a band of light fell on to his white cuff. With an effort Hunter kept his eyes on the clock. 'This is called "shading",' said Calvin's voice. 'I am controlling the amount of light which falls upon the print. A delicate operation.'

'Twelve,' said Hunter. The switch clicked back, and the light inside the head of the enlarger was extinguished at the same time. The room was darker.

'Good!' said Calvin. He seemed excited. 'Now we'll develop!' He took a pair of surgical scissors and snipped round the edge of the paper, which was still quite plain. His hands were golden in the amber light. He laid the paper down and cleaned a pair of tongs with a strongly smelling rag.

'Hold the print with these tongs,' said Calvin, 'and move it in the solution as I told you. Soon you'll see the picture appearing. It's like magic. I never get tired of seeing the picture come.'

Hunter took the tongs awkwardly and picked up the piece of paper.

'Wait for the clock,' said Calvin. 'Now.'

Hunter plunged the print into the solution and Calvin began to count. Hunter stared at the white paper as he moved it gently about. Nothing was happening. 'Twenty-five,' said Calvin. Then something faint and greyish began to appear. Hunter could see the outlines of human figures. 'Thirty,' said Calvin. The picture was coming. 'Thirty-five,' said Calvin.

Hunter uttered a piercing cry and dropped the tongs into the solution. He turned on Calvin. 'You devil!' he cried. 'That's why you brought me here! You devil!'

'Look out!' cried Calvin, 'you'll spoil it!' He moved, thrusting Hunter aside, and seized the print, dipping it into the water and then into the fixer; and as Hunter reached out to snatch it from him he hurled it into the bath. Stumbling after him, Hunter fell to his knees on the edge of the bath. In the deep swirling water he could see the print turning rapidly over and over like a falling leaf. He plunged his arm in, coat sleeve and all, in a vain attempt to catch it as it swept madly round with the circling water. He touched it but it escaped, turning and turning its image towards him and away. Hunter grovelled upon the slippery edge of the bath. At last he caught the print by a corner and drew it out. He stood up, the water dripping from his coat, and examined the print carefully. What it represented was Rosa in the arms of the Lusiewicz brothers.

Hunter looked at it for a moment and then tore it to pieces. He raised his eyes to where, very close to him, Calvin was standing. He was immobile, his face half gilded, staring at Hunter with an expression of triumphant intensity. Both men were breathing heavily. Hunter said nothing, but without warning he lunged violently in the direction of the enlarger. Like a flash and with the precision of a machine Calvin put out his foot, and as Hunter tripped he took his arm in a crushing grip and forced him to the floor. Hunter looked up at him wide-eyed, and as his arm was released and he rose, Calvin was standing between him and the negative. Then Calvin turned slowly and in a leisurely manner removed the strip from the enlarger, replaced it in the book, and put the book in a cupboard, which he locked, and pocketed the key.

Hunter stood perfectly still. His face was blazing and he was struggling for breath. He was very near to tears. He tried to say something, and as he unlocked his throat his eyes spilled over. He reached out for the rag which lay on the electric plate close to his hand and applied it to his face.

'Don't get that stuff in your eyes,' said Calvin, 'unless you want to be blind!'

Hunter's eyes began to hurt violently. Choking with rage and exasperation, he knelt down beside the bath, groping his way, and began to bathe his eyes with the swirling water. The water trickled on to his waistcoat and down his neck. Still the hot tears were coming.

Calvin stood beside him, looking down curiously. 'Why are you so upset?' he asked. 'This seems to me to be a fuss about practically nothing. In that picture your sister is as beautiful as a princess and just as proper. It's a very fine photograph and not, if I may put it so, over-exposed!'

'You're a devil!' said Hunter, still choking. 'I didn't know anyone could exist like you!' He had given up any thoughts of dignity and knelt in a pool of water at Calvin's feet. 'Where did you get that picture?'

'I took it myself,' said Calvin.

'I don't believe you,' said Hunter.

'Why not?' said Calvin. 'Do you imagine that your sister would have arranged to have it taken? I'd no idea, incidentally, that she had so much hair.'

With a cry like an animal, Hunter reached out and grasped Calvin's legs with all his force. For a moment they swayed, and then Calvin brought his hand down like a hammer on the back of Hunter's neck. He fell, half-stunned, and then was conscious that Calvin was propping him against the wall and dashing water into his face.

'Really, Hunter,' said Calvin, as he hurled another handful of water, 'you do surprise me! I hope you don't mind my using your Christian name? I feel by now that I know you quite well. I must say that I neither intended nor expected this undignified struggle. But perhaps I am to blame. This childish device of letting you print the photograph yourself only occurred to me at the last moment, and I'm afraid I was carried away by my instinct for the dramatic.'

'Stop!' said Hunter, shielding his face. He buried it in his hands and sobbed for a moment. Then he was silent.

'That's better!' said Calvin. 'I really do apologize. Here, get up and sit in this chair. It's so wet on the floor, you must be soaked to the skin.'

Hunter got into the chair. Then he stared at Calvin, his mouth open and his face and hair soaked with water and tears. His eyes were still burning violently. Automatically he rubbed the back of his neck.

'Look here,' said Hunter at last, 'have you shown that picture to anyone?'

Calvin looked at him with a look which was almost tender in its intensity. 'Listen, my dear boy,' he said, 'let's be simple about this. There is one person who, I imagine, you are particularly anxious should not see this picture. Now, I have *not* shown it to this person, nor does he know of its existence. I say this, and it is true. You may say, how do I know that you're telling the truth? To which I answer, you don't know – but, from your point of view, I may be, and you can't afford to gamble on it. Therefore, for all practical purposes, you had better assume that this picture is still, and so far, a secret between you and me and the camera.'

'From what I know of you —' began Hunter.

'You know nothing of me,' said Calvin, 'so let's leave personalities out.'

'You beastly contemptible shit of a crook,' said Hunter. 'What's your price for the negative?'

'Dear me!' said Calvin, 'see how high the seas of language run here, as Wittgenstein would say!'

'What's your price?' said Hunter.

'A small one,' said Calvin. 'Just the *Artemis*. And if I may once more abbreviate our conversation, if you say "How can I trust you?" the answer is that you've got no choice.'

Calvin was standing beside the table with his hand upon the head of the enlarger. Hunter, who had composed his face and dashed the wisps of dripping hair out of his eyes, glared up at him.

159

'Why did you imagine I would do business with you at all?' he asked.

Calvin spread out a golden hand, whose shadow flitted along the wall. 'It was a brilliant conjecture,' he said. 'I imagined that you would be concerned; and I've seen nothing to make me believe otherwise. Indeed, I must confess that the violence of your reaction has surprised me.'

Hunter held his head in his hands. 'I must have time to think this out!' he said.

'There is very little time, I'm afraid,' said Calvin. 'The annual meeting of shareholders is tomorrow.'

'Give me the negative,' said Hunter, 'and I'll do whatever you want at the meeting.'

'Sorry,' said Calvin, 'it is the privilege of the stronger to be the one who is trusted.'

'What's in this for you, Blick?' said Hunter. 'Why should you care so much about getting hold of the *Artemis*?'

'As I said,' said Calvin, 'you know nothing about me, and this is not the moment for teaching you. May I suggest that you give me an answer straight away? We've been making quite a lot of noise, and though Mischa hardly ever comes down here, he might just take it into his head to do so today.'

'*What?*' said Hunter.

'Oh, didn't you realize,' said Calvin. 'We are in the cellars of Mischa's house. I thought you might recognize the back way in — but I suppose there's no reason why you should.'

'Let me out!' said Hunter. He jumped up and made for the door.

Calvin barred the way. 'Careful!' he said. 'You're like a dog that's been in the Serpentine, throwing water over everything. Let me tidy you up a bit.'

Hunter stood like a child while Calvin set his tie straight, rubbed his face and head with a towel, and then combed his hair into place.

'I'm afraid you're very wet, but nothing can be done about that,' said Calvin, 'and I've made you late for your appointment. You'll have to take a taxi. Have you got enough money?'

'Let me out!' said Hunter.

'My dear boy,' said Calvin, holding him by the shoulders, 'may I count on you tomorrow?'

160

'Yes,' said Hunter. 'Now let me go.'

When Calvin led him out into the mews, he took to his heels without looking back. Blinded by the daylight, he blundered into a lamp-post and several passers-by before he finally slowed down to a walking pace.

THIRTEEN

At breakfast-time on the following day, Hunter Keepe found himself without appetite. He looked across the table towards his sister, who never spoke in any case at breakfast, and was grateful for the copy of *The Times* which, elevated between them by Rosa, concealed from him the surly expression which he guessed her to be wearing, and from her the shocked and despairing look which he felt sure he was not proving able to banish. He had not slept. The posed trio, which struck him hideously as a sort of *pietà* in reverse, which he had seen in the photograph haunted him throughout the night in various forms, sometimes still and sometimes diabolically animated. The pain which this vision caused him made a deep wound into which all lesser miseries flowed indifferently: the humiliation suffered at the hands of Calvin, the enforced loss of the *Artemis*, the possibility of Rosa's displeasure. As he looked at the front page of *The Times* which Rosa was holding within a few inches of his nose, Hunter wondered whether or not she would decide to come to the meeting. Late on the previous night he had forced himself to scribble down a brief and ill-written statement in which the sale of the *Artemis* was proposed. What he had not succeeded in doing was to imagine himself daring to present this shameful manifesto to his sister. He hoped ardently that she would not come. But beyond this he had no plan, and was indeed incapable of any sort of mental activity except that of brooding upon the pain of his situation. Hatred, shame and anger, not yet differentiated, shifted and struggled in his heart.

He rose from the table. Upstairs Annette, who since her liberation from Ringenhall had not made appearances at breakfast-time, could be heard turning on her bath. Hunter coughed and fixed his eyes on the luxuriant dark crown of his sister's head, now visible over the top of the newspaper. 'Well, I must be off.'

The meeting was due to begin at ten-thirty: but Hunter was impatient to be out of the house. He could not have endured a conversation with Rosa, and the very sight of her moved him to a deep distress.

'Good-bye then,' said Rosa, without looking up. She reached out for some more coffee. Hunter fled.

At ten-fifteen Hunter was already entering the West End hotel where meetings of the shareholders of *Artemis* traditionally took place. Hunter would not have troubled to hold the meetings, since they were now become such a farce, in these solemn surroundings: but the annual hire of a large conference room had once been presented to the *Artemis* by a venerable lady for a period of years that had not yet expired. So it was that Hunter would present himself annually, with a written report and a financial statement, before a long mahogany table and a set of empty chairs, where, alone or in the company of Rosa, he would wait for about three quarters of an hour before departing. In this way Hunter had exercised his constitutional tyranny of which the last act, he sadly reflected, would be the deliberate destruction of his mother's noble journal.

Hunter entered the conference room. It was deserted and unkempt, with most of the curtains still pulled across the tall windows. The management had ceased long ago to take the *Artemis* meetings seriously. Hunter pulled back the curtains, put the chairs straight, and sat down at the end of the table. He spread out before him on the green baize cloth the last twelve issues of the periodical. The room was very silent. He closed his eyes, which were still smarting from the infusion of chemicals and from the tears which he had shed during the night. A sense of total physical and mental wretchedness swept over him, and he laid his head on the table. Where he was and what he would do next he was not able to think out; he was only aware that what he had seen upon the photograph imposed itself relentlessly between himself and a being that he loved which had alternately the face of Rosa and of Mischa. Until he had done all that he could to erase that vision, he would not be able to rest; but he knew, too, that what he was to do today was only the first move towards its erasure, and that perhaps it would never be erased. The problem of whether he could trust Calvin hardly occurred to Hunter at all. It was as if the destruction of the *Artemis* was a symbollic act which higher and more terrible powers would take note of and count, somehow, to his credit.

The door opened, and Calvin came in. Hunter lifted his head abruptly. 'Excuse me,' said Calvin, speaking in the low voice of one giving utterance in a church or a museum, 'may I take the liberty of attending this meeting? I imagine that you expected me to come.'

'Of course,' said Hunter. 'Naturally you want to satisfy yourself that everything is in order. Please be seated.'

Calvin settled in a chair half-way down the table. They sat in silence. Ten-thirty struck. The silence continued. Hunter smoothed out in front of him the piece of paper on which his final statement was written. He felt like a victim of the Inquisition. The sound of the door opening again made him start like a guilty thing.

Rosa entered, saw Calvin, and stopped in her tracks. Calvin looked at her under his eyebrows and then dropped his eyes and began to examine his hands which lay before him on the table. He had the coy expression of one concealing amusement. Rosa advanced, picking her way like an animal inspecting some unforeseen phenomenon. She sat down directly opposite Calvin, without looking at Hunter, and then also lowered her gaze to the table. They sat in silence, all three. Rosa looked at her watch.

Hunter, who had been blushing ever since Rosa entered, cleared his throat and said in a husky voice, 'Shall I read the statement?'

'Please,' said Calvin, after a moment. Rosa said nothing.

Hunter looked at the first sentences and felt that he would be unable to read out this statement in the presence of Rosa. He took hold of the paper as if it were the steering-wheel of some vehicle which he had to drive along the edge of a precipice. He opened his mouth to gasp for breath and found that he had begun to read the first paragraph in a low monotonous voice.

He had not read very far when strange noises began to disturb the peace of the meeting. There was a screeching of brakes as several vehicles drew up simultaneously outside the hotel. This was followed by a sort of distant uproar in the entrance hall. Hunter paused to wait until this din should have died down; but instead of decreasing the sound now seemed to be coming

164

nearer. There was a commotion on the stairs, and then a brisk knock upon the door. A spectacled face underneath an extremely large hat looked in. 'Is this the *Artemis* meeting?' asked an elderly lady to whom the face and hat belonged.

'Yes,' said Hunter, shrinking back in his chair.

'Yes!' the elderly lady shouted out of the door. 'This way, ladies!' she entered the room, followed shortly by three companions of similar age and appearance. One of them, who thought she recognized Rosa, bowed to her and smiled. Then all four sat down and began to inspect Hunter and Calvin with an air of suspicion and curiosity.

Calvin turned sharply to Hunter, whose face expressed astonishment; catching Calvin's glance, he spread out his hands and opened his mouth. Calvin turned to look at Rosa, who was frowning fiercely at the edge of the table. The din in the entrance hall continued, and more vehicles could be heard arriving at the door. Voices were raised upon the landing, and a further bevy of elderly women came bursting into the room, talking loudly as they entered. The newcomers were greeted by cries from the four who had arrived first. Amid swirling of skirts and removal of gloves there was a good deal of hand-shaking and inquiries about health. An elegant woman whose white hair was tinted with blue bore down upon Rosa, who sprang to her feet and saluted her with respect. 'Mrs Carrington-Morris,' said Rosa, 'I'm so glad that you managed to come!'

Hunter, who had fixed his eyes upon Rosa in the vain hope of receiving some sort of sign, also rose to his feet, stood irresolutely, and then sat down again wretchedly. Under cover of the din, he said to Calvin, who was leaning across the table towards him, 'I didn't arrange this!'

'I believe you!' said Calvin.

At this point Mrs Wingfield arrived, forcing her way into the already crowded room, followed by several supporters. Her appearance aroused shouts of 'Camilla!' and at once a number of ladies were crowding about her. Mrs Carrington-Morris, who was standing with her hand on Rosa's shoulder, waved a glove across the room. Mrs Wingfield was hatless, but her grey hair was sleek, and she wore a fine tweed dress whose age was betrayed only by its unusual length. She carried her head well thrown back and surveyed the scene with the air of a general

165

whose eagle eye can at once pick out the essential features from a confused ensemble.

It was clear by now that there were not enough chairs for this unexpectedly large gathering. Hunter, who had stood up again, was standing miserably beside his. Calvin was still seated, watching the scene closely with an inscrutable expression. Only one or two of the ladies were now seated. There was a general move to sit down.

Rosa turned to Calvin. Her frown had cleared and her face was unusually resolute and bland. 'Mr Blick,' she said, 'would you be so kind as to go and organize some more chairs? We seem to be short of them.'

Calvin got to his feet and Hunter tried in vain to catch his eye before he left the room. He reappeared shortly followed by hotel servants carrying chairs. A few more ladies were still arriving. The company by now amounted to more than thirty. The uproar was considerable.

Rosa's voice could now be heard rising above the din. 'Could everybody please be seated?'

There was a shuffling and scraping of chairs, and everyone sat down. As there was not enough space at the table, the company filled the whole room, scattered in irregular rows in a rough semicircle. With the clattering and the swish of long skirts subsiding and being patted into position, the voices gradually fell silent. At last the room was still.

As the silence continued, a number of people turned to look at Mrs Wingfield. Others fixed their gaze upon Rosa, or else looked to see whom their neighbour was looking at. Calvin looked at everybody in turn. Rosa looked at Hunter. Hunter looked at the table and saw with blurred vision the scrap of paper on which his report was written. Then he looked up and saw before him an astonishingly large number of venerable heads, some bearing the grey straight hair and purposeful expression of the reformer, others more conventionally decked with snowy curls and fashionable hats. Veils were being swept back, glasses donned or removed with a click, and one extremely old lady in the front row who was wearing a hearing-aid placed the receiver ostentatiously upon the table. Hunter swallowed hard and looked down again at his script. His mind became completely blank.

At last Rosa, her voice trembling slightly, said, 'My brother usually takes the chair at these meetings. Is it your wish that he should read out the annual statement about the *Artemis*?'

There was a silence. Then a lady with a ringing voice, who was wearing what appeared to be a mantilla, said, 'Is it in order for him to be chairman *and* to read the statement?'

Mrs. Carrington-Morris, turned with a gracious gesture to Rosa, said, 'In my view, Miss Keepe herself ought to be in the chair.'

Rosa said at once, 'I'd rather not!'

Mrs Wingfield, who it immediately appeared was a little drunk, called out, 'Never mind the details, we aren't in the House of Commons! Let the boy say his say.'

'Excuse me,' said the lady with the hearing-aid, 'I should be very glad, and I believe I speak for a number of others present, to be told what this is all about.'

'What do you mean, what it's all about?' asked a small tense woman with a grey fringe who seemed to find this remark very offensive. 'Surely we know why we are gathered here?'

'I certainly don't know why *I'm* gathered here,' said the lady with the hearing-aid. 'All I know is that yesterday I got a message '

'Perhaps it would be simplest,' the lady in the mantilla cut in, 'if whoever has got a statement to make could make it. I believe Miss Keepe's brother has got a statement to make.' She looked hopefully at Calvin.

'This is my brother,' said Rosa, pointing to Hunter, who was sitting like a man about to be electrocuted.

'Come on!' cried Mrs Wingfield from the back, 'we've been here half an hour already, can't you get on with it?'

Hunter cast a look of agony and reproach at Rosa, who was now looking in the other direction. Then he began once more to read out his statement.

'I can't hear,' said someone near the door. 'Would you mind beginning again?'

Hunter began again. His voice boomed in his ears, now loudly, now softly, like noises heard by a man about to fall asleep. He managed to get through two paragraphs.

'I don't understand any of this,' the lady with the hearing-aid said in what she probably imagined to be a whisper to her neighbour. 'It sounds rather a muddle, doesn't it?'

Hunter began to read the third paragraph. The proposal for

the sale, coupled with the name of Mischa Fox, occurred in the second paragraph. The third one elaborated financial details and technicalities concerning the shares. He suddenly stopped reading. There was no point in going on. He looked up and found forty pairs of eyes fixed on him intently. 'I think I'll stop here', said Hunter in a thick voice, 'and perhaps we can discuss the matter. If there are any questions I can answer —'

A confused hum covered his voice. 'Could you just explain who this young man is?' asked the lady in the large hat who had been the first to arrive, turning back to someone sitting behind her.

'Apparently he's Miss Keepe's brother.'

'Yes, but who is Miss Keepe?'

'Miss Keepe is *this* lady here.'

'Yes, dear, but who *is* she?'

'She's Maggie Richardson's daughter.'

'Oh, Maggie Richardson's daughter, of course! The boy doesn't look much like Maggie, does he?'

'Order, order!' said Mrs Carrington-Morris.

'Oh, get on with it!' said Mrs Wingfield.

'Look here,' said the lady in the mantilla, 'do I rightly understand that it is proposed that the *Artemis* be *sold*?'

'That is the proposal,' said Hunter.

'I don't think we can allow that, you know,' said the woman with the grey fringe who had the air of one who believed herself to be the only person present who really understood what was going on.

'It's a matter of financial necessity,' said Hunter. 'Perhaps I can explain —'

'They need cash!' shouted Mrs Wingfield.

'Why weren't we told of this before?' asked the lady in the large hat.

'Madam,' said Hunter, 'you have received a notice of this meeting every year. It's not my fault if none of you has ever taken the trouble to come!' He noticed with relief that his feeling of being cornered was turning from fear into anger.

A veiled lady who had not spoken so far leaned forward, rumbling like a clock before she gave utterance. 'Mmmm – do I understand you to say that it is proposed to sell the *Artemis* to – a *man*?'

Hunter gestured hopelessly. 'I've been running the thing for two years now,' he said, 'and after all I'm a man!'

A stiff silence followed this shameless declaration.

'It's all very confusing,' said the lady with the hearing-aid.

'I'm afraid,' said the woman with the fringe, 'that I find it far from confusing. The prospective buyer is someone who is not, to put it mildly, a supporter of female emancipation. To consent to this sale would be to consent to change the character of the paper altogether.'

'In fact,' said Hunter, 'the character of the paper has already changed. Since female emancipation has been achieved —'

'*What?*' said the lady in the mantilla. There was a general murmur.

'This young man is under the impression that women have been emancipated!' said someone at the back. There was a crescendo of voices.

'I confess I find this quite shocking!' said the woman with the fringe. 'Why, the very fact that the phrase "female emancipation" still has meaning for us proves that it has not yet been achieved.'

Calvin, who had been turning boldly to study each of the speakers in turn, said suddenly, 'Would you agree, madam, that the fact that the phrase "emancipation of the serfs" is significant proves that the serfs are not yet emancipated?'

There was an embarrassed silence.

'Who is that?' asked the woman with the hearing-aid, 'Is it Mr Fox?'

'Oh, no!' said Hunter in a shocked voice.

Calvin was staring hard at the woman with the fringe, who was looking red and uncomfortable.

'It *sounds* different,' she said with obstinacy.

'What sounds different?' said Calvin.

'He's so sharp he'll cut himself!' said Mrs Wingfield.

'This is like being in a madhouse,' said the lady with the hearing-aid.

'I think we should have a proposal to vote on,' said the lady in the large hat.

'Mmmm – I suggest that we break off for refreshments,' said the lady with the veil.

'That's a jolly good idea!' said Mrs Wingfield. 'Somebody find the bell and ring it.'

169

'In fact, I took the liberty,' said Mrs Carrington-Morris, 'of ordering tea and biscuits as I came in.'

'Here's the bell. Shall I push it?' asked the lady in the mantilla, who was sitting near the fireplace.

'Yes, dear, push it,' said the lady with the hearing-aid. 'We could all do with a cup of tea.'

There was a knock on the door and a waiter looked in. He asked, 'Is the lady here who ordered eight bottles of champagne?'

'That's right, bring 'em in!' shouted Mrs Wingfield.

'Really!' said Mrs Carrington-Morris.

There was a general flutter. Hunter tried to attract Calvin's attention, but Calvin had hidden his face in his hands. Rosa was sitting back, a little wild-eyed. A waiter brought in the champagne, followed by another waiter with a large tray of tea-cups.

'Where are the glasses, dolt?' said Mrs Wingfield. 'Or are we supposed to drink out of cups?'

'I must say,' said the woman with the fringe, who had recovered her confidence in the general confusion, 'I think this is scarcely tactful, Camilla. You can hardly have forgotten that some of us are members of the Temperance League.'

'Why shouldn't I have forgotten it?' cried Mrs Wingfield. 'I've forgotten almost everything, even important things. Why should I have troubled to engrave *your* prejudices on my memory? Open the bottles, waiter!'

'Well, I wouldn't say No to a glass of champagne!' said the lady in the mantilla.

The glasses arrived, followed by two large tea-pots and plates of biscuits. There was a scrimmage, in the course of which Mrs Wingfield struggled forward to the table and installed herself there with the bottles and the glasses. The teapots were passed overhead to Mrs Carrington-Morris, and one or two hats were splashed on the way with scalding tea.

'I still think,' said the lady in the large hat, 'that we should have a proposal to vote on.' A champagne cork popped.

'I really think I must go home,' said the lady with the hearing-aid to her neighbour. 'I believe things are going to get rough. I can't understand this meeting at all.' At that moment a wild gesture of Mrs Wingfield's disconnected the wire from her receiver and effectively cut her off from proceedings.

'I think the whole thing has been rather mismanaged,' said Mrs Carrington-Morris. 'I cannot blame Miss Keepe. I think —'

'Mmmm — pour out some tea, Ada dear,' said the lady with the veil.

'All right, if you want a vote, we'll have a vote!' cried Mrs Wingfield. People were moving from their seats and clustering round the tea-pots or round the champagne bottles. Glasses and cups were passed from hand to hand.

'I ordered this stuff,' continued Mrs Wingfield, 'to celebrate the liberation of our beloved paper from an impending doom. Before we go any further, let me give you a toast. The *Artemis*!'

As one woman the company rose, holding aloft their cups and glasses. 'The *Artemis*!' Only Calvin remained seated. Hunter, who had not managed to get hold of either drink, stood helplessly.

'That's all very well,' said the lady in the mantilla when she had drained her glass, 'but what are we supposed to be deciding?'

'Are we going to sell our beloved journal to this press lord — Yes or No?' Mrs Wingfield was swaying on her feet. Rosa was trying to persuade her to sit down.

'No!' said the assembled company, with varying shades of emphasis.

Mrs Wingfield sat down, 'Well, then,' she cried, 'you know what you've got to do! Miss Keepe, open the list of subscribers. You can put me down now for five hundred pounds. You'll have the rest later. What about it, Ada?' Mrs Wingfield leered across the room at Mrs Carrington-Morris.

'Certainly,' said the latter with dignity. 'I can't let Camilla outbid me. Put me down another five hundred pounds, Miss Keepe.'

Rosa had produced pencil and paper and seated herself at the table. With cries of enthusiasm, the others were soon crowding round her. The list lengthened.

Hunter gathered up his report and prepared to leave. He gestured to Calvin to accompany him. He had never felt so close to him. As he turned, he was surprised to find on Calvin's face an expression of delighted amusement; Calvin rolled his eyes and raised his hands to heaven.

'Let's get out,' said Hunter, 'before we're torn to pieces!' Calvin rose. He was shaking with laughter.

171

'Before the chairman and his mysterious friend slink away,' said the woman with the fringe, 'I should like to propose a vote of censure upon those responsible for ordering alcohol at a meeting of this kind.' Further uproar followed this. Hunter and Calvin made for the door.

'Were the Amazons teetotallers?' Mrs. Wingfield was crying. 'Was Mme de Staël? Was Sappho?'

The last that Hunter saw was a pyramid of excited faces, hats awry and mouths open, in the midst of which Rosa was still writing names and addresses. Her cheeks were flushed and her hair was beginning to come down.

FOURTEEN

John Rainborough was in a very bad temper. He felt himself to be the victim of gross injustice, indeed of a series of injustices designed to wound every facet of his personality. The trouble had started three days ago when Sir Edward Guest, seeing Rainborough passing by on the way to the canteen, had called him into his room, patted him on the shoulder, and started congratulating him. When Rainborough had looked startled, Sir Edward had said by way of explanation, 'I mean, of course, that splendid report by your young woman. You must have coached her a lot. It's a very useful bit of work. You'll hear more of this, Rainborough.'

Rainborough with stern self-command had smiled and accepted this praise with modest deference. He had even had the diabolical presence of mind to add that of course he hadn't really given Miss Casement much help, the credit must go to her, in a tone of voice which implied the opposite. When he emerged from the room, he set off at once in pursuit of his faithless junior. He was anxious to strike, and indeed striking was just what he felt in the mood for, while the iron was hot and before reflection set in to suggest to him that there were a great many possible ways of dealing with this situation.

He found Miss Casement not in her own office but in his, sitting thoughtfully on his chair and studying a file. Rainborough attacked at once.

'How did that report of yours get to Sir Edward?' he asked.

Miss Casement looked confused, even distressed. She made him the concession of getting up and refraining from the use of his Christian name.

'I'm extremely sorry,' she said. 'It was a mistake. You remember I put *For the attention of the Director* at the head of the draft? Well, as our little typist is away, I'd sent it with one or two corrections to the typing pool, and one of the new

173

typists, instead of returning it to me, just put it in the general out-tray, and so it got sent to the Director.'

'That's not true,' said Rainborough. He felt a profound desire to take Miss Casement by her elaborately permed hair and shake her until her teeth rattled. He opened the door of his room for her to go out. She went, with the air of someone who expects a kick from behind.

On the following day they had both sulked, confining their conversation to such brief remarks as the day's work rendered unavoidable. Stogdon's attempt to thaw the atmosphere by saying, 'Not very cheerful today, are we?' was greeted by a cutting rejoinder from Miss Casement which sent him away in a huff. Rainborough had to empty the out-tray himself at the end of the afternoon. It was then that, passing by the registry, he caught a portentous glimpse of Miss Casement, leaning against a filing-cabinet, in deep converse with Evans. He told himself immediately that there was nothing important in this. All the same the little picture haunted him. There was something about the intent and purposeful attitude of Miss Casement which made him feel uneasy. After all, as he had always suspected and had lately been able to verify, the girl was capable of anything.

The impression made by these calamities was, however, soon obliterated by the calamities which followed. The second day after the discovery of Miss Casement's treachery was the day before Mischa Fox's party. Rainborough had received his invitation at the end of the previous week, and had been delighted and relieved to see it. He took it as a sign that Mischa had not been offended by the curious circumstances of their last meeting. Rainborough, if he had ever cared to think about it, would have found now in his heart very little real fondness for Mischa, but an enormous concern about Mischa's opinion of him and about the continuance of their relations. It was essential for him to be able to continue to call himself Mischa's friend – although caring for Mischa or even wanting to be with him more than was necessary for the keeping up of appearances in, chiefly, his own eyes were not constituents of this strange friendship. So Rainborough was feeling pleased about the party, although he was not exactly looking forward to being there. He wanted very much to have been invited and to have been present; the hours of the party itself figured as a purgatorial period necessary for the attainment of the latter of these ends. Mischa's parties, as Rainborough knew from experience, were as often as not carefully constructed machines for the forcing of various plots and dramas; and this knowledge made him nervous, although he did not imagine that in this case he was likely to be cast in any central role himself.

The day had begun at the office auspiciously enough, with Miss Casement making obvious attempts at reconciliation: flowers on his desk, obsequious smiles, continually renewed attempts at small talk. Rainborough, who was too indolent to maintain the outward appearances of resentment, soon gave way before this barrage of goodwill, and closing up the black recesses of his heart, behaved to Miss Casement with his usual civility. It was then that she sprang her next surprise.

Rainborough was sitting with legs well stretched out, casting a dull eye upon the day's correspondence, when Miss Casement approached, and leaning over him said, 'John, might I ask you a favour?'

'Mmmmph?' said Rainborough.

'Would you mind taking me to Mischa Fox's party tomorrow?'

Rainborough stared at her. 'I can't,' he said. 'It's a private party. How did you know about it anyway? I can't bring along someone who isn't invited.'

'But I *am* invited!' said Miss Casement. She produced an invitation card from her pocket and flourished it in front of Rainborough's nose.

Rainborough jerked upright. Miss Casement's face was screwed up into the mask of someone trying hard to conceal a beam of triumph. 'But you don't know Mischa Fox!' said Rainborough.

'I've never met him,' confessed Miss Casement, 'but he must know about me. Anyhow, he's sent me an invitation.'

Rainborough felt a twinge of nausea at the idea of what 'knowing about' Miss Casement might possibly involve. He gave her a glare of hostility before he was able to compose his face.

'As I've never been to Mischa's house,' said Miss Casement, 'I was wondering if you'd mind calling for me on the way with a taxi, and, well, just coming in with me. I'd feel rather shy arriving alone.'

Rainborough twitched at her use of Mischa's first name, and grimaced at the idea of Miss Casement ever experiencing shyness: but he could think of no good reason for refusing. She had him cornered.

On the following day Miss Casement took the afternoon off and disappeared from the office at noon, presumably to make an early start on her *persona* for the evening. She was obviously very excited. Rainborough was left to speculate. He could get no further than the fairly simple idea that Mischa had taken it into his head to invite Miss Casement simply in order to keep his, Rainborough's, hands full and prevent him from competing for the attention of Rosa, should that lady chance to be one of the gathering. The other possible solution, that the whole thing was Calvin Blick's idea and was a case of pure mischief-making, he rejected on reflection. As it was, it was bad enough. That Mischa should know of Miss Casement's existence did not surprise Rainborough, who had long ago stopped being surprised at what Mischa knew. He did not imagine that Miss Casement could possibly think that he had himself put Mischa up to issuing the invitation. What he trembled at was the prospect of being forced to enter into a few hours of the Arabian Nights with that extremely determined young woman on his arm. Heaven only knew what would happen.

Half-way through the afternoon, after having got stuck with the crossword puzzle, Rainborough began to try to think of ways of getting out of the party altogether. He thought of feigning illness, of inventing urgent business in Devonshire, even of leaving the country: but he knew as he conjured them up that these escape plans were futile. A terrible curiosity drew him on. What did, however, demand satisfaction was his animosity against Miss Casement which, like a river fed from many sources, was now become raging and destructive.

After a while Rainborough hit upon a simple device. The party was due to begin at eight. It had been rather vaguely agreed between them that Rainborough should arrive with the taxi soon after that hour. Rainborough had suggested coming about nine-thirty, in the hope of curtailing his sufferings, but Miss Casement, who did not want to miss a minute of the proceedings, would not hear of this. Rainborough's new idea was to annoy her by arriving early. He particularly wanted to be able to see her before she had made up her face. He might even discover her half dressed. What Rainborough hoped to gain thereby was not a closer view of Miss Casement's charms; he wished simply to startle her out of her usual composure. This would have a further advantage. Rainborough, whose imagination had been busy, had conceived it possible that Miss Casement might be affectionate to him in the taxi. He shuddered at the thought that she might even take his hand. He had already made plans for seeing to it that they left the party in someone else's car; and Miss Casement, who might also have anticipated that they would not again be alone together, might have planned a prompt attack. If he could arrange for her to be discomposed and aggrieved at an early stage, he could thereby ensure that the atmosphere in the taxi was anything but intimate.

So it was that with a Machiavellian smile Rainborough arrived about seven-fifteen at the address in Hammersmith which Miss Casement had given him. He told the taxi which had brought him to return about an hour later, and he mounted the stairs. Miss Casement had told him to come straight up to the second floor. It was a big Victorian house which had been divided into small flats for business girls. Rainborough found Miss Casement's name on a door and knocked. There was a prolonged flurry. Then a figure in a powder-stained dressing-gown and with a head which Rainborough scarcely recognized opened the door. Miss Casement stared at Rainborough. He could see at once that he was not going to be disappointed.

'You've come bloody early!' said Miss Casement.

'Oh, have I?' said Rainborough. 'I'm so sorry. I mislaid my invitation. The party's at seven-thirty, isn't it?'

'No,' said Miss Casement shortly, 'at eight. Come in, though.'

'I can easily wait outside or go away for a while,' said Rainborough, coming in eagerly and sitting down on a sofa.

'You're sitting on my dress!' said Miss Casement. She pulled away from under him an armful of flame-coloured silk.

Rainborough looked about him – and at once he realized that Miss Casement's flat consisted of one room only. It was a small room whose faded velvet curtains and plump shabby plush furniture exuded a dusty smell which mingled with the odour of gas and face powder. The place was stuffy and over-

177

heated. In a narrow grate, surmounted by bright green tiles, a gas-fire, turned full on, burnt with a low shrieking sound. In front of it was a gas-ring, and a number of saucepans, some of which were clean. The floor and most of the furniture was covered with underclothing and silk dresses, the latter no doubt the record of Miss Casement's earlier indecisions. The dressing-table was stacked with creams, powders, rouges, lipsticks, tonics, fresheners, varnishes, removers, cleaners and other kinds of cosmetics. Above the divan bed, which was covered with small lacy items, was a small shelf which held a dozen Penguin books. None of this surprised Rainborough. It had only not occurred to him, although he knew that some unfortunate people had to do it, that Miss Casement lived in one room. He turned to look at her, and at once began to feel ashamed of his little plan, which was succeeding even beyond his expectations.

Miss Casement was standing irresolutely, holding her dress up against her and clutching the neck of her dressing-gown. Her hair was tightly done up in curlers and covered by a net. Her face, deprived of its usual crenellated frame, was also bare of make-up. Miss Casement looked paler and older. Her nose glistened and the skin was drawn tight about her eyes. Rainborough felt pity for her and turned his glance away. Among scent-bottles on the mantelpiece he noticed some animals made of glass and wood. In a moment he would begin to find Miss Casement's room rather touching.

'You'd better have a drink,' said Miss Casement grimly. She produced a sherry bottle from behind the dressing-table. A box of powder leapt to the ground and spilled on the carpet.

'Oh, hell!' said Miss Casement, and kicked it into a corner, where it overturned into a pile of pink silk things. She poured out a glass of sherry.

'Shall I go away while you dress?' asked Rainborough, now genuinely anxious.

'No,' said Miss Casement, 'stay where you are.'

She went out carrying the dress and banging the door savagely behind her. The was a sound of running water in an adjoining bathroom. A moment later she returned wearing the dress, but still without stockings or make-up. Rainborough knew that he was upsetting an established routine. He sipped his sherry and watched. Miss Casement tied a towel awkwardly

178

round her neck and began to smooth cream on to her face. Another woman, Rainborough reflected, might have turned the tables on him and found some way of turning the situation to her advantage. Not so Miss Casement, whose character in this respect he had judged rightly. With even a little grace in her person there was some intimacy, some complicity, which she might have drawn out of the scene; but she was still rigid with annoyance. How stupid she is! he thought to himself, and began to feel better.

'You could make yourself useful,' said Miss Casement, whose voice still sounded a little high-pitched and odd, 'by drying those stockings for me.' She pointed to a pair of stockings which lay across the fender. 'Hold them up a bit closer to the fire. That's right.'

Rainborough drew his chair nearer to the gas-fire and dangled the damp stockings to and fro in the heat. As he did so, he looked up at Miss Casement. She was putting powder on her face with an enormous puff. The familiar surface was beginning to appear. She threw her head back. Then she removed the hair-net and began to take out the curlers. Rainborough watched the transformation fascinated. A cloud of powder was floating across the room. It reached him and enfolded him, suffocating, sickly, synthetic. Through mouth and nostrils Rainborough drank it in. Miss Casement was shaking out her hair. The dark curls sprang to their stations. In a moment the whole mass had been released, not to ripple freely down Miss Casement's back but to protrude stiffly in pre-destined undulations. Miss Casement, who was now feeling better too, turned a little towards Rainborough. She took a hand-mirror, and parting her lips drew a thin red outline about them which she then proceeded to fill in. Her mouth, which was small, but failed to gain in width what it lost in length, opened at last to reveal a number of teeth. Lost in the detail of Miss Casement's face, it took Rainborough a moment to realize that Miss Casement was smiling at him. With a start he hastened to respond.

As he moved a sudden ball of agony collected in his right hand and shot violently up his arm. With a loud cry of pain Rainborough sprang to his feet. One of the stockings had come too close to the fire and the inflammable nylon had leapt in one great tongue of flame into the palm of his hand. He hurled the burning remnants into the fireplace, dropped the other stocking, and danced about the room hugging his hand under his left armpit.

'Oh, you fool!' cried Miss Casement. 'Those were my best stockings!'

'Damn your stockings!' said Rainborough, arresting his dance and trying to examine the damage. The pain as he opened his hand was considerable. He closed it again and put it in his pocket. He glared at Miss Casement. 'I'm badly burnt!' he said.

Miss Casement looked at him with exasperation. Then for a moment it seemed that she was going to laugh. But all she finally said was, 'What does one put on burns nowadays?'

'Oh, never mind!' said Rainborough. 'There's nothing one can do with a burn. For heaven's sake let's get out of here.' He sat down heavily on the divan and nursed his hand.

Miss Casement left the room. She returned a few moments later fully dressed and swathed in an expensive fur cape, which Rainborough immediately felt sure she had borrowed for the occasion. They looked at each other. Miss Casement's look expressed hostility, determination, and expectation: Rainborough's hostility, irritation and negation. They walked down the stairs together. The taxi could be seen waiting outside.

'Oh dear,' said Miss Casement, 'the taxi's been waiting all this time!'

Rainborough said nothing. They got in.

The taxi-driver turned round. 'You did say eight-fifteen to come back, didn't you, guv?' he said. 'I wasn't sure if I'd got it right.'

'That's quite right,' said Rainborough.

The engine started. Miss Casement turned upon him a cold pitiless look of understanding. Rainborough did not trouble to invent an answering glance. His hand was very painful indeed.

FIFTEEN

Mischa Fox's house was brightly lit. Every window was blazing. A carpet had been laid upon the steps, and there were flowers on either side of the door, metallic blue and red in the crystalline light from the doorway, and swaying slightly in the evening breeze. A number of onlookers had collected. The outer door was open, and through the glass of the inner door two footmen could be seen standing in the hall. The time was 8.30 p.m. Already the onlookers had been rewarded by the arrival of two famous personages, accompanied by a train of conspicuously dressed women.

Mischa Fox's abode, as was well known, had certain curious features. Mischa had had the fantasy of buying four houses in Kensington, two adjoining in one road, and two adjoining in the next road, and standing back to back with the first two. He had joined this block of four houses into one by building a square structure to span the gap. Within this strange *palazzo*, so rumour said, the walls and ceilings and stairs had been so much altered, improved and removed that very little remained of the original interiors. By now, it was reported, there were no corridors and no continuous stairways. The rooms, which were covered with thick carpets upon which the master of the house was accustomed to walk barefoot, opened directly out of each other like a set of boxes; and the floors were joined at irregular intervals by staircases, often themselves antiques which had been ripped out of other buildings. The central structure, which, it was noticed, had few windows, excited yet wilder speculation. Some people said that it housed a laboratory, others that it contained a covered courtyard with a fountain, and others again that it was a storehouse for art treasures which had been procured illicitly by Mischa and which were so well known that his possession of them had to be kept a secret. The more accessible parts of the house were known to be crowded with *objets d'art* of all kinds alleged to be worth a quarter of a million. This maze of splendours was described by Mischa's foes and acquaintances, according to taste, as 'mad', 'sinister', 'vulgar', or 'childish'.

The taxi containing Rainborough and Miss Casement drove up to the door. A footman handed them out. Rainborough paid the fare. The crowd watched. 'What's he tip you, mate?' someone asked the driver.

Miss Casement stood by uneasily, not knowing what to do with her eyes. They turned to go in. Miss Casement tripped over her dress and seized Rainborough's arm. 'Drunk already!' said the crowd.

They got into the hall. Rainborough was ushered one way and Miss Casement the other to leave their coats. Then they were led over silent carpets through a series of rooms and up a silent flight of stairs which rose directly out of one room and gave directly into another. They did not speak, and it was as if their feet did not touch the ground. Rainborough cast a quick glance at Miss Casement. Her lips were parted and he had never seen her eyes so wide open. He noticed, without surprise, that he was holding her hand. His heart was beating violently. A final door opened and they found themselves in a long room which was full of low and heavily shaded lights. There was suddenly a subdued murmur of talk. Rainborough let go of Miss Casement.

A figure came forward to greet them. It was Calvin Blick. In evening-dress he looked like a mixture of Baudelaire and de Tocqueville. He leaned towards Rainborough, whose eyes were just becoming accustomed to the dim light, and held out an arm which seemed to embrace Miss Casement and draw her closer to her escort's side.

'Ah, you've both arrived!' said Calvin.

Rainborough, who was not concerned to dispute this, and was anxiously looking about to find Mischa, did not reply. Mischa was not in the room. Someone gave him a drink, Calvin's hand was on his arm, and he was moving forward towards two men of Austro-Hungarian appearance who were standing near by, with attendant women who seemed to be all jewellery and no faces. Calvin introduced him and Miss Casement to the group. The men were apparently called Rosenkrantz and Guildenstern, or else Rainborough had misheard.

One of them made a polite remark to Miss Casement. Rainborough began to study his surroundings.

The room, as yet, was empty except for the small group to which he was attached, and one or two unrecognizable persons whom he could descry at the far end. It was an extremely long room and already rather stifling. The reason for this was not far to seek. Three of the walls were hung with tapestries which completely covered all the windows. Only the door through which they had come was revealed, the tapestries on either side being drawn well apart at the base and meeting to a point above the doorway. Rainborough looked at these hangings. He judged them to be French work of the fifteenth century. They were profusely covered with leaves and flowers among which ran, flew, crawled, fled, pursued, or idled an extraordinary variety of animals, birds, and insects. No human figures were to be seen. Rainborough noticed in a glance a hound loping amiably in pursuit of a rabbit, an astonished encounter of a hawk and a pigeon, and a unicorn holding a conversation with a lion. Then he shifted his eyes to the fourth wall, where a large gilt mirror towered above a fireplace where a log fire was burning. A white mantel-shelf was covered with French paperweights and small ivory figures. On frail tables along the walls the lamps were burning at regular intervals, revealing in circles of light the golden pallor of the Aubusson carpet. Half-way along the room in a large round bowl of green glass, surmounted by a coronet of lights, tropical fish swam idly to and fro.

Rainborough turned round and found himself face to face with Annette, who had just come through the door. Annette's eyes and mouth were open, as Miss Casement's had been. The first thing that she saw on entering was Rainborough, and she kept her gaze upon him, still gaping, while Calvin murmured greetings and handed her a drink. She walked towards Rainborough, who was discreetly detaching himself from Rosenkrantz. Guildenstern was still holding forth to Miss Casement, who was casting nervous glances towards Rainborough and Annette and was hardly able to answer him civilly. Rainborough turned and struck out boldly across the room to the fish-bowl, and Annette followed him with the docility of a young duckling which is supposed to follow the first thing that it sees.

Rainborough had not met Annette since the day when she

had visited his house. He looked at her now. She was wearing a sea-green three-quarter-length evening-dress, extremely *décolletée*. He peered at her breasts and her ankles; and he felt a sudden protective tenderness towards her. They leaned against the glass.

'Well, Annette,' said Rainborough, in the tone of a Victorian father coming upon one of his eleven children at her innocent play.

Annette shot him a dark look. 'Where's Mischa?' she asked.

'I don't know,' said Rainborough. 'He hasn't appeared yet.'

Annette studied the fish, and Rainborough studied Annette.

'Do you know anything about fish?' Annette asked after a moment.

'No,' said Rainborough. 'Do you?'

'No,' said Annette. They were silent.

Rainborough swallowed his drink quickly and someone refilled his glass. A few more people had arrived, amongst whom Rainborough recognized a well-known composer and two potentates from Fleet Street.

'Who is that girl who's staring at us?' asked Annette.

'That's a Miss Casement,' said Rainborough. 'She works in my office.'

'Oh,' said Annette. 'Is she a friend of Mischa's?'

'No,' said Rainborough. He felt unable to develop this, so they were silent again. Rainborough experienced a profound and anxious need to communicate with Annette. He wanted to say something which would be wise and reconciling, which would bind up all wounds and draw the child to his heart. He began to search for words.

'Annette,' he said, 'as one grows older one realizes that life has a great many random elements. One result of this is that there are a great many ways in which we can hurt and startle other people to whom we wish only good. For beings like us, patience and tolerance are not virtues but necessities.'

'When I'm patient,' said Annette, 'I'll be dead.'

This quick answer surprised and pleased Rainborough, who was trying to think of a rejoinder when there was a commotion at the doorway. They both turned. Mischa Fox came in, accompanied by Peter Saward. Rainborough saw that Mischa was holding Peter Saward's arm, and he felt a sharp thrill of jealousy. A wave of attention undulated through the room and everyone was looking towards the door. The conversation paused and then resumed. Rainborough could see from the corner of his eye that Annette was standing rigid, holding on to a fold in the tapestry. Miss Casement, who undoubtedly recognized Mischa from his photographs in the paper, turned crimson, to the astonishment of Rainborough, who had never seen her blush.

Rosenkrantz and Guildenstern were advancing with cries of joy and addressing Mischa in German. Mischa answered them in English, and presented Peter Saward. Rainborough noticed that Mischa treated Peter as if he were a celebrity. Rosenkrantz and Guildenstern noticed it too and received Peter with an attitude of reverence. Rainborough felt extreme irritation. He knew that this was the moment at which he ought to go forward and introduce Miss Casement, but he thought: he invited her, he can deal with her; and detaching himself from Annette, Rainborough sat down in a nearby chair. As he turned, he noticed Calvin Blick, who was leaning against the mantelpiece at the far end of the room, his gaze moving to and fro between Mischa and Rainborough, like a spectator at Wimbledon.

Then Rainborough saw that Mischa, leaving Peter Saward in the hands of Austria-Hungary, was turning towards Miss Casement. He shook hands with her, drawing her skilfully aside as he did so, with the words, 'You must be Agnes Casement. I'm so glad that you managed to come!'

'Confound it!' thought Rainborough. 'He even knows her Christian name!'

Mischa introduced Miss Casement to Peter Saward. Then he turned and surveyed the rest of the room. Rainborough made no movement. In a minute or two Mischa began to saunter lazily towards the fireplace, speaking to various guests on the way. He was wearing a velvet smoking-jacket and looked very much at his ease. Rainborough looked to see how Calvin would greet his master; but Calvin had disappeared. He must have gone through a doorway concealed behind the tapestry in the far corner of the room.

Mischa came up to Rainborough. 'John!' he said, 'Hello!' His eyes were gleaming with gaiety.

Rainborough resisted an impulse to rise to his feet. 'Mischa,' he said, 'you old rogue!'

Mischa sat down on the floor. Rainborough remarked the

relaxed grace of his posture and the extraordinary flexibility of his feet and ankles. The human foot, which is usually a stiff and jointed object, quite unlike the smoothly bending limbs of an animal, appeared in Mischa to have lost its rigidity. Rainborough, an agile man, but even in his youth robust rather than lithe, looked down at Mischa with envy as he sat, his legs tucked under him and the soles of his shoes turning upward, like an oriental sage.

Annette was still standing near them holding on to the tapestry and staring at Mischa. Mischa turned his head. 'Annette, come here,' he said, speaking as if to a child. He stretched out his hand.

Annette came forward cautiously, putting her foot down as if the floor might give way under her. As Mischa kept his hand outstretched, she took it, and he drew her down to sit beside him at Rainborough's feet.

'You two have met, I believe?' said Mischa. His eyes were wide and serene, like those of a happy animal.

'As you know,' said Rainborough.

'I like my friends to know each other,' said Mischa. 'Tell me, Annette, when did you say that your dear mother was coming to England?'

'In the summer,' mumbled Annette. She was looking down and refusing to meet Mischa's gaze. He put his hand under her chin and lifted her head; and she gave him without concealment a look of yearning which made Rainborough turn away in embarrassment and surprise.

'Do you think that Annette resembles Marcia, John?' asked Mischa.

'I've never met Marcia,' said Rainborough sulkily.

Annette was relaxing. She was finishing her second drink. 'What is that marvellous stuff?' she asked.

'You must excuse me a moment,' said Mischa. He was staring at the door. Hunter and Rosa had just come in. Mischa rose slowly.

Hunter advanced into the room. He was very ill at ease and obviously blinded by the dim light, which contrasted with the bright room outside, and by the haze of cigarette smoke which now darkened the air. He caught sight of Peter Saward and clutched his arm with piteous desperation. Peter greeted him warmly and introduced him to people nearby. Rosa meanwhile

186

stood stock still by the door and looked about for Mischa. She soon saw him and stood quite motionless, looking towards him intently. Mischa approached, and it seemed to the two who were watching a long time before he reached her. He took her hand and kissed it. Rosa said nothing, but turned and walked away to the farther end of the room, where there was an empty space. Mischa followed her, and they were to be seen a moment later in conversation. It was plain, that they were both much moved. Rainborough looked at them. They seemed immensely distant and inaccessible. He looked at Annette, and once more had to turn away.

Some more people were arriving. The room was now quite full. Rosenkrantz and a rather dull woman who appeared to be his wife bore down upon Annette, asking news of her mother. Rainborough had another drink. He began to feel calmer and more detached. His hand, which had been hurting him considerably, was beginning to feel better too. Round about him the chatter was deafening. Through the throng he could see that the tapestry had been swept back at the far end of the room to reveal an open window. In the alcove so created, beside a bright lamp, like figures on a stage he saw Mischa and Rosa with Peter Saward. Peter was sitting in a chair and leaning towards the window. Mischa and Rosa were looking down at him. Mischa was saying something with gestures.

Several drinks later Rainborough found that he was sitting on the floor. So were a lot of other people. A number of the celebrities seemed to have gone home, and the room was a little emptier, though the din seemed to be just as considerable. Close to him on the floor he discovered Mrs Rosenkrantz, who, it turned out, was not dull at all, but delightfully witty and attractive. As they talked, a familiar green skirt swept past, and Rainborough looked up to see Annette making for the mantelpiece like a shipwrecked man striking out for a raft. When she reached it she leaned against it heavily. She looked rather the worse for wear. Her face was flushed and her hair, which was usually unruly, was almost standing on end. There was a wild look in her eye. As she leaned there breathing deeply, Rainborough noticed Mischa, who was standing a little way off by himself and also watching Annette. It occurred to Rainborough at that moment that Mischa had been drinking nothing all the evening. He turned to explain this point to his companion. It turned out to be surprisingly complicated.

Annette was staring at the mantelpiece. In the centre of the shelf was a group of ivory figures of men and animals. She touched one or two of them gingerly with her finger. Then she became aware of Mischa. She straightened herself and patted her hair as he came towards her. A soft music was beginning in the background, and at the far end of the room someone was rolling back the carpet. A couple began to rotate slowly.

'What these?' said Annette, pointing to the ivory figures. Her voice didn't seem to be quite under her control.

'They're called *netsuke*,' said Mischa. 'They were made in Japan in the eighteenth century. People used to wear them on their clothes.'

'Was it magic?' asked Annette.

'No,' said Mischa, 'or only in the way in which magic can be part of ordinary life.'

Annette lifted one of them. It was an old man seated and leaning against a sleeping buffalo. She turned it upside down. It was carved underneath too, the man's naked foot turned back, his figured robe, the fur of the animal. She put it down. Next to it was a girl seated on a clam-shell, then a boy with his arm round the neck of a goat, an old man with a rat on his shoulder, a woman holding a fish. Each one she saw, represented a human being with an animal.

'You got real fish here,' said Annette. 'Let's see the real fish.' She turned suddenly and made for the fish-bowl. Mischa followed her. Annette looked at him from the other side of the bowl. She held the edge of it like someone about to do a handspring. Her eyes were flashing. Then she looked down at the fish. Intent upon their own concerns, the fish swam to and fro. The black sulky ones with the whiskers and the zebra-striped ones with the large fins swam slowly and lazily. The little shiny blue ones and the pale dog-faced ones swam quickly and nervously.

'What's *that* one?' said Annette, and thrust her hand into the water, pointing.

'Don't do that,' said Mischa, 'you frighten them, and you contaminate the water.'

Annette withdrew her hand. She stared at him for a moment. Then she plunged her whole arm into the bowl up to the elbow. The fish scattered in alarm.

Mischa did not move. 'Don't do that, Annette,' he said.

Annette slowly drew her arm out. The water ran down her dress, making a dark stain. She looked dazed.

'Come and dance,' said Mischa. He drew her across towards the music.

The little demon, thought Rainborough who had been watching, she wanted to force him to touch her! He looked about for Rosa and saw her sitting by the window talking to Saward. Hunter was on the dance-floor. Rainborough was just turning back to Mrs Rosenkrantz, who, it was becoming apparent to him, had the most wonderfully large eyes, when an apparition appeared which seemed to be located directly above his head. This apparition, when it came into focus, turned out to be Miss Casement.

Rainborough, who had temporarily forgotten about Miss Casement, surveyed her with interest. It was evident that as far as the drink was concerned Miss Casement had not been wasting her time.

'Sit down, sweetie,' said Rainborough, 'and let me introduce you to Mrs Rosenkrantz.'

'No!' said Miss Casement in a surprisingly clear voice. 'You get up!'

Rainborough found himself on his feet. Mrs Rosenkrantz seemed to have been suddenly vaporized.

'I must have some air!' said Miss Casement. 'I think there's a window here behind the tapestry.' She fumbled at a gap in the stuff.

'Yes, so there is,' said Rainborough. 'Here let me.' He pulled the heavy material apart and they stepped through. The tapestry fell to behind them and they found themselves standing in a bay window. It was extremely dark. Rainborough pulled up the sash and leaned out. He was looking into some sort of garden. He wondered where in Mischa's domain this garden could possibly be, and he tried to orient himself by the stars; but it was a cloudy night and the few stars that were visible did not announce any constellation that he could recognize. He drank in the cold night air. It was sobering.

'Let's sit down,' said Miss Casement, 'there's a sofa here.'

Trapped! thought Rainborough. He started to say 'No, let's —', but Miss Casement gave him a gentle push and he subsided on to the sofa. She sat down beside him. They looked at each other. Rainborough could see nothing of Miss Casement except the light reflected from her eyeball. Yet he knew, somehow, exactly what her expression was and exactly what she was going to do. She leaned forward and kissed him on the cheek. She had been aiming at his mouth, but missed it in the darkness. She tried again and found her objective. Rainborough remained quite still. There was a raging confusion inside his head. The bitch, a voice was saying, the bitch. He leaned towards her and began to kiss her brutally and indiscriminately upon her face and neck. He had never felt before that kisses could be so much like blows. Miss Casement became limp and he felt her sighing breath in his face. Rainborough stopped and sat back in amazement. 'John!' breathed Miss Casement tenderly. She took his right hand and pressed it in a fierce grip.

Rainborough suddenly became conscious of his hand in a wave of pain which rushed straight up into his head. He gave a loud cry and dragged it away from her. His burnt palm was searing him as if it had been flayed. He jerked himself back and fell off the sofa with a crash. Then light was streaming in upon him, someone had pulled back the tapestry and faces were peering through.

'Dear me!' said Calvin Blick, 'whatever is the matter? Have you seen a ghost? Why, you've got Agnes Casement in there with you! Having a bit of a wrangle, eh?'

Rainborough emerged, followed by Miss Casement, who was looking both dazed and furious and smoothing down her dress. She walked sharply away from Rainborough, who made a helpless gesture.

'Never mind!' said Calvin. 'More fish in the sea. Let me show you a picture of my sister, the one who's married to an engineer in British Honduras.' He drew out his wallet.

'I don't want to see your beastly pictures,' said Rainborough. He was looking at the dance-floor. Annette was still dancing with Mischa. Rainborough noticed that Rosa was leaning against the mantelpiece, fingering one of the French paperweights, and watching them closely. He thought that she looked very drunk. Peter Saward had evidently gone home.

At that moment Annette, who had been moving more and more sluggishly, suddenly threw her arms round Mischa's neck and sagged violently with all her weight, trying to pull him to the ground. Mischa, with an agile movement, slipped his head out of the circle of Annette's arms and she sat down heavily upon the floor. Several people laughed and began to help her up.

Calvin had taken out several photographs and was trying to attract Rainborough's attention. But Rainborough was now staring at Hunter. The boy had left the dance-floor and was looking open-mouthed and with a poignant expression of terror at Calvin.

'Here, look at this one!' said Calvin to Rainborough. He seemed to have noticed Hunter's terror and to be enjoying it.

'What's the matter with Hunter?' asked Rainborough.

He received no reply, for after that things happened very fast. Annette had got to her feet and was standing holding on to Mischa. Rosa was staring at them. Hunter's fear now rose to a frenzy. He could see Calvin holding up a photograph and waving it to and fro. He ran to his sister. 'Rosa,' said Hunter, in a tone of desperation. 'Do something! Create a diversion! Faint, scream, do anything!'

Rosa looked for a moment into her brother's terrified eyes. Then with a violent movement she turned and hurled the paperweight she was holding with tremendous force across the room. It caught the curving surface of the fish-bowl squarely in the middle and with a deafening crash the bowl broke into fragments. There was a silence in which the weary beat of the dance music was heard for a moment. Then everyone began to shout and precipitated themselves upon the remains of the bowl. The water spread in a great circle upon the floor, and within it the fragments of the paperweight were scattered like innumerable pieces of sugar cake. Suddenly fish seemed to be everywhere, gasping upon the carpet, clinging to the lamp-shades, sliding across polished tables, and wriggling upon chairs and settees. Helplessly, people began to pick them up and run about the room looking for somewhere to put them. Flowers were tossed away, and fishes snatched from cushions or plucked from under stampeding feet were hurled into the vases. One was dropped by mistake into a decanter of gin. Hands reached out and every hand clutched its coloured fish. Under the tables and chairs they scrambled to gather them up, and the room was full of cries.

'Stop!' said Mischa. He was still standing in the middle of

the dance-floor. He was as white as paper, as if all the blood had left his body.

'It's no use,' he said. 'They will not survive.' He turned and picked up a large china bowl whch had contained biscuits. 'Put them here,' he said.

Silence fell again. The music had ceased. Everyone came to Mischa, bringing the fish, and laid them in the bowl. He stood there like a priest. The last one was brought. But still Mischa stood there, rigid and white. For a moment it seemed as if he was going to faint. Then Calvin Blick came forward and took the bowl from his hands. Mischa turned on his heel and left the room.

Everyone stood there paralysed. Then they began to look at each other guiltily. Annette, who had been standing perfectly still on the spot where Mischa had left her, her hand raised to her mouth, was suddenly galvanized into activity. She spun round madly towards Rosa. 'You did that on purpose!' she screamed.

Rosa, who was leaning against the wall looking completely bewildered, turned towards Annette — and as she turned Annette launched herself upon her like a young tiger. Amid scandalized cries the two women reeled and fell struggling to the floor. Rainborough and Hunter ran to separate them. Calvin was watching with glowing eyes.

Rosa was the stronger of the two. As soon as Annette touched her she felt an enormous power inhabiting her limbs. At that moment she could have killed Annette, tearing her in two like a putty figure. Never had she experienced such a profound satisfaction of anger and hatred. In an instant she had Annette by the throat and was pressing her head back while with the other hand she tore at the bosom of her dress. The material gave way with a terrible rending sound. Then Hunter was between them, blindly pushing Annette away, while Rainborough pulled the girl to her feet. Hunter helped Rosa, who got up more slowly.

Annette wrenched herself free from Rainborough, who was trying to hold her arm and to expostulate. She stood for a moment with closed eyes, holding up both hands to support the front of her dress which was torn as far as the waist. Then she opened her eyes, looked about her, and suddenly ran out of the room.

192

Rosa shook herself like a dog. Her hair, which had been loosened by the struggle, cascaded down her back. She had been cut in the arm by some of the broken glass on the floor. People gathered round her. As she stood there looking at the blood upon her arm her eyes slowly filled with tears.

SIXTEEN

When Mischa had left the room, Annette had been in two
minds about whether to run after him or to spring upon Rosa.
Now having done the one, she had no thought but to do the
other. She ran through the door and found herself in an empty
room. She ran straight through a door on the other side and
into another room out of which a flight of stairs led down. She
ran down the stairs and then paused to listen. All the rooms
were brightly lighted, but there seemed to be complete silence
in the house. Then somewhere away to her right she heard a
door closing. The room in which she stood gave her no access
in that direction. She ran straight ahead into the next room
and found a door on the right side. She ran through another set
of rooms, breathless, her feet scarcely touching the surface of
the soft carpets; then a final doorway suddenly and unexpectedly let her out into the street.

After the lights within it was very dark, and the night was
enormous and silent with an intensity which for a moment
made her pause in awe. She was in an unfamiliar street. It was
a damp night, with rare stars. It was not raining, but it had
been, and a street lamp some way off streaked the roadway
with reflections. Annette began to walk slowly towards the lamp.
Her thin-soled shoes stuck to the pavement at every step.

As she neared the lamp she saw a figure ahead walking
slowly. With a mixture of terror and triumph she slackened her
pace. For a while Mischa walked on, and Annette followed
twenty paces behind him. He was carrying his jacket and had
rolled up his shirt sleeves, and walked with his head thrown far
back. She did not dare, she had no wish even, to catch him up.
To walk in this way behind him seemed to Annette already a
sufficient marvel. She walked after him softly, resolutely, tenderly, like a hunter; and after a minute she knew that he had
heard her footsteps. She walked on in a dream with both hands
clasped at her bosom to keep the torn dress in place.

194

After another minute he paused, and without looking round he made a curious gesture with one hand which Annette understood at once. Eagerly she sped forward and as she caught him up he drew her against him and they walked on so for a while with Mischa's arm about her shoulder. Annette was in a daze of beatitude. There was no one in the streets, which were silent except for the soft sticky sound of their footsteps and the irregular tap-tap of water dripping from the trees. Wet leaves leaned down above their heads. A drop of water fell on to Annette's shoulder and ran down between her breasts. They walked through a square. The dripping sound, which at another time would have made Annette sad, seemed to her now the very voice of the spring. The air was soft and warm and the springtime was falling off the trees and rolling in cool drops upon her skin. Then suddenly there was a clear distant sound, and then another – and then again the silence.

'A bird!' said Annette.

'Yes,' said Mischa.

'Why, it's morning!' said Annette.

She looked up, and the sky was changing to a dark overcast grey. She turned towards Mischa and found that now she could just see his face. He looked so melancholy that Annette wanted straightaway to take him in her arms. She felt, and with it a deep joy, the desire and the power to enfold him, to comfort him, to save him. She stopped walking and turned to face him. Mischa withdrew his arm from her shoulder and looked at her or past her with a patient vacant look. Now that the contact between them was broken Annette did not dare to touch him; with a gesture of helpless abandonment she let her hands drop from her bosom and the torn bodice of the dress fell towards her waist revealing two extremely round and white breasts. For a moment Mischa stood and contemplated her, as she rose like a mermaid out of the sea-green sheath of her dress. Then he sighed and very gently stretched out one hand and drew a finger down the outside contour of one breast.

After this he turned and walked on. Annette trembled, gathered her dress up and followed him, walking a pace or two behind. Mischa stopped and began fumbling in his pocket for keys. Annette saw that they were standing outside a garage.

'Is this where you keep your car?' asked Annette.

'Yes,' said Mischa. He was pressing the key into the lock.

'It's a long way from the house,' said Annette.

'No,' said Mischa, 'the house is here.' He pointed above their heads and Annette saw a line of lighted windows. They had come round in a circle. She shuddered.

'Let's go quickly,' she said. Mischa opened the door of a low grey car and she got in. The light came up on the dashboard, the engine gave a low purr rising to a roar, and then they were away.

The powerful headlights of Mischa's car showed to Annette first a long unfolding series of familiar streets, then a series of unfamiliar streets, then a great main road, and at last green hedges and avenues of trees and grass verges scattered with primroses and stained white with chalk. The car was climbing.

'Wrap that rug round yourself,' said Mischa.

Annette curled up in the front seat with the rug tucked about her knees. In the dim mysterious light that came from the dashboard she could see his profile. He never looked at her. She tried to remember, but could not, whether it was his blue eye or his brown eye which was nearest. It was too dark to see. Once they reached the open country the car leapt forward like a mad thing. An indefinite time passed. A grey hazy light showed woods and villages which touched the car for an instant and flashed by. But within, there was a deep quiet. Annette moved, and her knee touched Mischa's side. She said nothing, but as the speedometer needle reached seventy, she felt herself to be in paradise. She had never been so happy in her life before.

The car was descending. The wheels were grating sharply upon gravel and then grinding upon stones. Then suddenly Mischa began to brake violently and the car came bucking to a standstill. He turned off the engine. With the abrupt ending of its roar Annette could not at first realize whether what succeeded it was a silence or not. A thick mist surrounded them. Mischa stepped out of the car. Annette uncurled her legs. She felt very stiff. She opened the door and a cold wind blew straight into her face. She wished that the journey had not ended. She found herself standing upon damp stones and stumbled and almost fell. Mischa had moved ahead of her and taken a few steps. Then he stood still. A strange roaring sound was ringing in Annette's ears. It was very close, it was deafening. She took a step forward. Then she realized what it was.

196

Mischa had driven the car almost into the sea. He was standing now with the waves breaking at his feet.

Annette was completely dazed. She came down to stand beside Mischa, picking her way carefully across a line of crackling shells and yielding seaweed. It was a beach of large flat stones which crunched awkwardly underfoot. Annette felt suddenly in danger. The mist hemmed them in. She looked back towards the car. Only the tip of the radiator was visible behind her. The rest was lost in the mist. She looked towards the sea. She could see just as far as the place where the waves appeared out of the grey wall, already beginning to curl over and fall. They crashed violently upon the stones, came foaming forward in a great sheet of water, and then withdrew, drawing the beach after them with a rattling grinding sound. The endless rhythmical noise covered Annette and held her for a while motionless and appalled. Her hand at her breast became one with the intense beating of her heart. Then she turned to look at Mischa.

The amazement which had gripped her she read again upon his face. His lips were parted and his eyes seemed to start from his head. He was staring at the waves like a man cornered by a strange animal. Terror and fascination were upon his brow. When Annette saw him she was yet more afraid. He was breathing hard and every now and then his mouth moved as if he were saying something the sound of which was lost in the roar of the sea. Already the water was covering his shoes. Then he bent down, plunged his hand into the foam at his feet, and put his fingers to his lips. He licked his lips, tasting the brine.

'Mischa!' said Annette. She could hardly hear her voice, so deafening and continuous was the clatter of the waves upon the stones. He paid no attention. Perhaps he had not heard or perhaps he had forgotten that she was with him. Annette felt suddenly that she was alone upon the beach. The mist was lifting a little and the daylight was growing. Now she could see beyond the breaking point of the waves where the great rollers were coming in, their backs glistening in the silver light of the mist and the daybreak. Everything about her was beginning to glisten and become radiant with the unseen sun. She turned about and felt but could not hear the stones shifting and groaning under her feet. She was wet to the ankles. In an agonizing flash of memory the events of the night came back to her. She saw the fish lying struggling upon the dry cushions and upon the carpet. She wanted to weep, to scream; above all she wanted Mischa's attention.

'Mischa!' cried Annette, and seized him by the arm. He shook himself and moved away from her, his lips still moving, without turning his head.

Annette looked at him for a moment, her face screwed up with pain. Then gathering up her long skirt she turned from him and with a loud cry she began to run into the sea. After three stumbling steps through the withdrawing sheet of foam the next wave struck her at the knee. Annette kept her balance and managed to take another step. With an icy shock the water was swirling violently about her waist. She cried out shrilly at the intense cold. She saw the next roller rising above her. Her feet left the ground. Then she felt a fierce jerk upon her arm and Mischa was dragging her back out of the sea. Annette struggled, and for a moment they swayed to and fro upon the stones, and the great wave drenched them. Then as Mischa pulled her on, she slipped, grating her leg upon the shingle, and an instant later he had dragged her, half running and half slithering on her knees, well up beyond the water line.

Mischa turned on her. 'You little idiot!' he shouted, and shook her violently.

Annette sat down upon the stones. She was almost beyond thought and feeling. Her leg was hurting. She wanted nothing now but to be left alone. 'Go away,' she said to Mischa.

Mischa leaned over her with the face of a demon. He pulled her to her feet and dragged her to the car. 'Get into the back seat,' he shouted, 'and take your clothes off. Then put this coat on and put the rug round you.'

Somehow, trembling with cold, Annette slid out of the remnants of her green dress and for a moment she was naked, with one long damp leg trailing behind her on the stones and the other in the soft warmth of the car. Then she slipped on Mischa's velvet smoking-jacket, which had been left behind and was quite dry. She gathered the rug about her and collapsed on to the back seat. Then she saw Mischa. He had taken off his shirt and was wringing the water out of it. His chest and shoulders were entirely covered with long black hair which clung close to his body now in damp streaks. The hair of his head, darkened by the water, streamed down each side of his face and water-drops stood upon his cheeks like tears. When Annette saw this she began to cry.

With a tremendous jolt the car started. Annette closed her eyes, feeling the wet tyres slipping and grinding upon the shingle. The mist had turned from grey to silver and now to gold. Through clouds of gold they climbed up to the main road, and the long drive home had begun. The roar of the engine rose to a crescendo and Annette's tears flowed without intermission. She had never felt so wretched in her life before. By the time she was able to control herself a little and look at the back of Mischa's head, from which the sea-water was still dripping, they were passing through the outskirts of London. Mischa said nothing until, as they were nearing the Thames, he said, 'You'd better put your own clothes on again before you go in.'

Annette could hardly attach meaning to his words, but she managed, for the last time, to make the rags of the green dress cling about her. Then she pulled the velvet jacket on again. As she completed this operation she saw with astonishment that they were outside the house in Campden Hill Square. The engine stopped and made a terrible silence. Mischa got out and opened the door of the car.

'I can't go in there,' said Annette in a clear voice.

'Come along,' said Mischa. Again she had the feeling that he was not looking at her, that he was looking past her or through her. Annette unpacked herself awkwardly and hobbled out on to the pavement. Mischa went up to the door and rang the bell. Then he got into the car and drove away, leaving Annette standing on the pavement.

She stood there for a moment in a trance of misery, clutching Mischa's coat about her. Then she climbed up the steps and opened the door, which was unlatched. She began to trail up the stairs. As she passed Hunter's room he emerged and watched her. He said nothing. When Annette reached the landing below her own room she saw Rosa standing at the top of the flight of stairs. The door into Annette's room stood open. If only I could get that far, thought Annette. She was unable to focus her eyes on Rosa. She realized that she had the most terrible headache. She leaned against the banister to rest. Rosa was standing beside the door of her room like a fatal archangel.

'Wherever have you been, Annette?' asked Rosa.

Annette could think of nothing to say. She just felt too tired, far too tired. She pulled herself up another step. Then Rosa saw Mischa's coat.

'Annette —' said Rosa, and then stopped. For a moment the house trembled. Hunter began to say something inaudible on the landing below.

Suddenly Rosa turned into Annette's room and began to drag open the drawers of her dressing-table. She seized an armful of clothes and hurled them down into Annette's face. Then pulling out one of the drawers entire she upended it at the top of the stairs. A surge of silk and nylon came cascading down.

'Don't!' cried Annette. She took a step back and then tried to spring up the remaining stairs. But weakened as she was by cold and exhaustion her hands were slipping on the banisters and her feet slithering on the soft torrent of clothing. She lost her balance, fell heavily backwards, and crashed violently upon the landing at Hunter's feet.

Rosa, who had given a cry of alarm when she saw Annette fall, began to pick her way down, kicking the clothes aside. Annette was sitting on the landing rocking herself to and fro. She began to let out a high-pitched wail.

'Oh God!' said Hunter. 'Oh, my God!'

He tried to help Annette up, but she shook herself free and fell back wailing more than ever. 'I think,' she sobbed out, 'I think my leg's broken' – and she abandoned herself to grief. Rosa came and sat beside her upon the floor. Hunter could see that in a moment she was going to start crying too.

'Oh, my God!' said Hunter. He made for the telephone.

SEVENTEEN

There had been complete silence for some time in Peter Saward's room. It was late in the afternoon and the lamp on his desk had been lit for more than half an hour. Outside the window a sad green light still lingered under the plane tree. Peter was never anxious to pull the curtains. He was not afraid of the spirits who come to press against lighted windows. He had laid his pen aside and was looking gloomily at the sheets of hieroglyphs. They were as impenetrable as ever. At last he stacked them into a neat pile. Then he reached out for his paper-knife and drew towards him a pair of thick volumes which had just arrived from Paris. He looked at his watch. He began to cut the pages. A short time passed.

There was a knock on the door, and Mischa Fox came in. 'I'm late,' he said. 'I'm sorry.'

'That's all right,' said Saward. 'I haven't been wasting my time!' He swung his chair round and Mischa sat down on the floor at his feet. They sat for a short while without speaking, Mischa looking moodily into the corner and Peter Saward studying Mischa.

'You're looking tired,' said Peter Saward.

Mischa shook his head. 'Everybody has been going mad as usual!' he said.

'You make them mad,' said Peter.

Mischa considered this. 'I don't make *you* mad,' he said. He looked up at Peter. 'Did you hear what happened at the party after you left?'

'Yes,' said Peter Saward. 'Rainborough came and told me.' He frowned and shook his head.

'Ah, well —' said Mischa. He spoke with the air of someone who has got over with an unpleasant duty and can now get on to brighter matters. 'Did you get the photographs?'

'Yes,' said Peter. He pulled out from a drawer in his desk a large shabby book with a green cover. The book bumped to the floor and Peter followed it to sit beside Mischa. Mischa was already turning the pages, almost tearing them in his eagerness.

'Oh, splendid,' he cried, 'these are the best ones I've ever seen! So detailed, and not just the usual things. How clever of you, Peter!' He was like a child in his delight, he almost clapped his hands, and his face was transfigured by a look of mingled joy and pain, quite unlike the tense expression of irritated distress which it had worn a moment ago.

'Oh, if you knew, Peter,' said Mischa, 'how this moves me. How astonishing photographs are! There is a thing in my heart which these pictures touch and which will soon be restored to me. I feel it turning already. What a miracle it is to feel that, after all, nothing dies.'

Peter Saward was sitting awkwardly upon the floor, his arm resting on the seat of the chair. He was absorbed in watching Mischa. A sea of books surrounded them both.

Mischa had paused over a photograph. 'Do you see that little street?' he said. 'There was a shop there, you can almost see the edge of it, where I used to buy sweets. Our house was *that* way. There was a street and a square and then the street where we lived.' He turned another page.

'Now *here*,' said Mischa, '*you* should be able to tell me where this is! Can you say what would be just round this corner?' He showed Peter Saward one of the pictures.

Peter reflected for a moment. 'Your school?' he suggested.

'That's right!' cried Mischa. He was so delighted by this he almost embraced Peter. 'Do you know,' he said, 'since I last saw you I've remembered the name of the German schoolmaster, the one I was trying to think of. He was called Kuneberg.'

'Kuneberg,' said Peter Saward. He looked at Mischa, feeling again the puzzlement and tenderness with which these curious encounters always filled him. Mischa was a problem which, he felt, he would never solve – and this although he had got perhaps more data for its solution that any other living being. Yet it seemed that the more Mischa indulged his impulse to reveal himself in these unexpected ways to Peter, the more puzzling he seemed to become. It was now a long time since Mischa had taken it into his head to talk to Peter about his childhood; and since he had started to talk he had sketched a

202

picture of the most astonishing detail. At first Peter had not been at all sure that everything that Mischa told him was true; now he was certain that it was true as Mischa could make it and that the pursuit, here, of exactness and completeness was for him a terrible necessity.

Sometimes when they were together Mischa would sit for minutes on end trying to remember something, such as the name of his schoolmaster – and at such times his face would pucker and contract and become for the moment like the face of a child. It was Mischa who had suggested that a really good set of photographs might aid his memory further – and Peter Saward had been able to obtain some from a friend at the Warburg Institute.

'And here,' said Mischa, he had before him a picture of a fountain, 'there was a bronze fish. How strange, I had forgotten this completely! You can't see him here, he's on the other side. And the water came, not out of his mouth but out of his eyes. I remember asking my mother why he was crying. And in *that* square,' he went on, turning a page, 'there used to be a big fair every autumn. It was a terrible thing, that fair.' He fell silent suddenly, biting his lip.

'Why?' asked Peter Saward.

'There were – competitions, side-shows,' said Mischa, 'the children would all take part. And do you know what they would give us as prizes? Little chickens, a day old.'

'Oh?' said Peter Saward.

'Well, just that,' said Mischa. 'We would play with them until in a day or two they died. They could not survive. Everyone knew that. The fairmen knew, my parents knew —' His voice died away. Peter Saward looked at him quickly for a moment. Mischa's eyes had filled with tears. Peter Saward was not unduly startled. During these strange conversations Mischa often wept.

'I remember that so clearly,' said Mischa, 'the first time. I was very small. I could not understand what had happened to my chicken. Someone explained, as if it were the most ordinary thing.'

Peter Saward was silent. He felt, as he so frequently did during Mischa's reminiscences, tormented in some incomprehensible way.

'After that,' said Mischa, 'I watched other animals to see if they would die. But no – one does not see animals die. One is not so privileged. Even dead animals one does not see. Think of all the creatures that there are which live their lives about us, birds and animals and all kinds of insects. Helpless creatures and who do not live for long. Yet one hardly ever sees one dead. Where do they go to? The surface of the world ought to be covered with dead animals. When I thought about this,' said Mischa, 'I used sometimes to –'

'To what?' said Peter Saward after a moment.

'To kill animals,' said Mischa. He was sitting perfectly still, one knee raised and one leg curled under him. He stared through the wall as if he were seeing the past.

'Why did you do that?' asked Peter, very softly, speaking to Mischa's thought.

'I was so sorry for them,' said Mischa. 'They were so defenceless. Anything could hurt them. I couldn't – stand it.' Mischa's voice became almost inaudible. 'Someone gave me a little kitten once,' he said, 'and I killed it. I remember.'

Peter Saward looked at him again and looked away. He transferred his gaze to Mischa's hand, which lay on the carpet near to his own. It was trembling slightly, and to Saward's disturbed imagination it looked like some small and helpless creature. He shook his head. This was not the first time that he had been told of such matters. He asked himself what demon drove Mischa continually to uncover and to torture this strange region of sensibility – and as he did so he reflected yet again how strangely close to each other in this man lay the springs of cruelty and of pity.

'So poor and defenceless,' Mischa murmured. 'That was the only way to help it, to save it. So it is. If the gods kill us, it is not for their sport but because we fill them with such an intolerable compassion, a sort of nausea. Do you ever feel,' he turned to Saward, 'as if everything in the world needed your – protection? It is a terrible feeling. Everything – even this matchbox.' He took it from his pocket and held it up in front of them.

'No!' said Saward.

Mischa stared at him still for a moment, unseeingly, his eyes focused on the past. Saward, his attention shifting from the blue to the brown eye and back again, was not at once aware that Mischa was now watching him with a look of amusement.

'Oh, Peter,' cried Mischa, 'how patient you are! How good you are to me!' He was laughing. He sprang to his feet. He dropped the matchbox and kicked it expertly into the air as it fell. It sailed up and landed on the very top of the highest bookshelf.

'Let it stay there!' cried Mischa. 'Let it perish! Let it rot! What do we care?' He took Saward by the wrist and pulled him from the floor.

'Now, about these hieroglyphs, Peter,' said Mischa. He reached out and took one of the sheets and stood for a moment looking at it, his hand on Saward's shoulder. It seemed just then to Saward that Mischa was about to read out to him the things that were written upon the sheet. He could hardly bring himself to believe that Mischa could not understand it. As he looked down at the writing, with his brown eye visible, and his sallow hawk-like face, he seemed suddenly to Saward to be the very spirit of the Orient, that Orient which lay beyond the Greeks, barbarous and feral, Egypt, Assyria, Babylon.

'You should leave them now,' said Mischa. He spoke with authority. 'You'll never work them out. There will be a bilingual stone soon.' He threw the sheet back on to the desk and turned to face his friend. 'I have to go now,' he said.

Peter Saward felt sad. He had hoped for a longer visit. 'Will you take the photos with you?' he asked.

'No, you keep them,' said Mischa. He picked up the green book and laid it on the desk. 'I shall only look at them here. I keep my childhood with you.'

'Thank you,' said Peter Saward. He didn't want Mischa to go. He tried to think of some way of detaining him.

'Peter —' said Mischa.

'Yes?' said Peter Saward hopefully.

'Did Rainborough tell you — about the fish?'

'Yes,' said Peter Saward.

'Well —' said Mischa. He paused a moment, not looking at Saward, 'Good-bye, then.'

The door closed behind him. Peter Saward put away the paper-knife and took out his notebook; but it was a long time before he was able to write anything down. He wished that he had managed to say something to Mischa about Rosa. But what could he possibly have said?

EIGHTEEN

Rainborough was standing at the bottom of his garden contemplating the wistaria. From the wistaria he shifted his gaze to the daffodils, from there to the primulas, from there to the roses, which were already showing small and timid buds, and from there back again to the wistaria. The destruction of the wall was due to begin tomorrow. It was not this, however, which was chiefly occupying Rainborough's mind. Since the events of Mischa's party, now two days ago, Rainborough had not been near his office. He had rung up to say that he was taking some annual leave. After that he had answered no phone calls and had spent most of the previous afternoon sitting by the drawing-room window looking into the garden.

It was by the morning's post that he had received a letter from Sir Edward Guest saying that, as no doubt he knew, Sir Edward would, with much regret, shortly be retiring and that G. D. F. Evans had been nominated as his successor. Sir Edward enjoined upon Rainborough the importance of giving Evans the support of his, Rainborough's, unique gifts and experience in the crucial period of SELIB's development that lay ahead. Hereat Rainborough had the dubious satisfaction of knowing that he might have foreseen what would happen and that if he had troubles they were certainly ones which he had brought upon himself. It had been a bitter morning.

It was now the afternoon. Rainborough had by this time reviewed his career in detail, beginning at his kindergarten, and framed a number of unpleasant but not very new or original generalizations about himself. As this occupation was merely uncongenial and he suspected not even intended to be constructive, he soon transferred his energy to the more invigorating task of blaming others. The villain of the piece was of course Miss Casement; for although Rainborough could not rationally imagine that everything that had occurred had been planned and executed by her in detail, yet her peculiar treachery was the symbol of the whole catastrophe. Rainborough speculated idly as to whether it was through the defeat of Miss Perkins or by an alliance with her that the elevation of Evans had taken place. What was clear was that Miss Casement had decided, even without undue haste, that her superior was not a worthy vessel in which to embark her own ambition. Rainborough savoured carefully the impossibility of his position — and concluded that he would have to resign. At having been, as he put it to himself, outwitted by Miss Casement, he felt extreme chagrin — but his regret at the collapse of yet another section of his career was misted over by a dull fatalistic melancholy. His only other reaction, he was surprised to discover, was a sort of sadness and frustrated curiosity at the thought that when he left SELIB he would not see Miss Casement again.

As Rainborough returned his gaze to the wistaria, the fate of his garden came once more into his consciousness. He felt almost a gloomy satisfaction at the thought of all these disasters happening at once. On the following morning rough men would be trampling on the flowers and uprooting the wistaria. Rainborough had already decided to go into the country for several days. He had no wish to be present when the wall came down. He had intended, indeed, to be gone already; but still he lingered. I ought to pick all the flowers, he thought to himself, before they get beaten down. He stooped and plucked a daffodil. But then it suddenly seemed pointless, and he threw it back on to the earth. Perhaps he should have spent his time transplanting all these things; but there was nowhere to put them, and anyway it was the wrong time of year. He surveyed the scene. Then without premeditation he reached out and seized a clump of daffodils, crushing the long strong leaves together in his hand. He uprooted it and threw it on to he lawn. He advanced on to the flower-bed and began to trample about wildly, kicking out at plants and bushes, until one end of the bed was completely laid waste. At last he paused and looked at the wistaria. It was extremely strong and old. He put his hands round the trunk and pulled at it without making it as much as shiver. His right hand was still very tender and would not bear much pressure. He took a spade and began to dig at the root. The roots were as extensive and knotty as the branches. Rainborough took off his coat. He was sweating and panting.

He was still looking at the wistaria with an expression of tragic determination when the garden gate upon his left flew open. Rainborough was in the mood for portentous happenings. He turned hopefully. The visitor was Miss Casement. She was dressed in a coat of fine checks, and her make-up, which had become a shade darker, announced that the season was now to be thought of as early summer. She propped the garden gate open with her foot and stood dramatically in the gateway with the air of one posing for *Vogue*. Behind her in the road Rainborough could descry an extremely long red object which he made out to be a sports car. Rainborough had not seen Miss Casement since the episode behind the tapestry. When and how she had returned from Mischa's party he knew not.

'Well, my dear Agnes,' said Rainborough, 'this is an unexpected delight!'

Miss Casement stood for a moment hesitating, not knowing whether to be pleased or not at this unforeseen familiarity. She suspected Rainborough of sarcasm, a device which she herself could neither use nor counter. She advanced into the garden and the gate banged to behind her. Then she saw the carnage upon the flower-bed.

'Come here,' said Rainborough. Miss Casement, ready to melt, but not yet melting, came.

'Help me to uproot this damned wistaria,' said Rainborough.

'But why —' said Miss Casement.

'The wall's coming down,' said Rainborough briefly. 'What we need is an axe.' In a moment he had fetched one from the shed. He put it into Miss Casement's hand. She stood there staring at him, fingering her silk scarf with one hand and holding the axe in the other.

'I can't use it,' said Rainborough, 'because of the burn. Here — a couple of good hard blows across that root should do it.' He cleared away a little soil with his foot and pointed to the place.

Miss Casement plunged forward. The newly turned soil covered her smart tan shoes and her check coat was trailing on the ground. With a look of extreme fierceness she lifted the axe and brought it down three times across the thick root. Pierced to its golden interior, it was almost severed.

Rainborough was thinking of Clytemnestra. 'That'll do,' he said. 'Now we'll pull together at the trunk.'

He stood with Miss Casement, their feet deep in the earth, and side by side they began to pull. Rainborough inhaled a powerful smell of soil and Bond Street perfume. His bared left arm was braced against the tweedy sleeve of her coat, and their shoulders were glued together. Rainborough groaned. The wistaria was very strong. Then suddenly with a rending sound the trunk gave way and the great fan of branches came heeling over away from the wall. Rainborough and Miss Casement fell sharply backwards into a heap of upturned earth and uprooted flowers, and a great network of tiny leaves and twisted branches subsided to cover them.

Rainborough sat up, thrusting his head through the foliage. He saw before him the devastated surface of the wall, suddenly alive with hundreds of insects. He could feel something walking on his neck. He shook himself violently. Beside him Miss Casement was reclining on one elbow, trying to disentangle a piece of wire which had somehow got stuck into her coat. Her face was smudged with earth. Rainborough thought she looked rather improved.

'Are you all right?' he asked.

'Fine!' said Miss Casement without much conviction.

Rainborough reached out and took her hand, which was temporarily disengaged.

It was that moment which Annette chose to announce her presence by a discreet cough. Rainborough and Miss Casement turned about, their heads emerging from the tangle of leaves and boughs. Then they began to scramble to their feet. This was not easy. Annette, who was standing just outside the drawing-room doors, did not attempt to come to their aid. She was leaning on a pair of crutches and had one of her legs in plaster. She watched their struggles with interest.

At least Rainborough got to his feet and pulled Miss Casement after him without overmuch ceremony.

'Oh, let me *go*,' said Miss Casement, dragging herself free. Ignoring Rainborough and Annette, she began to examine the condition of her stockings and of a much-pleated nylon petticoat, a large area of which Rainborough could now see from the corner of his eye.

'What on earth are you doing?' asked Annette.

'Never you mind!' said Rainborough crossly. 'What have *you* been doing?'

'I fell downstairs,' said Annette.

Rainborough drew his hand across his brow. He could feel the earth mingling with his perspiration and coursing in muddy streaks down the side of his face. He felt a powerful desire to go indoors and lie down. 'Nothing serious, I hope?' he asked Annette.

'No,' she said, 'it's not even broken. They put everything in plaster these days.'

'Oh, do you two know each other?' said Rainborough. 'Miss Cockeyne, Miss Casement.'

'I believe I noticed Miss Cockeyne at the party,' said Miss Casement. She produced a pocket mirror and tried, with dabs of a damp finger, to remove some of the dirt from her face.

Annette smiled vaguely and turned back to Rainborough. 'I was wondering if you could put me up for a few days, John,' she said.

Rainborough stared at Annette. Miss Casement stopped what she was doing and stared at Rainborough.

'Why? How can I?' said Rainborough.

'Well, no one will help me,' said Annette, sounding pathetic. 'I can't go back to Campden Hill Square. Rosa won't have me.'

'I can hardly believe that,' said Rainborough. 'Where were you last night?'

'In a hotel,' said Annette, 'but it was so depressing and everyone stared at me so.'

'I'm just leaving for the country,' said Rainborough. 'I've got my rooms booked.'

'Is it far?' said Miss Casement. 'I'll take you there in my car.'

'Your car?' said Rainborough.

'Yes, it's new,' said Miss Casement. She opened the garden gate and propped it open with a stone. The long red object was once more visible. 'An M.G.,' said Miss Casement modestly.

'Don't go away and leave me, John,' said Annette. She was beginning to sound tearful.

Rainborough looked at the car and suddenly he felt weak at the knees. He was unable to drive himself. He adored women who could.

'I can't do anything with this leg,' Annette added.

'When the plaster hardens,' said Miss Casement briskly, 'you'll easily be able to walk with a stick. A friend of mine had an accident skiing, and she managed to walk perfectly well with her leg in plaster.' She shook her powder puff stylishly and then brushed the particles of powder off her coat. 'Are you coming, John?' she said. Her face was as bright as new.

'Look,' said Rainborough desperately to Annette, 'don't be foolish. We'll take you back to Campden Hill Square in the car.'

'It's a two-seater!' said Miss Casement.

'I'm not going anywhere!' said Annette fiercely. 'If you go away I shall stay here alone!'

'Excuse me,' said Rainborough, 'I must just go inside.' He ran through the drawing-room doors. For a wild moment he thought of rushing out of the front door and hailing a taxi. But his feet took him up the stairs. Coldly, he packed his case.

When he came back to the drawing-room Annette was inside reclining upon one of the settees. She looked at him with wide cool eyes. She saw the suit-case. 'Good-bye, John,' said Annette. 'Have a nice time in the country. Shall I forward your letters?'

'No,' said Rainborough. 'Can I do anything for you before I go?'

'Give me a cigarette,' said Annette.

Rainborough put the cigarette-box beside her.

'I suppose,' said Annette, 'that this is one of those random elements that you mentioned at the party?'

'Random as hell,' said Rainborough. He went into the garden. He could see Miss Casement sitting outside at the wheel of the M.G. He kicked away the stone from the garden gate and plunged into the car. The two doors slammed together.

NINETEEN

The wall had come down, and the view from the drawing-room windows of John Rainborough's house now showed a foreground covered with piles of masonry and white dust, a middle distance of brick-stacks, cement-mixers, and piles of sand, and a background of Nissen huts, one façade of the hospital, extremely Victorian, and a number of advertisements which were distantly visible in Upper Belgrave Street together with the red flash of passing buses. A noise of hammering was interrupted by intermittent crashes and various machines were grinding in the background. Burly men, blanched with dust, walked boldly to and fro outside the windows and conversed loudly in a dialect which Annette found almost totally incomprehensible. She had been alone now for two days in Rainborough's house. The scene outside the window had begun to upset her so much that she had finally pulled the curtains and lived entirely by electric light. She spent her time in the drawing-room and had occupied it mainly in tears and reflection on recent events.

At that moment, however, Annette had a fresh cause for grief. 'Would be!' said Annette petulantly, talking to herself aloud under cover of the din, 'just when I need him! Selfish boy!'

She picked up again from the floor the letter from Nicholas which Hunter had brought her that morning, and started re-reading it. When Rosa had arrived by taxi a short while after Rainborough's departure, Annette had carried out her threat and had refused to move. Since then she had been waited on daily by Hunter. The letter from Nicholas, which had been received with such joy and perused with such disappointment, read as follows:

Hotel Vincent
Cannes

Écoute, ma sœur. I have just taken a very grave decision – and you, as always, shall be the first of our family to hear

212

of it. (And for the moment, little one, the last. Not a word to the Olympians!) I have decided to join the Communist Party. This is not a quick or random decision but the inevitable outcome of my whole life. I expect it won't surprise you. No time to explain now all the arguments. I'll tell you when I see you. Meanwhile I enclose a book list. About your chucking Ringenhall, by the way, *j'en suis ravi*. I bet you've learnt more since you left than you ever did while you were there. *Je te félicite.* I never wanted you to be an English Lady (you remember how we swore once we'd *never* be *English?*) or to waste time acquiring the *mœurs* of a defunct class. About the book list, not all these books are quite O.K. — but a modern education must include an understanding of Liberalism. It is necessary, dearest Sis, to *have been* a Liberal! I've put asterisks beside the books which are really all right.

I've a project for going to Greece in the vacation. *Si tu es sage tu viens avec.* Reunion *alla casa Francolini.* Then we proceed *en bagnole.* Look decent when you come for heaven's sake. I want you to make a good impression. (*Especially not trousers. D'ailleurs, puisque tu manques complètement de derrière, c'est pas intéressant que tu portes des pants!*) Details of all this later.

Again, not a word about the C.P. to the Olymps. They'll have a fit. I must break it gently. If you write say I'm 'becoming interested in social problems', ho ho!! Be good, Sis. *Je t'embrasse.*

Nicky

P.S. I'm just going mad about chess. Try to learn before we meet. Get yourself a good textbook.

'*Nom de Dieu,*' said Annette, '*ça c'est marrant!*' She threw the letter to the floor. 'Chess! The Communist Party! Just when I need his advice. He obviously hasn't even read my letter properly.'

She wondered whether she should cry again. She decided not to. She was getting tired of crying. She felt no particular surprise at Nicholas's letter. The warning about not telling the Olympians was customary, only it usually referred to a motor race.

Annette was still wearing Mischa Fox's velvet coat. She had derived what comfort she could from the presence of this object, which she drew closely about her, hiding her hands in the sleeves and her face in the upturned collar. The pockets had turned out to contain nothing except a packet of Turkish cigarettes, which Annette had smoked religiously. She had hoped for visions, but none had come. Her plans for the future, in so far as they existed, were exclusively connected with the moment when she would return this garment to Mischa. She could not imagine that it was indifferently or by accident that he had let her carry it away. She had been presented with a valuable hostage and she would surely be expected to use it.

The failure of Nicholas's letter to throw any light upon the situation made Annette restless and then desperate. She felt that she must act. She got up and began to move out into the kitchen, lifting her petrified limb step by step. It was as if some god had touched her and she were turning into a tree-trunk. The limb was hard and heavy, and the rest of her body, deprived of its usual freedom of movement, felt unshapely and soft. Annette wondered what it would be like to walk normally again, lightly putting one foot in front of the other. What a marvel! Yet human beings did it every day without a thought! I'll have a thick ankle, thought Annette. I'm marked for life now like Rosa. It's all over. What was all over she did not specify to herself, but the phrase was adequate.

She made some coffee. In the kitchen the sounds of destruction were less deafening. I must see Mischa! said Annette. But she did not want to see Mischa with one leg made of stone. She felt herself accursed. It was still three days to the time when the hospital, who had been unable to find a fracture and had diagnosed a severe sprain, had told her to return to have the plaster removed. Suddenly it occurred to Annette that there was nothing to stop her from removing the plaster herself. After all the hospital wasn't God. She left everything and began to search through drawers and cupboards looking for a tool. She found a large chisel and carried it back into the drawing-room. She sat down on the floor underneath one of the lamps, turned back the cuffs of Mischa Fox's jacket, and began to chip fiercely at the cast. It was extremely hard; and after about ten minutes she had merely succeeded in covering the carpet with white powder and making her leg look very ugly indeed.

'Oh, hell!' said Annette. She threw the chisel away and took her head in her hands.

At that moment footsteps were heard coming across the hall and the drawing-room door was opened cautiously. Calvin Blick put his head round it. Annette, who would have been indifferent just then to the arrival of the Devil himself, looked up furiously. 'Well?' she said to Blick.

'Dear me!' said Calvin. 'Whatever are you doing, Annette? Can I help?' He came and squatted near her on the floor.

'I want to get this damn thing off,' said Annette, 'but I can't.'

'That's not the way to do it, you know,' said Calvin. 'Allow me. What we need is a sharp knife.' He disappeared to the kitchen and came back bearing a large carving-knife.

'This will do the trick,' he said. 'But wait, let's put some newspaper down on the floor, shall we? That's right. Now just keep quite still. Here, hold on to this chair.'

Annette sat rigid and kneeling beside her Calvin took the petrified limb in one hand. He began to drive the knife deeply in at one end of the plaster.

'Don't cut into my flesh!' said Annette.

'Don't worry,' said Calvin. He drew the knife firmly along the length of her leg. Then he put his fingers into the fissure and pulled. The plaster began to crack apart. Annette pulled too. In a moment, very white and putty-like, her leg was revealed.

'Oh, good! Oh, thank you!' cried Annette. She jumped to her feet, but immediately uttered a cry of pain and sat down again on the floor.

'Better take it easy,' said Calvin. 'You'll need a stick for a day or two. Here, let me massage you. That will restore the circulation.'

He sat down and began to massage her, moulding the flesh with strong firm movements. Between his hands, from the thigh to the ankle, Annette felt her leg slowly coming back to life.

'Now move it a bit,' said Calvin. 'Good, now try standing up again.'

Annette stood up and took a step or two. Calvin had gone over to the window and was drawing back the curtains. The daylight flooded in. It was a pale sunless day with a very white light. Annette flinched from the light, and then hobbled over towards the window. Together they looked out. The garden was full of workmen who had gathered there to drink cups of tea. They stared curiously at Annette and Calvin.

'How extraordinary!' said Calvin. 'I wondered what the noise was!' He looked with a kind of delight upon the chaotic scene.

'Mr. Blick,' said Annette, 'did you come here to bring me a message from Mr. Fox?'

'A message?' said Calvin. 'No. That person is out of the country anyway, he's gone to America.'

'Oh!' said Annette. She had not thought of this possibility. 'When will he be back?'

'I've no idea,' said Calvin. 'In a few months maybe. One never knows.'

Annette's face became stony with pain and with the effort to conceal it. In that case there was no future. 'Why did you come then?' she asked.

'I came to fetch the coat,' said Calvin cheerfully. He indicated Mischa's velvet jacket.

Annette clutched it more closely about her. 'I won't give it to you,' she said.

'You will, in fact,' said Calvin, 'or would you rather that I took it by force?' His tone was cheerful and conversational.

'I won't give it to you,' Annette repeated.

Calvin turned slightly towards her. He took the sleeve of the coat lightly between a finger and thumb.

'Come now, Annette,' he said. The men in the garden were still watching them with interest.

Slowly Annette took off the coat. She threw it on the floor and kicked it. Then she walked away from the window. Calvin picked the coat up and dusted off the white plaster which was adhering to it. He prepared to go.

'Don't take on,' he said to Annette. 'The notion that one can liberate another soul from captivity is an illusion of the very young.'

'Go to blazes,' said Annette.

It was a few hours later. Annette stepped out of the house in Campden Hill Square and pulled the door to softly behind her.

She was holding a small package in her hand. She was glad that she had managed to slip in without meeting Rosa. She had no wish to repeat the uneasy interview of a few days ago. She had tiptoed up to her room. Everything there had been made neat and tidy again. There were even flowers upon the dressing-table. The jewels which had been on show, folded carefully in their velvet cloth, had been put into the top drawer together with the rest of the collection. Annette had poured them all into the leather bag in which she kept them when she travelled; and with this wrapped in a large handkerchief she had stolen from the house.

Limping heavily, she returned to the taxi which she had instructed to wait for her on the other side of the square.

'Where to now, miss?' said the taxi-driver.

'Lambeth Bridge,' said Annette. It was a warm and windy afternoon, and the taxi rattled away through a gale of blowing branches and white clouds. Blossoming trees greeted it from either side as it sped towards the river. Usually Annette enjoyed riding in a taxi. It made her feel as if she were taking part in a conspiracy. But today both fantasy and reality were darkened by the blackness of her mood. She lay back, and taking her leg on to the seat beside her began to rub it vigorously, imitating Calvin's movements. This made her leg, if anything, more painful, but it eased her heart.

They came to the river. Annette paid the taxi-driver and limped on to the bridge. She had chosen Lambeth Bridge because she thought it would be the least frequented of the bridges in central London; and in fact there were very few people about. The tide was in and the Thames was rushing beneath her, adorned with tiny waves and crests of white. She walked to the centre of the bridge, and took the leather bag out of her pocket. She looked down. It was a long way to the water. She felt suddenly rather faint, and had to hold on to the parapet, grating her wrists upon the stone. She wondered whether, if she threw the bag as it was, it mightn't perhaps float on the water. She decided she had better throw the jewels in one by one, or else strew them broadcast.

The sun came out from behind a cloud and the small waves far below were glistening as if the surface were already covered with gems. Annette opened the bag and drew a stone out at random. It was the large ruby. For the last time she fingered it

217

with love and pain. It was so light and insubstantial, it was as if the wind would blow it away. With a quick movement she flung it from her. It curled over and disappeared into the air. She did not see it hit the water. She took out another. It was a small but very perfect diamond that a diplomatic acquaintance of her father had given her in Switzerland. Already it was made of light. She threw it far out into the glittering space above the river and the same air spirit took it and it vanished. Annette was leaning excitedly over the parapet. Her lips were moist with saliva and her eyes were dazzled. She fumbled for another stone. She did not see Jan Lusiewicz until he was standing close beside her.

'What you doing now, Annette?' said Jan.

Annette started and shivered. Jan looked like a figure in a dream. 'I'm throwing my jewels into the river,' she said.

For a moment Jan did not seem to understand. Then a look of amazement and horror came over his face. In a scandalized splutter his English almost left him.

'You not do so!' said Jan. He reached across and imprisoned her right wrist.

'Why not?' said Annette, not resisting him. She had had rather too much fighting in the last few days. 'They're mine! You can throw one or two in if you like.'

'Why you throw them?' asked Jan, holding on.

'Because —' said Annette. She could not manage this one. 'Let go!' she said.

'Not!' said Jan. 'Why you throw jewels when I and my brother starve?'

'You're not starving,' said Annette. 'I'm sure you've got very good jobs. Let go of me or I'll shout for a policeman.'

Jan looked at her. Annette was excited, but she was calm compared with Jan. His face expressed by turns and all together distress, cunning, avarice and sheer astonishment.

'You give me some to throw,' said Jan.

'No!' said Annette. 'You wouldn't throw them, I know!' She felt a desperate need to get the jewels somehow into the river. If they didn't go in something terrible would happen.

They stood together, as if hand in hand, at the centre of the bridge, like a pair of lovers. Annette began to struggle in a surreptitious way, trying to twist her hand out of Jan's grip. As she moved she saw that a policeman was coming towards them along the opposite pavement. His tall peaceable form drew nearer and nearer. Annette relaxed. Jan saw the policeman.

'If you speak to policeman now, or later either,' said Jan, 'I will kill your brother!'

This threat was so unexpected, so terrible, and so terribly uttered that it froze Annette completely, and it did not occur to her until afterwards that it was an absurd menace uttered at random. They stood still, locked together and gazing into each other's eyes. The policeman passed on with a slow stride. For a moment they were alone on the bridge.

'Oh, you swine!' said Annette, in a misery of helplessness.

'You give me this now,' said Jan. 'I keep it for you till you are wiser.' He began to twist her wrist. With a gasp Annette let go of the bag, and at once Jan had left her at a run.

Annette looked after him until he disappeared along the Embankment. Then as she turned to leave the bridge she realized that she was still holding one jewel in her left hand. She opened her palm to see what it was. It was the white sapphire.

TWENTY

Rosa was sitting in the drawing-room thinking by turns about Annette, Mischa, and the *Artemis*. It was two days now since Annette had disappeared completely, and Rosa was feeling extreme remorse. Annette had been so intractable when she had gone to fetch her from John Rainborough's house that she had decided to let her stay there. Rosa had imagined that twenty-four hours of solitude would be enough to cure Annette of her refusal to return to Campden Hill Square. But Annette had dug herself in, and Rosa had had to send Hunter to wait upon her. On the third morning Hunter had arrived to find Annette gone, her bed not slept in, and only the remains of the plaster cast whitening the drawing-room floor. Since then no one had seen or heard of the girl. Rosa resolved to wait another day and then, if she could find out nothing, to telephone Marcia. Rosa did not look forward to this telephone call.

As for the *Artemis*, the situation of that journal seemed to have improved without having been very much clarified. As a result of Mrs Wingfield's intervention, a number of promises of money existed on paper amounting to nearly sixteen hundred pounds. Of these generous donors only two, Mrs Carrington-Morris and a Mrs Jolovitz, whom Rosa had identified as the lady in the mantilla, had so far paid up. With these monies Rosa had settled the bill of the paper merchant and one or two other items; there remained, however, the larger bill of the printer, to say nothing of debts of honour to various contributors to whom Hunter had unwisely promised fees. And even if the sums guaranteed eventually did materialize, they would only rescue the periodical from its immediate difficulties. What Rosa wanted, and what she had hoped that Mrs Wingfield would offer, was a regular subsidy.

Since the shareholders' meeting Rosa had called twice at Mrs Wingfield's house, but on each occasion Miss Foy had opened the door and announced in a loud voice, 'I'm afraid

Mrs Wingfield is indisposed,' after which she had added in a piercing whisper, 'She isn't really, you know!' – and then, with many gestures of frustrated goodwill to Rosa, closed the door.

Between Rosa and her brother, on the subject of the latest turn in the fortunes of the *Artemis*, there had been a mutual refraining from recrimination. Each had tried to spring a surprise on the other, and each was grateful not to be reproached for it. Concerning the future of the journal, Rosa had not yet been able to bring herself to torment Hunter. She felt that, for the moment, the boy had had enough.

As Rosa sat moodily turning these matters over she suddenly heard noises coming from upstairs. Hunter, she knew, had just gone out, so who could it be? The sound, as she listened, seemed to come from Annette's room. Rosa felt a thrill of relief. Annette must have come back! She jumped up and went to the bottom of the stairs and called. There was no answer. She began to mount, and as she went she rehearsed her good resolutions. Rosa was well aware that she had never taken the trouble to get to know Annette. Now some of the facts had been thrown in her face. The rest she would study henceforth with the patience which she ought to have displayed from the start. She knocked on the door and then opened it.

Reclining on the bed was Stefan Lusiewicz. Rosa stood there immobilized with astonishment. Then she came slowly into the room and shut the door. Stefan lay like an animated corpse, following her movements with his eyes.

'What do you want, Stefan?' asked Rosa. It was, as it happened, more than two days since she had seen the brothers. After the incident with Jan, Rosa had detected a certain coldness in her reception; but this had almost immediately vanished and everything had seemed to be as usual. She could not interpret Stefan's sudden appearance – but it chilled her blood.

'What is it?' she asked.

'Nothing,' said Stefan. 'Come near, Rosa.'

Rosa stood holding on to the door handle, as if it were a precious link with the outside world. 'Are you all right?' she asked.

'Very fine,' said Stefan. 'I take rest, that is all.' He stretched and yawned, changing his position. Then he laughed shortly. 'I

221

know you glad to see me, Rosa,' he said, 'but you not look so. Why you not smile?'

Rosa found herself trying to smile. It was almost impossible. 'You frightened me,' she said. This was terribly true.

'I bring my suit-case, see,' said Stefan. He pointed to a large case in the corner of the room.

Rosa looked at it and trembled. 'What's in that, Stefan?' she asked.

'What does man put in suit-case?' said Stefan. 'Pyjama, toothbrush, towel, vest – all like in English exercise book!' He laughed again.

'Look here,' said Rosa. 'Stop mystifying me, Stefan. What do you want?'

'I want nothing, I say,' said Stefan. 'You not ask Hunter all time what he want. I live here now, I stay here, this room my room. That girl Annette go away. I come. That is all.'

Rosa felt as if the temperature of her body were sinking violently. She tightened her grip on the handle of the door. 'You can't do that, Stefan,' she said. 'Annette is coming back to this room. In any case, this house belongs to Hunter and me.' It was an odd, almost apologetic, way of putting it.

Stefan was not smiling. 'It is big house,' he said. 'There is room for all.'

'Not for you,' said Rosa. 'You know Hunter wouldn't stand it. Anyway, it's impossible for every sort of reason.'

'If someone go,' said Stefan, 'it is Hunter to go, not me.'

'Oh, stop this nonsense!' cried Rosa. 'You must have gone mad. What about Jan? What about your mother?'

'Is nothing now,' said Stefan. His voice seemed suddenly several tones lower.

'What do you mean "is nothing"?' said Rosa. 'Try to speak English!'

'She is dead,' said Stefan. 'I clear her away like old sack. I bury her in the garden.'

'You're mad,' said Rosa.

'She is dead,' said Stefan, '*gaudeamus igitur*.'

'I don't believe you,' said Rosa. 'Where is Jan?'

'Jan is gone,' said Stefan. 'Jan is bad man. He go away. Will never come again, never.' He sat up suddenly. 'Now is only you,' he said.

Rosa sat down in a chair. She did not know what to think or what to believe. 'Stefan, tell me the truth,' she said.

'All this is truth,' said Stefan. 'If you not believe, what I can do? Go and look at our room. All is changed, all gone. Never again you see Jan or that old woman. All gone, I tell you, Rosa.' His voice now had the repetitive cadence of a lament.

'What are you going to do?' asked Rosa.

'I tell you hundred times,' said Stefan. 'I stay here. Now you are mother, brother, all. I stay with you.'

Rosa threw up her hands. 'It's not possible,' she said. 'Anyway, I don't understand. I just don't understand.'

Stefan, who had been sitting on the edge of the bed, came near to her and smiled for the first time.

'You soon understand all,' he said. He bent down towards her and his eyes blotted out the room. Without touching her he spoke very close to her face. 'I soon give up factory too.'

'And how will you live?' said Rosa.

'I live with you,' said Stefan. His voice was soft and caressing. 'You give up factory, and we live with your money. You are English lady, you have money, you tell me so yourself.'

'You're mistaken, Stefan,' said Rosa, looking into the cold eyes.

'We see that soon,' said Stefan. Then he laughed. 'Perhaps I joke about this. We see soon.'

A door closed downstairs. 'That's Hunter,' said Rosa.

Stefan stepped back. Then he began to fold himself lazily on to the bed until he was reclining once more. 'Go then,' he said, 'and tell Hunter that now I am here.'

Rosa left the room and began to go slowly down the stairs.

TWENTY-ONE

Hunter woke up and looked at his watch. It was only three. He had slept for an hour. Now he knew that he would not sleep again. He tossed about in an agony of discomfort. It was as if the room were disintegrating round him. He expected to feel things falling on his face. Then something did run across his cheek. He sat up, brushing it away with horror. It must have been a spider. He sat for a while with his hands round his knees. These three o'clock awakenings when one starts up, imagining that one has a mortal sickness; and indeed this is true. Life is that sickness, and at that cold hour one can realize it.

For Hunter this was the third night of sleeplessness. A hundred times during every night he heard the footsteps coming from upstairs towards his sister's door. He knew that this was imagination and that Rosa's door was locked. But he could not prevent himself now from getting up again and going to stand on the landing. He wanted very much to go and wake Rosa, but he knew that she would only send him away angrily. There was nothing to be said, nothing to be done. Rosa had not explained Stefan's presence in the house. She had only said to Hunter, 'Put up with him. He'll soon go away.' But Hunter strongly suspected that Stefan had no intention of going away. He could see that Rosa was afraid; and like a child that sees its mother upset, he felt the foundations of the world rocking. Especially he felt that he ought somehow to deal with the situation. The notion that Rosa was expecting something from him had increased since the previous afternoon, when she had suddenly asked him to go with her to the house in Pimlico. There had been nothing to see there but an empty room; which was what they had expected. But Hunter was both moved that Rosa should have depended on him, and terrified at the sense of responsibility which this dependence was beginning to awaken.

Since the arrival of Stefan, Rosa had given in her notice at the factory and had stopped working at once. It was as if she were clearing the decks for some terrible struggle. Only, Hunter thought, the protagonist might turn out to be not her but himself. He had a sense of being hemmed in by evil. This feeling, as he stood now in the darkness of the landing, listening for noises, became overwhelming. He went back into his own room and put the light on. He lit a cigarette. He wondered whether Rosa was asleep. What she now did with her days he did not know. She left the house early and returned late. He knew that she had called in vain on Mrs Wingfield, and that she had made an equally vain attempt to see Annette, who had been discovered to be staying in a hotel at Maidenhead. Annette had left the hotel just before Rosa arrived. Rosa had told him these facts, but without revealing her state of mind.

If only I could sleep, thought Hunter. Then in the morning I might know what to do. His bed, crumpled and undone, was the very image of sleeplessness. Hunter was beginning to know the real torture of insomnia — the terrible continuation of one day into another. I shall become ill, he told himself with relief. But then the twisting and turning of indecision began again. Ill or not, he must act. The centre of Hunter's anguish was the knowledge that he, and he alone, was in possession of the weapon which could destroy his sister's tormentor. Hunter had cherished, with anxious care but without much further reflection, the information which he had gained on the day of his visit to John Rainborough's office. The Lusiewicz brothers were born east of the Line. They were in England illegally. Rainborough had said that if this became officially known they would be deported. So, Hunter told himself, he had after all got the whip hand. But what was he to do with it? To hold a weapon is one thing and to strike is another.

Hunter was not a man much addicted to harming his fellows. The harm which Hunter had done in his life had usually been done accidentally in the course of seeking easy and unobtrusive ways forward for himself. He was an animal whose protection was not teeth but flight and camouflage. However just the cause, he shrank from the dealing of blows. He shrank in this case particularly because of the extreme obscurity of the situation: he was, as usual, in the dark about what exactly Rosa wanted, and whether she might not be right in thinking that Stefan would soon go away. Hunter also disliked the idea of harming anyone, however detestable, in this particular way. He would, he thought, have been more ready to act if there had been some definite crime which he could bring home to Stefan, and from which the punishment would follow automatically. But, on the one hand, what Stefan's crime consisted in was very unclear – Hunter shrank from considering how far his sister might not have brought all her troubles on herself – and on the other hand what Stefan would be punished for if Hunter moved would be the fact of having been born east of a certain arbitrary line. As Hunter very much disapproved of a world in which people were penalized for accidental facts of birth, he especially hated the notion of using such a weapon against even his worst enemy. There was, further, the practical difficulty of invoking this cruel power against Stefan without hurting a lot of innocent people as well. Hunter was alive to all this. A tender conscience was among his assets. Strong nerves unfortunately were not.

Neither had Hunter forgotten the card which Calvin Blick was holding in his hand. After the débâcle of the shareholders' meeting, Hunter had written to Calvin saying that he hoped that Calvin did not imagine that he had intended this and that he would be glad to see Calvin any time to discuss what should be done, as he did not regard the question of the *Artemis* as closed. Hunter did not like remembering this letter which he had written in a moment of panic, and which smelt both of servility and of disloyalty to Rosa. However, Calvin had not replied, so that here too Hunter was in the dark. This anxiety was strangely joined in his mind to the distress caused him by Stefan's presence in the house. It was as if these two menaces were echoes of each other – and although Hunter knew that he could not by destroying one destroy the other, yet the two conjoined to make him feel the urgency of his sister's peril; and in the background of it all stood the figure of Mischa Fox. It's all out of proportion, said Hunter to himself. The shapes that surrounded him, he told himself again and again, were grotesque shadows of realities; and he could perhaps have convinced himself of this if it had not been for the spectacle of Rosa's fear.

Hunter had been sitting on the edge of his bed with the light on for nearly an hour. Tears of misery and frustration were coursing gently down his cheeks and falling off on to his pyjamas. He got up at last and drank some water and put his face into the wash-basin. Then he said to himself, I can't stand this any longer. He went out again on to the landing. There was no sound from Rosa's room. He began to mount the stairs. The light from his bedroom showed him the stairway and his own enormous shadow sliding on ahead of him until it reached as far as Stefan's door. Silent and barefoot he followed it. At the door Hunter stopped. His terror made him unable to breathe quietly. He gave a sort of choking sound which he felt must be ringing audibly through the house. Then he tried the handle. The door was unlocked. In a moment there opened before him the dark void of the room. He stood upon the threshold, knowing that he must be clearly visible in silhouette from within, and as he stood there trembling he felt himself to be more victim than actor. He wondered if the Pole was awake. He had come to wake him — yet he was silencing his movements in a sweat of terror in case he should wake him inadvertently or find him already wakeful. The darkness and stillness of the room continued unbroken. The idea came into Hunter's head that perhaps Stefan had gone. He fumbled in the pocket of his pyjamas for a box of matches. He dropped two on the floor before he managed to make one strike. He moved the flaring flame away from his dazzled eyes and looked towards the bed. Before the tiny light went out he saw that Stefan was sitting up and looking at him.

If Hunter had seen a corpse quicken he would not have been more scared. He almost turned and bolted. A very dim illumination came as far as the doorway from his own door on the floor below. But in Stefan's room the darkness was like velvet. Hunter took a step back and struck another match. From the way in which he immediately found Stefan's eyes fixed on his own he felt sure that the Pole could see in the dark. The match went out. He sank on one knee.

'Listen — ' said Hunter. His voice, coming out of hours and hours of silence and darkness, seemed to him like a voice heard at the bottom of a well. As he spoke he knew that he had committed himself to action, and the fear that had been fluttering about him nestled down in his heart.

'Listen,' he said, 'I want to talk to you, Stefan.' He spoke very quietly, hardly above a whisper. He needed desperately to hear Stefan's voice, to be persuaded that it was not a demon

227

but a human being that lay before him; and as he unexpectedly uttered the Pole's Christian name he felt it as an appeal to the community of human beings with each other.

'What you want, coming here at night?' said Stefan. He also spoke softly – and as Hunter heard the hatred in his voice he thought: he believes I came to kill him. At this thought Hunter almost groaned aloud; and what he felt most immediately was the danger to himself.

'I mean you no harm,' said Hunter. This was a lie, but as he saw himself in the role of a murderer he had suddenly to say it.

'But you must leave this house,' he said. At this he struck another match. He needed to see Stefan's face.

The Pole was sitting bolt upright now and had cleared the bedclothes aside as one who prepares to defend himself. His long neck and white chest were bare, and there was no fear in his expression, only extreme venom.

'Why?' said Stefan.

'Because my sister wishes it,' said Hunter. The match went out.

'If your sister wish it she say it,' said Stefan. 'Is between me and her. You little boy keep out or you get hurt.'

Hunter felt a tide of incoherence rising within him – and at that moment the thing he feared most was not the violence of Stefan but the proximity of tears. He moved closer to the bed and pinched his fingers savagely upon his thigh to stop the tears.

'She does wish it and she has said it,' said Hunter. His voice was beginning to tremble. 'You get out of this house or you're the one who'll get hurt.' His face was screwed up in the darkness in an agony of self-control.

There was a sharp hissing sound and sudden light. Stefan had struck a match. It flared between them for a moment revealing Hunter's burning cheeks and eyes and the intent white face of the Pole.

'I am master in this house,' said Stefan. He said it in a slow almost contemptuous way which made Hunter breathless with anger.

'We – we – we'll see,' said Hunter, stammering with fury and confusion. 'I've given you a chance. You drive me to it. I can have you turned out, turned out of England if I want to. I know where you were born. It was east of that line. You know what that means, don't you? It's not legal for you to be here. If I tell

228

you'll be deported tomorrow. I give you warning. If you don't leave this house, I'll have you turned out of England.' At last hatred and anger had made him brave. He was leaning over the Pole and spitting the words into his ear.

There was a silence. As he waited for the reaction, Hunter's courage began to wilt. Then Stefan struck a match and lifted it between them like a torch with a gesture which was almost leisurely. His eyes pierced Hunter as if they were trying to brand him before the light was gone again.

'Listen you now,' said Stefan, and then his voice continued in the dark. 'I tell you something true. If you make such trouble for me I kill you.' He spoke slowly and there was something cold and objective about his tone which made it impressive. 'I not say this for threat. I tell you it as fact. If you do this thing I hate you so I kill you. I not want to perhaps, but I cannot stop myself. It will be so. I swear it by Holy Mother of God.'

Hunter rocked to and fro in the dark. He was very close to Stefan now. As he felt the reality of the threat spreading through his blood he shook in a crisis of helplessness and despair. 'No,' he said, 'no! You must leave this house! You must leave this house!' He rocked about and his breath came in a low humming moan.

Stefan struck another match. In the golden light their faces stared, close together, Stefan's tense with hatred and Hunter's crumpled with misery.

'I say I am the master here!' Stefan said. He whispered the words, but they echoed like thunder inside Hunter's head. Then, before the match was extinguished, Stefan's hand shot out and grasped a lock of Hunter's yellow hair. He drew Hunter's head back until the eyes were ready to spin from their sockets. For an instant he held him so. Then with a quick movement he brought the lighted match close to Hunter's face and set fire to the lock of hair.

The hair sizzled and flamed up. With a scream Hunter leapt to his feet. He beat his head with his hands. A sharp pain was searing his forehead. A terrible smell was in his nostrils. It was dark now, and Stefan was laughing. Hunter blundered towards the door. He almost fell out of the room and down the stairs towards the light, holding his head in his hands.

On the lower landing Rosa appeared in her nightdress. 'For God's sake, Hunter!' she cried. 'What is it?'

Hunter kept his forehead covered and pushed past her. 'It's nothing,' he said, 'I just hurt my head. It's nothing.' He went on down and into the kitchen. Rosa followed him in and shut the door behind her.

Hunter was fumbling awkwardly in a drawer. After a moment or two he let everything drop and turned round and buried his face in Rosa's shoulder.

TWENTY-TWO

Although Rosa did not know about Hunter's secret weapon, she had no difficulty in reconstructing in outline the events of the previous night. It was now 9 a.m. and she was drinking coffee and observing her brother, who was sitting with a white bandage tilted over one eye like a drunken maharajah and looking more wretched than Rosa had ever seen him look.

'Eat something, Hunter,' said Rosa. But Hunter just shook his head miserably.

Stefan, who had not yet carried out his threat of retiring from work, had disappeared at an early hour to the factory. As Rosa looked at her brother, she felt tempted to rush upstairs, throw Stefan's goods into the street, and barricade the door. But she knew that at the moment she was simply not able to do it. Hunter hung limply upon her spirit. He filled her with feelings of softness and despair. She needed some stronger ally before she could bring herself to be completely ruthless.

She had thought of going to Peter Saward for help. But what could Peter do? He, too, affected her with something of the same soft protective and yet helpless feeling that she had in relation to her brother. Saward had for her the dear authority of a father, and yet, too, something of a father's remoteness. In Rosa's mind he represented the sweetness of sanity and work, the gentleness of those whose ambitions are innocent, and the vulnerability of those who are incapable of contempt. He would be unable to conceive of such a character as Stefan Lusiewicz: more important, he would be unable to understand that part of Rosa herself which answered to Stefan; and Rosa had indeed very little wish, in this matter, to instruct him. She decided that only darkness could cast out darkness.

Her argument, if it was one, was designed merely to reach a conclusion which she had already reached on other grounds. Stefan had come from a place far outside the world of rules and reciprocal concerns and considerations in which Rosa mostly lived. Stefan did not belong to human society. This was why Hunter was powerless against him. The children of society could only be seared by such a contact. Nor could Rosa herself summon up the kind of strength required to do battle with such a being. Only some spirit which came out of the same region beyond the docility of the social world could do this work for her. Rosa knew that she must go and see Mischa Fox.

Rosa was not surprised at the inevitability of this conclusion. Like all emotional rationalists she had in her nature a certain streak of superstitious fatalism. At certain moments she was prepared to let go and allow herself to be carried by a stronger force; and if she later demanded of herself an account of these surrenders there was usually a selection of labels ready made to bring the violence of the spirit under some clinical and domestic heading. In this case, however, the demon of unreason did not come to Rosa wearing a psychological disguise but bearing the name of a friend. Where Mischa was concerned, Rosa was prepared to believe anything. When she felt that she had to go to Mischa she was quite ready to acknowledge herself to be under a spell. It was as if the climax was come of perhaps years of preparation: and suddenly all the force of those years was to be felt in the pull which drew her in spite of herself towards him. She knew that even if at that moment Mischa were oblivious of her existence, yet he was drawing her all the same. She was reminded of stories of love philtres which will draw the loved one over mountains and across the seas. She rose from the breakfast table.

'Hunter, stop looking so wretched!' said Rosa crossly. 'Shall I give you some brandy?'

'I don't want any brandy,' said Hunter without looking up.

Rosa shook him gently by the shoulder and then went to put her coat on. She opened the front door. The morning blew in upon her, rather warm and perfumed with earth and trees. Rosa suddenly began to feel strong. She drew the door slowly to behind her and began to walk along the pavement. She turned the corner into the sunshine. As she walked, she saw something out of the corner of her eye which seemed for a moment like her own shadow. Then looking down she saw that it was Nina the dressmaker who was running along between her and the railings, a pace or two behind, not quite decided how to attract her attention. Rosa looked at her with surprise.

She usually saw Nina indoors and was struck now by the oddness of her colouring, the gold of her dyed hair and the profound darkness of her eyes. Dusky roses were upon her cheeks, but across the crown of her head there was a black line where the new hair was growing at the base of the golden poll. Nina is neglecting her appearance, thought Rosa. She smiled down.

'Miss Keepe,' said Nina, still dodging along by the railings, 'might I speak to you? Have you a moment?'

'I'm going somewhere just now,' said Rosa, 'but do walk along with me if you like.' They waited at a kerb and crossed a road.

'By the way,' said Rosa, 'I wonder if you've seen Miss Cockeyne lately?'

'I haven't seen her for a long time,' said Nina. 'I hope she is well?'

'So do I!' said Rosa, turning to bow to Mrs Carrington-Morris, who was passing at a slow pace in a Rolls Royce. Rosa was beginning to feel astonishingly cheerful. I am driven to it! she kept saying to herself, I am driven to it! And this, instead of being a cry of despair, turned out to be a song of hope and delight. She wanted to laugh out loud. They were descending towards Kensington High Street.

'She is still with you in London?' asked Nina.

'Who? Oh, Miss Cockeyne, yes,' said Rosa. At that moment she caught sight of Miss Foy with a shopping basket on the other side of the road. 'Excuse me for a moment,' said Rosa, and dashed across.

Miss Foy's hair was standing on end rather more than usual and a smile was creased across the wrinkles of her face.

'How is Mrs Wingfield?' asked Rosa.

'Perfectly well, Miss Rosa, perfectly well,' said Miss Foy, 'but perverse, you know, difficult and perverse. Just keep on calling, you know. She likes you to call. Yesterday you didn't call and she was quite disappointed. She kept asking, hasn't that girl come yet?'

'Would she have seen me yesterday?' asked Rosa.

'Seen you? Oh, dear me, no!' said Miss Foy. 'But she wanted you to call. She *will* see you, Miss Rosa, just be patient. She's an old woman.'

Nina had followed Rosa across the road. 'May I introduce,'

said Rosa, 'Miss – er – Nina, Miss Foy.' Rosa could not always remember Nina's surname at short notice.

'We met at your house once. I remember this young lady,' said Miss Foy kindly.

'Oh, did you?' said Rosa. 'Good! Well, now I must be getting along.'

She strode on down the hill, followed by Nina. Now they were almost at the High Street. Everything will be all right, thought Rosa, everything will be all right. She had a vision of herself, Hunter, and the *Artemis* all somehow encircled by a beneficent power. Without thinking what she was doing, she began to run. Nina ran behind her.

'I'm so sorry!' said Rosa. 'I just forgot for a moment.' They had arrived at the High Street. It took them some time to get across the road.

'How are you getting on, Nina?' asked Rosa, when they were on the other side. She struck down a side street in the direction of Mischa Fox's house. She felt almost ready, with power and impatience, to fly through the air.

'I have some problems,' said Nina. Rosa was now walking so fast that Nina had become quite breathless with the task of keeping up with her.

'Life is a series of problems!' said Rosa merrily. Proceeding slowly towards them along the pavement, she saw the lady with the hearing-aid who had been able to make so little of the events of the shareholders' meeting. Rosa saluted her with an elaborate series of flourishes of the hand, beginning some ten yards off and continuing until they passed each other. The lady with the hearing-aid, who had not recognized Rosa, turned round in puzzlement and then went on, shaking her head.

Rosa laughed. 'She doesn't know who I am!' she said to Nina. They negotiated another busy road.

'The traffic in London just seems to get worse and worse doesn't it?' said Rosa.

'Yes,' said Nina.

Now they were almost at Mischa Fox's house.

'How are you getting on, Nina?' asked Rosa. 'Oh yes, I asked you that, didn't I. I do hope these problems aren't really bad ones. If I can ever be of any assistance —'

'Ah, yes!' said Nina breathlessly from behind Rosa's elbow. 'I would like to ask your advice!'

234

'Never be afraid to ask advice,' said Rosa. 'People try to be far too independent of each other. I'm just going in now to ask Mr Fox's advice.' They stopped on the pavement.

'Mr Fox —?' said Nina. For the last ten minutes Nina had been seeing nothing but the sleeve of Rosa's coat. Now she looked up and saw Mischa Fox's house towering above her, window upon window.

'Some other time —' said Nina. 'I'll call again.' She turned about and bolted away down the street.

Rosa looked after her in surprise. Then she turned and looked at the door of the house. She forgot Nina completely. She mounted the steps.

Now that Rosa was face to face with the door of Mischa's house, she felt her exultation beginning to fade away. What remained behind was an iron resolution and a longing to see Mischa so strong that she felt she would have been able to walk through a wall. She rang the bell. In a moment or two a servant appeared. He threw the door wide open and Rosa stepped into the hall. The servant asked for her name and her business. Rosa had the feeling that she was both recognized and expected. Yes, it turned out that Mr Fox was at home and would see her at once. It was only then that it occurred to Rosa how very improbable it was that either of these things should have been the case.

As she followed the servant she had to hold her two hands to her breast to stop her heart from starting through her flesh. They walked from room to room. In one of the first rooms, which seemed to be a kind of small drawing-room, Calvin Blick was reclining upon a settee reading a book. He nodded amiably to Rosa as she passed through, as if her appearance were the most ordinary thing in the world. At last they reached a door at which the servant knocked cautiously. Then he opened it for Rosa to go in. She entered. The door closed behind her.

She was in a big room with windows on two sides. She looked about in confusion, a little dazzled by the extra light. Then she saw that Mischa was standing quite near her, leaning against a bookcase. Rosa leaned back against the door. Now that she was in Mischa's presence, she felt a slow but steady relaxing of tension. She felt no need to say anything, no need even to look at him. She glanced about the room and then walked over to one of the windows. As she turned, she heard a strange sound. It was Mischa laughing. Then Rosa began to laugh too, a profound laugh of relief and pleasure. Suddenly she was unable to control the muscles of her face; she covered it for a moment in case it should tell of too great a joy. They walked towards each other and when they were a few feet apart they paused.

Rosa stopped laughing — but the great rift which their laughter had made remained open, and through it they looked at each other. What have I been doing all these years? Rosa wondered. She took another step and felt that her knees would give way. She saw Mischa's face as if it were suddenly stripped; and she was sure that no one had seen this unprotected face of Mischa since the last time, many years ago, when she had seen it herself. She took a final step, and he caught her arm. Locked together, they turned about and fell to their knees and then sank slowly sideways on to the floor. For a moment her eyelid fluttered under his mouth like a bird. Then they were exchanging long kisses like people after an exceedingly long thirst who drink at last.

Mischa pulled her up to a sitting position. He sat beside her cross-legged. He looked small and gay, like a tailor in a fairy-story. 'Well, Rosa?' he cried.

Rosa drew her hand across her brow. 'I'm lost,' she said, 'lost in a forest.'

'Just go on a little way,' said Mischa, 'and soon you'll hear the clop-clop of the axe. Then go on a little way farther and you'll come to the woodcutter's cottage.'

'No,' she said, 'to the enchanter's house.'

Rosa looked at him. It was like looking into a mirror. It was as if her own spirit had imprinted itself upon him as they embraced and now looked back at her wide-eyed.

'How strange,' said Rosa, 'I never noticed before that we resembled each other.'

'It is an illusion of lovers,' said Mischa. He rose and helped her to her feet.

'Mischa,' said Rosa, 'I need your help.' They sat down close to each other in chairs. Rosa then noticed with surprise that she was in the room in which the party had been held. The furniture was the same, only the tapestries had been taken away. She looked at the place where the bowl of fish had been and as she did so a seam of memories was uncovered in her

236

mind, deeply buried memories of the grief which she had made for Mischa many years ago, and the grief which he had made for her.

'Never mind it, Rosa,' said Mischa. He was reading her face.

'Look here,' said Rosa, 'let's be business-like.'

Mischa laughed again. 'How like you that sounds!' He took her hand.

'It's very unpleasant,' said Rosa. She had given some thought to the question of how much of the Lusiewicz story she should at this stage reveal to Mischa. She had decided beforehand to tell him the absolute minimum. Now, moved by his presence and startled by her own joy, she wondered for a moment whether she should not tell him everything. But caution returned to her like the renewed pressure of a cold hand, and she did not change her plan. She did, however, introduce one unpremeditated modification into her tale; she spoke only of Stefan. She did not mention the existence of Jan. In the story as she told it there was only one Lusiewicz. It was quickly told. Mischa watched her closely as she spoke, and Rosa wondered how much he was able to guess of the many things which she was leaving unmentioned. He asked no questions, and all he said when she had finished was, 'Hmmm. May I use any methods I please?'

Rosa inclined her head. She felt as if she were selling herself into captivity. But to be at his mercy was at that moment her most profound desire. If there had been a fire between them she would have leapt into it.

'Thank you,' said Rosa. It was like the end of a very long discussion.

'There is something I would like to talk to you about, since you're here,' said Mischa, 'I see you so rarely.'

Rosa was aware of a change of atmosphere, a deep shift of situation. This too reminded her strangely of the past, and of times when week after week and month after month it was as if Mischa were dragging her by the wrist through hell. There was a demon in Mischa which she had never been able to know and which had never allowed them to be at peace. Always at the last moment and without apparent reason there would come the twist, the assertion of power, the hint of a complexity that was beyond her, the sense of being, after all that had passed between them, a pawn in Mischa's game – and with that twist the structure of tenderness and of delight, ever so little shifted, would suddenly seem to her an altogether different thing. It was this demon which, in the past time, had defeated her, and from which she had in the end had the strength to flee. Now, with a shiver, she heard its voice again in Mischa's apparently innocent remark. She felt, all the same, that she knew what was coming. But his next words surprised her.

'It's about Peter Saward.'

TWENTY-THREE

Annette had stayed in five different hotels in the last seven days and her powers of endurance were almost at an end. During the first two or three days she had telephoned Mischa Fox's house at intervals of a few hours, for on reflection she had decided not to believe what Calvin had told her about Mischa's absence. But on each occasion she had been politely told that Mr Fox was not at home. She had also sent three letters to Mischa, and a reply-paid telegram, but without any result. Then a hopeless apathy came upon her, and she sat in her hotel room all day in a stupor. She left each hotel only because she feared that the management might conclude that she was ill or mad, and either question her or try to communicate with her parents. She knew in her heart that Mischa did not want to see her; and she told herself that if this was so she did not want to live.

She stepped out on to the platform of a big London terminus carrying her suit-case. She walked slowly towards the exit. She had no idea where she was going. Indeed, she had nowhere to go. Annette felt that she had been driven in a small circle, and that now all her possibilities of movement were exhausted. She passed a telephone box. Annette believed in the telephone. She paused to look at it. It was warm and red and brightly lighted. It seemed to her suddenly like a little shrine. Like a traveller who casts himself in desperation before a saint at the wayside, Annette entered. She lifted the receiver as if she expected to hear from it immediately some message of hope. Then she knew what she must do. She was amazed that she had not thought of it earlier. She knew also that it was her last card.

She opened her bag and fumbled for Nicholas's letter. It gave the address of the hotel in Cannes and a telephone number. She picked up the phone again and asked for Continental.

'I want to make a call to Cannes,' said Annette – 'Cannes in France.' As she said this it seemed as hopeless as asking to be put through to Valhalla. But the operator took it calmly. Yes, it appeared that it was quite possible for her to speak to Cannes; it would cost her nine shillings for three minutes.

Annette began to pour pieces of silver out of her handbag on to the floor of the box. Meanwhile, beside her ear a long corridor of sound was opening out telescopically, section after section, and the last piece was to contain the voice of Nicholas. English voices were speaking to each other in a space of sound – and now suddenly clear and crisp a French voice had joined the conversation. Annette imagined that she could hear the waves of the Channel breaking across the line. A voice in Paris was speaking to a voice in Provence. Annette waited. The intensity of her desire to speak to Nicholas was almost depriving her of breath. At last far away there was the sound of a telephone ringing, a French telephone, a telephone in a hotel in Cannes. A voice announced the name of the hotel. The intermediate voices turned about, speaking back again in the direction of Annette. '*Vous avez la communication, Londres,*' said a distant voice.

'Speak up, you're through,' said a voice close beside her ear.

'*Je voudrais parler avec Monsieur Cockeyne,*' said Annette. She found she was hoarse and had to clear her throat.

'*Avec Monsieur qui?*' said the French voice, rather impatiently.

'*Cockeyne,*' said Annette, and spelt the name out.

'*Ah, Cockeyne,*' said the French voice. '*Attendez un moment. Qui est à l'appareil?.*'

'*Sa soeur,*' said Annette. The pressure on her heart relaxed. She kissed Nicholas's letter.

A moment later the voice was speaking again. '*Monsieur est parti, il est parti ce matin. Non, il n'a pas laissé d'adresse.*'

Annette put the receiver down slowly. She trailed out of the telephone box. She trailed along the street, touching walls and railings with her hand. Now at last she knew what she was going to do. Annette had been deeply impressed by the failure of her attempt to sacrifice her jewels. It had not entered her head to pursue Jan Lusiewicz or to attempt to retrieve her property from him, since she regarded him as the messenger of fate. Her symbolic gesture had been rejected. Annette left her suit-case at a cloakroom and then she took a taxi to Campden Hill Square. Her plans appeared suddenly small and clear and inevitable. Life had become simple again. She would kill herself.

The intention appeared already conjoined with the method. In one of the cupboards at Campden Hill Square Rosa kept two bottles of sleeping-tablets which she had told Annette were quite enough to be fatal if taken all at once. Annette felt her mind narrowing to a tiny focus. She wanted those two little bottles with the desperation of a lover. She did not conceive that anyone would hinder her; and no one did. The front door was locked, but she let herself in with her key and walked straight to the cupboard. The two bottles were there, and she pocketed them. She looked into her own room. It looked as if someone else were living there. She walked down the stairs again, quietly but not on tiptoe. There were sounds from Hunter's room, but none from Rosa's. She left the house, banging the door. The taxi was still waiting. She gave the name of a discreet and expensive hotel near Hyde Park where her parents sometimes stayed.

The taxi sped away through Kensington. Annette examined the bottles. Rosa had stopped using the tablets some time ago and each bottle seemed to be quite full. Annette hugged them to her. She wanted to be alone with them. She gulped for air, and forced herself to look out of the window. She was impatient for the journey to end. She was still in the world.

The door of the hotel appeared at last, very tall and white. Annette went through it. 'I should like a room facing the Park,' said Annette.

Her voice came out with difficulty. Through a veil she looked into the eyes of the receptionist. He replied very quietly, almost in a whisper, as if he knew what it was that confronted him. Annette walked up the stairs with extreme slowness. The room was big, with two great windows which opened on to a balcony. Outside, and beyond the road, lay the Park. Women with perambulators were parading in the green walks, and down long vistas of trees children bowled hoops while dogs ran barking behind them. Someone was flying a kite. Annette looked out. Already they seemed to her as remote as figures painted in a book of hours.

'End this farce,' said Annette aloud. She was alone now. 'End this farce.' These words seemed to express the essence of her resolution.

'Why continue in pain?' she said. She looked at the people going to and fro in the Park. Through holes in the clouds a pale sunlight fell upon them in shafts.

'End this farce,' she said. She sat down on the edge of the bed with her eyes glazed. She was the centre of an extraordinary solitude. Her head was growing and growing until it enclosed the whole world. Annette was no longer present. She was become the boundary of the universe and within her all things lived and moved and had their being. Death could not change her now more than she was already changed. 'End this farce,' said the moving lips of Annette.

The telephone rang. Annette started violently and lifted the receiver. It was the management asking if she wanted anything. No, she wanted nothing. She put down the receiver. As she thought, raggedly and incoherently, of what she was going to do, the thought of Mischa was scarcely present to her mind. What came back to her now were the sensations of childhood: the loneliness and boredom and fear of strange places, the hurry and the noise of a world which was never her own, the alien odour of the expensive hotel and the long-distance train. These were the things that had prefigured the present moment.

She took the two little bottles out of her handbag. Is it enough? she wondered. Then she had another idea. She lifted the telephone again. Yes, after all she would like something. Could they send up three bottles of gin? Annette had read in the papers that sleeping-tablets taken after alcohol were twice as deadly.

The waiter came in. Annette did not look at him, but she could see from the corner of her eye that his attitude expressed curiosity and impertinence. He put the bottles on the table.

'Pardon me, miss,' said the waiter, 'how many glasses shall I bring?'

'One,' said Annette. 'Oh, I mean six, please.' She did not want to arouse suspicions.

'Is there anything else you'd like for your little party?' said the waiter. 'Olives are nice, cheese straws, crisps, we can even do you a —'

'Nothing else,' said Annette. The waiter went away. He returned with the glasses and then went away again.

Annette got up and walked about the room. She opened a

bottle of gin and poured out a glassful. She drank it rapidly. At once she began to feel a bit different. She drank a little more gin. No half measures, thought Annette. She listened to the silence in the room. To die in silence. She turned about savagely. If she could only pull the hotel down on top of her, leap into a roaring fire, blow herself up with a bomb. Anything rather than this silent ending. Within her desire for annihilation a destructive frenzy awoke to life.

'End it!' exclaimed Annette. She hurled her glass into the fireplace. She looked at the gin bottles and at the row of glasses, and a macabre idea came to her. A party. Why not? Slowly she lifted the receiver and dialled John Rainborough's number. She would be attending her own wake.

Rainborough was sitting in his drawing-room trying to make up his mind to telephone Agnes Casement. He had promised to ring her during the afternoon, but had kept putting it off. It was now becoming, in equal degrees, both essential and impossible that he should do so at once; and as he meditated upon this, turning it into a problem of metaphysical dimensions, it gave him the image of his whole life. For Rainborough was now engaged to be married to Agnes Casement. How this thing had happened was not very clear to Rainborough. Yet it was, he was determined to think, quite inevitable. That much was certain. Must face up to my responsibilities, said Rainborough vaguely to himself as he contemplated the telephone. Need ballast. All this wandering about no good. Must root myself in life. Children and so on. Marriage just what I need. Must have courage to define myself. Naturally, it's painful. But best thing really. That's my road, I knew it all along.

These thoughts floated in fragments on the surface of his mind; but underneath there was fear and horror and sheer astonishment. How on earth had it happened? He remembered for the hundredth time the scene in the country lane. The open car was at rest under the opening fans of a young beech tree. The dewy cream of blackthorn was spreading through all the hedges. Beyond a five-barred gate lay a water-meadow rank with kingcups. Miss Casement's perfume was mingled with scents of pollen and manure. Far away there was the sound of a tractor. A bird began to sing in the beech tree. Rainborough had asked her to marry him. He wondered why; and the thought came to him that what had really happened in that moment was that he had become engaged to Miss Casement's red M.G.

The telephone rang. Rainborough started guiltily and lifted the receiver with a sickly look. But the voice was not that of his bride-to-be. With pleasure he recognized the voice of Annette. He greeted her effusively. A party! How splendid! And straightaway. Just what he felt like. Yes, he'd come at once. So glad she was better. Lovely to see her. He jumped to his feet. As he was leaving the house he remembered that he had not telephoned Miss Casement. He returned gloomily and like a man in a play he spoke his lines. It was not difficult to think of a plausible falsehood. He reflected that this would not be the last. He felt that his marriage had already started.

Annette was telephoning the house in Campden Hill Square. She reckoned that at this hour Rosa would be sure to be at work, and that she might find Hunter alone. Hunter answered the call and exclaimed with delight and relief when he heard Annette's voice. Yes, he'd come at once. How unfortunate that Rosa was out. Yes, at once. After that Annette sat holding the receiver in her hand for so long that the management sent up to ask her either to replace it or to make her call. She dialled Mischa Fox's number. The usual voice told her politely that Mr Fox was still away. She asked for Calvin Blick. In a moment Calvin's voice was heard.

'Mr Blick,' said Annette, 'I'm afraid that I was rather rude and distracted last time we met. I'd be very glad if you could come and take a drink with me now in a quieter atmosphere.' Calvin was glad too, he was delighted, he looked forward, yes at once.

Annette sank back into the chair and drank some more gin. She was glad to think that representatives of both Mischa and Rosa were going to be present. How she would make them sorry, those two! – and for a moment it seemed to her as if it was they who were about to be put down. Annette began to prepare the scene. The room had a bathroom attached to it, and here Annette secreted the two little bottles. She ordered some more gin and some vermouth and some champagne. It occurred to her to wonder whether she should pay the bill. But then with an inward jerk which was half sickening she realized that she had already left the region where one pays one's bills.

In the country which she had entered now gin and French was free.

Calvin Blick was the first to arrive. Calvin, who never took things at their face value, looked curiously at Annette. He could see that she had been drinking. 'No, thank you,' he said. 'I never touch the stuff.'

While Annette was ordering orange juice, John Rainborough came in.

Calvin, who seemed to be in a very cheerful mood, greeted him noisily. 'Why, you're looking feverish, my dear Rainborough!' he cried. 'Too much work at the office, eh? You administrative birds are never done!'

'I've resigned,' said Rainborough sourly.

Calvin, who had been aware of this for several days, began a rigmarole of exclamations of surprise and embarrassing questions to which he already knew the answer.

Hunter came in. He looked very dismayed when he saw Calvin, whom he had not seen or heard of since the night of Mischa Fox's party. Annette had withdrawn into a corner and was starting on her fifth glass of neat gin.

'May I do the honours,' said Calvin, 'if Miss Cockeyne will allow me? What's yours, my dear Rainborough?'

'I'll have some champagne,' said Rainborough. And added, After all I've got something to celebrate! This, however, he said to himself only. Concerning their intentions he had sworn Miss Casement to secrecy. This was a device to keep the realization of his fate from too rudely and rapidly flooding through his own consciousness.

Hunter accepted a little gin, and then went up to Annette, who was standing staring at them all with a strange smile.

'Annette,' he said, 'please come home to Campden Hill Square. Rosa is very sorry for all that's happened and wants you to come back.' Rosa's sorrow was Hunter's conjecture; but he looked upon Annette with real concern.

'Home!' said Annette, catching on the word. 'Cam' Hill Square isn't my home. I have no home. I'm a refugee!' She looked at them all defiantly. They were looking at her.

'I'm going to end this farce,' said Annette. She poured the rest of the gin down her throat.

'I say, steady on!' said Hunter.

'What price the School of Life now, Annette?' said Calvin.

'It's the end of term,' said Annette. She turned her back on them and looked out of the window. The Park was darkening. A band of dark clouds lay across the sky, and underneath it was the last pale brilliance of the evening. The trees were starkly revealed, every leaf showing. The children and the dogs had gone home. Lovers strolled here and there along the avenues. As she watched, the scene was fading. A blue which was of the night was spread upon the darkness of the clouds.

'Put on the light!' said Annette. She began to draw the curtains.

'Do come home!' said Hunter, in a low voice.

'Let her be!' said Calvin.

Annette went into the bathroom. She opened the first bottle and poured a number of tablets out into the palm of her hand. She filled a tumbler with water. As she did so she saw her face in the glass. Her eyes had become very large and black and her face stared back at her like a wild face in a dream. As she put one of the tablets into her mouth she watched herself in the mirror. It was easier that way. She swallowed the tablet, and then several more. It was slow work. Her throat seemed to be closing up against them. There was a roar of laughter from the room behind her. Annette poured some of the tablets into the water but they failed to melt. She searched round for something to crush them with. Lying on the floor behind the foot of the washbasin she found a toothbrush, left behind no doubt by the previous guest. She picked it up, but rejected it as unhygienic; then it occurred to her that this didn't matter now. This was a shock. She began to crush the tablets, drinking up the powdery liquid as she did so and adding more water. In this way she finished up the whole of the first bottle of tablets. She started on the second bottle. She found that she was unable to stand, and sat down on a chair. It's working already, thought Annette.

Someone was knocking on the door. Hunter's voice said, 'Annette, are you all right?'

'I'm fine,' said Annette, or something in her head said that, and some noise came out of her mouth. How interesting this is, thought Annette. It will be fun to describe it all to Nicholas. Then the thought followed, I shall never tell this to Nicholas. Only a few tablets remained in the second bottle. Annette put it down. That was enough surely. She was beginning to feel very strange indeed. Her thoughts were moving extremely slowly.

'So this is what it is like,' said Annette half aloud. One's thoughts become so slow, like a clock running down. And never to tell Nicholas.

Annette opened the bathroom door and entered the bedroom again. There were some people there and their mouths were round with laughter. Annette picked up the gin bottle and began to pour out some gin with a shaking hand.

'Annette!' said Hunter close beside her. 'You've had enough to drink.' The gin was splashing over Annette's hand.

'End this farce,' said Annette. She licked the gin from her hand. Then she began to study her hand. It struggled before her like a dying animal. It *was* a dying animal. Her poor hand, it didn't want to die. She had not asked its permission.

'My poor hand!' said Annette. Then she found that the tears were quietly flowing from her eyes. Perhaps they had been flowing for a long time. She stared at her hand with fascination.

Rainborough and Calvin were looking at her curiously. 'What's the matter with your hand?' said Rainborough. 'Have you cut it?' He took her hand and inspected it.

'Oh, Annette, don't cry!' said Hunter. He sounded as if he were going to cry too. 'Here, have some more gin.' He filled up her glass and then his own. Annette began to sob hysterically.

'The girl's had far too much to drink,' said Rainborough.

'I don't know,' said Calvin. 'I think there's something else. Annette! Annette!' he called to her loudly, as one might to someone who was already far away.

Annette swung round and subsided into an armchair. Hunter knelt beside her. A black ring was closing upon her field of vision. Somewhere in the centre a light still flickered and she saw the faces of Rainborough, Calvin and Hunter bent over her. Incoherent with sobbing she grasped Hunter by the shoulder. He put his arm about her. 'Stop it, Annette!' cried Hunter in anguish.

Annette was trying to say something, but only sobbing cries would come out of her mouth. It was terrible to hear. 'I've – taken – poison,' she gasped out at last, scarcely audibly through the high continuous wail which was issuing now from her lips.

'What did she say?' said Rainborough.

'She says she's taken poison!' said Hunter.

'She's drunk!' said Rainborough.

'No, I think it's true!' said Calvin, and his eyes were shining.

At that moment the door of the room burst abruptly open and two tall figures came striding in.

'Andrew! Marcia!' cried Annette, and fell back in her chair.

The trio grouped about her, Hunter supporting her shoulders, Calvin peering closely into her face, and Rainborough stooping and holding her hand, were for an instant petrified with amazement. Then, guiltily, they sprang apart. Annette's parents bore down upon her. From either side they raised her up. She hung limply from their long arms.

'She's poisoned herself!' cried Hunter shrilly. 'We must have a doctor!'

After that the room was full of cries and activity. Annette's mother was saying something very rapid and high-pitched in French. Annette's father was asking the management to put him through to a hospital. Annette was moaning with her eyes half closed. Her father was slapping her cheeks and asking her what it was that she had taken. Hunter was uttering incoherent lamentations. Rainborough was explaining to no one in particular that he had not had the faintest idea until two minutes ago that Annette – the thing was unthinkable – really he had had no idea. Calvin watched and poured himself out a little more orange juice. Men in black coats came in followed by men in white coats. The doctor was saying something to the manager of the hotel. Annette was now lying quite limp and quiet. Her father was searching the room.

Rainborough emerged from the bathroom. 'This is what she took,' he said. 'It looks like sleeping-tablets. Luminal, probably.' He held up the two bottles.

Hunter dabbed his eyes. 'Let me look,' he said. He examined the two bottles. Then he sat down on the bed and began to laugh helplessly.

'The boy's hysterical,' said Rainborough.

For a moment Hunter was speechless with laughter. When at last he was able to stammer out a few words he said, 'Annette's suffering – from too much gin and an overdose of Milk of Magnesia!' He rolled back among the pillows.

TWENTY-FOUR

It was about an hour later. In the hotel room there remained now only John Rainborough and Marcia Cockeyne. Hunter had accompanied Annette and her father to the hospital. Calvin had disappeared; and it was some ten minutes since Andrew had telephoned to say that Hunter had indeed been right, and that Annette was by now almost recovered. After she had been extremely sick, her mistake had been explained to her. It was a long time before she was convinced. At the moment she was weeping tears of rage.

'How did you know where to find her?' asked Rainborough.

'We went of course to Campden Hill Square,' said Marcia, 'and there quite open upon the table was a note which Hunter had left for Rosa to say where Annette was. So we came at once.'

'Won't you have a drink now?' said Rainborough.

'*Mais oui*,' said Marcia, 'some champagne perhaps. We have something to celebrate, no?'

This phrase made Rainborough sigh deeply as he poured out the champagne. He then took a liberal quantity for himself. 'May I order you a taxi?' he asked.

'But no,' said Marcia, 'I have my own car outside. Let me rather take you home.'

Rainborough thanked her and they prepared to leave. He helped her on with her coat. Indeed she was beautiful. She had the same pale skin and small head as Annette, but a straighter nose and more luxuriant chestnut hair which fell in a rolling mass on to her neck. Approaching near to this radiant stuff, Rainborough inhaled a perfume which made him pause in astonishment. After the harsh sweetness which emanated from Miss Casement and Miss Perkins the scent of Marcia was of a celestial subtlety. It was not exactly a scent of flowers. It was more like a scent of wood. Sandalwood perhaps, thought Rainborough. He had never smelt sandalwood, but he suddenly felt sure that it must smell like this. It occurred to him, suddenly that the whole extraordinary ensemble of powder, perfume and paint which gave so artificial a surface to Miss Casement lay upon Marcia as a natural bloom. She was an exotic flower, like flowers which Rainborough had seen in southern countries, which were hardly like flowers at all, yet were undoubtedly products of nature. Rainborough's norm was still the wild rose, although he no longer even desired these simple blossoms.

With an effort he restrained himself from plunging his nose into the shining mass of Marcia's hair to smell it ecstatically. The coat was now on, and Rainborough walked politely round to the front. Here he observed her eyes, which were of a rather dark flecked blue colour and set wide apart. Upon the wide expanse between them how glorious a privilege, thought Rainborough, it would be to imprint a kiss.

Marcia was saying something for the second time.

'Oh yes!' said Rainborough, and told her his address. They walked together down the stairs.

Outside it was night. At the door, revealed in the bright light of the portico, stood a black Mercedes. Rainborough stumbled towards it submissively and stooped into its soft red interior. He lay back helplessly on the cushions. With undisguised admiration he watched Marcia start the engine. It was dark in the car. Rainborough sat with one leg curled under him watching in the rapidly passing illumination of street lamps and neon signs the beautiful profile of his companion appearing and disappearing. When they reached his door it did not even occur to him to ask her in, so inconceivable did he find it that they should have to part so soon.

Marcia came into the house. Rainborough put on lights and fires. He pulled the curtains to conceal the wrecked garden, pale with fallen stones and builders' timber. Then he poured out drinks for Marcia and himself. The sandalwood perfume filled the room. He offered her a cigarette and struck a match. As he held the flame up, lighting the pallor of her face, his hand was shaking violently.

Marcia took his wrist between two cool white fingers and held his hand steady while she lit the cigarette, looking all the time into his eyes. '*Mais qu'est-ce que vous avez?*' she said. 'You are distressed, Mr Rainborough. My little girl will be all right. But you are still upset, I think?'

'Yes,' said Rainborough. To hell with your little girl, he thought. He realized he was drunk. He had a feeling of ground subsiding far under his feet. 'Yes,' he said, 'I have various troubles.'

Marcia drew at the cigarette. Then she suddenly handed it back to Rainborough. He put it to his lips. It was like a healing draught.

'You are worried, yes,' murmured Marcia. She sat down on a settee and motioned Rainborough to sit beside her. He sank down.

'Perhaps I could help you,' said Marcia. 'But first you must tell me everything.'

To Rainborough's astonishment that was exactly what he proceeded to do. The whole story of Miss Casement came out. It sounded grotesque; but it gave him an extraordinary relief to tell it as a story. To place Miss Casement in the framework of 'And then she . . .' set a blessed distance between them.

Marcia listened with a gentle slightly clinical air, nodding her head. '*Que tu es drôle, mon cher!*' she said at the end. 'But you do not love this woman at all, I think?'

'No,' said Rainborough. 'Yes, I don't know. She fascinates me.' He saw Marcia's hand lying beside him on the cushions. It resembled Annette's hand. Rainborough's head reeled. He stood up. 'I'm in a muddle!' he said.

'You want to escape, I think?' said Marcia.

'Yes, exactly,' said Rainborough, 'escape, yes, yes! But how?'

'You do not love her,' said Marcia firmly. 'This first must be clear, not only to think but to feel. Ask yourself what is the thing about her that is most unpleasant that you remember?'

Rainborough reflected. For a moment he could think of nothing graver than the fact that she had been so bad tempered when they had missed their dinner at Henley because he had been so long in making his proposal. Then he thought of her behaviour to the little typist.

'Now tell this to me in detail,' said Marcia.

Rainborough did so. He felt that he was being guilty of the basest treachery. It was a delicious feeling.

'Now you must go away,' said Marcia, 'at once.'

Rainborough stood before her helpless and incoherent. Fierce hatred for Miss Casement possessed him, while Marcia swam before his eyes, strangely disintegrated into hair and hands and lips. 'How can I,' he said, 'at this hour, and where to?'

'You will go to our villa near Saint Tropez,' said Marcia. 'There in the south it is already summer-time. Here is the address. I will send a wire to the servant, and to some friends of ours who live near. You have no business here to keep you?'

'None!' said Rainborough.

'Why do you wait then?' said Marcia. 'Relax, *mon cher ami*!'

'I haven't got a ticket or any French money,' said Rainborough frantically.

'I will give you money,' said Marcia, 'and we will book you a ticket by telephone. For what do you keep a telephone?' In a moment she was talking to the airfield.

Rainborough walked or staggered once round the room. He felt pain and exultation. Irrevocable things were happening. 'I can't go without telling her,' he said.

'Tell her then!' said Marcia, 'or shall I? You leave it to me, yes? What is her telephone number?'

Rainborough uttered the number.

'And excuse me,' said Marcia, 'what is your Christian name? This is necessary too.'

'John,' said Rainborough, 'John, John, John!' He repeated it passionately as if he were casting down his personality at her feet.

Marcia was speaking again on the telephone. Very far away, already in some other world, Rainborough could hear the voice of Miss Casement.

'John asked me to tell you that he is going away . . .' Marcia was saying. Her foreign tones were like green honey.

Rainborough sat down. He wiped his brow. For a moment the pain in his heart seemed a little like pity. Then a great wind was blowing through him. It blew right through him without any hindrance. He was empty. He left the room to pack his suit-case.

'Your plane leaves in an hour's time,' said Marcia's voice. 'I will take you to the airfield. Do not forget your passport.'

A few moments later Rainborough was going out of the front door with Marcia. He slammed the door to behind him. He got into the Mercedes.

TWENTY-FIVE

It was a few days later that a question was asked in Parliament by an obscure Conservative M.P. concerning the status of certain European workers who held permits for an indefinite stay in Great Britain. The M.P. wished to ask the Home Secretary whether he was aware that a number of individuals who had been trained for work in this country under the so-called SELIB scheme were strictly ineligible under the terms of the agreement. This question followed, as it happened, upon a charge, which was being levelled against the government of the day, of irresponsible management of monies donated by American organizations. This country, it was argued by an Opposition group, was forgetting upon which side its bread was buttered. The phrase 'after all, we Europeans —' uttered by a Socialist speaker in the ensuing debate was greeted by cries of 'Look here!' and 'Don't exaggerate!' The whole matter received considerable publicity. The obscure M.P., having performed his task, sank again into the tranquillity of the back benches. It was generally agreed that some-one must have 'put him up to it', but no one could make out who had done it or why, although one or two well-known names were mentioned.

For a day or two the evening papers put the discussion into the headlines. HOME OFFICE TO SCREEN SELIB WORKERS. *Deport Illegal Migrants says M.P.* On the second of these two days Rosa returned to Campden Hill Square to find that Stefan Lusiewicz had disappeared. He had vanished as completely as if he had never been there. He left no trace in the house. Rosa noticed his departure with a dull satisfaction. Since her visit to Mischa Fox she had scarcely noticed his existence. It was as if, as soon as she had seen Mischa, Stefan had already been blotted out of her life. Other problems now engrossed Rosa. It was as if the years had rolled away and she was once again involved in the old coil: what was Mischa up to, what did Mischa really think, what did Mischa expect of her, what was she to do about Mischa? What had chiefly stunned her on the occasion of her visit to him was his determination to talk about Peter Saward, and even to speak of Peter's attachment to Rosa.

Rosa had, she imagined, been prepared for anything when she went to see Mischa. She had been ready to be snubbed and humiliated. She had also been ready for an affectionate welcome, to be followed by some sort of renewal of his suit. Rosa had not made clear to herself whether she wanted this or not. In any case it had not happened. It had seemed rather as if Mischa were pressing the suit of Peter Saward, although nothing had been said which could unambiguously be read in this way. What does he want? Rosa wondered. Does he want to keep Peter and me together in a cage? She was, it occurred to her, singularly without information about the relations of Mischa and Peter. Or was this move designed perhaps rather to divide her from Peter and make her feel disgust and impatience about him: possibly to arouse in her the sense that it was certainly not with Peter that she would ever link her fate, and so to enlighten her about her true feelings?

But what were her true feelings? The only thing which Rosa did feel as a result of Mischa's tender concern about him was an extreme irritation with Peter Saward. She knew this to be irrational and unfair – but its inevitability inclined her to think that this was perhaps just what Mischa wanted. She then did her level best to feel the opposite. Later on she told herself that she was attaching an undue importance to the whole thing and that Mischa had not meant anything in particular; but this view she in turn rejected on the general *a priori* principle that Mischa never failed to mean something in particular. He is cutting my links with other people, she thought suddenly, he is blocking my routes of escape. She now no longer troubled to regret her action in seeking Mischa's help. It made no difference. Whether she ran towards him or away it was all the same.

As Rosa revolved these thoughts in her mind she was sitting beside Hunter's bed. He lay there before her as helpless as in childhood. Hunter was ill with a mysterious illness. He had a high fever and intermittent delirium. He lay at present in a comatose slumber. The doctor had confessed himself puzzled, had declared the boy to be in no immediate danger, and had

254

said that there was nothing to be done but to keep him quiet and see what happened. Rosa had her own theories about the cause of Hunter's sickness, but as these were too fantastic to reveal to the doctor she kept them to herself.

When the scandal about SELIB had broken as a result of the question in Parliament, Hunter had been amazed. How very odd that it should have happened now, he kept saying to himself. But his triumph at the discomfiture of Lusiewicz and his subsequent departure was clouded by the thought that the Pole would certainly regard him as responsible for this timely development. Hunter feared for his life; for he very heartily believed the threats which Stefan had uttered on the occasion of the striking of the matches. He began to have vivid nightmares in which he would hear the Pole creeping down from his room above and fumbling at Hunter's door. These were varied with hardly less unpleasant dreams in which Calvin Blick was to be seen displaying innumerable pictures of Rosa dressed in black stockings. From these nocturnal entertainments Hunter would be awakened by the pain of his burnt forehead, which seemed to be refusing to heal. A feeling as if all the skin of his face were being drawn towards a hole in his brow persisted all day and as much of the night as was spared from the sequence of nightmares. In despair Hunter had cut off his yellow hair as far back as the crown of his head, and now he did not dare to venture out into the street. He became a sick man.

He was now wakening slowly from sleep. The room seemed to be full of light and darkness which was scattered about it in intense patches. The light was dazzling, and the darkness was oppressive, as if the room were full of dark objects. One of these objects seemed to be lodged on Hunter's chest. After a while it occurred to him that the light was so dazzling because it was daylight and not electric light. He began to puzzle about what time it was. The darkness now seemed to be gathering together into one part of the room and had something of the appearance of an enormous black spider which was crouching in the corner. One of its legs touched Hunter's bed and made him shudder continually. Somewhere in the lighted portion of the room he could see his mother sitting. Her head was thrown back and she was looking away from him out of the window. Her black hair was tumbling down her neck in the way in which he had so often seen it. She was frowning. And now someone else was in the room too and the voices were beginning to fly about above his head. They were booming inaudibly like a loudspeaker system that has gone wrong. Now they were loud, now they were soft. Hunter lay quite still and listened.

Rosa was surprised to see Mrs Wingfield coming into the room. She jumped to her feet.

'It's a fine thing,' said Mrs Wingfield, 'when *I* have to come and look for *you*!' She was wearing her corduroy trousers under a tweed cape, and an old-fashioned pair of horn-rimmed spectacles.

'I'm so sorry,' said Rosa, 'the last two or three days —'

'Don't apologize!' said Mrs Wingfield. 'Foy ran me across in the car. She's waiting outside now.'

'Oh, let me ask her in —' said Rosa.

'On no account!' said Mrs Wingfield. 'If she likes to play the faithful retainer, let her, I say. You wouldn't believe, incidentally, what a speed fiend that woman is. She almost touched fifty coming across the square. What's the matter with the boy?'

'We don't know,' said Rosa. 'Oh, my dear, hello!' This latter exclamation was directed to Marcia, who had just put her head round the door.

'May I come in?' said Marcia. 'How is poor Hunter?'

'Much the same, I'm afraid,' said Rosa. 'Mrs Wingfield, may I introduce Lady Cockeyne?'

'Ah, you have seen the newspapers!' said Marcia.

'Indeed I have,' said Rosa, 'and may I congratulate you? Marcia's husband has just been honoured,' she said to Mrs Wingfield.

'If you call *that* an honour,' said Mrs Wingfield, 'your poor mother must be spinning in her grave like a teetotum!'

'Is Hunter asleep?' asked Marcia.

'Yes,' said Rosa, 'he's very comatose. Nothing rouses him.'

'It is strange, is it not?' said Marcia. 'It is as if someone had cast a bad spell on him. Do you believe in love potions and in spells which bring to people illness and death?' she asked Mrs Wingfield politely.

'No, of course not!' snapped Mrs Wingfield, 'but I believe in the unconscious mind, and that's quite enough moonshine. The boy must have been brooding on something. He probably suffers from guilt feelings. Has he committed any crimes lately?'

'No,' said Rosa, 'he hasn't committed any crimes.'

'I don't know what you mean by that,' said Mrs Wingfield, 'and am in too much of a hurry to ask. I came over to tell you that I don't want your brother to have anything further to do with the *Artemis*.'

'Are you the person who decides?' asked Rosa.

'Your tone is sarcastic,' said Mrs Wingfield, 'but let me wipe that look off your face by telling you that in fact I *am* the person who decides. I own the *Artemis* now. The largest shareholder was Mrs Carrington-Morris and I bought her out three days ago. She may have conscientious objections to alcohol, but she had none to taking the suitably large sum of money which I offered. I've also bought out all the other shareholders except you. No, don't look hopeful, I don't mean to offer you anything for your shares. So now the paper is mine, and I propose to dispense with the boy.' Mrs Wingfield peered down at Hunter with an expression of interested disgust as if he were a dead mouse which the cat had brought in.

Hunter turned on the bed. The voices still boomed and buzzed somewhere above him. Far away someone was uttering his name. A strange perfume floated on the air like the scent of forests where he had been as a child. He heaved his chest up and drank it through mouth and nostrils. In the lighted portion of the room, rather still and far away as in a picture, he could see a beautiful lady. She looked familiar, and yet she was not anybody that he knew.

'A film star,' said Hunter aloud; 'must be a film star.' Film stars always looked like someone one knew. She was wearing a leopard-skin coat and she bent towards him with such a sweet look of concern. But as she moved, the spider moved nearer too and its many-faceted eye was suddenly close above him. In its glassy surface he could see himself reflected once, twice, a hundred times. He turned away in horror and buried his head in the pillow.

'He is awakening!' said Marcia. 'He said something. What was it?'

'What do you want me to do with the *Artemis*?' said Rosa. She felt very tired.

'You make me sick!' said Mrs Wingfield shrilly. 'Why don't

you put up a fight? I'd give the whole thing to you tomorrow i
you had any blood! As for your brother, he's obviously dying o
anaemia!'

'Don't shout, Mrs Wingfield,' said Rosa, 'you're disturbing
him.'

'And let me tell you,' cried Mrs Wingfield rising to her feet
'I'd have left you all my money too if I'd thought that you had
any blood in you! You've missed a quarter of a million, my
dear Miss Keepe, just reflect on that! No blood, Miss Keepe
that's the trouble with you, no blood!'

Mrs Wingfield had left the room and was going noisily
down the stairs.

'*Tiens!*' said Marcia.

Rosa shrugged her shoulders.

'Has there not been too much noise,' said Marcia, 'besid
what may indeed be a bed of great sickness?'

'Hunter's all right!' said Rosa, and she prodded the side o
the bed irritably with her knee. Hunter murmured something
inaudible.

'I came to say good-bye,' said Marcia. 'We go on Friday to
Dalmatia for our holiday.' She was looking radiant.

'I am so glad,' said Rosa.

As Hunter watched, the spider was getting bigger and
bigger. Now only a small patch of light was left within which
he could see his mother's face. At last this too was disap
pearing.

'How is Annette?' said Rosa.

'So well, my dear,' said Marcia. 'So well, so young. Do no
worry at all about Annette.' She touched Rosa's arm. 'Do no
worry about anything.'

'I am so glad,' said Rosa. 'I am so glad. I am so glad.'

TWENTY-SIX

Nina the dressmaker was packing her suit-case. She packed only a few clothes and the things which she called her original room, the things which had travelled with her everywhere. They were not many. Some photographs, an embroidered cloth, a Bible which had belonged to her mother, and three wooden horses which a peasant had carved near the place where she was born. As she packed, her tears fell steadily over her hands and into the suit-case. She no longer troubled to wipe them away. She turned round through a haze and stumbled about in the forest of unfinished dresses. From a distant drawer she brought a warm jersey and put it into her suit-case. She would need that where she was going. But where was she going?

Three days ago Nina had received a communication from the Home Office asking her to present herself at a certain department in Westminster, and adding that failure to do so would render her liable to prosecution. For Nina too had been born east of the line. She had not obeyed the summons. Now in a fever of haste she was packing to be gone, at every moment expecting to hear upon the stairs the tread of the police who would come to take her away. She had read everything that the newspapers had to tell her about her situation; and she had no doubt that if she fell now into the hands of the State she would be deported at once back to her own country. And I would rather die, thought Nina, I would rather die.

She had finished packing her case. Everything was ready. She looked into her handbag. She had in it a very large sum of money and her passport. She stared at her passport, and it seemed to her suddenly like a death warrant. It filled her with shame and horror. She took it in her hand and it fell open at the picture of herself. It was an old picture taken in the worst days of her fear. At the Nina whose hair was golden a younger black-haired Nina stared back, anxious, haggard and fearful.

Here was her very soul upon record, stamped and filed; a soul without a nationality, a soul without a home. She turned the faded pages. The earlier ones carried the names of the frontiers of her childhood, frontiers which no longer existed in the world. The later pages were covered with the continually renewed permits from the Ministry of Labour. The Foreign Office which had issued this document had disappeared from the face of the earth. Now nothing could make it new. It remained like the Book of Judgement, the record of her sins, the final and irrevocable sentence of society upon her. She was without identity in a world where to be without identity is the first and most universal of crimes, the crime which, whatever else it may overlook, every State punishes. She had no official existence.

Nina put on her coat. She must lose no more time. She had already wasted two days in distress and indecision. She had made an attempt to see Rosa, but Rosa had told her shortly that her brother was very ill and would Nina come back another time. Another time will be too late, Nina said to herself with the slowness of grief, there is no more time. She had walked home, dragging her feet at a slow pace. Then at last it had come to her that she must run away. After that, she had acted with desperate haste. She had had to wait until the banks opened and she could draw out all her money. Then she had packed up her things and now she was ready to go. But where she was to go to she had not clearly conceived. In the first moments of her decision to fly she had decided to go to Eire. She was not sure whether a passport was needed to get into Eire. She was not sure, and there was nobody, nobody, whom she could ask.

She stood there with her coat on and her suit-case packed, and looked about the room which she had already abandoned. Then suddenly it seemed to her impossible that she should be allowed to leave the country. Every port would be watched. She pictured once again the sort of scene in which she had so often taken part, the scene at the frontier where she watched and waited while uniformed men examined her papers; the long time of waiting until the man who had taken her passport away should return with a surly look, as if she had wasted his time, to tell her that her papers were not in order and she could not pass. I couldn't stand it again, said Nina to herself, not again. She sat down on a chair.

A loud sob escaped from her like a live thing bursting from her breast. It now seemed to her quite useless to try to fly. She would only be arrested as she was about to board the boat. There was no escape. The men in uniform had only let her run ahead of them for a little way. Now once more they were close behind. They had not really let her go, they would never let her go. It was useless to fly and impossible to stay. Only one frontier remained, the frontier where no papers are asked for, which can be crossed without an identity into the land which remains, for the persecuted, always open.

She got up and started to walk up and down the room. She began to pull her coat off. Tears seemed to come now from her eyes and nose and mouth as if her whole being were dissolved into water. Her coat fell to the floor and she trampled across it. Then she began to pull out from its hiding-place in the bale of cloth the map of Australia which she had cherished there for so long. She opened it and laid it flat and looked at it for a while. Then she left it where it was and continued to walk about, treading upon it and striking the walls with her hands. Her tears began to abate. She could not remember that she had ever cried so much.

As the crying ceased, it was replaced by a low and regular wailing sound which came from her lips, without her will, in a rhythmical cadence. It rose and fell like a song. She had heard lamentation like this in her childhood, but she had never understood it. Now she knew how it was possible to sing in the presence of death. People whom she had known long ago came to her now, not clearly seen but present in multitude, in a great community. She held out her hands to them across the recent past. She stumbled across the room and opened the window very wide. Hazy with sunshine and budding trees the afternoon was revealed. She mounted on a chair.

As she sat upon the window-sill, she swayed to and fro with the continuous rhythm of her song. The sound became higher-pitched and the rhythm faster. The noise seemed now not to pass her lips but to issue out of her head. As she rocked and swayed, like one beguiling a child or a physical pain, she looked back across the room above the colonnade of dresses murmuring now in the warm breeze from the window. She saw the crucifix upon the wall. I forgot it, thought Nina. How foolish. But now it doesn't matter. She looked at it, and as she looked she saw it for the first time in her life as a man hanging most painfully from his hands. How strange, she thought that I never saw it in this way before. How he would have suffered, she thought, if he had been mortal. But all that time he knew of paradise, he spoke about it to the penitent thief. It was not the senseless blackness of death, the senseless blackness as it was for her. Then her thoughts coiled back: if not so for him, then not so for her. If for her, then for him too. A dark confusion rose to cover her. For an instant she felt the terrible weight of a God depending upon her will. It was too heavy. Her song came to an end. She gathered her feet under her and pitched head first from the window.

TWENTY-SEVEN

The train was running along with its wheels in the sea. Or so it seemed to Rosa, as she sat at the window, wishing that she could feel the cool water rising about her knees. After black tunnels, between dark pillars, there could be seen at intervals the Mediterranean, intensely blue and scattered with dazzling points of light. It was late afternoon and intolerably hot. Rosa was extremely tired, burdened with the long journey and the weight of her decision. The smell of the train and the heat of the afternoon enclosed her like a winding-sheet. It required an effort to move her limbs. She glanced down at her watch. Still half an hour to go. The train roared into another tunnel. Rosa closed her eyes. If there were any exhilaration in being in hell it would be of this kind.

It was immediately after Mrs. Wingfield's visit that Rosa had suddenly decided that she must act. Reflection and counter-reflection about Mischa Fox had brought her to a point of disequilibrium where rest was no longer possible. She had now no doubt but that Mischa's curious behaviour at their last meeting was designed to produce exactly this frenzied state of mind. But the diagnosis did not cure the condition. She had left the house meaning to call on Peter Saward. But the way to his house seemed to be lined with telephone boxes. Rosa had never in her life noticed so many telephone boxes. They stretched before her like monoliths that mark the way to a temple; and in each one of them a picture of Mischa Fox was hanging up. Rosa looked in at the black telephones as she passed. In each one of them the voice of Mischa Fox was lying asleep. When she came to the last one before Peter Saward's house she entered it and dialled Mischa's number.

Ringing up Mischa was always a discouraging experience. Half a dozen different voices might be heard at the other end of the line before at last there was the voice of Mischa; and it was impossible not to believe that all the nameless speakers were still somewhere upon the line, listening to every word, and that this was exactly what Mischa desired. Nor was it ever possible to identify these voices with real people in Mischa's entourage. They were anonymous voices by whom the caller was interrogated, stripped, and often finally rejected. On this occasion it was without much hope of really establishing contact with him that Rosa lifted the receiver. It was simply that she needed to do something, to perform some action in the real world, and to charm herself for a moment out of the world of thoughts and ghosts. She lifted the telephone as one might light a candle in a church, without belief, and yet obeying a need for ritual.

A woman's voice replied and asked her to hold on. Then a man spoke, asking her name and her business. Rosa gave her name and asked for Mischa. There was a long silence. Then she heard the voice of Calvin Blick. Calvin was friendly, apologetic. Unfortunately Mischa had left London and would be for some time resting at his villa in Italy. Did Rosa know the address? Here it was in any case, perhaps she would like to note it down. Mischa would be very sorry that he had missed her in London, very sorry indeed. Had she got a pencil to write down the address? Good, good. In the middle of this Rosa rang off. That was settled then.

She went on as far as Peter Saward's door. Then it occurred to her that it was not settled at all. She stood quite still for five minutes outside Peter's door. Then she turned about and ran back the way she had come. The need for action, so far from being satisfied by mere ritual, was grown within her into an obsessive fury. She called on Miss Foy and asked her to be so good as to look after Hunter. Then she took a taxi to Victoria.

Rosa reflected, as the train was leaving Naples, that perhaps she ought not to have left Hunter alone. But then she told herself again that in fact she was now doing the thing which would be of most help to Hunter; and more deeply still she told herself that what drove her now, half blindly, onward was not only her own will but Hunter's. About what was to come she reflected not at all. She had never visited Mischa's Italian villa, nor had she ever met anyone who had, though she had heard various fables about it. She knew its address, which for some reason had always been engraved on her mind, without needing to have it recalled to her by Calvin. And it now seemed to her that she had always known that it was a place to which she would go.

The rhythm of the train altered, and as it became slower the beating of Rosa's heart became faster. She had not told Mischa that she was coming. How she would reach the villa, and what she would find there when she arrived, she had not even dared to imagine. Perhaps, she thought, she would simply take another train back. Perhaps she would do that. She could, even now, do anything that she wished. Nothing irrevocable had happened yet. She picked up her suit-case and went into the corridor. The train was now running along in the open. On the inland side hills were to be seen, spotted with olive trees, with sad cracks running down their woody sides like the tracks of tears. Behind them were mountains, brown and purple in the late afternoon light, and very softly contoured as if a great quilt had been thrown over more jagged shapes that lay beneath. The train began to stop.

Rosa got out on to the small station. She was the only passenger to leave the train. It was a lonely remote little station, with no houses round it and a single square ochre-coloured building which housed the station offices. Rosa stood on a path of sharp stones beside a dusty grove of oleanders and waited for the train to go on, so that she could cross the line. It went away, curving away inland towards the hills and leaving her behind in a sudden silence. Her feet crunched on the stones. Then she crossed the rails and gave up her ticket. She emerged from the station and found herself at a little crossroads which was deep in white dust. She looked about her.

Then she saw on the left, stark as a little picture in the heat and silence of the afternoon, something which made her stand quite still. At the side of the station, drawn a little off the road, was a smart *carozzella*, with tall red wheels, one horse in the shafts, and a white fringed awning, which was tilted at a drunken angle over the driving-seat. In the driving-seat, with his head fallen sideways so that he was almost toppling out on to the road, was Calvin Blick. He was fast asleep. The horse, whose head was drooping so that its nose was almost on the ground, appeared to be asleep too. As it breathed, at long regular intervals, it raised a tiny cloud of dust upon the ground below its nostrils. Rosa put her hand to her heart and began to laugh.

Her laughter wakened Calvin, who jolted violently upright

and opened his eyes. His movement wakened the horse, who lifted his head and set loudly ringing the five bells which grew upon a little tree upon the harness at its neck. Rosa went on laughing. She had never felt so pleased to see Calvin Blick.

'Dear me!' said Calvin. 'Well, you've arrived at last! This is the third train I've met today. Get in quick before the animal lies down.'

'But what are you doing here?' said Rosa. 'You were in London.' She was feeling enormous relief.

'Ever heard of aeroplanes?' said Calvin. 'Swifter, in this case, than the thoughts of love, I flew with British European Airways.'

Rosa stepped into the body of the carriage, which tilted perilously towards her as she set her foot on the step. Calvin adjusted the wide-brimmed straw hat, shook the reins vigorously, and shouted '*Avanti!*'

The sleepy horse set itself in motion, and the jerky movement of its body communicated itself to the *carozzella*, which moved forward in an irregular impulsive manner. The little bells upon the harness began to ring, the polished tin upon the collar sparkled in the sun. A cloud of dust arose above the tall wheels, and through it Rosa saw the countryside unfolding. It was a bare countryside, pale with rocks and dust, where the olives and vines which rose upon shelves above her were grey rather than green, and weary with the heat even in this early summer. Between light brown curves of hill she saw through the blue haze white farms, scanty as bones, and beyond them now and then the dark line of the sea. There was an intense evening light which now mottled with colour the mountains farther away and drew the sky downwards like a silk cloth. Rosa breathed in the warm air. It was long long since she had been in the south.

She could have wished that the drive would last forever. She had never felt closer to Mischa and more totally at her ease in this proximity. In the poverty and beauty of that denuded landscape she embraced him. It now seemed to her strange that she had imagined Mischa's Italy so differently, almost as a tropical paradise. She now saw that it could only be like this. The *carozzella* rattled through a small village, and a crowd of children shouted after it. The white doorway of a church appeared round a bend in the road and was gone. Then there was a procession of heavy carts, drawn by little donkeys scarcely out of the womb. Then the countryside again. They were moving faster now. Rosa sat up and leaned forward. The air smelt of dust and sea and unknown flowers and the south.

The carriage suddenly left the road and began to climb up a little track. The horse which had, after a fashion, been trotting, slowed down to a walking pace. Calvin jumped off and began to lead the animal up the slope. Rosa could see white walls appearing at the top of the hill, and a shallow roof which had once been red but which now, following the colour of the countryside, was paled towards a ruddy grey. The declining sun struck the side of the wall, dazzling Rosa with a rectangle of gold. She covered her eyes. She was still dazzled as the carriage turned into a small courtyard and she stepped out almost into Mischa's arms.

'Come inside,' said Mischa, 'you must be very tired.' He was completely calm. An Italian youth was unharnessing the horse. Calvin had disappeared.

Rosa followed him across the courtyard, and as she went, black hens with crests like scarlet flowers scattered on either side. They came into a dark room. For a moment Rosa could see nothing. Then she saw dimly Mischa's profile close by, and his soft voice said, 'Your room is just here, on this side of the house. Maria will bring you cool water from the spring. Come back when you are ready. Then we will have a meal.'

Maria, who seemed to consist of a large white apron and an even larger white cap and two black smiling eyes, showed Rosa into her room, and then returned bringing two jugs, one of hot and the other of very cold water. The room was dark, only a little light filtered through the tightly closed shutters. When Rosa's eyes became accustomed to the obscurity she saw a stone floor, an iron bedstead with a gay counterpane, a washstand with bright Italian jugs and basin, a gilded settee and a chair to match. This was all the furniture. Then she went to the window. With difficulty she undid the shutters and forced them outwards.

The square of landscape leapt into being, quivering with light. The intenser illumination of the later evening drew from the pale country the colours which the earlier sun had hidden, gentle browns and golds, while the occasional olive tree displayed a darkening green, ready to turn to black. Before her,

267

framed by the hills, lay the sea, streaked now with golden lines, its blue turning to amethyst, its dazzling surface resolved into an inward light. It glowed like a great window of stained glass. Rosa looked down into its depths. It lay very close to the house, but far below it, and past a curve of the hillside she saw a section of the stone steps which must lead from Mischa's door down to the beach, of which from here she could see only a tiny yellowish triangle. Directly in front of her window was a wide terrace with a stone parapet which swept round to what she took to be the front of the house, which faced the sea more squarely. Her own room was in a wing which jutted out at an angle to the main building. The terrace was empty. There was a smell of mint and the sound of a spring or fountain falling. Rosa stood there for a long time. Then she turned back and began to pour out the cool water. The warm evening followed her into the little room.

A little while later Rosa joined Mischa in the room where she had left him. She now made out that this was the central room of the main building, which served both as drawing-room and dining-room. It was simply furnished in an inconsequential style. A table was laid for a meal. The room was still dark and shuttered. Mischa's darkened face spoke to her again. 'Maria isn't quite ready yet. Come out on to the terrace.'

He pushed open two doors at the end of the room and Rosa followed him out. Then she received the full splendour of the view which she had seen only in part from her bedroom. The sea lay before them between two bare golden hills, and the steps could be seen intermittently, twisting and turning downwards towards a long line of sand where without waves the sea ended, quiet as a lake. The sea circled the horizon, enclosing a bowl of warm air, and on the farther hillside the shadow of the mountains crept slowly up, changing the gold into an obscure brown. They crossed the terrace. A line of slim cypress trees led down towards the valley, which was already dark for the night. Far beneath them a dog was barking. The sound came circling up like a bird to vanish into the wide circumference of the evening sun.

Rosa looked at Mischa. He was gazing down into the valley, and she had never seen him look so subdued. When he was aware of her eyes he dropped his head still lower. She realized that she would not know his mind until the following morning.

He moved away from her towards the far end of the terrace, and there Rosa saw the fountain whose voice had haunted her. Out of a rudimentary lion's mouth water was pouring into a long grey trough. As Rosa came near she saw that the trough was a stone sarcophagus, on the edge of which figures were carved, marshalled in an irregular line. A depression at the far end of the trough let the water fall again in a second shower to seep away through the gravel at the corner of the terrace.

Rosa sat down on the edge of the sarcophagus and plunged her hand into the cool water. As she drew it out she could feel the water evaporating at once into the warm air and the last rays of the sun. A few drops remained, and for a moment she still felt them cool upon the collected warmth of her flesh, and then her arm was dry. She plunged it in again. Mischa was standing beside her with a glass of wine. She took it in a dripping hand and he sat down opposite to her on the edge of the sarcophagus.

Mischa was silent. He shook his head several times as if to indicate that he would speak if he could. Rosa tasted the wine. It was harsh but refreshing.

At last she said, 'It is a very beautiful landscape.'

'It is a very poor landscape,' said Mischa. There was no reproach in his voice.

He was not looking at her, but was gazing at the ground. Rosa looked down too and saw that the gravel surface of the terrace was covered with living creatures. Ants passed by carrying heavy burdens. Poor dried-up beetles walked or staggered on their way. Large green grasshoppers paused immobile and almost invisible and then sprang suddenly out of sight; and here and there were patches of red which were ladybirds, enormous and without spots. As Rosa looked it seemed to her as if the whole scene had been conjured up by Mischa simply for her benefit. If she were to go away, all this would vanish too, and Mischa would be left, haggard and staring, in some place unimaginably stripped and denuded. At the last stroke of the clock all these things would return to their natural shape too.

Rosa shook herself. She pointed to a pair of grasshoppers. 'Are these cicadas?'

'No,' said Mischa, 'no one ever sees cicadas, they are only voices.' He spoke sadly, but under the mutual awkwardness Rosa now felt a deep accord.

A lizard came suddenly on to the parapet near to Mischa. It stood tensely still, and in the horizontal sunlight its small body cast a big shadow. With an easy sweep of the hand Mischa caught it and drew it on to his knee and held it for a moment with both hands cupped. His face lit up with animation and pleasure as he looked down at the panting belly of the lizard. It lay still in his hands.

'Give him to me!' said Rosa. She stretched out her free hand.

'Be careful how you hold him,' said Mischa, and he put the lizard into her palm.

Rosa's fingers closed upon it maladroitly. In an instant, with a quick twist, the lizard had sprung away from her on to the ground, leaving its writhing tail behind in her grasp. With a cry Rosa dropped the tail upon the gravel. It lay there still twisting and writhing. Mischa picked it up quickly and threw it over the parapet. They looked at each other wide-eyed with a sudden fright and distress.

'He'll soon grow another one,' said Mischa, and his voice was trembling. Then he took her wrist and drew her towards him. The wind tilted into the fountain.

TWENTY-EIGHT

On the morning of the next day Rosa woke early. She remembered at once where she was, and remembered how Mischa had shown her to her room at an early hour on the previous evening and had then disappeared. A little later she had heard his feet going away down the steps. She had lingered at the window, looking out into the warm dark, but had been able to see nothing except for one moment when the headlights of a car suddenly showed her in sharp relief a row of trees upon the other side of the valley. After that she slept, grateful to be left alone.

She sprang out of bed now and threw the shutters wide. The scene of yesterday was quite transformed. The sea was now pale and almost colourless, yet at the same time brilliant, a sea of liquid light. It merged without a boundary into a sky which at the horizon was of an equal pallor, though changing at the zenith to a very pale vibrating blue. Here and there in the far distance, as if suspended motionless between sea and sky, there were small sailing-boats with triangular sails. Rosa stared for some time into the great field of light. Then she looked to each side at the hills, and saw upon them, with the different falling of the sun, great rocks and hollows and contorted trees. Below her she made out the winding channel of a tiny stream, perhaps the same stream which flowed through the stone sarcophagus. At one point, far down, it crossed the steps in a wide sheen of water.

Rosa told herself that this was the day that would decide her fate. She said this to herself with emotion, but without fear or distress: for it was not, she felt, as if she would have to struggle this day to make her destiny. Her destiny was already made. The day would do no more than announce it to her. She would await the announcement with calmness and with open eyes.

She turned away, leaving the window wide open. The morning shadows fell like water upon the stone floor. She dressed quickly and was already finished when Maria came to call her. Rosa's Italian was crude, but she understood that the master had gone down to the sea, and would be glad if the *signorina* would join him there, at the bottom of the steps, after she had taken her breakfast. This, it seemed to Rosa, was characteristic. She sat down to her bread and coffee in the central living-room, sitting beside the doors, and letting the light from the great scene outside fall upon her face and breast. Soon she would go out on to the terrace and look down to see if she could discover Mischa on the beach. And a little after that she would descend the steps, but very slowly, and walk through the water of the stream. And a little after that. Rosa felt that her breath was coming now with deep slow movements, as if the whole rhythm of her being had been slowed down. Her heart was beating only very gently and lazily. She felt an enormous serenity falling upon her like a blessing. She drank the coffee. She had no desire to eat. Then she went back to her room and did her hair again, very carefully. She came back through the living-room, and pushing open the doors, set foot upon the terrace.

As she did so she heard someone call 'Miss Keepe!' Rosa turned sharply. Standing at the other corner of the terrace, beside the house, was Calvin Blick. Since yesterday she had forgotten his existence. She was reminded of it now with a shock which made her turn cold with an anticipation of ill. She stood motionless staring at him, and her lazy heart gave one jerk and then began to beat with furious speed. She said nothing.

Calvin came towards her along the edge of the house, trailing his fingers on the wall. 'Could I have a word with you?' he said.

Rosa turned, her heels grinding on the gravel. She nodded, and stepped back into the semi-darkness of the room. There was something in Calvin's tone which made her suddenly and profoundly sick at heart.

She drew a chair up to the doorway and seated herself. Calvin stood beside her, half in and half out of the door, looking down. Then he passed by her into the room. Rosa's breakfast was still there undisturbed. Calvin poured himself out a cupful of warm milk and drank it solemnly, mouthing the liquid roundly, his tongue darting into it like a fish. Then, leaning one hand upon the table, he turned to face Rosa. She thought that he was looking excited. She had never seen him display emotion. She watched him tensely.

'I realize, Miss Keepe,' said Calvin, 'that this is a serious moment in your life.'

A spirit spoke into Rosa's ear and told her to spring up now before it was too late and run away quickly down the steps. But some stronger power made her stay.

'I believe,' said Calvin, 'that at such moments one should have, as far as possible, all the facts before one.' He spoke as if he were uttering a premeditated speech.

'You will say,' he went on, 'quite rightly, that the problem is, what are all the facts? Let me reply at once that I do not presume to know. I am only concerned to help you on one or two very small points without in any way knowing what difference I shall be making to the whole picture as you see it.'

'You don't want to help me,' said Rosa. Her voice was very deep with emotion. She did not imagine that anything trivial was at stake. 'Let us be frank at least.'

'As you will,' said Calvin. 'In fact, my state of mind is neither here nor there. It is simply that I cannot allow you to proceed without saying what I want to say and saying it now.'

It seemed to Rosa that he spoke with a kind of sincerity. She waited, containing her heart with her hand. 'Go on,' she said. 'But I can't promise you any discretion.'

'It won't be necessary,' said Calvin, and he smiled a smile which made him look to Rosa more familiar.

'First,' he said, 'and without comment, this.' He drew something from his pocket and handed it to Rosa.

She tilted it into the light. It was the photograph of herself with the Lusiewicz brothers. For an instant the shock was intense. A whiteness rolled through her head and she dropped the photograph on the floor. Calvin picked it up with a deferential gesture, and gave it back to her.

'Thank you,' said Rosa mechanically. She laid it on the table.

'Of course,' said Rosa, 'that flash of light. I ought to have guessed. Who took this photograph?'

'I did,' said Calvin, keeping his eyes down.

'Ah —' said Rosa, and she shook her head with an air almost of pity. 'Has he seen it?'

'I have no secrets from him,' said Calvin.

'Has he seen it?' she repeated.

'Yes,' said Calvin. 'After all, I was instructed to take it.' He looked at Rosa, and his face glowed now with a purposeful look that was almost like gaiety. His eyes opened wide and sparkled as he looked down at her very intently.

'I don't believe you,' said Rosa. Her gentle smile was frozen with anxiety. She spoke still in a low voice, like a voice of compassion.

'Your family is hard to convince!' said Calvin. He began to move to and fro behind the table. It was as if he wanted to dance. He kept looking delightedly about the room and then looking back at Rosa. 'That little photo has done a lot of work!' he said.

Rosa stared at him and the smile faded from her. After a moment she said, 'Did you – show that picture to Hunter?'

Calvin nodded, his eyebrows going up and down and his teeth glistening. 'Hunter was anxious that a certain person should not see it!'

Rosa looked at him. She was maintaining her detachment. 'You astonish me,' she said. 'You not only attempt to blackmail me with one story and Hunter with the opposite story but you have the insolence to admit it.'

'Yes, yes!' said Calvin. He was looking at her eagerly. He could not keep still. 'Exactly, exactly!' He seemed delighted.

Rosa put her hand to her head. 'It isn't possible —' she said.

'Why not?' cried Calvin. 'You will never know the truth, and you will read the signs in accordance with your deepest wishes. That is what we humans always have to do. Reality is a cipher with many solutions, all of them right ones.'

'By boasting in this way,' said Rosa, 'you surrender your power.'

'Power!' said Calvin. He was speaking very fast. 'Do you imagine that any real power lies in these mechanical devices? I have done nothing for you and your brother but provide you with rather grotesque pretexts for doing what you really want to do. The truth lies deeper, deeper. It is always so!' He spoke with enthusiasm, leaning towards her across the table.

'You are completely mad!' said Rosa. 'And I don't believe you. And in any case it doesn't matter, it doesn't matter. I can't think why you should imagine that we cannot know the truth. And I can't think why you should imagine that it matters.'

She covered her face with her hands. She could feel Calvin's glance penetrating her, like a sharp tool that searches for a weak place which it can prize apart.

'Is that all you have to say?' said Rosa. Her voice was beginning to tremble.

'No!' said Calvin. He was calming himself. He now had the deft exultant look of one who is the master of a still difficult game. 'No! This was just the overture designed, shall I say, to put us into the proper mood. Let us indeed agree that it doesn't matter. My function, dear Miss Keepe, is merely to bring one or two small facts to your notice. I have no wish to discuss or to persuade. So may we now, under your permission, proceed to exhibit number two.'

He produced from inside his coat a copy of the *Evening News*, which he unfolded carefully and spread out before Rosa on the table. It carried on the front page the story of Nina's suicide.

Rosa drew the paper towards her. 'I didn't know – about this,' she said.

The newspaper attributed Nina's death to the publicity given recently to the position of a certain category of aliens, of whom, it appeared, Nina was one.

'Very sad, isn't it!' said Calvin.

Partly for her own sake Rosa needed to read his face at this moment. She lifted her eyes; but the effort was too great, and she saw his head hazy and distorted in a cloud of tears.

'But,' said Rosa, and after the first words her voice came quite clearly, although the tears were coursing down her face, 'surely they wouldn't have done anything to Nina?'

'That's the sad thing,' said Calvin. 'Of course they wouldn't. After all, it's England. It's like the Duchess in *Alice*. No one really gets beheaded. Someone writes to *The Times* or to their M.P. long before that happens. None of these people will be deported. One or two individuals, who had bad consciences for other reasons, may find it prudent to disappear – but no one else will be interfered with. Nothing would have happened to Nina, except that she would have had to fill in a few more forms. Someone ought to have explained all this to her.'

'Who would have believed,' said Rosa, with a wail in her voice, wiping the tears away with the back of her hand, 'that Nina would have been so foolish —'

'She was very isolated,' said Calvin. 'She was peculiarly isolated, and very near to despair in any case.' He was leaning close to her as he spoke the words, and uttering them carefully and clearly. 'Someone ought to have explained things to her, someone who knew her situation through and through. As it was, she was just an incidental casualty —'

'Stop!' said Rosa. 'You've made your point!' She got up, and stepped out of the doors on to the terrace. The warmth of the morning sun took her in a golden embrace. Its touch was hateful to her, like the taste of food after a death. She stood still for a moment, and Calvin came and stood behind her shoulder. She shivered to feel Calvin so near, and began to move away from him.

'I cannot think,' she said, 'why Mischa has not killed you years ago.'

'Mischa did kill me years ago,' said Calvin in a soft voice.

Rosa's movement brought her near to the parapet and she saw with astonishment that the great pale shining sea was still there; only a little blue had leaked into it now out of the morning sky. She gazed down at the beach.

'Do you see him?' said Calvin softly.

Rosa looked. 'No,' she said.

'Look through these,' said Calvin. He whipped out a pair of binoculars. He trained them like a gun upon the scene below. Then he handed them to Rosa. '*There!*' he said, pointing. 'He's quite still, so he's hard to notice.'

Rosa looked through the glasses. A section of beach sprang into view, very close and quite deserted. She could see the crystalline lights on the sand and the very small ripples at the edge of the sea. She moved the glasses slowly along. Then suddenly there was Mischa. He was sitting on the sand, barefoot, with his trousers rolled up to the knee, and the soles of his feet touching each other like a pair of praying hands. He was looking towards the horizon. The shock of seeing him was so great that Rosa lowered the glasses at once. When she lifted them and found him again he had got up and was standing with his feet in the sea. He stooped down and picked up something which seemed to be a starfish, and after looking at it, threw it far out into the water. Then he turned about and looked straight into Rosa's eyes. She flinched and handed the glasses back to Calvin. She could not believe that Mischa could not see her face and soul. For an instant, but only for an instant, she believed that he knew and intended all.

'He's seen us!' said Calvin. 'He's waving!' Calvin began to wave vigorously. 'Wave!' he said to Rosa, 'or he'll think something's the matter.'

Rosa waved. She could now see a tiny figure far below agitating its hands. She turned to look at Calvin. He was looking down with a tender predatory expression.

'You know how to protect your own,' said Rosa. She turned away and crossed the terrace, stumbling as she went.

'Where are you going?' said Calvin.

'To pack my suit-case,' said Rosa.

'I'll tell Lucio to get the car,' said Calvin.

When Rosa came back a moment later with her things the car was already waiting in the front courtyard. Maria's son Lucio was at the wheel.

'He will take you to the station,' said Calvin. 'There's a train for Naples in less than half an hour.' He opened the door of the car.

As Rosa was about to get in, he captured her hand. She did not try to free it but looked at him. 'It's odd,' she said, 'in the past I always felt that whether I went towards him or away from him I was only doing his will. But it was all an illusion.'

'Who knows,' said Calvin, 'perhaps it is only now that it would be an illusion. I am sorry.'

'What will you do?' said Rosa.

'It is rather what will he do,' said Calvin. He made as if to kiss Rosa's hand, but she pulled it away from him and got into the car.

A great cloud of dust arose as the car went down the track that led to the road. By the time it had quite cleared, the car had vanished, and even the sound of the engine had died away into the motionless landscape that leaned over towards the sea. Calvin Blick stood quite still until the sound had gone. Then he turned about and ran through the house and across the terrace and began in desperate haste to descend the steps.

TWENTY-NINE

The Orient Express was flying southwards through Europe. In a first-class compartment Sir Andrew Cockeyne was kissing his wife passionately. Annette had lingered in the dining-car, and for the moment they had the compartment to themselves. Andrew loved his wife; but he was never sure whether in marrying him she had got what she wanted. He had soon learnt, he had learnt it on his honeymoon, not to question her about her feelings. But he still hoped, although he knew that this displeased her scarcely less, that he might read his answers in her eyes. Somewhere deep within, a light shone which could reassure him for ever. But this reassurance was something which, deliberately or not, Marcia had always withheld from him. She would not permit him to look into her eyes. She was never still, and when they embraced she would hide her face. So she escaped him, always evading the point of rest and contemplation towards which he always wished to draw her; and when at times he caught her head, violent almost with hunger for her gaze, she would move restlessly, tossing her hair, twisting her body, and turning away her eyes like an animal. Andrew sighed, and tried now to draw her down on to his shoulder — but with a quick movement she freed herself.

'*Attention, violà l'enfant!*' said Marcia.

Annette entered the compartment and beamed benevolently upon her parents. She took the corner seat and settled herself, yawning and drawing up her legs. Her cheeks glowed like peaches, her arms were already becoming tawny with sunshine, and the parting of her hair shone like precious metal. She arranged her skirt about her in a great fan. Andrew looked upon her with astonishment. Then he looked at his wife. Marcia was bending upon Annette a look of intent understanding which seemed to make her face grow rounder and her eyes larger. Marcia was quite still now. Andrew looked from one to the other. He did not know which was the more mysterious.

Annette was stroking her slim legs. 'Look, Marcia,' she said, 'that ankle is quite well again now. You couldn't even tell which one it was.' With a flash of coloured petticoats she lifted one leg right up until it pointed at the roof.

'Annette!' said Andrew.

Marcia laughed. Annette laughed too, and settled herself again, posing her right hand ostentatiously upon her thigh. On the third finger, set in a gold ring, was the great white sapphire. As the train swung round a bend, the sun blazed suddenly in at the window and set the sapphire alight.

'Pull the blinds down, Annette,' said Andrew.

'Well, only a little way,' said Annette, 'because I want to look out.' She adjusted the blind and curled herself up, crouching on the seat and leaning her cheek against the lower half of the window. As Andrew saw in profile her fresh untroubled face he felt for a moment a sense of puzzlement, perhaps of awe, almost of resentment, at her vitality.

Annette was absorbed in watching the landscape. A house, a dog, a man on a bicycle, a woman in a field, a distant mountain. She looked upon them all enchanted, lips parted and eyes wide. It was like being at the pictures.

'Look! Look!' she kept saying to Marcia. 'Look at those cows, how very red they are! Look, there are crows sitting on their backs, like in the – Oh, look at the little dog, it's barking at the train! Why, there's a house just like our house at Vevey! Do look, Marcia! What a lovely avenue of trees! Oh dear, it's gone.'

And while Annette looked at the world, Marcia looked at Annette, and Andrew looked at Marcia. Then the train stopped at a tiny station and there was a sudden silence. Annette ceased her chatter. She opened the window. In the sunny quietness she could smell the dust and hear the sound of the cicadas. She knew that she was in the south.

The train began to move again very slowly. The little station disappeared and a row of pine trees were drawn away to reveal a deep valley. In the valley there was a sparkling river, and beyond the river there was a great row of arches.

'Oh, look, Andrew!' said Annette. 'What's that, over there?'

'It's a Roman aqueduct,' said Andrew.

'Where did it go to?' said Annette.

Andrew began to explain. But already she was no longer listening. Soon, soon, soon she would see Nicholas. She would have a lot to tell him.

THIRTY

It was raining. Peter Saward was standing at the window watching the rain as it fell into the little dark garden, finding its way through the great leafy tree that took up most of the space between the walls, running along the leaves and the branches, and falling into enormous pools on the bare earth. The large wet surfaces of the leaves, weighty with moisture, drooped and swayed in the sharp wind that was blowing. As he watched the falling water, Peter whistled softly to himself, imitating a bird. Then he turned away from the window into the darkness of the room. The silence of the room was profound and familiar, as if all the books were breathing quietly. He stood quite still for a long time, looking into the obscurity with unfocused eyes.

There was a strange flurry outside the door. Peter Saward started. Then the door was flung wide open and in the sudden light from the hallway he saw Rosa, her clothes all darkened with the rain, standing before him. She stumbled in, and the room became dark again. After the first moment Rosa did not look at him. She murmured, 'Thank God!' half under her breath, and then began shaking herself like a dog.

'Don't do that, Rosa,' said Peter, 'you're throwing water all over the books.'

'Damn the books!' said Rosa. She slipped out of her coat and dropped it on the floor. Peter picked it up and hung it carefully over the back of a chair. Rosa sat down at the desk and began to undo her hair, which was extremely wet. Heavy with rain, the dark tresses fell down over both shoulders.

'Poor thing, you're soaked!' said Peter. 'I'll open the stove.' He pulled apart the two iron doors and a bright glow lit up the room, reflected in the polished side of the desk and revealing the colours of many thousand books.

'Come near,' said Peter. But Rosa did not move, and kept mechanically combing out her hair with her fingers, while the water still dripped on to the floor from the hem of her skirt.

Peter stood over her awkwardly. 'I'm so glad you've come,' he said. 'I was just watching the rain. It was looking so beautiful,' he added, in case this should sound like a complaint.

'Funny thing,' said Rosa, 'I thought you were dead.'

'Why ever did you think that?' said Peter. 'I'm not, as you see!'

'I don't know,' said Rosa, 'but in the train I suddenly felt quite certain that you were dead. I saw it all, like in a vision. I saw myself arriving here. The front door was locked and I had to ring, and Miss Glashan came and told me very gently that her lodger had passed away. And then she let me come into this room and I saw that it had all become a senseless jumble of objects that someone would have to come and sort out and cart off.'

'Well, it ain't so,' said Peter. 'Here, have a cigarette.' He always kept cigarettes in his desk for Rosa.

'No,' said Rosa, 'those ones have been there for months.' She moved closer to the fire.

'Where have you been?' asked Peter.

'I went to Italy,' said Rosa, 'to see Mischa. But it was no use.' Her tone forbade further questions.

'Have you – been to Campden Hill Square?' asked Peter.

'No,' said Rosa, 'I came straight here from the station. You don't happen to know how Hunter is, do you?' She wrung the water out of the ends of her hair and began to dry her cheeks with a handkerchief. Her wet face glowed red in the firelight.

'Here, how stupid of me!' said Peter Saward, and he fetched her a towel. 'Hunter is completely better,' he said. 'He's up and about again, so Miss Foy told me.'

'I'm not surprised,' said Rosa. She shook her head slowly to and fro and sighed.

'Did you know,' said Peter Saward, 'that Mrs Wingfield has died?'

'Oh —' said Rosa. She threw the towel to the floor. Her forehead was still glistening with rain. 'Oh —' she said, 'I am sorry. Poor lady! How strange. My dear mother loved her, I remember.' She drew her hand across her brow and her eyes.

'Miss Foy was looking for you,' said Peter Saward, 'to tell you about the will.'

'Oh, the will!' said Rosa. She picked up the towel again and bundled into it the mass of damp hair that fell into her lap and began to rub it vigorously. 'What got what, pray?'

'Mrs Wingfield left you all the shares of the *Artemis*,' said Peter Saward, 'and an annuity of five hundred pounds so long as the journal continues in publication with you as its editor.'

Rosa laughed shortly. 'Five hundred pounds!' she said.

'Do you think she was mean?' asked Peter.

'No!' said Rosa. 'Intelligent! What got the rest?'

'She left the rest to Miss Foy,' said Peter Saward.

'Oh, good,' said Rosa. 'I am so glad! Was there plenty?'

'Plenty,' said Peter Saward.

'Whatever will Miss Foy do with it, I wonder,' said Rosa.

'Give it to you, if you aren't careful,' said Peter Saward.

'I don't want it,' said Rosa. 'You and Hunter can have it. Poor Mrs Wingfield —'

'Rosa,' said Peter Saward, 'did you hear about Nina?'

'*Yes*,' said Rosa. 'For God's sake, Peter, sit down somewhere. You make me tired standing around like that.'

He sat down in an armchair near to the stove and Rosa left her chair and sat down at his feet. She leaned lightly against his knee while with both hands she spread out her hair like a great net to dry. For a moment they rested so, she melancholy and thoughtful, he observing her, suddenly immobile with contentment. Outside the window it was night-time.

'This room looks different,' said Rosa. 'It looks emptier. What have you done? I know what it is — the sheets of hieroglyphs aren't there. You've put them away.'

'Yes,' said Peter, 'that's all over.'

'What do you mean, all over?'

'Well, they've found a bilingual near Tarsus, a big thing – it tells everything.'

'It tells everything?' said Rosa. She knelt upright before him. 'You mean all your research is wasted?'

'Well, yes, I suppose so,' said Peter. 'I was off the track anyway. I was quite wrong in thinking that the language was Indo-European. It turns out to be a sort of Mongolian tongue. The bilingual gives quite enough vocabulary to decipher most of what we have.'

'What was that stuff you were always poring over, what did it mean?'

'It's too soon to say in detail,' said Peter, 'but it seems to be mainly accounts of battles — quite interesting — they establish —'

'Never mind what they establish!' said Rosa. 'So all your work was for nothing, for nothing!' She spoke half angrily, half in grief.

'Well, what can one do?' said Peter. 'One reads the signs as best one can, and one may be totally misled. But it's never certain that the evidence will turn up that makes everything plain. It was worth trying. Now I can go back to my other work in peace. There's nothing to be sad about, Rosa.'

She knelt before him and her black hair fell about her almost to the ground. She put a hand on his arm.

'Peter,' she said, 'what would you think of the idea of marrying me?'

He looked at her calmly and a little sadly. 'You can imagine, my darling,' he said, 'how much it moves me to hear you say this. But you don't really want it. Some god or demon makes you say it, but you don't really want it. Ah, if only you did! But you don't.' He put his hand under her chin and looked into her eyes. She stared back at him fiercely.

'Some god or demon!' said Rosa. 'No, no! Won't you believe me?'

'No,' said Peter. He moved his hand up the side of her cheek and took a strand of warm hair which he drew across on to his knee.

'No,' said Rosa, and her voice was breaking. 'You won't believe me, you will never believe me now. Peter, I'm going to cry. Find something quick to distract me, show me something.'

Still holding her hair, he reached out with the other hand for the green book of photographs which lay on the desk near by. As he opened it before her and began to turn the pages, she saw the pictures through a gathering haze of tears.

'See,' he said, 'here is the old market square and here is the famous bronze fountain, and here is the medieval bridge across the river . . .' He turned the pages. 'And here is the cathedral . . .'

THE UNICORN

A calm lovely woman sits barefoot in her drawing-room in Gaze Castle, dressed in a yellow silk dressing-gown. She is a prisoner cared for, loved even, by dark maids, a powerful ex-lover of her absent husband, a bitter, yearning female cousin, a blue-eyed clerk and a dangerous golden youth ...

'She is at the top of her form in *The Unicorn* ... an absorbing tapestry of luxurious depravity and diabolism'
New York Times

£1.95

THE BELL

A number of eccentrics join forces to establish a lay religious community in Gloucestershire. But the ancient conflict between religion and sex is not to be easily set aside. The pious and peaceful scene so eagerly sought after is transformed into a complex struggle of secrecy and suspicion.

'Not a dull page or slipshod sentence ... *The Bell* shines with intelligence'
The Observer

'At once hypersensitive and deeply resilient, combining a feminine sensibility with a sharp and masculine mind ... *The Bell* establishes Miss Murdoch in the forefront of living English novelists'
Sunday Times

£1.95

Under The Net	£1.25 ☐
The Sandcastle	£1.25 ☐
The Bell	£1.95 ☐
A Severed Head	£1.25 ☐
An Unofficial Rose	£1.25 ☐
The Unicorn	£1.95 ☐
The Red and the Green	£1.25 ☐
The Time of the Angels	£1.95 ☐
The Nice and the Good	£1.25 ☐
Bruno's Dream	£1.50 ☐
An Accidental Man	£1.75 ☐
Henry and Cato	£1.25 ☐
A Word Child	£1.25 ☐
The Sea, The Sea	£1.95 ☐

All these books are available to your local bookshop or newsagent, or can be ordered direct from the publisher. Just tick the titles you want and fill in the form below.

Name ....

Address ....

....

Write to Granada Cash Sales, PO Box 11, Falmouth, Cornwall TR10 9EN

Please enclose remittance to the value of the cover price plus:

UK: 40p for the first book, 18p for the second book plus 13p per copy for each additional book ordered to a maximum charge of £1.49.

BFPO and EIRE: 40p for the first book, 18p for the second book plus 13p per copy for the next 7 books, thereafter 7p per book.

OVERSEAS: 60p for the first book and 18p for each additional book.

Granada Publishing reserve the right to show new retail prices on covers, which may differ from those previously advertised in the text or elsewhere.